THE FEW
THINGS I
KNOW ABOUT
GLAFKOS
THRASSAKIS

THE FEW

THINGS I

VASSILIS VASSILIKOS

KNOW ABOUT

TRANSLATED FROM THE GREEK BY KAREN EMMERICH

GLAFKOS

SEVEN STORIES PRESS

NEW YORK ≈ TORONTO ≈ LONDON ≈ SYDNEY

THRASSAKIS

The quote attributed to Sartre in chapter four is from
Jean-Paul Sartre, *The Family Idiot*, translated by Carol Cosman
(University of Chicago Press, 1981).

SEVEN STORIES PRESS
140 Watts Street
New York NY 10013
www.sevenstories.com

In Canada
Hushion House
36 Northline Road
Toronto, Ontario M4B 3E2

In the U.K.
Turnaround Publisher Services Ltd., Unit 3
Olympia Trading Estate, Coburg Road
Wood Green, London N22 6TZ

In Australia
Tower Books
2/17 Rodborough Road,
Frenchs Forest NSW 2086

Library of Congress Cataloging-in-Publication Data

Vasilikos, Vasilåes, 1934–
[Glaukou Thrasakåe. English]
The few things I know about Glafkos Thrassakis / Vassilis Vassilikos;
translated from the Greek by Karen Emmerich.
p. cm.
Originally published: Athåenai: Livanis, c1996.
ISBN 1-58322-527-7
I. Emmerich, Karen. II. Title.
PA5633.A46 A8813 2002
889'.334—dc21   2002013866

9 8 7 6 5 4 3 2 1

College professors may order examination copies of Seven Stories Press titles
free for a six-month trial period. To order, visit www.sevenstories.com/textbook,
or fax on school letterhead to (212) 226-1411.

≈

BOOK DESIGN BY POLLEN, New York
PRINTED IN THE U.S.A.

CONTENTS

I love this book more than any other I've written thus far. The reason is simple: it is the only novel I wholeheartedly adopt as an expression of the self as a third party. . . . I'd call it a biogranovel, an autonovegraphy, a novistory. . . . But those terms would all be mistaken: because there is, too, a reworking of the essentially autobiographical material, a distance between the experience and its recreation. The book first circulated in three separate volumes. Then in one, then two. Later on there was a fourth volume, the "Undiscovered Stories." . . . Finally, all that gushed forth again in a new form. *Glafkos Thrassakis*, the chronicle of a Greek of the diaspora, is presented here in its definitive, reworked form.

This note by Vassilikos appears on the back cover of the nearly 800-page 1989 Gnosis edition of *Glafkos Thrassakis;* readers of the time most likely accepted its assertion that this edition presented the "definitive" reworking of three volumes published during 1974 and 1975 and of the 1979 *Undiscovered Stories of Glafkos Thrassakis*. In fact, the 1989 edition gave way seven years later to the "revised, definitive" Livanis edition, which was itself amended by a further sixty pages of text, bound separately but packaged and sold with the book. As the narrator explains in the prologue to this longest, most outward- and inward-reaching of Vassilikos's works, the text defies a definite conclusion, since he (the narrator, and also Vassilikos) can never bring himself to stop writing and set the manuscript aside. Perhaps this is because *Glafkos Thrassakis*—considered by some to be Vassilikos's greatest work, superior even to his celebrated *Z*—draws its material largely from Vassilikos's own life, as attested by his 1990 autobiography *Memory Returns in Plastic Sandals.* Indeed, as the note above suggests, *Glafkos Thrassakis* might be considered a kind of fictional biography of a nonfictional individual: Vassilikos himself, who continues to rework this "autonovegraphy" as his attitude toward the details of his (and his country's) past are transfigured by the passage of time.

To date, *Glafkos* has accompanied Vassilikos—the author of over ninety books translated into thirty languages and Greece's ambassador to UNESCO since 1996—through almost three decades, returning in ever-evolving forms. This translation represents yet another continuation of the *Thrassakis* tale. Readers familiar with the original (though in the case of this book it is particularly unclear what that means) will note considerable differences between this translation and the most recent edition of the Greek text, upon which it has been based. In a series of meetings and conversations, it became clear to Vassilikos and myself that my translation would transform the text yet again—not only by moving it into a new language, but by modifying its structure and content as well. During our first meeting in Athens, Vassilikos decided to cut from the English version the 200-page "Roman Notebooks." Written after his return to Greece following the fall of the dictatorship in 1974, this section belongs, Vassilikos said, to an entirely different chapter in his life; perhaps a translation of the "Notebooks," he said, could form a future sequel to this English edition. Subsequently, over the course of several months and with the invaluable help of Avi Sharon, minor cuts were made throughout the remainder of the text.

These changes, while quite unusual in a translation, mirror the history of the text in its original language, as the book's complicated life continues in its English-language afterlife. They reflect the general trend, in the decades-long process of revision the book has undergone, toward streamlining, clarification, and making more discrete the interwoven threads that constitute this multifaceted narrative: Glafkos's childhood during the second World War; his life in exile during the dictatorship of 1967–74; the unpublished short stories described and discussed in the "Findings of the First Sack"; and the biographer's own tale of growing instability due to his psychological identification with the subject of his study.

Many names and events that provide a context and framework for the book may prove unfamiliar to readers removed from the sociopolitical history of twentieth-century Greece. Foremost among these historical conditions are the German Occupation and the Civil War, which formed the backdrop of Vassilikos's early childhood, and the colonels' dictatorship of 1967–74, which pushed many leftist writers and intellectuals (Vassilikos among them) into exile abroad. Despite the possible foreignness of certain references, I have chosen not to include footnotes in this text, as that would create an air of academicism out of keeping with the more freewheeling, "anti-statistical" approach taken by the narrator, as by Vassilikos himself. My hope is that this translation will allow the English-language reader to approach the history behind and around the text through the text itself, through this "biogranovel," this "autonovegraphy," this "novistory."

I would like to express my gratitude to Avi Sharon for his assistance and advice throughout the process of translation and editing. Many thanks also to Peter Constantine for his encouragement and support; to Jill Schoolman and Leah Swann, my editors at Seven Stories; and to my parents and brother, David, Helen, and Michael Emmerich, for their careful reading of multiple drafts.

KAREN EMMERICH

THE FEW
THINGS I
KNOW ABOUT
GLAFKOS
THRASSAKIS

INTRODUCTION

WHAT STANDS out in this piece, apparently by the same anonymous painter, is the movement of the central figure's hand as he raises his glass to propose the standard "To your health," and his glinting glance fondly embraces his companions—friendly faces, elderly, red-cheeked and gentle, people who look like they could never wish evil on anyone, much less commit it.

We have a bit more information about this piece, thanks to an explanatory note found tucked into the back right corner of the canvas as if hidden away in a cupboard. Moreover, the amateur painter seems not to have known that in order to stretch the canvas properly, he had to hammer open the crossed supports of the wooden frame. Thanks to that ignorance, the painting has been preserved for us in all its detail, while on a well-stretched canvas, the acrylic paint would have cracked, split, splintered with time.

From the slip of paper found in the hollow formed by the two embracing supports, we learn that the painting is called, "The Return of Glafkos Thrassakis to His Native Land in the Year 1976 A.D." The *Encyclopaedia Universalis* informs us that Thrassakis was:

> . . . *the pen name of Greek writer Lazarus Lazaridis, who was obliged to live far from his homeland by a cholera epidemic and a conviction under Law 509, decided by a military court in his absence, for illegal trade in antiquities, or "the removal of an essential part of the state." Thrassakis published very few works during his lifetime. Most of his writings remained unpublished and were entrusted to the library of a major American*

3

4

university, where he later intended to settle as a writer-in-residence and revise these writings at his leisure. Yet that dream was never realized. Due to an inconceivable twist of fate, Thrassakis was devoured in New Guinea by a tribe of cannibals who later became vegetarians, around the time that one of the Rockefeller sons was also captured and eaten. The only proviso concerning the donation of his papers to the aforementioned university was that, in the event of some unforeseen accident, they were not to be opened until twenty-five years from the time of his death—which is to say, in the year 2003.

The specific reasons that forced Thrassakis to live the greater part of his life abroad remain unknown. When in 1976 he was finally able to return to Greece, his friends organized a celebratory dinner at the Grigoris Taverna in the Athenian suburb of Kifissia. Searching through publications of the time, we find mention of this event in a bi-monthly column in the literary journal *New Stove* (Vol. 292, no. 478, 59):

It was with infinite pleasure that our country's cultural community welcomed the lifting of the ban prohibiting the return of distinguished comrade Lazarus N. Lazaridis, better known in these circles by his pseudonym, Glafkos Thrassakis. During his years in exile, Thrassakis served as our literary ambassador to the West, cultivating a hotbed of Hellenists and translators at the Institut des Langues Orientales, where he earned his living teaching Modern Greek literature with the amiable philhellene and stunning philologist Henri Soupault. Among those in attendance were . . .

These names don't interest us, since they no longer mean anything. What does interest us are the faces and their expressions, which can be made out only with difficulty, hidden as they are by the shadow that falls from the arbor above the outdoor gathering—a shadow that allows the amateur painter to concentrate not so much on the specific features of the individual guests as on his attempt to capture in snapshot images the intense emotion that presides over the table, images which he brings to life for us in the clearings and glades of his painting.

The light in the painting is dramatically Attic, the kind of light that bestows on each object, no matter how small, the essence of its earthly existence, transforming the courtyard of the Grigoris Taverna into a garden of delights. Judging from the slant of the light, it must be about one-thirty or two in the afternoon. The table is spread with all the taverna's specialties: broad beans in tomato sauce, meat patties, triangular cheese-pies, pickled sheep's eyes, potatoes with oregano, fish-roe salad, and last but not least *moustalevria*, since, according to the article in *New Stove*, it was this dessert of must and hazelnut flour that Thrassakis missed most of all during his twenty-year absence. The article continues:

> *In his toast, Thrassakis said, among other things, how deeply moved he was to find himself again among these old comrades who had all started out together, so many years ago, as servants of the same priestess: the Art of the Written Word. He remarked sadly that not everyone was there, but added, "It's as if they were here with us, because their writing speaks for them—those works that have conquered time."*

It must have been incredibly painful for him to see all these people seated around the table—Kadmo, Iro, Iannoula, Penelope, Michalis, Thomas—all these beautifully aged faces of gray-haired friends who had been teenagers when he left, white-haired friends he had remembered through the years as men in the prime of life, and a few women (muses of his youth?) who were now sweet-faced grandmothers. He must have been hit by a kind of sudden spiritual emptiness on seeing them there, like transformed heroes from Proust's last volume, in which time acquires the density of matter—so that, in abolishing matter, time ends up becoming an organic part of nature itself. . . . The painting exudes the warm calm one feels when he senses himself approaching the end of his earthly journey.

Later on in his speech (as reported, once again, in the bi-monthly column), Thrassakis spoke of the absurd position of the emigrant, the expatriate, the exile, the refugee, the resident alien—a historically legitimate position whose significance has almost been recognized. But what is the fate, the finale of even the most successful of exiles? Take, for example, Francisco Portas, Thrassakis suggested. Born in the Cretan city of Rethymno, Portas studied philology in Padua, became a teacher in the Greek community in Venice, and later found a position in the Italian Court in Modena, where he was inducted into the city's famous Academy. Then, suspected of harboring hostility toward Protestantism, which had just begun to permeate the city of Modena, he left for neighboring Ferarra, where he went on to pursue a brilliant academic and intellectual career. He then made his way across all of Europe, finally settling in Brussels, where he lived for a full thirteen years, teaching Greek to exalted personages of the time. He continued to publish Greek books with Latin commentary (Pindar, Apollonius, Sophocles, Xenophon, Thucydides, Aristotle, Euripides, and the rhetorician Ermogenis) until his death in 1581, crotchety and tempestuous to the very end, and to all appearances unsatisfied with the course of his life. No matter how far the footpaths of exile led him, two things seem never to have left his mind: a desire to cultivate and enrich Greek letters, and nostalgia for his homeland.

Thrassakis, the article tells us, ended his moving speech with the lines of Ronsard, the French poet of the *Pléiade* group: "Greece bore me, France buried me. / Normandy will keep me here to rot. / O, proud fate that oppresses all men / and makes a Greek die in Constant."

It is still early for us to enter into a discussion of the reason or reasons why Thrassakis left his native land. From some of his writings we can deduce that he must have been strongly affected by the death during the Civil War of his brother Markos Lazaridis, a well-known "captain" in that organization falsely condemned for "the removal of an essential part of the state." Perhaps Thrassakis had suffered from a kind of overdose of Greece and decided to go cold turkey, like teetotalers during the American Prohibition. If in fact he did return—which remains a good subject for further investigation—it may have been because he instinctively sensed that he would meet his untimely end in exile yet again, just two years later. At least, that is, according to the *Encyclopaedia Universalis*, which gives the year of his death as 1978, when he was devoured by cannibals who later became vegetarians.

But what really concerns us is not so much the painting itself, as the identity of the self-taught artist. We know that this work, like the previous one, was completed in 1976 or shortly thereafter. But why did the artist choose to paint this particular scene? Perhaps he was acquainted with the deceased? Perhaps Thrassakis had described the celebration at the Grigoris Taverna to the painter, who then decided to recreate the feast on canvas? Perhaps the painter himself was among the guests that day? Or perhaps he was simply flipping through *New Stove* one day and happened to read the column and began to identify with the deceased, involuntarily putting himself in his place—and so, in substituting himself for Thrassakis, depicted the scene as if he had been the one to return to his homeland after such an extended absence? In this case, it seems likely that the painter would have painted his own friends around the table, and that he himself would be the central figure gazing fondly at his companions and raising his glass to begin his toast. . . .

The anonymity of the painter and the enormous lapse of time since the painting's completion preclude the formation of any "categorical accusations," which would, at any rate, be of little interest to anyone. We can only suppose that the amateur painter, perhaps not wanting to inflict on his friends the anguish of return he had felt that year (but what year, we might ask, and why this anguish of return?) disguised himself under the cover of another—a double, a mirror, a reflection—and took an existing person as a persona, an existing name as a pseudonym, in order to express himself more freely under the guise of a third person.

PROLOGUE
BIOGRAPHICAL INFORMATION

*The researcher's job is to create forms, means of access, tools,
keys, just as the writer's job is to render them useless.*
—Panayiotis Moullas

THIS INVESTIGATION, which could be called *The Few Things I Know About Glafkos Thrassakis*, has no pretensions of ever achieving its ultimate goal, since such an inquiry ends only with the researcher's death.

With a public notary you can tell just from glancing at his records what kinds of people he met, what dealings he had with different business ventures; but with a writer it's extremely difficult to track down the true stories that gave birth to the legends, especially if there isn't much concrete evidence to go on. It's like a field of untouched clover: a deer bounds across and the clover springs up again as it passes, erasing the animal's tracks. Unless we have some kind of real evidence, it's almost impossible for us to retrace a life spent on the fringes of life—and, more specifically, on the fringes of history.

My desire to write about this life evolved from my fundamental opposition to the dead silence and stagnation that characterized Greece at the time. I wanted to go abroad. So I proposed a study of Glafkos Thrassakis's life and work in the European Common Market. Almost immediately the Common Market, with the resources at its disposal, granted me a fellowship to support my research.

Not that Thrassakis had any particularly strong ties to the Common Market, though one source identifies him as a translator for the first delegation of Greek workers to enter the Market around 1955. Apart from a single letter, which we will examine later on, he himself left no written evidence of this excursion, though a verification of his presence would prove extremely useful in illuminating certain particularly shadowy facets of his work. For example, a certain phrase springs to mind from an early, unpublished piece: "I descend into the darkness of the earth as if into the darkness of the womb"—which, written in 1956, can refer to nothing other than his experience (if confirmed) in the Belgian coal mines.

The claim that Thrassakis might have had something to do with that first group of immigrant workers is supported by an article announcing their arrival in a Greek-Belgian magazine, which notes the presence beside the representative from the Labor Department of a young interpreter in thick glasses (which Thrassakis surely would have been wearing by then), whom the Belgian trade unions asked to stay and help keep an eye on those first three hundred Greek workers—who, finding themselves face to face with Italian immigrants, were reliving minor episodes from the recent war between Greek and Italian forces. However, despite exhaustive research, no other mention of him was uncovered, which suggests that Thrassakis did not accept the proposal—primarily because, as the magazine hints, his thick glasses would have made it difficult, if not impossible, to descend into the deep shafts of the mines.

≈

IN A MANNER I will soon describe, I verified the information the encyclopedia had to offer: At the age of 45, Glafkos suffered the same fate as the young Rockefeller; he was roasted and devoured by the savages of New Guinea. Glafkos happened upon some religious feast honoring the warriors who had fallen in battle against another tribe. To the cannibals, this man who appeared out of the blue on his raft, having crossed the straits of the sea, seemed like a gift sent by their god for the feast. And so—disregarding the laws of the jungle, the attempted intervention of the Dutch missionaries, any thought of ascertaining the identity of their future victim, and so on and so forth—these savages immediately undressed, roasted, and ate him, spitting out nothing but his bones, which they couldn't manage to swallow.

It was in Delft, a small city in the north of Holland, as quiet and scentless as a tulip, that I finally managed to locate the bishop who had been in charge of all missionary affairs in New Guinea at the time of Thrassakis's death. The bishop then sent me to

Leiden, where at long last I met with a pastor who was able to confirm that the man the cannibals had devoured was in fact none other than Glafkos himself.

With nationalist movements sweeping over the countries of the so-called "Fourth World," this pastor ended up being the last missionary to abandon New Guinea. Since then, the pastor now told me, his country, deprived of its colonies, had shrunk—but not his religion, which feeds off the wealth of its colonies in the Afterworld (and here he quoted a line from Lorca about the poet's hometown of Granada, which has no other port than the one formed above her by the starry sky). After this sudden shrinkage, when its all-consuming tentacles were cut off from the sources of raw materials the colonies had provided, Europe had sought to create its own union. That, the pastor said, was why the Common Market had decided to fund my research on Thrassakis: it wanted to show that the cannibals were still savages, and still needed the light of civilization to lead them from the darkness of the jungle.

I was falling from the clouds. So they'd had an ulterior motive in supporting my research? What they really wanted, those capitalist leeches, was to prove their own superiority?

No, not at all, the good pastor insisted, wanting above all to encourage me in my work, instead of discouraging me before I had really even begun. As far as he could tell, there was no ulterior motive; I was free to write whatever I pleased.

"Yes," I answered, "but always with my hero's well-known end in mind."

"But think of Christ, who was crucified," he said. "Can anyone write about Christ without referring, if only implicitly, to his crucifixion?"

Then he pointed to a drawbridge just like the one Van Gogh had painted, lifting itself to let a boat pass in the canal below.

We were walking together through the city of Leiden. The slow quietness of the streets; the fresh air, free of exhaust; the quaint houses, unchanged from the time of the great Flemish painters; the pretty northern blonds riding by on their bicycles and the long-haired boys who waved to them, all came together to create a calming, soothing atmosphere.

"So you witnessed his sacrifice?" I dared to ask as we left the city's museum, which was rich with curios from the early colonies. It had started to drizzle, and the pastor opened his umbrella.

"No, of course not," he said in his excellent English, pulling at his dog's leash as it strained to sniff at another passing dog. "But the chief of the tribe, a friend of mine, told me about it afterwards, as if it were something perfectly natural—after all, this white man's arrival had coincided with the climax of their ritual orgies." The pastor described the victim for me, and from his description, I realized that it had to be Thrassakis. (Here I should mention that it was the pastor's statements to the press, badly translated in the Greek papers of the time, that had first sparked my interest in the "Thrassakis case.")

"He was unlucky," the pastor continued as we walked toward his house, and I felt for the first time as if I were under the surface of the sea, so strong was the reptilian feeling that washed over me as the sky gradually darkened. "He was dreadfully unlucky—if that wind hadn't come up and sent his pirogue down the Sepik River, through that narrow pass, he wouldn't have landed on the stretch of shore belonging to the cannibal tribe that captured him, but would have reached another, rival tribe, whose members would have made him their king, since just then they were expecting the arrival of a white god. So the next day I sent David their way, a young Englishman who will surely go on to write amazing things. Remind me to tell you about him sometime."

By then we had reached his house, where we parted ways, though I didn't rule out the possibility of another meeting with him in the near future. His dog had loved the smell of my shoes so much that it whimpered from behind the door as I left.

≈

STARTING AT THE END, with Thrassakis's death, and trying methodically to work my way back to the beginning, as one might start at a delta and climb back to the river's source, was for me the only way. This amphisemic progress of sources and mouths was more helpful to me than helicopter flights over unfamiliar mountain ranges could ever have been. Anyone can talk about the end of a life, but few can speak of a soul's creation, of the influences and elements a root absorbed before it met its familiar end. Thrassakis, who belonged to a restricted nation, was in no way exempt from the common fate of his colleagues and comrades: the loss of correspondence and important juvenile writings (the only ones to survive were those saved by a certain mad aunt), as well as the complete lack of bibliography and of any biographical materials whatsoever. The few surviving photographs from his childhood years add to our picture of him, but offer no explanation. They show him as a round, chubby baby with a mop of curls, perhaps because his mother had wanted a girl and dressed him as such until the last possible minute, when he was old enough to start school. Each photograph is a dead drop of rain, a dead tear. So how can you yourself cry? Whatever else that might have offered a bit of light with which to peer down into the well is gone.

Which is why my first task was to visit Brussels, where Thrassakis spent an important segment of his adult life. As he wrote to a certain friend and "biographer," he would have preferred Charleroix, a city he knew from the trams of his youth in Thessaloniki. If he ended up in Brussels it was only because, as he wrote to his friend, "cities choose their people, not the other way around."

According to the leftist literary critic Pavsanias Alipastos (surely a pseudonym), he chose Brussels because it was then the site of NATO headquarters, and Thrassakis, an agent in the guise of an intellectual, played the role of NATO ghostwriter. However, this hypothesis is not only entirely unfounded, but it shakes the very foundations of the doctrine of free will. Does everything always have to boil down to political motivations? Can't a man be just a man and nothing more?

According to our point of view, Thrassakis chose the city as his site of more or less permanent residence because, raised and fattened on French, he found in Brussels all the advantages of a major European city without any of the usual disadvantages. Besides, it had a larger stream of immigrants passing through. Some of the taverna owners in Brussels remember him to this day. Something as small as a plate of stuffed cabbage leaves could make him almost happy. Every so often he would paint a mural or two. Every so often he would dance a *zeimbekia*. Which, incidentally, brings to mind one reason some people thought he was gay: he had once studied classical ballet. But he just liked to dance. He needed to express himself. He was self-sufficient in his solitude. Until, that is, he met the woman who would later become his wife. But I believe my own wife will be writing extensively about that.

And now, before I proceed, I would like to address all those who ask, whenever the name of the unlucky writer comes up in conversation, why he never wrote a "cyclical novel." By "cyclical" they mean total, rocklike, complete. Perhaps he hadn't had the necessary experience? Hadn't lived the necessary sum total of life? Perhaps he just didn't have time before his untimely death? Or perhaps some such novel is to be found among his manuscripts in the special collections branch of the university library? His friend and classmate, his supposed "biographer," informs us that when Thrassakis was more stationary than he should have been, he was overcome by an impatience that spread over his body like swarming ants. He suffered. He wanted to move. With the outbreak of World War II, he had lost time at the very outset of life. So, like all runners who have fallen behind at the start of a race, he was always hurrying to make up for that loss. Hence the fragmentary aspect of his published body of work.

≈

A FEW DAYS ago someone asked me if Thrassakis was really a cosmopolitan writer. He hadn't read anything by him, but that's what he'd heard. I told him that the fact that Thrassakis chose to live as a citizen of the world didn't necessarily make his work cosmopolitan—perhaps he was confusing Thrassakis with his fellow writer Cosmos Politis? No, he was talking about Glafkos. So I explained to this man that Thrassakis had been an uprooted Greek who kept moving to whatever city Alexander Onassis had just left. His movements from one place to the next had as a necessary condition that he never find himself in the same city as "*le Grec.*"

Why exactly he sought comparison with that baron of wealth was and remains unknown. Since the two of them had never met, most likely it reflected a kind of wounded pride: "I'm someone too, since I'm avoiding him." As for the fact that he avoided airplanes at all costs, that had a logical reasoning behind it. He had left his homeland by plane and had sworn never to board one again, except to return.

The reason he left is common knowledge: the "cholera" epidemic forced him to leave, after first mowing down all his nearest and dearest.

≈

GLAFKOS, MASTER CHEF of atzem pilaf. Glafkos, dream interpreter who doesn't believe in dreams. Glafkos this, Glafkos that. An investigation without material evidence is a hopeless endeavor. Did he have a bank account? If so, what kind of deposits did he make? Where might Glafkos have wandered, in search of what thing? What was he missing, what did he miss? Was he weighed down by a house? Did he feel an obligation to certain mentors? What was his relationship with the telephone? Did he disapprove of hijacking airplanes? When did he learn to drive? How many car accidents was he in? Did he vote? If so, in which elections, local or national? What party did he vote for? Was he in the clear with the national authorities? Did he have a police record? What did he think of the crisis in the Middle East? Did he take part in anti-Vietnam demonstrations? Did he offer monetary support for the Peace Boat? What size shoe did he wear? Did he prefer laced shoes or slip-ons? Was he color blind? Why in his entire published body of work does he never mention the color yellow? Was he scared of the color, or simply unable to see it? Did his short-sightedness—the result of adolescent masturbatory tendencies—get better or worse with age? What was his relation to the anarchist organization that placed a bomb in the NATO headquarters in Brussels? And what about food? Did he eat meat or vegetables? Which did he prefer, white wine or red? Did he stop to answer polls in the street? What was his stance on the oil crisis? If he had to choose between two TV channels, one showing a soccer match and the other a program about a mission to the moon, which would he have chosen? If he had never been born, would the world have been any worse off? Or did he, as a consumer, indirectly aid in the processes of production? Did he tie neckties with a thick or thin knot? Judging from photographs he seems to have preferred triangular knots. But who will ever be able to answer any of these questions?

And there are lots more unanswered questions. We know from photographs that he smoked a pipe instead of cigarettes or cigars. But at the post office, did he prefer to lick the stamps or to use a wet sponge, if there was one on the counter? Getting into a taxi alone, would he sit in back or up front next to the driver? Did he like Turkish baths? Was it his fear of accidents that made him always choose one of the last cars on a train, or was he simply too lazy to walk to the front? Did he go to church? Did he like Beethoven or Brahms? We know from his writings that he preferred Tebaldi over Callas, but what were his favorite Verdi arias? Mountains or sea? Tuberculosis or malaria? Lebanon or Libadia? How little we know of a man's life. . . .

There is one serious problem (see the *Encyclopaedia Universalis*) hindering any investigation into the life and work of Glafkos Thrassakis: the works he wrote after leaving Greece (which, of course, constitute the great majority of his manuscripts) were sold, still unfinished, to an American university that believed Thrassakis might acquire some measure of fame after his death. Actually, after the publication of the English translation of *Prinos II* he received several offers from various universities in the U.S. to teach for a semester or two as a visiting professor, as well as an offer to write for or be written up in (I haven't quite figured that out yet) the international *Who's Who*, and then the fateful proposal from a university in Massachusetts to house his manuscripts, memoirs, letters, and so on in the special collections wing of its library.

Perhaps because Thrassakis happened to be experiencing considerable economic difficulties; or because as a boy, as he describes in one of his texts, he had witnessed the plundering of the manuscripts of the Agios Theros monastery, which were sold by the kilo to half-witted middlemen; or because (and this last possibility seems, to me, the most likely) he sensed that the end of his earthly journey was not far off and hoped to settle down in the U.S. and revise his manuscripts, giving them their final form before offering them to publishers for translation, he decided to send three bags of his papers to Massachusetts.

I wrote repeatedly to the university library explaining that I was preparing an extensive study, the first of its kind, on the life and work of Glafkos Thrassakis. I even had the Common Market's Ministry of Culture ask on my behalf for permission to access that valuable archive. I would not remove any document, I said, from the holy space of the wing in which his papers were being held. If I found something absolutely essential for my work, I would photocopy material within the library itself under the watchful eye of its accommodating staff.

Unfortunately, the answer that came back was negative. The "prematurely departed Greek writer," the letter said, had left explicit orders that in the case of an accident the three sacks were not to be opened until twenty-five years after his death. What did he think he was hiding, the confidential files of a new Kennedy case? Did he take himself so seriously as to believe that twenty-five years after his death people would still be interested in his non-existence?

I still want to go, and thanks to the fellowship I have the funds to get there. I'm all ready to set off in search of the lost treasure, but I keep tripping up on the secret of a bank that doesn't want to hand over its keys. So I'm obliged to turn my attention to the things he wrote while still in Greece—and of those I prefer the unpublished texts discovered in the basement of one of his aunts who went mad, believing herself to be Beethoven's granddaughter.

So I chase after him like a dog following its master's trail, knowing I'll never manage to find him if I depend only on smell—for his scent is lost in Rotterdam, where he boarded the ship for New Guinea, from whence he never returned.

One thing remains in doubt: why did Thrassakis prefer to entrust his manuscripts to the States, and not to the Old World? He wasn't so naïve as not to realize that the United States was first on the list of nations bound to suffer attack—cities and towns would be bombed, and the people, with their fragile, untried skin, would bear the trials inflicted on them by the law of historical responsibility. Just as no man can live without suffering some kind of wound, he knew that all countries will eventually experience war on their own land. So Europe, which had by then retired from her military career, had a far safer future than America, who was still waiting her turn in line.

I am of the belief that Thrassakis's complicated relations with America have not yet been explained. An alumnus of Anatolia College, a private high school in Thessaloniki maintained by American sympathizers of the East, wouldn't he have had a strong bond with that country? According to one account, he became a leftist because he had studied at Anatolia. According to another, in 1947 during the Civil War when the College was besieged by guerrilla fighters, he and some of his friends snuck off the campus at night and brought the guerrillas food stolen from the school's cafeteria. And finally, a completely unverifiable account claims that Thrassakis (then Lazaridis) had thrown a kind of primitive molotov cocktail at Purefoy, the American Consul in Thessaloniki, who had come up to the College to hand out that year's diplomas. (Purefoy, I should note, became something of a symbolic name, since he had come to Thessaloniki in order to prepare the groundwork for the purifying "distilleries" that were soon to come.) Whether this bomb actually went off or not, the name of a Lazaridis is mixed up in the affair, and when the Tupamaros in Latin America, worthy continuers of the trend Thrassakis had begun, later killed Purefoy in mid-journey, Glafkos dedicated a battle hymn to them.

To be honest, I find nothing in all of this para-philology but the strong foundations he was given at a very young age by the luxury of having at his disposal an entire library that included even the early works of Ritsos, during the very height of the guerrilla war. And, of course, the foundations of his strange sexual tendencies, prematurely developed in the closed, entrenched camp of the boys' school. And when, at a ripe age, he shouted out the familiar slogan, "Out with the American Bases," the bases to which he referred must have been none other than the American foundations upon which, as an adolescent, his personality had been built.

≈

THRASSAKIS WAS the uprooted exile *par excellence*. The reason for his exile was, as mentioned before, "cholera." (I should explain that "cholera" was what they called the junta back then. And Thrassakis was anti-choleric. Which is to say, an anti-junta intellectual.) But even after the epidemic had passed, he was still not permitted to return home, because there was a charge against him, decided in his absence under the quaint old Law 509—which, in order to discourage another theft to rival that of the Elgin marbles in 1844, found illicit dealers in antiquities guilty of "the attempt to remove an essential part of the state." The police claimed to have found in his possession an amphora from Thassos which he was taking out of the country to sell illegally abroad. These days there is no doubt that their motives were purely political: they planted the amphora in his bag in order to relieve themselves of his presence and influence inside of Greece. Abroad, they knew, he could play only a minor role.

Surely a more resourceful government could have found some more effective way of disempowering him. Because by disempowering him only politically, they left him what really mattered, the marrow: his work.

But now that work is buried in America, and he himself was gobbled up long ago in New Guinea. What, then, is left?

Because I've thought about it a lot: the map is altered only by earth-shattering upheavals. The passage of winged gods (poets among them) leaves no more mark on a wall than the death rattle of a butterfly. What did Thrassakis want from life? To make wine into spirit. But the spirit departed and all that was left was the wine that ate away at his liver. Chasing his shadow, which was chasing him, he passed through the world like a movie screened on the crumbling wall of an outdoor theater—because the wall has no memory. The wall cannot remember. He passed majestically, like a helicopter's shadow over rooftop terraces where rich women lie sunning themselves in the nude, seeing the helicopter only at the exact moment when it's blocking the sun from their bodies. The absence of sun marks the presence of the comet that hides it. So, he passed through life like a human comet, leaving a long trail in his wake—a trail which, however, the wind soon made its own.

≈

THE WOMAN who had helped me get the fellowship wanted to see me. She was a countess, a little flighty, then living in Copenhagen. I went up north by train, hoping for an extension of the fellowship, or a raise at the very least.

She welcomed me to her country estate, which was an old manor house. She openly confessed to me that she had gotten me mixed up in the monograph. Her country's representative of cultural affairs in the Common Market, she had, she confessed, been in love with Glafkos, and she now wanted someone to immortalize his form.

I explained my difficulties to her. I explained that there can be no Common Market without a Common Quest. The problem was, in the end, a matter of so-called free time. The gaps in buildings are what keep the bricks together. For some the gap is great, for others almost non-existent. And so the workers . . .

She cut me off, saying that Glafkos's problem had always been women. Uncertain of himself, he constantly sought confirmation.

I told her that my wife, who was researching Glafkos's relationships with women, would gladly come up to meet with her. The countess got angry. The other women, she said, were of no interest to her. She had suffered enough from Thrassakis's wife—now she was supposed to suffer from the wife of his biographer, too? And right then, she threw herself on me. She said I looked just like him. So much that for a fraction of a second, she had thought I was him, that she was speaking to him. And that's why she threw herself on me.

I left with a deep doubt in my mind: perhaps she was clinically depressed? If she was any indication of what Glafkos's life had been like, I completely understand why he might have preferred New Guinea. . . .

PART ONE
NOVEL

I won't relate yet again the history of this important discovery or give another detailed description of the contents of the find. Besides, that history remains quite uncertain on many points. We know almost nothing of the works to which it refers. The thirteen volumes, or fragments of volumes, discovered in 1945 include about 49 texts, all in the Coptic language, which most likely represent the fourth- or fifth-century library of a Gnostic community in Lower Egypt. Here I deem it necessary to note that some of the writings, those included in the Jung codex, are influenced by the teachings of Valentinus. Indeed, they are. But I will only note those texts that contain an immediate bearing on our topic.
—Henri-Charles Puech,
  In the Pursuit of Knowledge, p. 93

Chapter One

I

The Tigers

SOME TIME had passed since I had abandoned all attempts to continue my research, hindered primarily by a lack of funds, when I received an unexpected letter from the U.S., from the main office of the Tiger Club (something like the Lions Club, known throughout the world for its philanthropic work) regarding the difficulties I was facing in completing "our" work. As a society to which Thrassakis had belonged, the Tiger Club was willing to contribute to the cause.

I immediately set out to ascertain whether or not the deceased had, in fact, been a member of the club. I knew he'd been mixed up in lots of things. At the branch office in Athens (26 Valaoritos, third floor) I learned that while he had never actually been a member (he possessed neither the necessary career accomplishments nor the corresponding financial security), he had once travelled to the U.S. as a Tiger scholar—though, to be sure, "against his will."

Knowing Thrassakis's character, familiar with the simpler as well as the more complex problems my hero had faced, that "against his will" set me wondering. And I was right to wonder. I had hit a vein. But first, let me finish my own story.

On returning to Athens after my visit to the crazy woman in Copenhagen, about whom I will write more later, I had made up my mind to withdraw from the "case." So how had the Tiger Club come to learn of my "difficulties"? Who was starting these rumors, leaking these things I was sure I'd never told anyone? Was it the dead—who, they say, still speak, demanding justice? Or perhaps some chance firing of fate had brought news of my predicament to the ears of some Tiger big shot, and thus they had decided to help me out?

In return for the money, my only obligation would be to attend one of their banquets, where the Tigers—the members of the club, that is—mimicked the beasts of the jungle. And I certainly had no objection to going once and honoring the custom by howling along, since I could then make myself festively absent from all the other banquets of the year.

But did this mean I'd have to become a member? No, they didn't insist on anything of the sort. Like most masonic guilds, they permitted tremendous individual freedom. Without ever saying it openly, though, they hinted that the committee would more readily approve the proposed "contribution" if I agreed to become a trial member. How? Simple: by filling out a short, standardized form.

I was supplied this form by the branch office at 26 Valaoritos, third floor. What they wanted was exactly what the American consulate required before it would approve a visa to the U.S.: a declaration that you were not, had never been, and would never become a member of the Communist Party or supporter thereof. "A rather outdated regulation," the exceedingly courteous Tiger in the office explained to me, a rule *datant* (he had studied French) from John Foster Dulles and the Cold War era, "but unfortunately it's still in effect, since you could live two lives back to back in the time it takes to amend a law." If he were figuring 75 years as a median life expectancy, this was a roundabout way of reminding me that a disgraceful number of unjust laws haven't changed in the 150 years since the liberation of Greece itself.

That "against his will" meant, then, that Thrassakis had signed the form. So it must still exist somewhere, that slip of paper he would have seen as an emblem of shame which would mark the rest of his life—since for him the "I never was" would weigh, in the end, less heavily than the "I will never become." The mortgaging of the future was, for Thrassakis, an act far more barbarous than the denial of the past. (I, however, am of the opposite opinion: to deny something that hasn't yet happened, and which, according to the laws of probability, might never happen, isn't nearly as serious a matter as to deny something that happened, to deny the person you were—to deny, in short, your past.)

I then politely asked if the local Tiger representative would be willing to provide me with a Dutch or Swedish application form, from which the offending clause would no doubt be absent (for the form changed, chameleon-style, from place to place, according to each country's history and level of economic development). I was sure, I said, that neither the Dutch nor the Swedish chapter of the Tiger Club would ever ask candidates to sign that kind of statement of repentance. Referring then to my own case (after all, reasoning is like strategic warfare: it should always take the immediate situation into consideration, and not just the normative abstraction), I went on to say that while I had never been a Communist, as my police record could confirm, and while I was fairly certain that I would never become a Communist, I was unable to offer my full guarantee, since such a guarantee would constitute a restriction of my personal freedom of action.

"But it's just a formality, purely routine. The big fish are all in cahoots," he sighed bitterly. "The rest of us will be squabbling till the end of time over paleontological differences."

The man seemed to be forgetting—and, of course, I lost no time in reminding him—that in the long run the "rest of us" always end up paying for the quarrels between "big fish."

He threw me a discouraged look. *That's why we Greeks, as a nation, will never get ahead,* his eyes seemed to be telling me. *It's always, "Not you, me," and, "Not me, you," until along comes some guy like Koemtzis who knifed a man to death just because some band played the other guy's song instead of his.*

Yes, but—I mentally objected—*at least Koemtzis had the guts to do his "laundry" out in plain sight. What about the silent crimes of the Pentagon or the tanneries, where they clean hides with no one around to see?*

My Tiger was one of those Greeks caught up since birth in the craze for all things American. But whereas true Greek-Americans at least have a true nostalgia for their ethnic homeland, these Greeks, who have never even left home, never cut the umbilical cord that ties them to their land, imitate their cosmopolitan counterparts with the awkward manner of apes monkeying humans—since humans (as, after Darwin, no one can doubt) have never stopped aping.

So with an atavistic movement (and in a moment I'll explain why I characterize it as such), I ripped up the form, right there in front of the local Tiger representative. His only response was to let out a groan. As I later learned, in moments of anger the trusty Tiger doesn't swear or curse the gods, in whom it is doubtful, anyhow, that he believes. No, the Tiger just groans—which is why once a year, at the banquet, he howls like a beast, symbolically venting the anger of man at the injustice of God the Creator.

I learned about the atavistic nature of the event just described from an old woman in Olintho, on the Halkidiki peninsula—a woman as wrinkled as a Corinthian raisin, as the Russian poet Siniavskii might say, since that's the only Greek product that appears to have made it into the Soviet Union. Atavistic because it reminded the old woman of another, previous event still engraved on her memory, so deep was the impression it made on her. It was an ordinary morning in the Lazaridis house, where she worked as a maid. Lazos's father always got up first, drank his tea, and before leaving for work to earn the family's bread and butter, would call in to rouse his loafer of a son, who was inevitably lazing in bed or dawdling at his desk with his pencils. But on that particular morning, the maid, now a decrepit old granny who always votes red, heard the father threaten the son: "Either you sign or . . . ." That "or," the grammatical disjunctive, could signify nothing other than a real-life disjunction from the conjunction of the couple—which is to say, from his parents. But Lazos grabbed the paper and tore it in two, saying something like, "I was and am and will continue to be a Communist"—which, in turn, compelled old Lazaridis to reply, "Do you see this hand? You know only one side of it, the indulgent side, the side that gives. May you never meet the other."

What was at stake here, as the maid later learned, was the contested question of the fellowship. His family wanted to get him off their hands, and had found the Tigers, who were willing to pay. But Lazos didn't seem too eager to abandon the family hearth. Thus, according to the maid, the quarrel between father and son.

During the difficult years of the German Occupation, it seems that his father had, as a "leftover" democrat, and without understanding its tie to the Communist party, supported the guerrilla army of EAM (National Liberation Front). But during the liberation celebrations, he was alarmed to see Thessaloniki's Aristotle Square flooded with red flags. Among the members of the crowd was the dental assistant from his office, Fofo, who was also carrying a red flag. Old Lazaridis slapped her right there in the middle of the square—an act that Lazos, still a child, seems to have seen and heard, and for which he never forgave his father. At such a young age, he was of course unable to explain the act in ideological terms, so he interpreted it emotionally. He reasoned that his father, secretly in love with his assistant, was jealous at seeing her happy and carefree, celebrating with her friends, dancing in the streets after four years of occupation.

But perhaps this incident wouldn't have made such a lasting impression on him if it hadn't been followed shortly afterwards by the girl's death, which, like all deaths, was unjust and unexplained. Fofo, headed for her hometown of Kavala to serve as a juror in the people's trials of those who had collaborated with the Bulgarian Nazis, was killed when the bus she was riding in was blown up just outside of Pravi. Back then the young Lazos couldn't yet comprehend how her death was the result of ongoing class conflict. And so he wrote, "Night, black night / pushed threateningly against my windows," equating night not so much with death as with the dark workroom where the assistant had developed x-rays of customers' rotten teeth. To the young Lazos, Fofo had seemed like a priestess of darkness.

Thus we reach the logical conclusion that the political rift between father and son arose not so much from any substantial ideological differences (after all, both represented the same class interests, since Lazos would eventually inherit his father's estate) but from the emotional toll that darkened the passage out of the long tunnel of the Occupation.

And so, years later, in ripping up the application form for the Tigers Club, Lazos was unconsciously avenging the unjust loss of his father's assistant—a loss that came not with Fofo's actual death, but at the moment when his father had slapped her in the middle of Aristotle Square for carrying a red EAM flag.

As for me, what "atavistic" memory might have driven me to tear up, for the same reason, that very same form?

II

Glafkos Thrassakis's First Notebook

SPERLONGA, 1973

[On the cover:]

You aimed high and reached your goal.
Bravo, my child, bravo.

[Inside:]

1
Magical hand of the sun
that calms the waves
quivering like the fleece of sheep
from fear at the thought
that you might abandon them.
Sun, loving father,
you know how to soothe them,
assuring them that what will follow
is none other than the great night itself.
And you, Grandfather,
with a whole lifetime of stories,
you know how to unwind
the fabric from the big skein
in half-yards, meters, yards,
leaving two chance inches
for the good customer: me.

2

The ferocious battle lasted all day long, as we watched their colossal struggle. Wherever one of them left an opening, the other would spring out. If the clouds won in the end, it was only because they were lower than the sun, just as the bedraggled proletariat defeats the emperor who, from his great height, is unable to reach down and overpower his erstwhile subjects. The sun claimed victory only when it dropped down to the level of the clouds. And then it would shine out thunderously from beneath their round bellies. The sea stood as witness and mirror to the entire battle, as calm and unstirred as an ice rink. Later on it would host a peaceful, anaemic moon.

None of us had any doubt as to what the final outcome would be. Whenever the sun seemed to triumph, sending out its blazing rays, the vapors rising from the sea kept swelling the ranks of thick cumulus. So there was an uneven give and take. Of course if the storm were to break and the sky to lighten, the sun would rule alone in its splendor. But if something like that ever did happen, it would only happen the following day. In the meantime, today's generation would be footing the bill—if there's anyone around who still supports that theory, so widespread in crypto-Christian and proto-Communist years.

The worst, however, was after the sun's defeat: for a while the clouds held its memory, the way the down of a mangled chicken will linger on a fox's fur.

3

"The sea glistened." He wanted to write the words in capital letters to stress their significance. No telegram, he said, is ever written in prose. Capital letters are like newspaper headlines—the more important an item of news, the bigger the letters it demands. Outbreaks of war, earthquakes and military coups, appreciations and depreciations of currency, hijackings and sudden deaths take up the greater part of the front page, announced in letters as large as the top line of an eyesight chart. If dinosaurs had known how to read, they would have needed colossal letters, huge as mountains, to correspond to their

gigantic retinae. For in any given optic range, the size of the signifier should reflect the significance of the signified.

And yet "THE SEA GLISTENED" is still no more than a dark smudge on dull paper. Here by the water I can see these myriads of silver scales—"the sun crushing diamonds"—and I can hear the lapping of waves, the sputtering of a motorboat going out to pull up or throw out its nets, and the salty air around me completes this sensation of sea. But for someone reading in some frozen corner or sunless hole, coughing from the stench of the toilet or all the cigarettes he's been smoking, in the smog and the fog of the city, with unpaid bills hanging from plastic memo pads—for someone like that, the phrase, "It glistened, the sea," can never transcend the confines of language to go beyond the phrase itself. If only he could see it, enjoy it, sit in the feast of the sun and let the soothing strokes of the sea wash over him—then it would really mean something to him. A memory, at least.

What we need, then, is to change not literature but life.

A cliché—or plissé, as my grandmother's seamstress would say.

4

I had forgotten even the fact of my own mortality, so absorbed was I with the thought of death. I had forgotten that, a creature of the earth, I belong on and to this earth that traces its circles around the sun—until yesterday, watching the waters of the sea rise, even in the absence of storm, to cover regions I had thought belonged to the inviolate sovereignty of dry land, I suddenly remembered how, as the earth's accessory, I too should submit to her deterministic laws and accept the seasons as passively as the stars, which are, people say, bound by love to their orbits.

5

Today the sea seems carved by the experienced hand of some sculptor/tamer of beasts. Today the horses of breaking waves greet the sea ceaselessly with their hoofs. But the sea's embrace does not hold me, for I, expanding, use her juttings of land like long nails to clean out the ears of seashells, through which to hear more clearly the ocean's roar.

6

These people, at least, resemble something, remind me of something: They're like old shoes you find at the edge of the sea, washed up by the waves, still hold-ing the memory of the legs that bore them, the ankles they enveloped, the bunions that banished them. They're nothing like the plastic bottles that waves harry and harass, bottles as anonymous as the stuff they're made of, as ignorant of history as the machines that made them, as irrelevant as a plastic ear in the empty gash where Van Gogh cut off his own, deaf to the voices of the world.

7

The cuttlefish was rotting on the beach below a happy cloud of insects. Soon there was nothing left of the slimy, trembling flesh except white bones—the memory of snow on a towering mountaintop—a whitewashed thorax where I might clean my pen, so as to write with it more easily.

III

Two Vignettes From the Past

Middle-aged Mr. Evlampis, whose prematurely white hair adds a little some-thing to his charm, enters the living room with birdlike movements that enchant the ladies, many of whom think him a rather frivolous type, though his jokes and pleasantries amuse them. An eternal adolescent, he seems never to take anything seriously. Only his melancholy wife seems to consider her hus-band's antics no more than smoke and mirrors. Whenever they play cards, whether he wins or loses, Mr. Evlampis always leaves in the same good mood as when he came. On Sundays he takes his boat out to fish on the Thermaic Gulf, sticking close to the Sailing Club and the Yacht Club, never venturing too far into the open waters. His child, a lymphatic little boy, sickly and weak (he was born during the Occupation and, you might say, inherited the short-

ages and shortfallings of the time) comes along with him in the small boat,
stolen from Penelope Delta's In the Secret Places of the Swamp. *But Mr.*
Evlampis—of whom I can remember nothing now but his gestures, the con-
jurings of his hands, which have remained engraved on my memory as if
carved into some soft and lasting dough—is dead, has been for thousands of
years. He always had something "scrumptious" to say to amuse the ladies, all
except his wife. Was it she who died first and he who followed? Or the other
way around? Which of the two? Who could tell me now? And even if someone
were to know, what difference would it really make?

≈

And here is Mr. Kopanas, springing up from memory, short and plump, in all his
Zakynthian cleverness and Corfuscian charm. He takes off his hat and leaves his
umbrella at the door, thanking the maid ever so politely with a deep smile as she
helps him off with his overcoat and hangs it on the rack. Snatches of conversation
drift out from inside. The other guests are already there, talking animatedly. Mr.
Kopanas fixes his tie, picks up the small bouquet he had set down on the hall table
and, as the maid stands impatiently behind him, makes his entrance into the house.

As soon as she sees him, the hostess leaves the card table with its green felt and
comes over to greet him. Mr. Kopanas kisses her hand and presents her with the
bouquet. The hostess, delighted, grabs his arm and leads him into the parlor. She
is slightly taller than he, but only because of her heels and the bun in her hair.

Mr. Kopanas is the head of the Drama School, the only one in our city. The
others will be established much later, a few more private schools, as well as the
one run by the State Theater. During the Civil War, Mr. Kopanas is the only
one who continues to stage our ancient tragedies. He also holds literary morn-
ings at the "Elysian" cinema house, reciting everything from Solomos to Cavafy
(very daring for his time, Mr. Kopanas, but then his boldness is exactly what
the women so adore). He speaks in a low, bass voice, rhythmic and melodic,
with perfect enunciation. This, above all, is what he teaches at his School.
Many of the School's alumni have gone on to careers in the theater in Athens.
As for Mr. Kopanas, he loves our own city and its people. He is particularly pop-
ular with members of the gentler sex, because he understands them. A jewel in

company, affable, sweet—if the ladies had been Catholic instead of Orthodox, they would undoubtedly have made him their confessor.

Mr. Kopanas never plays cards. Instead, he comforts the losers. He rarely sits down. He keeps an eye on his watch and always leaves exactly at eight.

Because Mr. Kopanas has a secret life—a life no one can see, not even through the keyhole—lots of things are said about him, lots of things are rumored. From Solomos to Cavafy.

Mr. Kopanas, who is exceedingly regular in his social calls, speaks untiringly of the problems of the theater, of the need to build up a local community (back then all the plays came from Athens), and whenever he notices that the children of some household show talent in the arts, he offers the parents advice, encouragement, and words of comfort.

Mr. Kopanas clearly plays a positive role in the life of our city. He even helps with performances outside the School. I remember him on those Sunday mornings at the Elysian—"Clang, clang, the monastery bells in the desert, clang, clang," his voice, too, ringing like a bell, and later, "Honor to those who in life define and guard Thermopylaes." Later that day I would use the typed program to take hot pans from the oven without burning my hand.

He had an irresistible sweetness, Mr. Kopanas. That sweetness is all I remember now.

IV

Childhood Years

THOUGH I am as yet unable to reveal the source, I hold as certain the intelligence that each time the young Lazos misbehaved, his mother would burn him on the behind with a match—a fact that might have led to the early development of retrogressive tendencies. Hunted, he would hide in empty suitcases (a classic symptom in imaginative young children who dream of abandoning the paternal fold) and gnaw savagely on his mother's leather belts, as a chained-up dog will gnaw on its master's leash.

That which is truly new, however (and which, if true, explains a great deal), is the intelligence (from, as always, a first-hand source) that during the second or third month of her pregnancy, his mother had tried to abort him using the primitive means available at the time—which is to say, the "spoon" method. Since this pregnancy followed soon after the birth of the eldest son—the famous guerrilla fighter Markos Lazaridis, who met his tragic end fighting for the people's army at Kaimak Tsalan—and since the firstborn son had been delivered by caesarean, it seems that his mother and her mother feared some complication and tried to abort the second child. But the spoon didn't catch him, the attempt failed, and the newborn came into the world with a feeling that never left him: that he was unwanted, living "by mistake." From a very early age he showed a clear preference for the male members of his family, for his father and the only grandfather he ever knew. We will discuss later on his relationship with the latter. As for the former, it suffices to say that on the day Lazarus came like another Lazarus into the world, his father, choked with guilt over his passive complicity in the attempted crime, triumphantly announced the birth to a gathering of Jehovah's Witnesses with the following words: "Brothers, it has just been announced that my wife has brought yet another Jehovah's Witness into the world!"—a pronouncement that was heard with joy, but only ever came half true. Yes, Lazarus would become a witness, but certainly not for Jehovah.

In his childhood records we also find reference to a very peculiar automobile accident. Lazos was waiting with his schoolbag slung over his shoulder on one of the town's narrow sidewalks (little more than fringes around the walls, so narrow that he later describes them as "laces" or "ribbons") to cross the street, when he saw a truck in the distance headed his way. He suddenly thought, "That truck might hit me." He insists that it occurred to him beforehand. But why? Why on earth would that truck have hit him? Though in fact it did, swiping him with its side-view mirror as it passed. From then on things are confused, and we are unable to construct a clear picture of what really happened. How did he end up under the wheels? And why? Black blood trickled from his head. Neither Lazos nor the patrol officer, the seamstress's husband, who happened to pass by shortly afterwards, can explain how it happened. The officer didn't see the boy being hit, he just found him there on the ground. He picked Lazos up and led him home by the hand and let him in through the basement to keep his mother from seeing him and taking fright—a fact for which our poet later offered another interpretation: when fate raises her hand against you, you lose your right to go in through the main door and have to use the servants' entrance instead. The scar on the boy's forehead stayed with him like a mark of shame, until as a teenager he read Herman Hesse's *Demian* and identified with the hero, who was also marked on his forehead.

But this chance occurrence developed into a kind of obsession with him. Just as they say, "Whatever you most fear will come true," Glafkos came to believe that whatever he imagined would actually happen. When the passing years showed that in fact the opposite was true, he reached, through a rather specious logical process resembling *reductio ad absurdum*, the opposite conclusion: whatever he thought up beforehand would never happen at all. And so he launched into a systematic attempt to foresee all the unpleasant things that could possibly happen to him, since in doing so he was sure to render all those unpleasant possibilities null and void. For example, leaving on a trip he'd say to himself, "I'll never make it back from Brussels. Something's going to happen to me on this trip." And when he came back safe and sound, he attributed his return to the fact that he had managed, through his anticipation of disaster, to stave off whatever had been slated to befall him. He always expected the worst, even when there was no earthly reason for fear. For example, he might have been walking down a country road in the sunshine on a beautiful spring day, arm in arm with his "little cloud." No threatening balcony looming above, no perilous flowerpot or roof tile. Level ground, no snakes, a plane-free sky. Not a soul in sight, no crazy man to gun him down. Yet even at this perfect, paradisical moment, he would say to himself, "But what if a meteor, hurtling toward Earth from millions of miles away, lands exactly on my head, just like last year in Texas in that guy Foster's fields?" And that thought would calm him. It was just the possibility of there being something he was overlooking, something he wouldn't manage to foresee in time, that made him anxious.

But could his method ever really bring him peace? Could it ever allow him to be calm and happy? Or was danger always waiting for him to let down his guard, so it could suddenly pounce before he had time to think it away? In this "Cassandra complex" from which he suffered, "good" was synonymous with whatever he wasn't thinking about. After all, since he thought away everything bad that could possibly happen, everything left unanticipated must have been pleasant. Thus he was always expecting joy without realizing he was expecting it—if that makes any sense.

≈

THRASSAKIS, now in his prime, writes:

I have a certain aversion that I'll just go ahead and spit out so we can be done with it once and for all: I can't stand seeing leftover wine kept in a bottle for the next day, or never. In pensions and resorts where dinner is included in the price of the room, they often keep your leftover wine for you, along with your own personal napkin. But is it really your own personal napkin, your own personal wine? Who can be so sure about that?

What I mean to say is, I don't like this presumed continuance, this assumption that the same thing will happen tomorrow as happened today, that the same person will come and sit at the same table and continue drinking from the same bottle of wine, a glass or two with his meal.

I reject such a tomorrow. (Thrassakis, *CDW*, Vol. I, 29)

Thrassakis is already more than well-known as a sum total of aversions, antipathies, neurotic dislikes. One of the lesser known, not entirely unrelated to the one described above, is that he could never write on numbered pages. The panic and fear that he wouldn't manage to fill those pages silenced any internal voice. His inspiration didn't want to be measured with milestones or progress charts. The numbers on blank pages inhibited his freedom as much as the ancestral "must"—submission to which he found quite unbecoming.

≈

EVEN AS A CHILD, Lazos had a habit of prettifying things in the retelling. After his accident, when he showed the scar on his forehead to his friends, he boasted that he'd gotten it chasing a colored butterfly.

The method of "once I foresee it, it won't happen" tripped up a bit with regard to a single but recurrent dream, in which he saw himself dying at the age of thirty-three. The dream's frequent repetition finally convinced Glafkos that it might actually come true, though he recognized his fixation on that particular number as a Christian complex that many writers and intellectuals had dealt with in the past, the prime example being Kazantsakis, who wrote his *Odyssey* in exactly 33,333 lines.

So, as a boy during the first years after the war, Glafkos dreamt of himself at thirty-three, running to escape some riot in the streets of Thessaloniki. Though it's not quite certain who exactly is involved, the setting is specific: the corner of Karl Diel and King Herakleus streets, directly across from a girls' school. The fighting is taking place somewhere around the church of Agia Sophia. Lazos is running, glad to have escaped, though he knows he won't be entirely in the clear until he can manage to turn the corner onto King Herakleus, heading towards Aristotle Square. And just as he reaches the corner, just as he's about to turn, a bullet comes from behind and sends him toppling to the ground.

No one can doubt the deep significance of this dream. For the awful truth is that the dream did, in a manner of speaking, come true: born in 1933, Glafkos was forced, as a result of the "cholera" epidemic, to abandon his homeland in his thirty-third year.

Many times I've asked myself what it would mean to have a Thrassakis among us today. He himself recognized that he was living in the wrong time. He was wrong for his time, that is, though naturally not the other way around. His era, with its heroic destructions of entire populations such as the Indonesians and the Vietnamese, with its triumphs in space and its heart transplants, had returned man to the primitive societies of mythic times, while Glafkos, an introvert, a man of closed spaces, of chamber music, never really took off, like the space ships of his time.

"Let's just keep the torch burning," he once wrote, "and perhaps someone else will come along to blow on it and help the flame grow, and pass it on to those who come later." A key phrase, this "passing of the torch," which one of his physics teachers had been wont to use. Like so many dirty old perverts, this teacher had an irrepressible tendency to moralize, droning on about "the flame of learning, the torch of virtue that is passed from hand to hand." Once when Lazos was collecting leaf samples for class, stretching to pluck them from the lower branches of some tree, he saw the teacher (now, rest his soul, among the tropical plants of Paradise) sitting there with an erection bulging in his pants, and the teacher sweetly invited him to come step on it in order to reach some leaves higher up in the trees. "The poor man died early, of a heart attack," Glafkos noted, "and in doing so, spared his family the pain of additional memories."

There is no question of our curtailing our study of Glafkos, since he offers a benchmark of our own fate as an unexpressed people. A people's youth reflects itself in the creations of its maturity, while the life and work of a writer, a poet, predicts the development of his country's fate. And yet . . .

V

Identification

And if I were not you,
perhaps you would be me?

THIS COUPLET, taken from Thrassakis's poem "Your Blood My Lie" (which he liked, friends say, to recite the other way around), brings us straight to the heart of that "and yet"—which is to say, to the problem of psychological identification. This is something that every aspiring biographer should know: a deep commitment to the subject of his study can often affect the biographer in unforeseen ways. Just as the psychoanalyst has to enter his patient's mind in order to help him "from inside" (and it has been shown that external help and support can never break down the high protective walls which a patient constructs around himself), I too had to work my way into Glafkos's skin, a fact that often made me live like a kind of Glafkos the Second or Thrassakis Junior.

To clarify: with all my efforts to stoop and drink from Glafkos's spring, I myself became the spring from which he drank (and indeed, he quite literally devoured my time, not to mention my money, since the wild Tiger money hadn't yet made its appearance). With all my efforts to bend and peer at him through a microscope, I myself became the microscope through which I was examining myself. I was no longer simply myself writing about Thrassakis. Instead, I had become he whom Thrassakis, in the Afterworld, watched writing about him, discouraged by the poverty of my imagination. And I can't blame him for that. If I had an imagination I'd have become a novelist, not a biographer.

And yet from the moment I become alienated from myself through his gaze, I find myself able to catch hold of truths which, in a state of conscious vigilance, escape me altogether. Looking up from one of his books to rest my eyes on the objects around me, I see him watching me, and can read in his eyes: "In order for me to stop being an abstraction for you, all you have to do is look at what's around you. Look at the Japanese screen with the swan. The coffee percolator. The shells on the mantelpiece. The dust on the window ledge. The faded curtains. The cigarette butts. And your typewriter where every day you machine-gun your thoughts onto the paper—which is to say, you machine-gun me, not at six meters distance, but six inches. Well, these are the kinds of things that surrounded me, too, when I lived." And so he, though absent, is able to take shape, while I, though present, evaporate—nothing is mine anymore, since he forces me to see with his eyes.

The fact that I was learning more about myself was perhaps the worst thing that could have happened to me, since psychological identification with another signifies nothing more than our own self-annihilation. Though how can you see yourself without first objectifying that self? But then—and here's the rub—who are you really writing about, if you can't even seriously claim that your subject is someone outside of you, and not you yourself? Why should anyone believe you? Because it does matter, in the end, to be believable. Yet no matter how much you might insist that your hero is not you but someone else, what do you do when that "someone else" returns to you your own image, like an undelivered letter whose sender and receiver are one and the same?

Then, naturally, you go insane. And when the person closest to you in the world, in my case my wife, is at the same time conducting research on the wife of that "someone else," a surely unprecedented identification of couples is bound to arise. In our case, I was him, my wife was her. If it's just you, you can hide this loss of self, you can cover it up—and if it doesn't show on the outside, you tell yourself, well then, it must not exist. Whereas once the problem is shared and discussed, once it's made an external fact, it suddenly acquires the multiple layerings and dimensions of the real. And really, where exactly was the line that separated us from them? Where did we end? Where did they begin?

At first our daughter Anna helped to keep us in line. Her ringing voice filled the house as she grew. And as much of a torment as a child can be, at least there would come a point when one of us could turn to the other and say, "Look. The Thrassakises didn't have kids. Since we do, we must not be them. We're the . . . " And we would laugh together over the joke about the crazy man who thought he was made of corn and was terrified he would be eaten by chickens. But at last we reached a point of advanced insight when not even children could save us, or dogs, or corn. Since all my formerly liquid assets were tied up in the construction of an apartment building, I borrowed some money to pay for a doctor, a psychiatrist.

It wasn't my first time. I wasn't a stranger to him. I had gone to him a decade before, and for years afterwards just seeing him on the street was enough to send me running in the opposite direction. Back then, as I recall, he advised me to get politically involved, to take some kind of action. (This was, of course, before my marriage.) And in fact I did get mixed up in politics, got involved, joined the Party, took action, until I was arrested and imprisoned, at which point all my angst and anguish disappeared as if by magic—not because I was suffering, but because for the first time in my life I was the object of concentrated, collective attention. People were paying attention to me, interrogating me, there were guards observing my every move, keeping track of what I ate, what I wrote, when I went to the bathroom. All of this raised me, first of all, in my own estimation, and later on helped to counteract the loneliness.

But this time the problem was different. The doctor confessed that it was the first time he had treated a couple together. Because that's how we went: as a single patient. Partly, of course, to cut costs, but more importantly because our problem was shared; it sprang from a single source. (I should note here that it always seemed a bit strange to me for a Greek to go to a psychiatrist. In our country there are so many more urgent problems that the luxury of psychiatry always seemed a little bit like going to a whore. On the other hand, I knew that our problem was clearly technical, as in Dostoyevsky's *The Double*, and thus could be solved only through scientific intervention.)

After the doctor had asked us a series of questions, primarily of a police-like nature (and though I knew he needed all this material before he reached a verdict, it made him seem more like an employee of United Detectives than a professor of applied biopsychology), he pronounced in his stilted Greek:

"There is simply no way of gaining immediate access to the experience of another. An individual who studies another individual's experiences has no other means of access than his own personal experience of that other. No one has the ability to hear with the other's ears or to see with the other's eyes. The only facts about the other that are available to us are those facts and events that we ourselves might relive as if we were that other. In which case the consciousness will once again register our own experiences and not those of the other."

And he wrote down the title of a book for us as if it were a prescription for some drug. The book was R.D. Laing's *Ourselves and the Other*, which offered a brief discussion of all the things he had been saying. He even had a few copies of the book to distribute, like the free samples family doctors receive from pharmaceutical companies and pass out to their patients. I took the book and flipped through it. It seemed very interesting, but what I really wanted to know was what exactly I should do.

"It's just a stage you're going through, it'll pass," the doctor said. "In the meantime, in order to break free of this tendency to see your own reflection in your 'recollection' of the deceased, one of you should take a break from your work on Thrassakis so that the other will be able to find in the companion of his or her life a relief from the study of death—which is more or less what your work amounts to, in the end."

When I told him that my wife wasn't researching Thrassakis but his wife, the doctor, who bore an uncanny resemblance to Giscard d'Estaing, let an ironic smile pass across his upper lip.

"We psychiatrists," he answered stiffly, "don't recognize 'couples' the way the church does. The problem, in your case, is a single one. That's why I recommend that one of you take a temporary break. The balance between the two of you will then restore itself to normal. And as a second step that should, in my opinion, follow immediately upon the first, I suggest you concern yourself only with his texts and not with the anecdotes or unofficial accounts of third parties. Limiting yourself to published texts will help you maintain a necessary distance. A printed, published text has an objective existence as an irrefutable document, like the fossils of leaves—they existed, they were written into the rock, they left traces behind. And so you, the researcher, the subject—or, shall we say, sub-*text*—can never identify one hundred percent with the object, the writer of the text, distanced as you are by the text itself. . . . "

The doctor assured us that he was at our disposal for whatever else we might need. No, he didn't want money—in this kind of post-operative situation, there was no charge for advice. When I tried to insist on paying him, he admitted that he too was a fan of Thrassakis, and would never dream of taking money from us. This knowledge, however, flustered rather than relieved me—I wanted to have the satisfaction of knowing that I had gone to a whore and paid for it. Whereas with all this love and admiration and so on, disaster still lurked close at hand.

Chapter Two

IN THE END, the local representative at 26 Valaoritos, insisting that I sign some version of the application form, provided me with one in English, intended for Dutch candidates, from which the preposterous anti-Communist declaration was missing. In its place was the question, "Were you ever a member or supporter of the Nazi Party," to which I didn't hesitate to write down my "No"—in fact, I must admit, I did so with pleasure. (In this regard, the fact that I'm utterly dedicated to my own beliefs and ideas really means that I am utterly dedicated to my own pleasure. Idea and pleasure are equated within me in an ideal, pleasureful rebirth. The idea of the Nation, the pleasure of my People. I leave guilt to others.)

The most important aspect of the grant coming my way from America was not so much the money itself as the vague promise that the Tigers, as a society, would help me gain access to Thrassakis's confidential papers. The head of the special collections department of the university library that held Thrassakis's files was himself a Tiger, and there had always been a strong network of solidarity between the society's members, just as after 1950 Greeks who had been abroad together in exile or imprisoned on the barren island of Makronissos always helped one another out, no matter where they ended up afterwards, as if there were some kind of Makronissos Association, unofficial, unregistered with the courts.

This human need to form groups, flocks, herds, ultimately derives from our animal origins. This need has always been more developed in the U.S., not because the people there are more like animals, but because there are simply more of them, and the geographical distances between them are so enormous—so naturally there's a greater need for the society, the club, the clan, the Ku Klux Klan.

During those days of suspense, I went one evening to a bar on Kidathenian Street in Plaka. While I was there, two clean-shaven young American sailors came in and turned the place upside down. They had drunk ouzo on top of vermouth and lost control. We easily overpowered them and turned them over to the police, and all of us, owners, waiters, and customers alike, went to the station to testify. The two sailors, who claimed they had been so drunk that they couldn't remember anything, offered only the standard, two-syllable "Sorry." Then suddenly a group of American naval officers burst into the courtroom, enraged, and we all watched with amazement as they whisked the sailors out of our hands and headed back to the base, where they would try them according to their own laws. Plaintiffs and judges alike were left high and dry. During the Turkish Occupation, of course, the Kadi had enjoyed complete jurisdiction over the accused. But back then we were, so to speak, under the fez. How could we explain it now that we were supposedly a free nation? I thought bitterly of how I would soon be taking money from Yanks like that.

However, I quickly comforted myself with the thought that the Tiger Club was an international organization. It may have been founded in the U.S. and have its central office there, but wasn't the United Nations also based in New York? Wasn't NATO supposedly a "European concern," despite all its American troops? It was, I told myself, as if I were taking money from the World Bank, not Chase Manhattan. Besides, if you start looking everywhere for American infiltration, there won't be a single crumb of clean bread left for you to eat.

But what exactly did Thrassakis do as a Tiger scholar in America? Who exactly were the Tigers, anyhow? I would find out only by following in his footsteps, by doing more or less the same things he had done. However, the Tigers weren't giving me the kind of fellowship he'd had, just a lump sum so I could continue my research on their former scholar. With this material difference in our respective situations, my strange sense of psychological identification with my subject—which was really starting to worry me—should have stopped then and there. But still I kept hearing a voice inside of me: "Not Yiannos, Yiannakis. Not Thrassos, Thrassakis." And I would see a vision of myself in the middle of a glimmering bouquet of light that spread its rays over the deep waters, as my own reflection looked up at me from the waves at the stern of my boat.

Before I follow the psychoanalyst's advice and turn to a discussion of Thrassakis's writings, I want to make a quick jump in time to satisfy the reader's curiosity as to who exactly these Tigers were, and say a few words about the first Tiger banquet I attended in the U.S. I was in a small city whose two main arteries, seen from the airplane as I landed, formed a cross that divided the city into four quadrants, with smaller roads radiating outwards from the center like beams of heavenly light. But you don't have to see the city from above to realize it was a Christian creation. All you need to do is look at a map: Church Street, Temple Street, Cathedral Street. There are no clergymen among the Tigers. At the airport, though, it seemed like everyone but the priests was waiting to greet me: the manager of the largest funeral home in town, a real-estate agent, the vice-manager of the water company, an orthodontist of Greek descent, an ophthalmologist, and a retired history professor, now in his eighties, who remembered, oh yes, the "fiery Greek," by which he meant Thrassakis, who had also passed through their city—how many decades ago?—during his visit to the U.S.

As soon as we had all filed into the private room at the restaurant which the Tigers had rented for their banquet, the doors were shut behind us. Whoever showed up afterwards had to pay a late fee determined by chance: the smiling, rosy-cheeked treasurer spun a wheel, and the latecomer had to pay in dollars whatever number the pointer stopped on.

It was a tradition that every Tiger visiting from abroad had to greet his dinner companions with his country's roar. So I roared in Greek, then spent the rest of the evening answering questions about Greek shipping magnates and how many drachmas there were to a dollar. The ancient professor remembered that they had asked Thrassakis almost exactly the same things, only back then they were all worried about Frederica, who was still queen and had just undergone some sort of operation on her ear.

This was the kind of small but saving difference that helped me, during the course of my stay, hold on to the belief that I was not, in fact, Thrassakis.

And these, in short, were the Tigers—not of the jungle, but of America.

≈

I'M LIKE AN ocean liner that has its own special machines for desalinating

water during overseas voyages. I too bottle my experience for travellers, for those
burning with fever. I'd like my "rest-in-peace" to be a spring, Virgo's spring.

(*CDW,* Vol. II, 38-39)

PERHAPS A FEW sentences from the first volume of his *Collected Works* should be added here: "The wind tangles itself in the ropes of the masts. How distant Rotterdam already seems!" (I suppose it must have been in Rotterdam that he boarded the ocean liner which took him to the States.) He continues:

> *There are almost three thousand people on land and at sea working to keep this ship running. As for me, I sell about three thousand copies of each of my books. If I die, I'll leave three thousand readers as orphans. And when they retire this ship—despite all its prestige, they say it doesn't turn a profit for the company—three thousand families will go hungry. And this ship will be a veteran ship.*
> Veteran, *a key word in Seferis's* Days.
>
> *All those things we note from our lives, from our hopes and feelings, are simply the few phrases in a thick book which we underline as we read, phrases that touch us in some way. And yet out of all the phrases we might underline, we mark only the ones we come across when we happen to have a pencil in our hand. While the others, which escape our underlining, might well be more important—more deadly, even. And so for whomever eventually inherits our library (the person most likely, that is, to read our own reading of the book), the only indication of what we liked, of what caught our attention, will be what fate permitted—fate, that is, as embodied in the presence of a pencil. Fate, in short, as coincidence.*

(*CDW,* Vol. I, 86)

Let us leave the illustrious pencil and focus instead on the chance aspect of writing—"chance," here, in the sense of "opportunity," as in "free time." Because that's what it's really about: art as an interlude from life, a parenthesis within life, and never life itself. Art, *point mort,* the dead space between inhale and exhale, when oxygen stands motionless in the lungs for a fraction of a second before becoming filtered air, transformed octane that was once a component of inorganic matter and is now the very essence of the "life-giving source"—in short, of man himself. Here we should note that in the passage above, the book of chance comes from *elsewhere*—which is to say, it is given, as Moses's ten commandments were given by the Prophet on the Mount. Life is given to us. (It doesn't matter, in this context, that they tried to kill Moses. That has nothing to do with the specific paragraph we're analyzing.) Others bring us into the world, handing us a book which we are invited to read, a book essentially independent of us, since we never asked to come here—not because we didn't want to, but because we were never given the chance: It was already decided, already written by fate, and the only freedom we have is to stress whatever moves us in the fate of that book, whatever impresses us or concerns us in some way. Yet even that is decided by fate! By whether or not we happen to have a pencil in our hand.

Necessity and chance, then, are interpreted by Thrassakis according to biblical (and, of course, bibliographical) prototypes. So the role of the creator, he seems to be saying, is perhaps simply to remind us again of forgotten things, to underline the already-written, as the sculptor gives to a barren rock the shape of his own suffering.

He felt redundant. He had the nagging feeling that he was entirely removed from the processes of production, that he existed only as a consumer. In "Posterity" (*CDW,* Vol. I, 25-26) he compares himself to a tractor trailer with 33 tires, of which only twelve are actually working most of the time. The other 18 (not counting the three spares) constitute the truck's reserve for when it needs to gain speed quickly on vast highways.

So why isn't he gaining speed? Perhaps he's overloaded, or perhaps the right roads haven't yet been built? "I pass through large towns," he writes in "Posterity"—referring, we assume, to Thebes—"where Oedipus is still killing Laius, where the wide Plataeas of the Persian War still haven't fought their battle. I go slowly." If he feels weighed down, it's because he has things to say. And he doesn't speed, he can't speed, because he hasn't yet reached the open, liberated roads. He is, then, both the driver shifting gears and the trailer carrying the weight. He is both peddler and merchandise. Both the rug and the foot that steps on it. The steaming shit and the still-gaping sphincter. Victim and victimizer. Weight and scales. Libra and Virgo. Button and Buttonhole. Keyhole and lock.

But not, however, the key. Thrassakis's entire method is to let you peep through the keyhole at the debauchery taking place inside the room, at the way the room is decorated, he even lets you listen to the music—*sotto voce*—and yet he never opens the desired door.

As my own wife explained to me rather convincingly, Thrassakis and his wife suffered from what you might call the "umbrella syndrome": as the couple walks side by side in the rain, the two adjacent domes of their umbrellas create a distance between them that reinforces the principle of non-intervention. Even if their tips are round, each umbrella's daggerlike spoke-ends threaten to put out the other person's eye. Support for this theory is found in the short story, "Erotic Metastases, or Penis Tricks":

> *During the first blush of love the couple squeezes together under a single umbrella. In the second phase, the two umbrellas chafe one another like bats. In the third phase, the little child-sized umbrella between them keeps the bigger umbrellas from colliding, and everyone is made comfortable. And if there is no child? Then the two umbrellas keep scraping one another—but they do not part.*
>
> <div align="right">(<i>CDW</i>, Vol. II, 36)</div>

≈

ONE QUESTION that immediately presents itself is, Why is the best Thrassakis the paid Thrassakis? He himself confesses that commissioned books and articles and translations always came out better than his "unprompted" or "spontaneous" writing. (Though as he notes elsewhere, even so-called spontaneous writing is always driven by something, always springs from somewhere. And that "somewhere," that "something," whether rock or spring or watchtower, is always given, always ready-made.) Might his civic consciousness or professional consciousness have served him better than the part of him that worked solely for its own enjoyment? If so, was it the concerned citizen who won out in the end, or the fortune-telling gypsy with seductive eyes, the Sylvana who cannot see the future until you cross her palm with silver?

Thrassakis writes:

My own personal history bores me unimaginably. There's nothing more tiresome than describing in the third person, or through some hypothetical first-person narrator, something that's actually happened to me. It's only when I enter the other's skin, when I identify with his fate, share in his secrets, that I feel like I'm performing a creative act. I feel good, lawfully disguised. What I mean to say is, it's easier for me to tell a story well, to make it come alive, if it never actually happened to me. Reality is constricting, and inferior to the imagination. I prefer to overcome myself through an imagined other, thus finding the thread that will lead me from the Labyrinth.

(*CDW*, Vol. I, 106-107)

A few pages later, with reference to payment:

"Really," Argyris was telling me the other day, "the greatest valuation of my work is when someone buys one of my paintings." And he insisted on explaining to me, as if I didn't understand—because according to him I can never understand, since I don't have to make a living from my writing—how he takes that money not at face value, but symbolically: "It's a way for the other to show that he values what I do. Because in the chaos of emotional confusion"—and here he played with the word, pronouncing it as "Confucian"—"where everyone has his own personal theory about art, why should the best critics necessarily be those paid by galleries and agents? Or by collectors? Why should I listen to some guy someone else is paying to say what he says? Why don't I just listen to the guy who's buying my work?" Argyris, who lives and works in Modena, was right, of course, particularly about his own art—painting.

The fact that Thrassakis himself briefly lived in that same Italian city of Modena is shown by a letter he wrote to his wife, who at the time was still in Brussels:

I finally found a little hole, a nest to shelter our love. So I'm telling you—come. Right away. Leave everything there just as it is, leave the keys with the doorman and come with a suitcase of spring clothes. The place is small and dark, with a single ray of sunlight that falls in at five in the afternoon, but it's comfortable. There's no phone, but a compagno—that's the word for "friend" here—promised he would get that taken care of through the municipal office, which is "on our side." On the application form I wrote that I need a phone because I have severe psychological problems, and in moments of crisis I have to be able to call my psychiatrist—you, my dear. That's what the compagni told me to do: "Either write that you're a nurse or that you have some chronic illness. Otherwise they'll never give you a line." I chose the second, knowing you'd be angry. My dear, it doesn't matter. Come as you are. Together we'll make a stir. The Italian compagni are really something. They're all talk, all fanfare and promises, but I prefer a false good word to sincere silence. As for the rent, it's practically nothing. Of course there's hardly any nightlife at all in Modena. All the bars and restaurants close at five to midnight so the night patrol won't catch them open. But they never take up the chairs in the central square. We can go and sit there, my dear, and dream out loud as long as there's moon in the sky.

(As for the "single ray of sunlight," let's not forget the short story "Around a Table," in which the main character, who relies like a heliotrope on a similar beam of light, spends his days shifting his little table to follow the beam as it moves. Only on cloudy days can he surrender himself to a kind of nirvanic state, now that he no longer has to move.)

Italy in those years was characterized by a climate of ascent. After a generation of fascism the antifascist powers were strengthening constitutional freedoms, though of course without actually being able to change the constitutional clauses themselves. But the progress they did make was no small thing. The ship was travelling on the open sea with all its spare parts on board. It depended on no foreign workshops, no foreign tools. On the other hand, thanks to the catalyst of Gramsci, the Party was able to go its merry way without joining forces with or even recognizing anything to its left. It lapped up cream like the *pater familias* picking the best cherries from the bowl. At that critical point in Italian political history, not even hatred could factionalize the Left. After all, the specter of fascism wasn't far away.

And Thrassakis? He felt like an outsider. He was, as he himself acknowledges, involved in the processes of consumption rather than of production, a position that bred all sorts of complexes, of the weight-of-the-world variety. After all, he sat around eating the prepared food of his wife's dowry, of inheritances, fellowships, gifts from the Party. And so he remained constantly vulnerable to boredom and angst, to the heartburn of longing, to *ennui*—classic symptoms of the socio-economic class to which he belonged.

In a letter to his friend Thomas (one of the few who kept Thrassakis's letters, because he happened to be an alphabetologist and kept practically every letter he ever received), he once wrote:

> *I feel like a traffic light at an outdoor market where all the streets are blocked off. The light changes from red to green without it meaning anything, since the whole road is thick with stalls. And people flow by, back and forth, loitering, stopping to look or to buy something, but no one ever notices the traffic light, since there are no cars to use it. Every now and then a motorcycle sputters through, carrying goods to the market, but not even its rider pays any attention to the light. Standing there in its uselessness, serving nothing and no one, the light feels stupid, unreasonable, insane—and yet it doesn't stop breathing or winking at the pretty housewives who pass by without even honoring it with a glance. Yes, that's more or less how I feel. I eat and sleep and work—red, yellow, green—always cut off from the traffic around me, always outside the processes of circulation, since all these efforts mean nothing in the end.*
>
> *But my existence does serve a purpose. I consume power. I live, Thomas, in the realm of consumption. And believe me, this sense of not participating in the processes of production is so utterly disheartening. I seem to myself like some ornamental object: An old, romantic traffic light that a passerby might look at with curiosity and perhaps a twinge of pity, as it keeps repeating those same convulsive changes over and over like a robot, as if there were still cars waiting at the corner. The worst of all is that you get used to it. And if I feel redundant in a farmer's market, a place where ordinary people come to buy and sell their ordinary goods, imagine how I would feel in an entire state ruled by the people. The middle-class clerk just scrapes the walls of his house when it needs replastering. The proletarian knocks it down and builds a new house in its place. And all the wreck really needs is a bulldozer to clear it away.*

I don't believe that any analysis of this passage would add much to the deep self-knowledge that Thrassakis had already acquired as a mature intellectual. What we're missing is information. The specifics.

There are, however, a few things we know for sure. Modena was such a small town that the couple couldn't bear to stay there for more than a month or two.

So they went to Bologna, and then to Parma, Sienna, and Florence, ending up in Rome. It was an era in which thousands of Greek students, overflowing from our country, ended up in Italy, where they went to the universities without even taking entrance exams, to learn Italian for a year. The central squares in cities all over Italy were literally occupied by Greek students, and the childless Thrassakises, travelling from city to city, easily found people to talk to each evening, thus renewing their ties with their native land.

He writes again to Thomas:

> At the train stations in Germany, you find a Greek expatriate community so unorganized, so underdeveloped, so troubled, that you, the intellectual, are flooded with anguish. But here in the Italian squares, these hordes of Greek students with their long hair and attitudes of suspicion make you believe in our nation, that we can survive—and then if you're a writer to boot, like I am, you see all these young Greeks as future readers.

And later in the same letter, "I'm talking about literacy. About the stuff of reading and writing. That, at least. The basics. The firsts."

≈

THOSE WERE difficult years. Nothing like our own times, when we know that the new year will come in and go out again through the same hole. For Thrassakis those years must have been full of agony and uncertainty. Historians never speak the whole truth. We have to look at a civilization's most sensitive indicators in order to ascertain what kind of seismic tremors it really suffered and withstood. But Italy is a strange place, where people walk and leave no footprints behind. First Kalvos, then Thrassakis. As hard as I searched for some old relation, some meaningful thread, I found nothing. In Italy there are castles to protect the villages from non-existent pirates, and the people in the cities seem to move in closed circles. How could our hero ever have managed to break through? I'm afraid he and his wife must have found themselves alone together in a circle of solitude.

Because it's a known fact that he didn't manage very well with the language. Perhaps that's even why he wanted to live there for a while, in order to be able to write. "When everyone around you," he writes, "is speaking a language you don't understand, you acquire a kind of independence of thought: even in a bustling *trattoria* you can shield the thread of your thoughts from external invasion" (*CDW*, Vol. I, 23). (Though the reference to the *trattoria* seems to place this sentence in Italy, Pavsanias Alipastos maintains that "*trattoria*" should really read "*kuchen local*," since Thrassakis was surely referring to German, a language which throughout his life he remained utterly incapable of learning, most likely because it reminded him of his childhood and the Occupation. Alipastos asserts, moreover, that Italian, so closely related to French, which he spoke quite well, could do nothing other than saturate Thrassakis's hearing.) A bit later, Thrassakis writes:

> *Swedish, for example, has a crude, enchanting music that lets me directly into the rhythm of a language and a people. I drink in the sounds and grow instantly enthralled as I see, through them, landscapes and images: tree-lined lakes, Swedish furniture, a simple salt-shaker, a square plate. A world that's homey and warm, built to protect man from the great frost of nature lurking outside. And the sounds, the deep cavernous vowels and almost nonexistent consonants, ring in my ears like pebbles in a dry riverbed, as a trickle of water jostles the rocks against one another.*

French and English, which he spoke well, really made him suffer. Not always, of course. There were times when he even enjoyed sitting at a table in the corner of some café and listening in on the people next to him, losing himself in their world, their problems. (People often think that their problems are unique, that their sufferings, their hopes and disappointments are the first and last on this earth—they have no inkling of the commonness, the utter banality of their concerns. Which is why, though they might claim to be unhappy, Thrassakis calls them "happy beasts.") But at other times he was so absorbed in his own worries that he resented anything that threatened to tear him from the insularity of his mind. So he took shelter in unfamiliar languages and dialects. As, for example, in Berlin, both East and West.

And Alipastos is right about that, at least: in Berlin, whenever he wanted to write, Thrassakis would take refuge in the *kuchen local*. Though with the grayness of life in the German Confederacy, so sharply contrasted to TV's fantastic kaleidoscope of colors, he suffered such horrible aversions to all kinds of *wurst* that he could easily shut himself up for days in his room and work. (On these trips the couple usually stayed with a friend whom they saw only in the evenings.) "And whenever I want," he writes to Thomas, "I go out and walk down to the train station, which is teeming with Greeks."

His own language doesn't bother him in the least. Greek is a constituent factor in his mode of expressing his "problem." Indeed, in the final analysis, the problem is none other than the language itself, just as the "medium is the message," and the medium an artist uses determines the subject of his work. So, listening to the Greek men at the railroad station talking about women, there was nothing to keep his stream of thought from following the line upwards, for example, to the problem of women's liberation. The Greek he hears when eavesdropping works like the amplifier in a stereo—it opens out the sound, amplifying it in his mind. Foreign languages he understands are like interference on the radio. Foreign languages he doesn't understand are like umbrellas under which he takes shelter, or clods of dirt that he pushes off if they start to weigh too heavily on him.

That's why one day when he sees someone sticking something onto the window of a train as it pulls into the station in Rome, something that looks at first like a political poster but turns out to be a sticker that reads "*Esperanto*," he wants to run and catch up with the guy, to share with him his own deep desire that everyone speak the same language, to talk to him about the sheer ridiculousness of being unable to communicate—no, it's simply too much to bear. But the fugitive missionary of the new religion has already vanished into the humming station, while Thrassakis, chasing after him, keeps bumping into annoying *cicerone* trying to offer him illegal taxis and cheap hotels. The *Esperanto* man is gone—but not the hope he represents: as Glafkos looks up and sees the little hand of the big clock fall, flinging a new minute into the world, then resting till it's time to fling out another, he thinks that perhaps time really works for those who love the future of the human race ("Patra-Brindisi," *CDW*, Vol. II, 48-50).

He is not, then, a fanatic. He is perfectly willing to suffer linguistic alienation for the sake of a common, pananthropic language—as long as he's not the only one. He remembers with fear how once, as a young boy, he and his friends had all agreed to turn off the lights and pull down their underwear. But when the lights came back on, he found himself the only one with his pants down, the others all fully-dressed, pointing at him and laughing. That's why he always insisted that collective action be finalized ahead of time, so there wouldn't be any tricks. He would agree to sacrifice his linguistic independence, but only on the condition that everyone else sacrifice theirs.

Chapter Three

Our age is tricky, full of pitfalls and traps. We move forward
blindly in the dark. The achievement of unexpected accom-
plishments is countered by the conspicuous depreciation of
all desire. The violation of every basic demand. "Hold on,
George." "But it hurts, Claude, I'm suffering." "Hold on,
George, you're the leader of a nation." "What does that
mean?" "It means that you represent a people." And he held
on, at least on the outside, while inside he rotted away. And
the people, who were rotting on the outside, had nerves like
scaffolding and beliefs like electric generators.

(Variation on P. Palaiologos's editorial concerning
the death of French president George Pompidou,
as the Greek reporter imagined him, and the
mourning of his wife, Claude, *CDW*, Vol. II)

THRASSAKIS, forced to live far from his homeland, enriched our country's literary tradition with his treatment of the theme of exile. In lyrical, nostalgic passages about once-loved footpaths, crossroads and corners, he enriched a theme
by now so familiar to us: the theme of return. Countless times he dove into the
bottomless depths of memory to bring up rare and hard-to-find rocks.

My relationship with the homeland is like that between the earth and the
smallest planet in the solar system: whatever weighs .04 kilos on the planet
weighs 2.5 kilos for me, since I have a different stratospheric structure. The
atmosphere weighs more heavily on me.

We will return later on to this motif of earth, planet, and sun—for now I'll refrain from offering my own analysis of his life as a "displaced person," since a thorough analysis can already be found in Thrassakis's published body of work. I want simply to direct the reader's attention to the phrase "exile with an automatic telephone connection," which recalls Lenin's "Socialism with electricity." What does it mean, exactly, this parachuting phrase, which in the entire body of his discovered work we find in just a single letter, written to his close friend Thomas?

In this letter Glafkos admits to Thomas how much he has changed since Greece was connected to Europe's automatic telephone network. That day marked a substantive change in his relationship with his country—for naturally, the possibility of immediate communication radically changes the mentality of the emigrant. As he writes in one characteristic passage:

> *It was one thing to be a Spanish political exile in '39, and quite another today, in '73. The former lived through his memories, his reflections, his relationships with other exiles. The exile of today picks up the phone, dials a few numbers and has a direct connection with the "land of nostalgia."*
>
> *Letters, photographs, the news someone brings [you] in person from the homeland, all resemble those platonic intimacies you share with a lover. Whereas talking on the phone is like going to a prostitute: You pay through the nose, you 'do it,' you finish and leave, having obtained only a deeper void.*

It is precisely this "deeper void" which our poet describes for Thomas, apparently after a long talk with him over the phone:

> *In the old days when you called up the international switchboard and asked to be connected, you could wait five, ten, twenty minutes, half an hour, an hour, two, sometimes even three on peak days like New Year's or May 21, the name day for Saints Constantinos and Eleni, or if tanks had appeared in downtown Athens—so you had all that time to prepare yourself psychologically, to chew everything over, to torment yourself, to freak out, to get drunk, even, on waiting. But now that prep time is gone. These days you just get annoyed if your call doesn't go through right away, if it's a little slow in hooking itself,*

sucker-like, to that invisible network. And believe me [I'm not sure exactly what kind of psychological insecurity it reflects, but this phrase, "believe me," often turns up in his letters to Thomas], I'm quite experienced in all this, since for a long time I had a free phone line at my disposal, and I milked it for all it was worth until the bill came and the people at the organization (an international institute researching air pollution) politely asked me never to set foot in their office again. Remember back then, when we talked almost every day? You were always saying, "Hang up, hang up, don't talk away all your money." And I always answered, "Someone else is paying."

Still, the exasperation you feel when you don't get through right away is a kind of saving grace, because it has to do with the here and now, and not the there and then which is the torment of every expatriate. The here and now isn't so much the connection with the outside world. It is, above all, the phone itself, the circular dial, gray or black, sometimes red, though in my case it was mustard yellow. By now I've learned how to sniff things out, I can tell how things will go from the very first number I dial. But what does that mean, really, to "sniff things out"—to smell space, to smell chaos? I'm not talking metaphorically, not at all. I mean it literally, as something that depends entirely on the senses. Or, if you like, on something beyond the senses, on the kind of extrasensory skill that true mediums possess: the ability to hear the almost inaudible noises that follow the dialing of each number, those smallest cracklings of infinity, the displacement of infinitesimal specks of dust in the primordial chaos that separates you from me. Just like when we were kids and we'd glue our ears to telephone poles, listening for what we called "messages from the beyond," or "the chorus of angels." I decipher these faint signals according to a certain code that tells me beforehand if the call will go through or if I'll end up again in the wide humming of infinity. That's what I mean when I say I can "smell" chaos. It's like those cylindrical nets for catching eels, where the eel swims further and further in, thinking all the while it's going out—each number sticks to the one before with a certain sound, forming part of a frame that narrows toward the end of the sack.

I don't know how I do it, but I'm rarely wrong. And so when everything seems to be going just fine and then all of a sudden I get a busy signal because the "other"—you, for instance—is on the line talking to someone else, the curses start raining down— "Dammit, you idiot, get off the phone, don't you know I've been trying for ages to get through?" But of course, how could you know? Though all that yelling and swearing, that ranting and raving is, in the end, redemptive—because, as I said before, it has to do with the here and now.

"Hello? Who's calling?" His or her voice comes across from the other end like a slap in a drugged man's face. The narcotic of time suffers complete and utter defeat. The effect of that "Hello?" is truly staggering, because the other—you— answers as if this were just any old call. For the expatriate, the emigrant, the exile, the "displaced," there is no greater pleasure than having the other treat him, even for an instant, as if he really were there, close at hand, "in place." He gets caught up in the momentary illusion, and wants so badly to keep up the game as long as he can, to keep the other thinking that he's there, close by. Because when the capsizing of reality is accepted by both parties, reality itself changes. And so that everyday, curt, concise, common, utterly common "Who's calling?" becomes something that the exile, the 'displaced,' holds on to and treasures like a momentary whiff of some scent which he bottles and stores away in his memory, to use later on against the narcotic of time.

Then comes the moment of recognition. And believe me, Thomas, in the days of my extensive dealings with the long-distance company, I often hung up before I even said my name, letting the person on the other end think something had gone wrong with the connection. Because afterwards everything changes. The voice on the other end takes on false tones of astonishment and delight, asking, "What's up, man? Where are you calling from? Oumeo? Where's that?" (Like a knife, his ignorance: if he doesn't even know where Oumeo is, how can you know, since the last thing you want to believe is that you're actually there? I'm speaking, of course, about unassimilated exiles—for the assimilated, everything changes radically.)

"You sound just fine, like you're right next door." That's usually what comes next—"just fine." But the "like" hits you like a poisoned dart in the chest, though you went in completely unarmed. Because without meaning to, the other has marked the distance that separates you from him: he's sitting on an axis of reference, while you're searching through him for the broken axle that left you stranded in the middle of the road.

What I'm saying is, no one should ever go in unprotected. Our culture, capable of yielding the greatest pleasure, can also produce the greatest sadness. Or rather, the suffering it causes equals its most astounding achievements. So the caller should never fall into the trap of mentally placing himself "over there." Because, in the end, he is "over here"—which is to say, not there. Oumeo and Athens are separated by an infinite abyss.

Of course what is for you the undesired self-distancing of the other is also, for him, a form of self-protection—for him, you constitute a dangerous emotional element, the nitro-glycerine of memory. And so, surprised by your call, not having had time to prepare himself to confront you, he resorts to the old karate tricks of human relations, knocking you to the ground with a Bruce Lee punch, pushing you and your black belt of memory outside the ring of his everyday reality. Because he too has to live. And who says you have the sole right to nostalgia? What if he too longs for the "far-from-here"? What if he's jealous of your life in the Laplands? Or still thinks you're as happy as a clam among the kaffirs?

So your friend offers a last defense from the trenches: "And the kids, how are they?" Words that define distance, tabulate time. After the momentary mirage, you're back in the desert again. And the only reason camels don't kill themselves crossing the Sahara is that, like it or not, they have water stored in their humps.

But the real kicker, Thomas, is when there's some marginal, minor character sitting there with your friend who also wants to say hello, to send you a "hey" from the homeland. So your friend—a junior clerk, a fruit thief from the days when the garden was unguarded—says to you, "Hey, Yannis is here. He says hi. Hold on a minute, I'll give him to you. Hey, Yannis!" And Yannis or Pavlos or Nikos or whoever he is comes to the phone. He's younger than the two of you and has never met you, only heard the stories. So he has respect— and that's the real killer.

An end, there is no end to the longing. The only "as if" I don't hate is the one carved beneath the bust of Papadiamantis on Skiathos: "As if there were no end to the longings and sufferings of the world." Because it's true. There is no end. After every phone call I would go back out to that awful office full of foreign secretaries who took vacations in Greece where the air pollution isn't as bad because our country is technologically underdeveloped. Do you understand? I would return to my own reality, which I hated: the secretaries, the

desks and chairs, the statistics on air pollution and raging tuberculosis taped
on the walls. And I had the sickness of sighs. I was sick of it all. I was horri-
fied. And I'd go out and gorge myself on fries.

From this letter, so eloquent in its discussion of estrangement, we are left with no doubt in our minds that Thrassakis counted the automatic telephone connection as one of the "frustrations" of exile. Thrassakis's own definition of "frustration," an English word that has no precise equivalent in Greek, is rather idiosyncratic:

Something that interrupts you during something sweet, or leaves you with an
aftertaste of sweet, or has no other sweetness than the anticipation of a sweet-
ness that never comes, and the anticipation is never the same as the sweetness
itself, but something else entirely, a weak substitute.

(*CDW,* Vol. I, 347)

Thrassakis himself put together a list of the frustrations endured by the exile, the emigrant, the immigrant, the displaced, the depatriated, the filed, the enveloped, the passportless. Let's take a look at that list.

I

NEWSPAPERS FROM *"down there."* Because they offer a slice of life, but only a censored life that has little to do with uncensored reality, which never comes across in the papers. Glafkos writes:

As the years pass, the exile's original attempts to read between the lines of his
country's censored papers inevitably ends up in his reading only the lines them-
selves, just as after years in jail the prisoner no longer sees the spaces between
the barbed wire that surrounds him but the wire itself, an impassable barrier
stretching endlessly to the horizon.

Which means not only that the sixth sense becomes second nature, but that whatever sticks around wins in the end. At first when he read the papers he understood what wasn't being said. But with ages of silence, those silenced things ceased to exist, until all that was left were the words on the page. A lie kept up for years acquires a claim to verisimilitude—and so the distorted picture the newspapers gave of the dictatorship somehow became the true picture. With time, the exile no longer gets anything more than the "inxile" from reading his country's censored papers.

2

ENCOUNTERS WITH ACQUAINTANCES, tourists just passing through. Thrassakis calls them "reality-shrinkers" or "partial messengers," since they only tell you what they think you want to hear. Keeping in mind the medico-judicial diagnosis of "cholera" that banished you from the homeland, they talk about the injustness of the epidemic, about the deaths, their own family dramas, the economic crisis, until you're reduced to nothing more than a huge humming beehive of human suffering: holes everywhere dripping poison. And they think they're giving you what you want.

They have a whole repertoire of topics they think you might like to hear about, now that you're cut off from the reality of your land—everyday problems, joys and sadnesses, match-makings and marriages, ambitions and disappointed dreams. Yet they reveal only as much as they believe belongs to your restricted range of reception—and so, as a result, that range just shrinks and shrinks even more. And though you want so badly to comfort yourself with the thought that nothing changes—the world is as it was, life hasn't changed, people's problems are basically the same as they always were—you can't help but wonder, "Can cholera really still exist in this world, for them to be talking about all these suffering people?" These fine patriots insist on telling you about all those suffering from "cholera" back home, as if secretly seeking to vindicate you, as if saying, "It's a good thing you haven't come back." But you take it the opposite way, telling yourself, "The breach is deep and unbridgeable. Almost no communication anymore." And so the "shrinkers" end up drenching you in the same bitter waters as the foreign radios and the foreign newspapers that live off the deaths of others, reporting arrests, kidnappings, train crashes, workplace accidents, crises, and strikes, while thousands of trains arrive safely on time, thousands of airplanes take off and land without falling from the sky, thousands of children are born, millions of letters reach their addressees, workers all over the world end the work day unharmed—no, the newspapers only report the unique, the exception, that which constitutes "news." As for the rest, silence and ashes. For a while they never even mentioned the mass movements until they reached peaks of individual despair and became mobs. Then, yes, they run, write, inform. They tell you crudely, "Why don't you kill yourself, we'll make you a hero. Then your dreams will be worth something after all."

And so, like an undelivered letter, I no longer expect anything of anyone. That's why I don't accept prescriptions from doctors, which in the end offer relief only to the curer, not the patient. As for the "reality-shrinkers," instead of distracting or relieving your repressed emotions, they just burden your scales—already unbalanced enough—with their own weight. They see you as a symbol of their own privations, partly because your deliberate absence gives shape to those lacks and shortages—and there, at your altar, they leave their offerings: sunburnt pistachios from Aegina, Kalamata olives that are split and rotting, Turkish delight missing its dusting of powdered sugar, stale honey cakes from the year before last. Since you embody their anguish by living abroad, it's hard for those still living at home to express that anguish before you. The "reality-shrinkers" see you as the antidote of the evil which has befallen them, no longer measuring you in human terms but in terms of the calamity— "cholera"—that sent you away. And so you cross paths and part again having never really communicated at all, with a deep satisfaction in never having mentioned what was really going on.

3

THE RADIO. More specifically, the stations of the western Peloponnese, which transmit the longing for the East to the fringes of the West. In endless pages Thrassakis describes the Ilias Tower as the antithesis of the Greek broadcasting that comes out of Munich. Because while the station in Munich addresses itself to the more or less permanent emigrants who have established themselves in Germany, the Tower sends its messages to all those travelling at sea. Thrassakis copies down the couplets: "I have my father's house in Mani / And a bachelor pad in Pasalimani." But in the absence of any dialectical (which is to say, critical) relationship with the audience, these songs, repeated again and again, ultimately produce the same result as the newspapers: they fossilize memory, these pre-recorded programs that drone on and on, never managing to relieve the longing of the exile, whose heart aches for his distant home.

What, then, is the request, and what its requested catharsis? Thrassakis finally settled the issue thus: none of these "alienated" forms of communication live up to his expectations. The only driving force that prods people to keep up the fight for communication is self-deception, which he describes as a vast gas station constantly refuelling the conscious advance of humanity. Which is to say, pity if the utopians were to disappear.

The false (dissonant, out-of-tune) life of the *émigré* has certain axes of reference which Thrassakis tried to pinpoint as well as he could, so that those who came after him wouldn't fall into the same traps he had. (This was, of course, a utopian (atopic, placeless) wish that nevertheless presupposed the existence of a base, a state, from which those others could emigrate. He did not foresee the fated dissolution of that state.) The False Life does not enjoy the support of the Historical Becoming. It is false in the way a falsetto is false. And so the cross-sections of the "national body" lie in concentric circles, each an even falser version of the one before. False farce of Mr. Farsakoglou.

False *falsetto*.

≈

THRASSAKIS, a single slice of that national body, destined to become a great writer, was meant to live a long life. With a very few exceptions, most great writers have been people of great age—if not utterly ancient when they died, they at least managed to sail smoothly into their eighties. Because, Thrassakis reasoned, if a writer managed to live into his eighties, friends and enemies alike would hail him with whoops of joy, first as a biological phenomenon, and then as a robust intellectual presence. If the goal of art is, in the end, to conquer time, to abolish the oblivion of forgetfulness, what could be more beautiful, more moving, than a runner on the intellectual track (Etiamble's "*athlète complet de l'écriture*") who wins this race *in body* as well? The *embodiment* of victory has the power to move even the most motley of masses. It shows how the origins of art as a therapeutic act were slowly forgotten as art came to be valued in its own right, until writers of remarkable age like Hugo and Tolstoy brought the issue of the healing, even life-preserving, nature of art once more to the fore. Furthermore, when the creator himself becomes an archive of life, the archivists are able to classify him all the more easily while he's still alive, on the basis of his living testimony. And if the critics of his generation—always the enemies of an author's youth—pass away before the author himself, their successors will be able to view that author with a kinder eye, since by the time they get to know him, he has reached another, more mature stage in his life and work. Thrassakis, familiar with these processes, knew he'd have it made if he could just manage to reach fifty-five. That's why after turning forty he plunged with such devoted haste into the revision of his unpublished body of work. But he didn't manage to finish in time—time caught up with him.

≈

IN RELATION to the earthly present of his homeland, Thrassakis compares himself to the dead dwarfstar Mercury—which, according to the data gathered by the satellite Mariner 10, is "the most intriguing of planets, due to the great extremes it exhibits, covered in craters and enveloped in a "very thin atmosphere of poisonous gases," which render "the sustenance of life on the planet almost impossible." When the satellite finally sent these data down to earth, the scientists, who had been working unsuccessfully on the project for years, fell into dejection and disappointment, as had happened previously with the moon. In the case of blood and urine samples, "negative results" means good news, but in the sciences it only means that they haven't really found anything at all. The report continues:

> Mercury, like the moon, has been hit by meteor showers. Essentially lacking in atmosphere, without water and with a temperature below freezing in the shadows of its mountains, Mercury is a planet entirely unsuited for human life. It is, to be precise, a dead planet, the closest in the solar system to the sun, at a distance of 57 million kilometers, as opposed to the 157 million kilometers of Earth. Thus the distance of Mercury from Earth is estimated at 100 million kilometers.

Soviet astronomers, however, opposing the views of their American colleagues at NASA, insisted that Mercury's atmosphere contained rare gases such as neon, argon and helium.

Thrassakis's psychological identification with heavenly bodies reflects one of the most complex problems presented by the condition of exile. I am unable to comment further on this experience, because, thank God, it is entirely foreign to me. All I can do is show understanding and respect for a man who wanted his longing to take on such cosmic proportions.

≈

THE LITERARY culmination of Thrassakis's experience of exile is to be found in the short story "LANWAIR" (*CDW*, Vol. II, 65-69), which I would never have examined in detail if I hadn't discovered entirely by luck (a luck which, as one can see, has rarely made its appearance during the course of my research) an interview published around that time which most likely served as the inspiration behind the story. Let us not forget the passage quoted above in which Thrassakis compares himself to an ocean liner that produces its own potable water during its overseas voyage. However, despite this presumed self-sufficiency, an artist of any sort necessarily draws on the reality around him, working with bits and pieces that catch his attention, that engage his sensitivity, that spark him to transmit the messages he receives in wavelengths uncommon among common beasts. But what exactly is "LANWAIR"? I will reprint the article's title and subtitles as they originally appeared, so the reader can see it more or less as the deceased must have done:

The "Lanwair" Plan

THE NEW "LANWAIR" PROPOSAL
FOR THE GREATER ATHENS AREA

Mr. Doxiadis explains why he prefers
Makronissos over Spata and the Greek National Airport

68

LANWAIR = LAND – WATER – AIR. In Greek, *GINERA* (*GI – NERO –
AERAS*); in French, *TERMERAIR* (*TERRE – MER – AIR*); in German, *LAN-
WALUFT* (*LAND – WASSER – LUFT*); in Italian, *TERMARIA* (*TERRA –
MARE – ARIA*); etc.

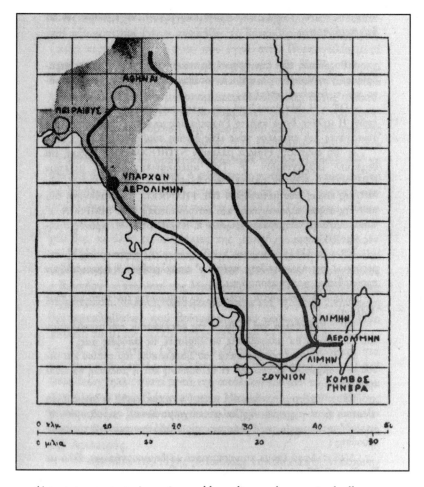

*Airport, two ports, train station and long-distance bus terminal, all concen-
trated in a single complex in the Makronissos–Lavrio region.*

Now that we've seen the etymology of these synthetic nouns, let us examine an excerpt from the interview that prompted the writing of Thrassakis's story:

EP: *Who first came up with the idea of building an airport on the island of Makronissos, who conducted the research, how long did the study take, and what kind of expenses were involved?*

DOX: *The idea was my own, and it grew out of several years of continuous research. The final study was conducted by myself and my colleagues at the lab, with the help of the following foreign advisors: the Swedish company Nitroconsult, specialists in rock-blasting; the American consulting firm Greiner, specialists in airport design; MIT professor of transportation engineering Dr. Frankel; MIT professor of aeronautics and astronomy Dr. Simpson; and Swiss airport specialist Mr. Rydingstam. The duration of the study was seven months and ten days.*

EP: *Do you think any of the alternative solutions that have been suggested for the expansion or relocation of the Athenian airport present possibilities for realization?*

DOX: *They are all entirely unfeasible, if we aim to respect the needs of the land and of the Greek people.*

EP: *More specifically, what is your view on the proposed expansion of the existing airport?*

DOX: *Such an enterprise would constitute a crime against the landscape, the Saronic Gulf, and half a million residents. The expense incurred and the pollution generated would be simply appalling.*

EP: *Are you opposed to the creation of a floating airport, an artificial island constructed on landfills, to be located somewhere in the waters in the vicinity of the capital?*

DOX: *Since we already have this island, why build another, incurring expenses up to twenty times as great?*

For those who haven't read it, let us briefly summarize the plot of Thrassakis's text. Comrade Katharosporis (whose name, which means "clean seed," symbolizes a generation dedicated to the ideals of resistance against the Nazi occupiers), returns to his homeland after years of exile. The dictatorship has fallen, martial law has been abolished, amnesty has been granted, progressive forces have taken over the country's government—all in all, something similar to what happened in Portugal after forty years of totalitarianism. The single-party state that had governed his homeland for all those years had forced Katharosporis, a supporter of multi-party Socialism, to remain outside the game, off the map, a non-player. Now he has come back in order to help to the extent of his abilities with the rebuilding of his country in the wake of the "tornado of the fascist military junta." (Thrassakis insisted on adopting his main character's style of speech in his own narration.) From the very moment of his arrival, however, this comrade—who, due to a stomach ulcer caused by the hardships of his long exile, can no longer drink anything but milk—can't stop himself from descending, step by step, the staircase of melancholy, plagued as he is by nostalgia for "the wings, the great wings of his youth."

Considering the source of the story's inspiration, the first blow is, of course, the landing of the Concorde at the new airport on Makronissos, where Katharosporis had once spent four consecutive years of internal exile. At first he doesn't realize where he is. The place seems vaguely familiar, of course, but because so many years have passed since his departure from Greece, he had been expecting to find everything changed—and besides (and here Thrassakis shows himself, for the first time, to be a keen psychologist), he could never have imagined that he would be landing at the precise place from which he had been expelled. (Immediately after his release from "Devil's Island," as Makronissos was called in those days, Katharosporis had passed over the mountains into Eastern Europe, finally settling in the West, where he had lived for the past ten years, after the schism of the Left.)

The irony of fate has transformed this same Makronissos into the New Parthenon of contemporary technology: two ports, to the left and right, both densely crowded with anchored ships, and a bridge two and a half kilometers long that connects the island—once a piece of the same flesh, before a geological rift had split it from the town of Lavrio across the strait—to that spot on the mainland where prisoners used to leave their hopes behind. And barely perceptible at the far end of the landing strip, on a small artificial island, the marker for blind landing.

At first he has no idea where he is. Since the old airport was also on the water, he always remembered it as being next to the sea, so it makes no particular impression on him when he sees the "glistening sea" (see: the "First Notebook")

from the airplane window, strengthened by a small magnifying lens in the corner (a Concorde novelty) which brings the shoreline and the straw roofs of seaside restaurants into close view.

He saw his friends often over the years; whenever they travelled abroad they
would stop by to see him. His relatives, however, were ashamed of him—"ide-
alist" was by far their kindest name for him—and as they had always avoided any
form of contact with him; he is now shocked to see how much the family has
changed. Unknown children of children, sisters of brothers, brothers of brothers, land-grabbers, brother-killers, divided all these years by bad blood . . . they've
all come running to witness the return of the prodigal grandfather. *Where am I?*
What is this place? his lost gaze seems to ask. "This is one of the most modern,
state-of-the-art airports in Europe," explains one of his nephews, a member of
the Olympic Airways ground personnel. "In a single peak hour it can accommodate up to a hundred and eighty take-offs and landings, a total of about
twenty thousand passengers."

Comrade Katharosporis has his reservations—not about the airport itself but
about the obvious pride this nephew of his takes in the place. He has his
doubts, too, about a young niece's excitement over some French floozy of an
actress who was on his flight and is now at the exit, surrounded by a group of
society reporters and gossip columnists.

His disorientation grows upon leaving the terminal, which faces west,
toward the island of Kea. Katharosporis, who has lived a clean life, with the few
but honest olives of his land, is bothered by all the signs in foreign languages.
He feels like he's in Lebanon or Caracas. He still doesn't know this is
Makronissos. Thrassakis, with O. Henry's technique of making the main
character the last to recognize his fate, leaves his hero suspended somewhere
between suspicion and presentiment, in the uncertain land of doubt that
gives fuel to the emotions.

Before the shock of his realization, I'd like to turn first to two subsequent
events that likewise upset the sensitized Katharosporis. The drama doesn't end
with his recognition of the island on which he had suffered, the island Andreas
Nenedakis once called "the island of It-is-forbidden." That same evening, a group
of veteran Communists take Katharosporis out to Plaka. What he had once
known as the Transfers Department, where he had been held overnight before

being sent to the island, is now a *boîte* with singers from "our side." Comrade Katharosporis can't manage to reconcile the past with the present, yesterday with today. It had been an important night for him, the night at the Transfers Department: at dawn his wife had come (just in time) to bring him a blanket and a few crusts of bread for his trip. Now he sits there, sipping a soda and listening to sad songs about "roads baptized with the names of foreign martyrs." Those last words make Comrade Katharosporis uncomfortable—they sound to him too much like "party martyrs." He is so sick of politics that he rejects all political art, even the mildest. He simply won't accept it. He wants art for art's sake. Yet he can't keep from thinking of the solitary night he spent in this basement thirty years before, not knowing whether the next day would bring exile or execution. "The people and places are ruined, corrupted," he thinks. "Back then the only music was the crackling of machine guns. Now here we are with our guitars, our accordions and violins. Poor Aris." (He is referring, Thrassakis tells us, to Aris Velouhiotis, who fought in the resistance and died in '45.)

His friends, all supporters of multi-party Socialism, see that he's suffering and decide to take him to a *bouzouki* joint on Alexandras Avenue for a taste of the "homeland." "The owners are on our side," they say. "The place just opened, we should try and give it our support." The bar, called "Kiss There" (which in Greek is a homonym for "prison"), is located in the old Averof prison. Katharosporis had been there more than once in the past. In fact he had once been something of a regular—though for different reasons, of course.

These days the prisons are *bouzouki* bars where they play the *rembetika*—"the good old songs"—that make his stomach turn. Is it from mixing drinks, or just too much] emotion for one day?

The musicians are playing at full blast, all the old favorites: "Echoing Mountains," "Moonless Night," "Sitting on a Stone." But Katharosporis isn't made of stone. Man is soft, "like a handful of grass." After the massive bloodshed of those years, as one of the vanquished, he has developed a metaphysical idealization of blood.

The Averof prison is now a *bouzouki* bar. The Transfers Department is a *boîte* for intellectuals. Makronissos is an airport. *Where am I*, he thinks.

Katharosporis dies shortly after, within three months of that night. But before we reach that point, let us return to Makronissos, where the first shock of recognition brings on a second, as the car he is riding in passes over the bridge that unites the island with Lavrio, as Hydra and Sounio are united in Jules Dessin's *Phaedra*. Suddenly something breaks inside of him. He turns to his sister-in-law, who is driving the car, and says, "Stop for a minute, would you?" There is no shoulder to pull off onto, but she obeys, because she's afraid of this bloodthirsty relative who would kill a man with the lid of a can if he had to—at least that's how she has been taught to think of him by family legends and the political propaganda of the Right. Comrade Katharosporis steps out of the car and, looking back at the island, wonders if this might be the place where . . . . Everyone's looking at him like he's insane. But according to Thrassakis, the Comrade won't be bullied, and walks over to the spot. He wants to see the rock from which, trying to get him to sign a statement of repentance, they threw him into the sea in a sack full of cats that, terrified of the water, scratched at him mercilessly with their claws. He wants to see the windswept hillside where they had eaten bean soup on their very first night on the island. He wants to see the island of pain, the island of old comrades now gone—he wants to honor the island not for what it is, but for what it once was.

In the meantime, an endless line of honking cars and busses has gathered on the bridge behind his sister-in-law's car. Life, we see, refuses to wait for the Comrade's memories to unfold. There is a statute of limitations on memory. Capitalist society moves forward by erasing memory, negating history. But Katharosporis has no desire to move forward. As at the end of Papadiamantis's *The Murderess*, he wants to end his life there, "on the neck of sand that links the rock of the hermitage with dry land, halfway across, midway between divine and human justice." But for Thrassakis, the murderess is life itself, with its unstoppable, irreversible forward motion, its lithium of forgetting.

The scene is incredibly moving, one of the best our deceased comrade had to offer. The island on one side, Lavrio on the other, as Katharosporis stands, remembering the heated conversations he'd had with their party leader, there with Lavrio just across the water, exactly where they were headed now, on this bridge. . . .

No, the shock is too much for the comrade to absorb, to take in, to digest. Though he has finally returned, he has done so only in order to die more easily.

And the story ends with the obituary that appears a few months later in the Old
Fighters' newspaper:

We will always honor the memory
of the fighter Katharosporis

*On the morning of Saturday, March 2, Comrade Pavlos Katharosporis left us
forever.*

*From an early age, Comrade Pavlos committed himself to the struggle of the
Greek people and the working class. He fought against the German occupiers,
against the levelling obscurantism of the reactionary powers of the Right. He
was imprisoned and exiled for his efforts. The people, however, honored him
with their trust.*

*Our remarkable comrade had all the qualities of a true fighter. He was a
courageous, dynamic, modest, combative, and tenacious defender of the people's rights. But his life came to an end before he could see his dreams come true
or his struggles bear fruit. In his last words to his wife and child, he spoke of
Greece's continuing struggle, of unity, organization, and undying effort.*

Chapter Four

AN INDIVIDUAL'S childhood years are perceived by everyone but the child himself. Though others can see him, the child cannot see himself. This is why it is so particularly unpleasant for an adolescent to listen to adults reminisce about what he was like as a baby. Though his likes and dislikes are already more or less formed, the adolescent hasn't yet reached the point of maturity at which he can look at himself from the outside—he hasn't, in other words, developed the double understanding of himself and his shadow. Like a cat, he sees his reflection in the mirror and doubts his own image, unable to understand its relation to the light. Similarly, our relationship with ourselves can only be a product of omnipotent time. Time, like boiling water, exists only above a certain temperature. Time exists at neither seven nor seventeen degrees Celsius. Time exists only in the cellular alteration of the organism, when new cells retain the memories of old, dead cells, just as literary schools give way one to the next in genealogical succession. But the child, in the absence of any objective standard of comparison, lives one-dimensionally. Glafkos remembers himself as a child only through the descriptions of others. Alienated through their gaze, he becomes what they want him to be. In some other period of his life he might have tried to resist, to remain himself, but as a child he is left with no other option, and submits to the interpretations of others.

When he runs toward his reflection, Gustave does not so much imagine that he will see himself as that he will see himself seen so as to adjust his image in the sight of others. But this is what he is forbidden to do; man's relation to his reflec-

tion resembles what the psychologists call the double sensation: *if my thumb touches my index finger, neither of the fingers is truly an object for the other since each of them is at once seeking and sought, feeling and felt, active and passive.*

(Sartre, *The Family Idiot*, 29)

Thus it is difficult, if not impossible, for us, in the absence of any records that might direct our research, to look back on Thrassakis's childhood years. As Glafkos observes:

When the inspiration provided by others runs dry and I don't feel like writing some kind of fairytale-drama, I turn inwards, go rooting through my ancestral trunk to see what's buried deep inside. That way, even if I'm lying through my teeth, I'll only be wronging myself. That doesn't mean that in writing about others I wasn't also searching for myself. That's why now, in searching for myself, I'm essentially seeking someone else, a third person.

(*CDW*, Vol. II, 201)

But if what he remembers is what others have told him, and what they've told him is what he remembers, one thing is certain: he remembers his hometown of Kavala very well. His family's two-story house beneath the Swedish consulate, near the Koufler villa and the church of Agios Yiannis; "1914," the year the house was built, in iron numbers above the balcony. The best thing about the house was the view. Built high on the hill, the house looked down on the stadium, the mill, the barracks; and from the eastern window, the church of Agios Pavlos, the Ottoman aqueduct, the lighthouse, the port. Leaving the house, he would thrash his way through the stifling maze of narrow streets that ran in between the tobacco plants. It was impossible to work himself loose once he got caught, but there was no other way to get to his grandfather, the pay clerk at the Georgis-Nikoletopoulos Mill. When Lazos saw him sitting there behind the grating of the cashier's cubby-hole, a prisoner of the company he believed he was serving, the whole world became a locked money-box. And his grandfather the only man who held the keys to those mythical riches.

The young Lazos remembers even more clearly his grandfather's decline after they fired him from his position at the mill, giving him a lump sum as compensation but denying him what really mattered: the joy of having something to do.

Within a year of unemployment he had faded, wasted away, lost his hearing, grown sick and hunched, battered and bruised. Young Lazos's repeated trips to see the foremen, Mahairas and Dantiras, even Nikoletopoulos himself (Georgis was nothing but a name, perhaps invented for purposes of tax evasion), all came to nothing. "He's way past retirement age," they told him. "But he's a good worker," Lazos argued, "everyone knows him. Every single man who comes to pick up his pay check. Besides, he saved the plant from the Bulgarians." All in vain. Capitalism calls for the constant renewal of its labor force. Thus Lazos could date his first stirrings of hatred for the capitalist system to when his grandfather was fired.

If the title of grandson offered Lazos a certain relief, it was because that role camouflaged a subconscious wish for patricide. As a son, he shared his father's last name, and was expected to follow a certain career path. His mother's father, on the other hand, had a different last name, one to which no one would compare him, one that wouldn't remind anyone of anything. Thus his grandfather—who released him, as it were, from the prison of his family—belonged entirely to the realm of myth.

That sense of myth was constantly being checked by the family consciousness, which placed Lazos in a specific, painful historical context: the attempted Venizelist uprising of '35, in which his father had played a leading role, and then the Metaxas dictatorship, the war, the occupation. But his grandfather escaped classification. He was simply a Macedonian fighter, a "Bulgar-eater" (or rather a Bulgar-killer, since he ate not Bulgarians themselves but only Bulgarian products: throughout the occupation, when his family was living in Thessaloniki, young Lazos sucked on the Bulgarian candies his grandfather would often send from Kavala).

Unlike Sartre, grandson of the great Schweitzer, Lazos remembers his grandfather clearly, telling tall tales about jungle beasts that were afraid of fire—tales from his days as a lion hunter in the Amazon where he would swing from tree to tree, using his enormous belt like a lasso. Lazos would get caught up in the tales his grandfather told every Saturday evening as they filled shotgun shells to take with them the next day on their hunting trip to the Sari Samban plain, between the cities of Xanthi and Eleftheroupoli.

These preparations lacked even the slightest hint of violence. It was more like cooking, with his grandfather, the expert chef, keeping careful track of the amounts of spice. His grandmother always made sure to be out of the house, since her husband would take over the table where she often played solitaire in the evenings beneath the room's only bulb. Lazos remembers how many different kinds of shot they had: little shot for birds, bigger shot for rabbit and partridge, round shot like uncrushed peppercorns for geese, and fat shot as round as peas for wild pig or in case they came across some bandit out on the plain. His grandfather would measure the gunpowder carefully, like a barman pouring out whiskey, while young Lazos watched, checked the shells, and carefully placed the ready ones in their cases.

The next morning, as the dogs watered Kostas's ox-cart with hot piss, he would think about wood-pigeons, a strange kind of bird his grandfather often talked about while firing luckless shots into the air: *Perhaps I'll see them again?* When there were no wood-pigeons or pheasants, they picked melons from the fields in the plain. No matter how hot it was outside, when they broke open a watermelon, splitting its heart in two, the inside was always cool.

He remembers clearly each and every one of their "campaigns." When it wasn't hunting season, his grandfather would take him to the mill, where hungry sparrows were the only grain filling the empty silos, or to the wharf, where even the rats were starving. They would buy fresh *loukoumades*, the dough still warm, from a corner store, and every shopkeeper they passed would call out a greeting. Young Lazos was an integral part of his city, his surroundings, his place. When the mythical priest passed by, shrouded in the cloud of his cassock, peeling bark off the trunks of acacias, he would ask his grandfather about the saying, "Even a priest has to wait his turn," and what it meant to be a priest, and why you had to wait your turn. His grandfather, not a religious man in the least, would point first to the church of Agios Anargyros, then to Agios Silas. Then to the mountain. They would find rabbit there.

It was into this house, built in 1914, that Lazos was born in 1933 under the conditions outlined above, having narrowly escaped the spoon of an attempted abortion. His room at the back of the house looked onto a plum tree that blossomed each spring. Lela lived across the way. One night they caught her with no panties on and she screamed. She, he remembers, was the only one who didn't treat him like a child.

Back then Kavala was a beautiful city. The house, nestled among gardens and yards. The trap door. The chicken thief his grandfather shot from the terrace with one of the shells meant for wild pigs, wounding him in the knee as he ran past the church of Agios Anargyros.

He remembers well how he, too, used to kill the wild doves called "*dekaochtoures*" because their call sounded like "*dekaochto*," the Greek word for eighteen. Birds fat as pigeons and calm as rabbits. The heat was absolute, scarcely eased by the breeze that clung to the clothes hanging on the line. His afternoon nap in the cool of his dark room, like the massive watermelons keeping cool in the shade of the kitchen table. Waking up in the late afternoon, he looked down at the city spread out below, motionless under the knife of the sun. He could guess the time from the size of the puddle around the ice, delivered and melting outside the door.

What he remembers most of all from those years are the moments captured in what photographs have remained. He remembers marmalade on a slice of bread. But what came before? He searches and searches, but finds nothing more. Time present and time past get confused inside of him, as in Eliot's famous line. The basement was really the ground floor, if you went in through the neighbor's yard, like that burglar did. What was it he stole? Sheets. He was betrayed, though, by their blinding whiteness in the night. They shone like a full moon in the dark. And then the war. The Bulgarian officer who killed his grandfather's dog just for fun. Later on, Glafkos would write his first poem about that very dog.

Every afternoon as he walks down to pick up his grandfather from work he comes to the fork in the road where the public park begins. One fork leads to his grandfather at the mill, the other to more tobacco plants. In the middle of the fork is the clubhouse with the big mirror in the hallway, frequented before the war by members of Kavala's high society. Dancing, late-night parties, holiday banquets. And jealousy, which ruins expensive dresses (his father had once ripped his mother's dress on the way home because she had danced with another man). He remembers. He remembers well.

The tobacco workers in the public park at noon. Watermelon and feta. Fresh fish and cured sardines. Work starts again at one. At six they knock off for the day. But there is no one among them as old and withered as his grandfather, the petty clerk.

There is no way we can fully understand the "Thrassakis problem" without a historical investigation into the site of his Second Refuge: Thessaloniki during the guerrilla war, where he was sent to study at a private American school. One day he suddenly finds himself trapped between the twin parentheses of the city gates, which seem to him like one-dimensional pyramids, like movie sets, or the façades of West Berlin houses. Though he remembers quite well the station in Kavala from which he left, he seems not to remember (which is to say, he never describes) the bus stop where he got off in Thessaloniki. He rejoices on the day he leaves Thessaloniki to return to "his city, Kavala." His grandmother is making homemade ice cream for him when he arrives, throwing rough grains of salt into the outer part of the bucket to keep the ice from melting, and his grandfather lights the wood-burning water heater so Glafkos can have a real bath instead of just washing himself at the basin.

The questions of "for whom does the bell toll" that he had asked as a young boy after the defeat of Korista, and then of Argyrokastro and Tepeleni, Glafkos now asks about his Uncle Panagis and his Uncle Stavros. On Thassos he had learned of the successes of the illustrious Greek army. As a refugee in Thessaloniki he learns of its failures. He learns of defeat. And there is no end in sight. "Night, black night / pushed threateningly at my windows." He gets scared each time the bus to Kavala has to pass through the narrow streets of Stavros, where partisans are blocking the streets. It was there, after the Liberation, that the bus blew up, the one his father's assistant Fofo was riding on her way to Kavala to serve as a juror in the people's court.

Strange things. Years later, he still celebrates his grandfather's name day, July 20, the feast of the Prophet Elijah. Because he believes that the best and noblest way to achieve the ideal patricide is through the adoration of the grandfather. This bridge between grandfather and grandson, passing over the father, describes an imaginary arc of avoidance. When his father fails in his attempt to kill the neighbor's rooster that always wakes him up from his afternoon nap, grandfather and grandson, the hunter and his young apprentice, exult in the father's clumsiness. And just for show, the grandson kills another *dekaochto* or two.

In summer, when everything stands motionless under a midday sun that blanches all movement, one of these dumb doves often comes to rest beside the decorative roof tile and starts to sing: *dekaochto, dekaochto*. Glafkos, who has been lazing in the sheets, gets up, picks up his rifle and loads it, then carefully opens the shutters. If the fat bird hasn't heard the noise and flown off, he takes aim at it through the branches. Almost simultaneous with the crack of the gun, the bird falls, hit as much by the heat as by the bullet. The panicked hens start cackling, the dog in the corner of the yard starts to bark, and the neighbors wake up, grumpy and displeased.

As a flag-carrier in the school parade, he was accused by his religion teacher of trying to hang his cap on the cross at the top of the flagpole he was holding while the classes were waiting in the churchyard of Agia Sophia for the parade to begin. Standing there in the yard, he got mad at some of the scoutmasters in shorts and called one of them a bore and told him to stick the flagpole up his ass—which the scoutmaster immediately related to the dour religion teacher, who told Lazos to go and confess his sin to the principal (an American psychologist and ace basketball player brought over by the Marshall plan). Nothing doing. He would prefer, Lazos said, for the teacher to go and turn him in, upon which he would be asked to apologize—but for him to go on his own, no, it was simply out of the question. Lazos knew the religion teacher had it in for him because his father was a Jehovah's Witness. Short, bald, and nearsighted behind glasses that made him look like a Japanese submarine officer, this grand inquisitor of a teacher now blamed him not for what he had done, but for not daring to confess his guilt. And so the young student came to internalize his guilt, transforming it into a lack of courage to confess his crime—but what crime?—and thus the boy came, bit by bit, to hate this teacher with his eyes that closed in their pockets, and told him rebelliously that Christ had asked his disciples to take weapons and go into the mountains if they wanted to follow him, but the apostles just domesticated God's word, housewived it, tidied it up, carried their submission to the level of slavery. At this the teacher crossed himself, his heart butchered like a cock thrown into the foundations of a house so the household will take root—as indeed it did. But what awful inhabitants lived there.

He remembers the sweets he used to eat during recess. And the mention of Cavafy's "He Asked About the Quality" that earned him a three-day expulsion. If he had to read Cavafy, one of his teachers asked, couldn't he at least choose "Thermopylae"? (When he later went to visit the place, he was glad he hadn't taken his teacher's advice: Thermopylae was nothing but American bases and radar—all of it, like his former principal, brought over by the Marshall Plan.)

But it's wrong to interpret those days in retrospect. The comfort offered by temporal distance is like economic ease: it makes a crisis pass more easily. Back then, during the frequent crises of his adolescence, there was no temporal comfort. It was all or nothing. And there was no one to blame. His Greek teacher, fattened on the hollow nuts of the Great Idea, a hunchbacked devotee of the poet Palamas, had cried in Constantinople, looking out of the steamboat at the cupolas of Agia Sophia, while Lazarus, in complete harmony with the little Turkish tour guide, kept quoting—instead of "Ours again, in time"—"The here and now is ours."

All of these figures—the philologist from Grevena, the mathematician, the big-chested chemistry teacher, the physics teacher, a fairy who died young of a heart attack, the Judah of a theology teacher, the principal-slash-psychologist-slash-basketball player, and the American singing instructor—all served, at the height of the Civil War, as forewarnings of the "cholera" that would break out later on. There were also clear indications even then in the Thermaic Gulf, though it wasn't yet clear whether or not Purefoy's microbe contained choleric leanings. And if it didn't, it certainly acquired them upon the construction of Tom Pappas's refinery.

He remembers certain small characteristic details, though most of the picture has been whitewashed over, like in the tiny churches in Thessaloniki's Upper City, whose frescoes have been eaten away by the damp. Flora, who survived Dachau, and his Armenian friend who sold dried fruit. Flora took him to synagogue, the Armenian to his church. He remembers. He remembers well.

And he's still afraid of never passing his final exams. He has nightmares of never graduating. Grown-up, in waking nightmares, he thinks he's been left behind. Just as later in the army everyone else is discharged, while his discharge is delayed for endless years. The recruits, the reserve officers, the draftees all feel sorry for him as they come and serve and leave, while he, relegated to the border patrol, remains unable to leave, because some civil servant somewhere has forgotten to file his release.

Chapter Five

MY SENSE OF identification with Thrassakis had once again become asphyxiating. It cycled through the course of each week. Monday always started out well, because we spent Sundays in the country with our little girl and some friends. Far from my worries, I would find myself again connected to people who loved me. Tuesday was great. And even Wednesday, I daresay, was still mine. But on Thursday I fell, slipping once more into the Other. On Friday and Saturday I would talk like Lazos, think like Glafkos, like Thrassakis. It was hell. And I would wait anxiously for our Sunday trip into the country, where I could find myself once more.

My psychiatrist assured me that things would be better as soon as the fellowship money arrived, because then I would be able to leave for the States. He knew that whatever money I had managed to save over the years had been sunk into the construction of a building that was never completed, I don't know why, exactly, I never really figured it out, it seems to have exceeded height regulations or trod on some corner of city property. Anyhow, all my once-liquid assets just sat there, solidified, immobile.

I, however, saw this fact in another light. I had just launched into a study of one of Thrassakis's early stories, written while he was still in his teens. (I found it in the magazine *Spark*, put out by his university's student organization.) The main character is an angst-ridden young man (Lazos himself, of course) who suffers from the freezing of family funds in a building that remains unfinished because the contractor turns out to be a crook. The story takes place at a time when the Marshall Plan is throwing money into the European market, money that somehow always seems to end up in the hands of hustlers. The main character's father, hounded for his political convictions (as Lazos's father, a Jehovah's Witness, was hounded for his religious beliefs), is a sensible man who fears above all that his family might go hungry. So he abandons the political arena early on and invests his nest egg in the construction of an apartment building. When the building is finished, two of the apartments will be his, four rooms each. The family will live in one and rent out the other.

The building, of course, is never completed. It started out well, a concrete tree springing up fast from its foundations—first floor, second, third, fourth, each one celebrated with a bottle of champagne—until it reached the fifth, the second to last, and stopped. The contractor went bust, turned out to be a cheat. At first the news didn't seem so bad. Like all irrevocable events, it came softly, quietly, creeping humbly through the door with a bowed head—"I hate to bother you, but may I come in?" Only time would reveal the facts in all their horrid glory. The family's distress grew in geometric progression as the days passed, then the weeks, the months, until the building, half-finished, had already started to age.

In those days, naturally, Thessaloniki wasn't anything like the megalopolis it is today. And so the open wound of this unfinished house stood out like a sore thumb in the city center, at the corner of Venizelos and Egnatia. This corner, this crossroads of anguish, marked the father's path—and, by extension, that of his son. Because what else is the child, according to bourgeois law, if not the future inheritor of his family's property? With work on the building stopped, the young man sees his future blocked, his years of study solidifying into walls, his entire education no more than the blind, empty hole where a window should have been. And what sense is there in locking the contractor up in jail, where on top of everything else their tax money would be paying for his upkeep? Luckily the cotton and tobacco did well that year, so the farmers had money to pay the dentists and lawyers, and the family didn't go hungry.

One night the boy goes on his first date with a certain girl. He wants to take her to the movies, but she's afraid of the crowd. He suggests they go out into the country where the grass is tall, but she's scared of bugs. So he takes her to the unfinished building. He doesn't tell her anything about its history. Just that it belongs to his family. That it will be theirs, as soon as it's finished. They go up to the fifth floor and look out the open window at the traffic on the street below, the tram, the carts at the Caravan Seraglio across the street, which is also unfinished, but crowded with homeless. The fact that he's brought this girl to the source of his suffering shows that he's looking for something. But for what? Or whom? Does he want to take his revenge on his frozen future? On this solidified scourge? The girl is put off by the disgusting smells and the dirty words written on the walls, the dried dogshit, the watercolors painted in piss, and she gets up to leave. Then, to please her, he recites one of his poems:

The champagne flowed freely
but the flu rate
remained high.
To change its orbit, the planet
fell like a meteor
into the navel of the earth.

But the girl takes it the wrong way; she thinks he's making fun of her. Agony and barrenness again—blood-brothers in the Thrassakian text.

Into this strange situation in which I found myself with regard to my double— the lining in the suit I wore—came, at long last, the Tigers' letter. I knew right away it was the check. I've developed a way of sniffing out letters that are bringing me money. They're more anonymous, somehow, less ostentatious. And, like Faulkner, I held it up to the light. Indeed, the check had finally arrived. I opened the big book of signatures I had taken with me from when I worked at the American Express office in Syntagma Square, looking for the names that corresponded to the signatures. The first was a rather well-known individual, and I ran straight to the bank to cash the check—only to find out that the international exchange had closed that very morning, due to another depreciation of the Japanese yen.

So I left my check there to ripen; by the time I cashed it, the dollar had risen three percent. And I was finally ready to go: return ticket, a suitcase stuffed with clothes, microfilm, letters of introduction—everything all ready for the Big Trip.

≈

86

AND AT LAST I arrived in New York, where I had to pass through the same channels as Glafkos had upon his arrival as a Tiger scholar. I went first to the main Manhattan headquarters to see the arch-Tiger's gray-haired secretary, who talked to me for a long time about Glafkos. Of course she remembered him—and how! He combined the diffidence of an intellectual, she told me, with the boldness of a great lover. This combination, added to his rather charmless face, made him very "appetizing," she said, for the sort of young woman she had been back then, about thirty years before. No, his wife hadn't come over with him. Some difficulties concerning the second ticket had delayed her for a few weeks (the fellowship usually paid for just one, but by lowering the amount of his stipend they were able to buy a ticket for her as well). So Thrassakis, alone for that first while, ran from club to club giving the standard speeches and talks—something I too would have to do, though of course not at the same pace as he, just enough to show the club's members that their money was making men move.

When I asked her if she could tell me something specific about Thrassakis, she pleaded a faulty memory which, in order to protect a wounded ego, had erased everything from that period in her life, which had been a difficult one. Back then, she told me, she had just split up with her third husband, and he didn't take the divorce nearly as well as the others had—on the contrary, he had tried to carve her face with a razor, and had in fact succeeded (she showed me a small scar on her chin), and she had called the police, who locked him up in an insane asylum—and so, not wanting to remember a thing, she had uprooted that entire year with all its many misfortunes from her memory, just yanked it right out of her mind—and in doing so, had also obliterated anything she might otherwise have remembered concerning "your fellow countryman, who came here as our scholar," though he wasn't actually a Tiger himself. And that's why she didn't remember anything, except . . . except . . . she laughed, she was embarrassed even to mention it—really, the human mind was so strange, to think she would remember that, of all things—the phone rang, she picked it up and forwarded the call—yes, she remembered how that scholar, the Greek, suffered from terrible constipation during those first months. Since he always had to speak after the Tigers' meals, he was always incredibly nervous when he ate, and his stomach would just clench up like a vise and whatever he ate—because he had to eat, even if he wasn't hungry—didn't get properly digested, which created awful peptic problems for him later on.

Since she had been in charge of arranging all the banquets where he was to talk, he had asked her a thousand times if she could schedule his speeches before dinner, if possible, so he could sit down afterwards and eat at his leisure, and maybe even enjoy his food—"And since there are quite a few restaurateurs among them," she added, "the Tigers, as you'll soon discover, always stuff themselves to bursting." The arrangement he requested was, however, impossible, because the Tigers came straight from work and arrived at the restaurant so hungry that they had to gorge themselves first—"Isn't that so?"—or, as they put it, to quiet the little tiger in their bellies—"Only natural, right?"—and then, while digesting, they would sit back and listen to the evening's guest, usually a Tiger from some other continent or country. Sated, they gladly turned their attention to the guest's talk about foreign customs, other ways of life, how much a dollar was worth in his country and what he could buy with it. As for Thrassakis, they usually asked him about Onassis, who hadn't yet married Jackie, because Jackie wasn't yet a widow, and Jackie wasn't a widow because her husband wasn't yet President of the United States of America.

As she talked, I suddenly understood Thrassakis's aversion to the name Onassis, and why he always avoided whatever city was temporary home to that tycoon of wealth. Earlier in my study I interpreted this as a kind of disguised megalomania—the desire to acquire a kind of vicarious importance by comparing himself to "*le Grec*"—but now I see that the name was merely an unwanted reminder of his dyspepsia and consequent constipation.

But it was simply impossible, the aging secretary was telling me, for him to give his speeches before dinner. Instead, he would sit and eat in the seat of honor next to the Tiger president, while the fact that he would soon have to stand and speak was eating him up inside. So he suffered from intestinal blockage and later experienced horrible difficulties back at the hotel.

This, then, was the only thing the secretary could remember about Thrassakis. And she sent me in to see her assistant, who would take care of all the practical details of my own stay.

≈

I SHAT REGULARLY. Not much, but regularly. Not, of course, with those prewar shits, when I would relieve myself once and for all. This new way was

more tiring, because I had to do it more often—but anything was better than
the constipation of my days with the Tigers.

(*CDW*, Vol. II, 103)

Today this use of "pre-war" is incomprehensible to a generation that knew other
kinds of lacks, without ever experiencing the poverty and suffering of World War II
and the Occupation. For the young Lazarus, the war marks a break, a turning point.
Hunger, thirst, anguish, and fear are all things that begin after the outbreak of war.
It makes sense, then, that "post-war" signifies poverty, malaria, diphtheria, civil war,
while everything "pre-war" is, on the contrary, synonymous with fertility and joy.

≈

THE ASSISTANT IN THE next room, sitting beneath an enormous poster of a
tame tiger from the 36th international Tiger conference in Caracas, with
William Blake's famous words embossed in yellow, was missing a finger. It had
been eaten by a seagull. She had been feeding French fries to her seagull friends
at a seaside restaurant in Galveston, Texas, and while the gulls were calmly and
amiably swooping down to grab the uplifted sticks of potato, some carnivorous
guy, a stranger in town—most likely come up from the southern shores of
Mexico, led off course by the Gulf Stream breezes—grabbed her finger instead of
the fry she was holding. At first she didn't realize what had happened. She
thought the snap she'd felt had been his wing hitting her hand. But then she saw
blood dripping from the sky and realized her whole finger was gone—Look, this
one, she said, spreading her hand out on the desk amidst the Tiger stamps and
memo pads and various stacks of papers concerning visitors' trips. It was a
pretty hand, the uninjured fingers long and smooth, while the one the bird had
eaten looked like a guitarist's finger bent in on itself in order to pluck the deep-
est notes from his instrument. She wouldn't have told me the whole story, she
said, if the restaurant in Galveston hadn't been owned by a Greek, Nick, a real
sweetie, known in the area as "Nick the Greek." When he saw what had happened
he ran straight into the kitchen, grabbed his rifle and started shooting at the gulls,
the jewel of his place—it was famous all over Texas for those birds, people came
from as far as Dallas and Houston to feed them. Of course he had been attacked

by the ASPCA for what he'd done, but Nick claimed that the gull was really a vulture, a "nigger eagle" (he really hated blacks, she told me, "But down there, you know, people are so different from us Northerners"). Anyhow, the birds never came back to his restaurant, and Nick the Greek wanted her to marry his son, but she was already engaged to a Tiger who worked for Texaco in Persepolis, and . . . she wouldn't have told me the whole story if I wasn't a Greek too, though certainly not a Nick.

≈

LET US EXAMINE the asphyxiating psychological climate that contributed to his "blockage": first of all, he was terrified of being mugged; second, he had suffered from food poisoning; and third, he was eternally unsuccessful in love— and so, cut off from all sides, he was forced to stay in this city. His prison was defined through the reductio et absurdum *of unfeasible solutions.*

(*CDW*, Vol. I, 100)

≈

AT THE FIRST Tiger banquet I attended, before we had even left the restaurant, a guy I would have described as rather unpleasant—if he hadn't happened to be a Tiger—came up to me and asked if I would be so kind as to give him a Greek coin of some sort; it didn't matter how little it was worth, just whatever I happened to have brought with me from Greece. He was a collector, he explained, and he permitted himself this un-Tigerlike habit of asking each newly-arrived scholar for a coin or two of his country's currency. "But for me, it's either the first day or never," the good American explained. "On the first day the coins are still hanging on him like droplets of rain on a man just in from the cold." In order to ease his guilt about asking, I explained to him that I wasn't actually a Tiger scholar but a biographer of a former scholar. But to him such details were meaningless. What he wanted was my money—for which, of course, he would fully reimburse me in American currency. So he met me in the hotel lobby early the next morning to collect the coins. Oh, I'll never forget the joy of imperishability in his eyes on seeing the first five-drachma coin! He grabbed it, raised it to his eyes and examined it with wonder. He had never seen a contemporary Greek coin before, only ancient and Byzantine ones. As a specialist in African coins, he explained, he was impressed by our own elegant representation of civilized themes. I gave him all the change I had, then and there. He wanted to pay for it. All in all it came to about a buck and a half, though of course I didn't take a cent. But I was struck by the sheer joy he took in all this, like the joy of a gold digger in the Wild West. I walked him to the door, and there in the sting of morning frost I understood for the first time, through the eyes of that Tiger, the passion of the collector, the thirst for that coin.

≈

I TOLD MYSELF I would pack my bags and leave. This awful weather, the rain, the heat, the humidity. The murderous wake-up calls that riddle you with gunfire as you lay defenseless in bed, before you even have time to put up a fight. What else can I learn here that I don't already know? I miss Glafka terribly. The lectures make me sick, and this awful weather. Spring, already late in coming, shows no sign of coming soon. Nothing but lightening and rain as nature, unprepared for the new anomaly of nuclear testing, struggles to adjust itself to the atmospheric conditions created by the blasts. There is no sadder day than May Day in Chicago, when you think back on the great heroic era of the working class, here in this "Hog Butcher For the World" (Carl Sandburg).

The wind blows, but the sails don't fill. They hang slack from the masts, withered as an old woman's breasts. And the keel, if it exists, plunges into the water's depths to escape the horrors of the surface. It's awful up there, the anchor murmurs as it drops quickly into the depths—or rather, as a man drops quickly into the depths with the anchor tied to his neck. A man who wanted to plant himself down there. To sprout at the bottom of the lake.

Everything happened so fast, in just a few seconds. From the time the bell rang to the time I opened the door, "the rhythm of the world changed within me." And only those little black flies that are always circling through the house—something between a moth and a fruit fly, black, like the ones you find hovering around plates in restaurants—only the flies weren't scared, but just kept flying—because, unlike the owner of the house, they're almost impossible

to catch. *Even if you catch them in your hand, they're still hard to kill—they're
so small and wispy they can take shelter in even the smallest fold of flesh. Only
the specially trained beaks of particular birds like phantoms or skylarks could
kill them—but the factories don't make birds like that anymore.*

*Greek turtles and frogs are exported primarily to France and Italy. These
harmless creatures are usually hunted at night on riverbanks and in bogs, with
flashlights and sacks. The frogs are particularly easy to catch, since they freeze
in the beam of the light. Then they're shipped live to Europe by plane.*

*I too decided to leave by plane from America, heading back to Brussels, car-
rying with me the semi-precious stone of my dumb load.*

*America was, in the end, a great disappointment: All that happened was
that I saw up close what I had feared from afar. Now what?*

(CDW, Vol. I, 101-102)

≈

THE NEXT DAY I set out for the university. I had written to inform them of my
arrival, so they were expecting me. But since my visit happened to coincide with
commencement, I was obliged to sit through the entire ceremony. I even listened
to the last few speeches. The robed professors and the students in their cardboard
hats seemed to be enacting the common law.

Though the university was in the center of town, the campus led a sheltered
life of its own. The wealth of greenery and youth seemed to cleanse the campus
of the guilty weight of the industries that maintained it. It was a greenhouse filled
with saplings that would later grow into the great trees of the jungle. But for the
time being, these young shoots and flower-decked girls still shone with hothouse
beauty and serenity.

I passed the Kissinger Wing, where the sorcerer-to-be had once studied, and
walked toward the library, crossing a quadrangle where squirrels scampered around
the roots of trees, sketching loose circumflexes in the grass. The traces of snow still
left in the shaded nooks of the library complex were as dirty as frozen guilt.

I was greeted by a librarian who spoke to me through a special voice muffler
that hung at his throat, allowing him to talk to the person beside him without
disturbing the others at work in the room. When he didn't need the machine he

could turn off it by adjusting a dial under his chin. With light, rhythmic steps, like Jesus walking on water, he showed me into a small inner room where there was coffee brewing. There, even after he took off the muffler, like an actor unclipping his microphone after a shoot, his voice sounded incredibly thin—atrophied, even. He told me that because of commencement the director of the special collections division, who had to attend the banquet at which the Kissinger Prize would be awarded to the top student in International Law, wouldn't be able to see me until the afternoon. So he, the librarian, was inviting me to lunch. Would I accept? Could I spare the time? It would truly be an honor for him.

My hostility for the country had flagged a bit since my actual arrival. What I was seeing wasn't the America of *coups d'etat*, of the Pentagon and the CIA, all those things we Europeans had learned over the years to suck on like candies. It wasn't the America of Manson and the Marines, of gurus, guns and Mafia cigars. A little grass might grow here and there for the druggies, but that was all. Even the street names—Temple Street, Church Street, Cathedral Street, Country Church Corner—put you in a different frame of mind: here, then, were the Byzantine monasteries, when all we knew were the blood-soaked rings of the Hippodrome and the orgies of the emperor's praetors. Here were the recluses' villas, the sanatoriums of the mind, where noise was kept at a minimum and students hunched over their books like bearded proselytes. In the cafeteria where we went for hamburgers and root beer, my nerves felt settled for the first time after the ordeal of the noisy Tiger banquets. We got in line, put whatever we wanted on our trays, then ate calmly and civilly in the blissful absence of pestering waiters. The fact that I didn't have to give a speech after the meal was, for me, the best thing of all.

The director of the special collections division of the Henry Kissinger wing of the university library (for obvious reasons I don't refer to the university by name, and since there are as many American universities claiming Kissinger as a former student as there are cities claiming to be Homer's birthplace, it would be almost impossible for the reader to pinpoint the exact location) picked me up from the cafeteria in his car. I noticed that where the antenna should have been, at the back right corner of the hood, there was a fishing pole instead—and what's more, it seemed still to be wet.

"It makes it so much easier for me to go trout fishing in the river here," said the director, who was as bald as he was sweet. "I take my car to the riverbank, where there are special little pullouts in the road—they call them 'fishing-ins.' Of course, I have to pay for the spot, but that way I can use the pole without ever leaving my car."

In fact, he said, his antenna was every bit as flexible as the sort of pole amateur fishermen tend to prefer.

"But I don't understand," I said, "which is it, pole or antenna?"

"Both," the good director replied. "A hollow pole on the outside, with an antenna running through it like a nerve. And it doesn't cause the least bit of interference on the radio."

You timeless Americans, I thought, *with your hobbies and your amateur certificates.*

The conversation that followed was just as difficult and disheartening as I had imagined. I had gone knowing, more or less, that he wouldn't give in, but I had held on to the hope that Kissinger's method of the "personal touch" might produce some unexpected results. Though I'd gone in completely aware of the obstacles before me, it was still something of a blow when all my pains and labors met with complete and decisive refusal. Despite my best efforts, Dean, as he had asked me to call him, remained not exactly unsympathetic, but strictly bound by the rules.

"This is our correspondence with the deceased," he said, handing me a folder. "Back when you first expressed an interest in visiting, I decided to show you these letters, so there would be no misunderstanding between us. After all, mutual understanding precludes misunderstanding." (This last sentence is, as the reader might recall, a one-hundred-percent Thrassakian phrase, though Dean's English version didn't have quite the same sense of career-soldier doubletalk as the Greek.)

"I've been wondering exactly why the library asked to purchase his manuscripts," I remarked before opening the folder of correspondence, which I was sure would be—as indeed it was—utterly uninteresting.

"Look at that red light that's watching us," Dean said with a deep sigh. "It's the same kind they have in department stores. Since the university, and the library in particular, has become a guardian of memory, an internal security sys-

tem has been installed that records our every move as soon as we enter its range,"
he said, pointing to the door of the storehouse of memory.

Poor Glafkos, I thought. *Even now when you're in the Great Beyond, your writings are kept under the Buddha's watchful eye.*

"But about the purchase of the manuscripts," I insisted.

"I must admit," he said, "your countryman wasn't exactly a big hit in the States. *Prinos II* was fairly well-received by the critics, and a myth of Thrassakis as an 'underground' writer started to grow, but he never really made his way *onto*, much less *off* the ground. He was, so to speak, buried alive, perhaps because his publisher didn't want to promote him, and didn't spend enough on advertising. So for us, it didn't make much difference whether we had his papers or not. Thousands of writers look to us with the hungry eyes of the immigrant who longs to become a citizen. It's a shame that we have to choose some over others. But even if our budget were five times what it is, it still wouldn't be enough.

"As far as your man is concerned, here's what happened: one of the city's most active supporters of our efforts, the Greek-American businessman Nick Polis, was offering to buy us the archives of a Greek writer fairly well-known in the States, preferably from Northern Greece, Macedonia if possible, because Polis was from Macedonia and had been pining all his life for real Macedonian yogurt, which in the States is almost always not Macedonian at all but Bulgarian. Polis was himself, of course, a big man in the dairy industry and wanted to Hellenize imported dairy products; he was ashamed that everyone thought they were Bulgarian, not Greek. He also sought a Greek Macedonia. And whenever Thrassakis gave us trouble over the money, Polis threw more and more our way.

"Here's the correspondence. It's at your disposal. Back then I hadn't yet been made director of the division, but my predecessor briefed me on all unresolved matters. . . . And of course the Thrassakis affair remains unresolved to this day, due to the binding clause that keeps his papers from being opened until twenty-five years after his death. Which is, if I'm not mistaken, thirteen years from now."

"Twelve," I sighed—my unlucky number—and picked up the folder containing the correspondence.

Good old Glafkos. His very first letter showed what a bungler he could be: he had written the letter on the back of a handwritten page of one of his own manuscripts. I asked for permission to photocopy the page, which they granted.

The rather mysterious text refers to someone who dyes his hair white in order to play a role in a movie for which, we surmise, he will be paid quite handsomely. During the course of the shoot he learns of the death of someone close to him, and in his utter despondency over the loss his hair really does turn white—only he doesn't realize it until the filming is over. And then . . .

Glafkos raises the price of his papers from letter to letter, with the excuse that the value of the dollar is dropping daily. Finally a price is agreed upon by both parties and a contract is signed, stating that within three months the existing "material" will be given over to the university, with the stipulation that the sealed containers holding the manuscripts are not to be opened "without the author's consent. In the circumstance of said death or debilitating accident"—what a wonderful paraphrase for the workings of the Devil himself—"the material received will remain sealed for twenty-five years from the date of this event."

I bowed my head, defeated. Though not before arguing, of course, that Thrassakis surely hadn't wanted all of his unpublished work to remain locked up in the dark archives of the library. The benevolent fisherman in Dean agreed with me, but the stubborn librarian insisted that he had no other choice than to respect in full the wishes of the deceased.

"But your predecessor, the Tiger, would at least have allowed me to flip through the papers in his presence, to see whether they were works of fiction or memoirs of some sort."

"I'm afraid," he replied, "that even the Tiger gives way before the professional responsibility of the guardian of memory."

Just then Dean reminded me more of a pallbearer than of any guardian of memory. He stood up and said he would take me to see the sacks—as if they were Egyptian mummies or something. He carefully opened the door and spoke into a closed-circuit phone, then we walked down a hallway, and at last they stood before me: three medium-sized sacks plastered all over with sealing wax the color of roof tiles. The seals looked like raindrops that had fallen from a great height through a thick cloud of red dust to land and freeze on the sacks, sealing them with the color of our earth.

"Those three," Dean said, pointing to the sacks, which had once held Brazilian coffee. *The corpse of the writer may have disappeared,* I thought bitterly, *but the corpus of his work has survived.*

The wing was encased in bulletproof Plexiglas. Thrassakis was flanked by a Czech poet on one side and a black poet on the other. Since their last names weren't anywhere near each other in the alphabet, I asked if they had ended up there by accident, or perhaps been shelved together because they had all suffered "accidents" of some kind.

"The library's special collections," Dean told me, "are based on a policy resembling Amnesty International's policy on political prisoners."

Seeing my baffled look, he explained:

"Just as Amnesty tries to focus their efforts on a range of political prisoners from the East, the West, and the so-called 'Third World,' hoping to demonstrate the truly global nature of political oppression, we too would like our collection to be representative of a global reality."

Dean then inserted a microscopic key into the thick pane of Plexiglas through which I was staring at the sacks. *Three drawers of material*, I thought, *all his belongings, his whole life, the dust of his days*. The tears springing to my eyes were tears of spiteful anger more than anything else. I'd come all this way, I'd gotten myself mixed up with the Tigers, I'd reached this far, and what did I have to show for it? Three silent rocks. Three pillows. Three—

"Here," said Dean, "the date when they can be opened: 2003."

"And it's only '89 now," I sighed. I thought about knocking on wood. But where? There was nothing but Plexiglas in sight. It's not so easy to find wood these days. Even wooden matches have disappeared from the market. Knock on Formica? Knock on steel? I don't know, neither of those has quite the same ring.

"You seem a bit upset," Dean said to me as he opened the drawer.

"Wouldn't you be, in my place?" I asked, looking at him for the first time with hate in my eyes.

"The regula-a-a-tions," he sighed, like Marilyn Monroe singing her famous song.

All for nothing, all for nothing, I said to myself, hissing on the inside like a snake. And out loud, "To come this far and learn nothing more than what I already knew!"

James-Bondish thoughts passed through my mind: I could take the guy's wife as a lover, steal that key and open one of the sacks. Or would it be more practical to kiss up to the old myopic spinster who worked in the library? Or dig an underground tunnel into the building? *Where are you when I need you, Bernardo*, I sighed to myself. *With a single magic stroke, you could free all these chapters from the frost of the Bank of Time, where they sit here earning no interest at all.*

It then occurred to me (though I should note that while I might not actually have thought of it at exactly that moment, for the sake of economy I'm putting it here, since that's where it really belongs, anyhow) that Thrassakis might have been bluffing. That he might have sent them nothing but air. . . .

I had rarely tasted such bitterness and gall—not since the time when, as a young boy, the remote control plane I had always dreamed of owning got tangled in telephone wires on its very first flight.

≈

THE NEXT DAY I went to find Nick Polis. Not the father, who was no longer living, but the son, Nick Polis Junior (or, to be precise, Nikos Polimeridis Junior), who spoke very little Greek. He seemed very polite and was particularly obliging to me. He invited me to stay at his house, which had once been his father's, and where Glafkos himself had once been a guest. Indeed, I would even be staying—just my luck—in the very same room. Polis Junior told me that though he himself was a Lion, he had lots of good customers who were Tigers, because his father, another "Nick the Greek," had been a Tiger, in fact the president of the Eastern division. And so Nick Senior had asked the previous librarian, also a lifelong Tiger, to buy the manuscripts belonging to Thrassakis, the Tiger scholar who had once passed through their city on a lecture tour.

"I know, I know," I said. "That's why I came to you."

As we were driving, Nick invited me to give a talk at the Hellenic Association to third- and fourth-generation Greek-American kids. They would understand my Greek, he said, if I spoke slowly and used simple words. When we reached his estate outside the city, I looked out at the view of the legendary river, and couldn't help being overcome, yet again, by a tumult of emotion.

Before I left, Nick gave me a notebook that Glafkos had left there.

Glafkos Thrassakis's Second Notebook

Prima Porta, 1973

I

IN MEMORY OF *Giangiacomo Feltrinelli. I can no longer see an electrical tower rising out of the green countryside without the awful image of his corpse coming to mind: stretched out on the ground at the base of one of those towers, legs blasted away by dynamite that, oddly enough, left his upper body completely untouched. Had there been some accident while he was planting dynamite, or was it a homicide in disguise? In any case, no matter what might prove true in the end, I've already formed my opinion of his murder, and this photograph has destroyed forever the sight of the scaffolding of electrical towers, which now look to me like . . . not electric chairs, even, but guillotines. The poetry of these acrobat skeletons stretching further and further toward the horizon, shrinking smaller and smaller into nothingness, linked by thick hollow ropes of wire where, instead of swallows, colored balloons sit and dream—this image has been engraved into my mind by the photograph of my fallen friend at the base of that tower.*

All the things I bottle up inside and never express linger on in well-locked storerooms. The basement light is dim. I feel imprisoned. And then all of life becomes one big warehouse, just as the sea, as Giangiacomo used to say, is a warehouse of water.

And the void cannot be filled by any green landscape like the one here, with its gurgling river and virgin grass.

Green is swallowed by green, melts into green. When there are clouds in the sky, it takes on endless shades and variations. There was a caterpillar crawling by on the grass. I threw a clod of dirt on it. It shat from fear, leaving a trail of white foam. Until then it had blended in with the grass, and passed unobserved. But now it has been betrayed, and can go nowhere in safety.

2

IN MEMORY OF Polygnotos Vagis, after seeing his nephew, my third cousin, this morning. Vagis left Thassos for America as a young shepherd, and went on to become a well-known sculptor. His works are to be found in many private collections and in New York's Museum of Modern Art. His nephew tells me that he used to fish the rocks he worked with out of the deep river that runs along the right side of that very same meadow where I sat earlier, writing about the innocent grass. According to this nephew, Vagis was consumed by the torments and anguish of exile. On top of all that, the owner of his gallery, a certain Iolas who was crazy about clocks, was domineering and exploitative. According to Iolas, on the other hand, Vagis died a poor man because, a cunning, distrustful Thassian to the very end, he refused to deposit his money in the bank, where it would have collected interest, but buried it in his garden, where the bills rotted in the soil.

Oxen fall off of Thassos's Mount Psario. After they fall, vultures pick the dried flesh from their bones, leaving them a glistening white. Back when he was a shepherd in the mountains, young Vagis used to say, "Man too is a carnivore, but with a difference: man can emigrate." So he decided to set off for America.

Vagis's comment reminds me of something my tenant in Brussels used to say: "Lions eat, get full, and withdraw into their dens. But no matter what man eats, he never gets full. So why shouldn't I like lions better?" My tenant, of course, had no idea that I myself was a Tiger.

3

HERE I BREAK in to inform the reader that I now find myself the guest of good citizen Polis, launching guerrilla attacks on the university library, trying to ascertain how many times *Prinos II* has been checked out, how badly it's been ravished by the pencils of admiring readers, hoping some inside connection, some helping hand will materialize. Here, in this very same room, Glafkos himself had once stayed. So the reader will understand why I've had to resort to what my psychiatrist calls "distancing pills," so as to keep myself from going insane.

4

ONE PROBLEM WITH Thrassakis was that he read his published texts more often than the manuscripts themselves. Because the final printed text offered a desired, even necessary distance from himself. And, at the same time, the impossibility of change.

A manuscript is something easily altered, a thing you can transform, and a thing that transforms you, while for him the typeset text was as irrevocable as a Supreme Court decision (the only possibility of appeal being the second, "revised" edition). Thus his dream was one of Brechtian distancing. . . .

5

THERE IS A KIND OF seasonal attrition from which Thrassakis, too, once suffered. I won't go into the details, because I would have to speak again of myself, living here in this same room, looking through the same window, no longer at one, two, three, four little shops, but at an entire supermarket.

6

THRASSAKIS HAD a compulsive need to reach the end of whatever notebook he'd started writing in. He would even fill pages that didn't excite him in the least, just as he always finished books he didn't like and would never dream of leaving a movie before the end. He'd rather sleep than leave. If he got there late and went in after the movie had started, he would stay and watch the next showing up to the exact point where he had come in, and then fuse the two halves together into a single plot, leaving, too, an overlap of twice-seen scenes, in order to catch the meaning.

I say this because all of his work (known to date) exhibits a kind of physical, epidermic contact with the paper, as if it were the crust of yogurt in one of those pre-war ceramic pots, or the skin of a woman he loved. He wrote as fast or as slow as his pen was able to slide over the page. When the paper sucked in the ink and slowed his progress, as if he were running in sand and sinking in with each step, he would try to find the right shoes, the right pen, to help him overcome this difficulty. He would write with the page on his thighs, not his knees.

Yes, he sometimes worked on the typewriter. But with the typewriter his thoughts had to pass through the given alphabet of the keys, while by hand he could form each symbol himself. With the typewriter the symbols were already there: all he had to do was hit them. Besides, as he notes, the machine chattered on unbearably. To Thrassakis, the difference between writing by hand and writing on a typewriter was like the difference between firing an old shotgun and an automatic rifle: Did the hunter with the automatic rifle really fare any better? Or did he just shoot more rounds, and with more misfires, more hot air, more empty noise? (Remember, here, his grandfather's wood-pigeons.) The current passing through the typewriter was no longer the current of inspiration, but the current provided by the electric company. An engine of so much horsepower instead of a cart with so many horses, a bulb of so many watts instead of a candelabrum with so many candles. His hands swarmed with the ants of ungrounded electricity.

So he went back to writing by hand, trying to mate pencil with paper, good gear on clean sheets. Not only did he collect pencils under his bed, as his family's old maid had told me, but he always made sure to have reams of paper on which to correct his mistakes, crossing things out, filling in the whiteness of those sheets.

7

THE THRASSAKIS OF REMORSE, of that guilty summer, Thrassakis of the pork chop, of his Glafka. *Basta,* enough. Suffer the little children to come unto me.

8

THRASSAKIS S RELATIONSHIP with alcohol, so much discussed by his enemies.

He found that whisky had lost its uniqueness—it had been biologically engineered, just like tomatoes. He ate tomatoes. But if it hadn't been for their color, he wouldn't have known them from potatoes. He only liked the whisky he saw in movies, the kind cowboys drank in the legendary saloons of the Wild West.

Of course he preferred vodka, and even more so as the ideological distance grew between him and Mother Russia (for he could see Russia only as a mother, and America as a kind of aunt). Vodka (the real kind, not Smirnoff, which was a product of the Cold War) let him partake in the endlessness of the steppes, in an infinite clarity, you might say, of emotion.

The drink he despised more than any other was Cynar, much advertised in his day, made with an artichoke base. He found the artichoke itself as senseless as an exploded hand grenade. He hated the tightness of leaves around the fuzzy heart, like a tight *komsomol* around its soft, pulpy instructor. The artichoke—the utter opposite of the explosive pomegranate—could, in his opinion, have produced no other beverage.

9

HIS PASSION FOR UMBRELLAS. Pointy ones, automatic ones, ones that opened up into globes. He liked the latter ones best. They were handy, they fit in your bag. Only he couldn't always open them: they had the springy elasticity of the sexual organ. The head of the umbrella, tucked into all those folds of fabric (read: underwear), wasn't easy to get out if the button didn't catch right. And if the rain came down in a sudden burst, the umbrella would get wet and turn to mere rags. There was, in other words, the issue of radial rising, which is why in this respect he preferred automatic umbrellas, which sprang up with a zoom of distress. Their heads were slim, though, while those of the globe-like ones were large and virile.

10

BOTTLED WATER. Tap water is unsafe, what with aging pipes and possibly poisoned reservoirs. So he drinks nothing but bottled mineral water. He prefers glass bottles. Apart from all the harmful substances they release into the water, the plastic seem somehow spineless to him, devoid of character. Plastic is cast in ready-made molds, while glass needs the divine breath of man to blow it out.

Chapter Six

A metal coin, falling on the kitchen tiles, can wake me up more easily than a burst of gunfire. Because gunfire covers over the entire surface of hearing, while the noise of the coin wakes up only a single nerve, which wakes me up in turn.

(*CDW*, Vol. I, 109).

"Adventurers of Love" Among the Cannibals

Kostas Makris, a Protestant missionary from Athens, went to live among the dangerous Yiali cannibals in the Seng Valley of Western Guinea, in an attempt to civilize this savage tribe.

A few years before, the Yiali had eaten two American missionaries, Phil Masters and Stan Deil. Since then no other white man had been allowed to enter their territory. Yet the Yiali showed a particular fondness for Makris, perhaps because the Greek missionary had gained enormous experience in approaching and dealing with cannibals from his work with several other savage tribes in New Guinea.

The Athenian missionary taught the cannibals to plant yams and other crops. "I'd like to build a little house here," he says, "and settle down here with my family. But . . . "

But there are plenty of Yiali still in Africa. And Makris still wants to continue his work as an "adventurer of love."
—Vassilis Kavathas

103

I MUST ADMIT that after seeing the fatal seals of silence that marked his manuscripts, I never would have been able to complete my research on Thrassakis if I hadn't gone back to Leiden to see the pastor once more. About seven years had passed since my first visit. Seven years since I decided to busy myself with the life and work of the deceased. (Though to be precise, it had been twelve years since the very first inklings of interest, elicited by the news of his death. But I don't want to discuss my own time, the time of the biographer, only that of the biographied—otherwise things will get too confusing.) I flew from New York straight to Amsterdam and checked into the Fterou Hotel, where I was welcomed with open arms. It was owned by three gay men, real queens, but clean. Sparkling. Even their big dog fawned over me.

I ended up at the Fterou because I happened to have the phone number with me. And I liked the neighborhood: bars and clubs, women, men, transvestites. After the puritan atmosphere of Massachusetts, I needed to unwind. Besides, it was right by the station, and the next day I would be taking the train to Leiden.

I have to say, I really like the Dutch. Their sense of humor more than anything. They don't take it too hard that they lost all their colonies. After brutish America with its raging capitalism, the refinement of Amsterdam was refreshing, like a Rembrandt painting after an exhibit of contemporary American art. (I'm not sure why, but lately my typewriter keeps misspelling the word: "Ameri*cant*.")

Irrational thoughts washed over me as I stood on the bank of a canal where I had also lingered seven years before. I think I must have already discussed the "seven-year itch." It has no metaphysical dimensions. People are just older, kids have grown up, goals still unachieved, the price of lamb's head higher, the changeless canals underbidding the houses in their ongoing auction. The canals here are like sentences: crowded on both sides by the bitterness of the unsaid, by rows of houses that once knew the likes of Anne Frank, while the ducks proliferate, punctuating the silent water.

But in closing, one cycle opens another. A cycle's end is always another beginning.

The pastor had retired. Yes, and now he was a pastor for retirees. So, a pastor once more. "We're like military men," he told me. "We can never stop being what we once were. The retired officer can't stop being a man of arms. And the pastor, even outside the divine liturgy, never ceases to be a vessel of God."

One thing that really shook me was his remark that, with the passing years, I was coming to look more and more like Thrassakis.

≈

NOW THAT THE interceding years had told their tale, the pastor felt he could speak frankly with me. No, he hadn't had any particular relationship with Thrassakis. His witness was the High Holy Palimsest above. They had met, yes, in one of those "sinful" Amsterdam bars, and had become friends. (The whole time he was talking to me, his dog kept rubbing up against my legs. Could he have recognized me, even seven years later, from the smell of my feet?) Back then the pastor had been on leave from his post in one of his Church's overseas dominions. Oh, things had been different back then. Certainly more romantic than today.

Back then Thrassakis, an admirer of "easygoing Amsterdam," had spoken to the pastor of his passion for freedom, his own personal freedom. He and his wife had been going through a rough time, and since they had no children, they had decided to go their separate ways for a while, until the separation could restore balance to their marriage. Glafkos was looking for somewhere to go. "At one time," the pastor told me that Glafkos had told him, "he might have considered going to Latin America. But just then it would have been hell for him to find himself there, a prisoner of the great political plots of the West. He wanted to go somewhere where nothing would remind him of the past. Somewhere where there was no such thing as a fluorescent light bulb. We were drinking together in the bar," the pastor continued, "when I first told him about New Guinea. I suggested that the virginity of the land and the roughness of the people—which might just have been kindness in disguise—might offer the best cure for his predicament.

"He seemed interested. He asked for more information, which I gladly provided. Everything else was up to the travel agent. And it all would have gone just fine, he would have gotten to where I'd sent him on exactly the right day, if that damned wind hadn't come up and sent his pirogue down a tributary of the Sepik, right into the hands of that terrible tribe that tore him to shreds.

"Me? No, I didn't find out right away, since I wasn't expecting to hear from him. It wasn't until much later that the rumors reached me of a white man who—"

"But why didn't you tell me any of this the first time I came?"

"Things are never that simple," he said, giving me a meaningful look and pouring a bit more Ceylon tea into my cup, pausing to give the silence the weight it deserved before continuing his tale. "Not wanting to worry his relatives before there was proof," he said, "I kept my suspicions to myself as to whether he might have been that man. When I discovered that he had no one in the world apart from his wife, I made those statements to the press that eventually brought you into contact with me."

I now found myself in a rather difficult position.

"Are you quite sure," I asked, "that it was his wife he was trying to avoid, and not a certain Danish woman?"

"The countess of the tower in Copenhagen?" he asked, looking at me curiously, as if wondering how I happened to have met her.

"Yes, the Danish cultural attaché to the Common Market."

"You met her?"

"Seven years ago she invited me to come see her concerning a renewal of my fellowship. When I told her my wife was researching Thrassakis's wife, she was furious. She threw me out of the house in seconds flat. And cut off my stipend."

"She came to me, too," the good pastor sighed, "after the statements I made to the press. She asked me, more or less, to give her the name of the tribe that had eaten him, so she could take a Danish TV crew out there to explore. 'Sounding the depths,' she called it. When I said, 'Madam, as much as you may have loved him, I don't think . . .'—well, she simply blew up. Went wild. Saw red. There aren't enough words in the world to describe her holy rage."

"She certainly lashed out at me, too," I said.

"She was one of many women who thought they had 'discovered' Glafkos. Besides, she fell in love with him during menopause, which is why—"

"It must have been her he was running from," I insisted.

"It's not out of the question."

"If Glafkos suffered, to a degree, from a fixation on the chase, the Danish countess surely suffered from an obsessive need to conquer. A dynamic woman. A free spirit. Too big for her country and her people."

The pastor was lost in memories. In mountainless countries like Holland and Denmark, you find people who are torn up on the inside, but without the external indication of visible quarries you find dug into mountainsides. In countries like that, insanity lets nothing show on the outside. First the Danish woman, and now the pastor.

(To keep myself thinking in terms of my place and my people, I brought to mind an image of young Lazos's legendary priest passing through the ruins in the cloud of his cassock, peeling the bark off the acacias. A friend of Aris Velouhiotis, raised in poverty, with raven's wings and an Almighty scowl. How different from this man here, this entomologist of disaster, this "adventurer of love.")

We walked down to the sea. The tide was drawing back, leaving boats stranded in the mud. Hordes of clam diggers with rolled-up pants and plastic buckets swarmed over the wet earth, digging holes here and there, becoming amphibians again. And I thought of how, back when a great civilization was blossoming in Greece, here there had been nothing but turtles and frogs. Products which Greece now exported to the rest of Europe, while importing radios and color TVs. And once again the injustice of being born Greek hit me hard in the chest.

"Breathe deeply," said the pastor. "The iodine in the air is good for the lungs."

There, against a background of gray, as his dog ran along the line of foam the waves had left on the sand, the pastor confessed that it wasn't love affairs or politics that had forced Glafkos into self-imposed exile in New Guinea. It was something much more specific, something simpler and more complex, like all things in this world: Glafkos was being chased by Interpol, not because of his youthful stories about the Thassian amphora, but because he'd gotten mixed up in a scheme for smuggling cigarettes. That is, he had agreed to play the role of contact for an illegal shipment, the job was botched, and he was caught and thrown in jail. When he got out, he preferred to move to another continent where the tentacles of the Interpol octopus wouldn't reach. The reason this story had never become public was that the police records of the time had referred to him by his real name, Lazaridis. He'd had a double identity, after all, two-natured, twin-souled. . . .

A bicycle ran over the wet sand, from which tiny bubbles emerged, betraying the vitality of the mud. The lighthouse, which had once flashed on and off for great vessels, now lit itself only for paddleboats. As for the boats stranded on dry land, for some reason they reminded me of phrases from Thrassakis's early works: *a vain attempt, we foundered in the shallows, we're stuck, and now . . .*

"It was a period in his life," the pastor began, "when Glafkos had urgent needs. Economic, I mean. They had thrown him out of UNESCO. They had fired a whole network of remarkable translators, wrongly suspecting them of being Soviet agents. So he had only two options left: smuggling cigarettes or smuggling weapons. He chose the first, thinking it the less dangerous of the two. But it turned out he was wrong: since the weapons factories are state-owned, the government cracks down less on weapons than on cigarettes.

"First of all, I must say he made a bad choice as far as location is concerned. The Italy of his dreams, the Italy of his 'personal renaissance,' as he said, had nothing to do with the real country, with the Mafia and its enemies. There's no doubt in my mind that his arrest was an inside job. There were people who had a lot to lose if that fateful boat unloaded its cargo before they managed to get rid of their own smuggled goods on the black market.

"He was drinking a lot back when I first met him. A real heavy drinker, but a good drunk. He never let his ugly side show, only his good side. But one night in Rotterdam, having come over from Belgium to let loose for the night, Glafkos got blind drunk and lost control. The blood test showed advanced levels of alcohol in his system. Here in Holland, we have rather philanthropic rules about alcoholism—they don't lock you up in a detox center, which can have rather unpleasant consequences, but in an ordinary prison, with invented charges of minor assaults, and you're so drunk when they arrest you that the next day you don't remember anything anyhow. So that's where Glafkos went through his detox cure.

"Who was it who said that prison, any prison, also imprisons your future life in advance? Voltaire? Solzhenitsyn? Because the people you meet in prison can often get you mixed up in other things later on. And that's precisely what happened to Glafkos.

"In the Rotterdam prison he met Vladimir, a Yugoslavian sailor from Split, who later introduced him to me, knowing my fondness for non-conformity. Ah, Vladimir! A drop of dew in the dry land of Leiden. Unlike most immigrants, the

Yugoslavians are very dynamic. They get around. They stir things up. You might not remember the famous Markovic case, but it went as far as the President of France. . . .

"To make a long story short, Vladimir became something of a fixture in my house. I liked him. Until one day he hoisted his sails and set off. He was going off to work in the illegal trade in guns and cigarettes. All with a base of operations in his homeland of Yugoslavia. That's where the guns were headed, in preparation for the overthrow of Tito, while the cigarettes, mostly American, left Yugoslavia for Italy. It was easy money—all you had to do was go along with the plan.

"When Vladimir left, he told Glafkos to think it over, he'd be in touch with him a week later, through me. I must admit that I sinned, too—the possibility of seeing my sailor again so soon was particularly appealing to me. So the whole plan had my blessing.

"Vladimir was one thing with me and another with his work. He'd been stealing from me all along, of course, but that's why I don't keep anything of value in the house, just plastic reproductions of all my great works of African art. I've donated the originals to the city museum, a rare collection that will later bear my name. But as far as his work was concerned, he was a man you could trust.

"Glafkos got a third of his share up front, as soon as he agreed to the deal. Vladimir brought it to him in cash. Since he didn't have an account in a Dutch bank—and back then it was hard for foreigners to open accounts—I had to step in. The banks had a special little window that was always open for trade from the colonies. I pretended that the sum belonged to a certain tribal chief I represented who earned money selling untreated crocodile skins.

"Not even the sickest imagination could have dreamt up that macabre scenario: my sailor, Vladimir, who is slowly eating away at me—and I like it— brings the money to Glafkos, who doesn't have a crust of bread to his name, and the money is deposited in the name of a chief who happens to belong to a branch of the tribe that will eventually eat Glafkos himself. And there it remains to this day, blocked, in the name of that cannibal dealer in crocodile skins.

"Vladimir came and told me what had happened in Italy. He was crushed. Glafkos had been pretending to go for a winter swim on a deserted beach with some sexy girl who was just there to keep him company and didn't know a thing. He was in contact with the boat through a CB radio. Then, just as the boat came into view, the *carabinieri* also appeared in the water. As soon as Glafkos saw the coast guard boats, he knew he was a goner, sold down the river.

"They threw him into one of the Palermo prisons that the mafia has turned into luxury hotels, where pipes running with whiskey come in under the foundations. When the mafia guys saw that they wouldn't get anything out of him—not because he refused to talk but because he really didn't have anything to tell—they tried sending him back to his country. But his country wouldn't take him back, since in the meantime 'cholera' had hit hard in southern Italy, with 288 dead, and they were scared that someone like him, who had left because of cholera, might just bring it back with him now. So he was transferred first to a prison in Spoleto, and from there to Bolzano, a city famous for its *grappa* made with Williams pears. It's a no-man's-land in Swiss Italy, or is it Italian Switzerland—the borders are almost non-existent—where they send people when neither country wants to take responsibility for a sentence. And just as the whole pears in bottles of *grappa* make the bottles seem smaller than they really are, while the pears seem larger, Glafkos, surrounded in nothingness, just stood up one day and walked out. Which is to say, the mafia let him go.

"He came to me. Not right away, because he was scared. First he sent word asking for money. I went to the bank, withdrew some of the money I had deposited in the name of the tribal chief, and sent it to him. During this whole adventure, Glafkos left his writerly identity behind. He wanted, he later explained, to leave a clean name for posterity. And so the name Thrassakis remained unstained.

"Then he told me about his desire to go to some other place, some other land, where he would know no one and no one would know him. Together we decided he should go to New Guinea, where I had my missionary post."

The sea was at low tide. A field of mud stretched before us, waiting for people to come digging for mussels and clams. Before I left, satisfied that I now knew the "whole truth," the good pastor gave me a manuscript Glafkos had left in his house, and which he was giving to me, he said, in order to sweeten the bitterness of my great disappointment in America.

Chapter Seven

I HAD DECIDED TO leave Thrassakis and his story on the back burner for quite a long stretch of time. You can't always be living with the dead. Reality throbbed around me. And so, not just because our psychoanalyst advised it but because we ourselves found it much healthier, my wife and I put the whole investigation out of sight, in the closet, so to speak. Sure, my wife might have been working in secret, researching the feminist movement and the role Mrs. Lazaridis (who never used her husband's pseudonym) had played in it, but she never said anything about it to me. And I might have been tracking down a few details about the "lost man," as components of "lost time," but I never mentioned any of that during our evenings together.

I had begun, however, to feel a strange attraction for my daughter. She had still been quite young when I first started my research on Glafkos, and hadn't elicited the kind of confusion I was now experiencing at the sight of her lively step. And so I can measure the ripening of my research in terms of my daughter's growing maturity.

Since I hate for other people to keep me over hot coals, I myself can't bear to toy here with the reader's impatience. The de-Stalinized Stalinist is the worst thing in the world, apart from the de-factionalized fascist. That's why I'm in such a rush to explain what happened between my second visit to Leiden and now, something that bowled me over completely: the old sailor Vladimir (once a friend of Thrassakis and the pastor's occasional lover) asked to see me. "I'm doubting everything," he said, "even my own doubt."

According to him, Glafkos wasn't eaten by cannibals. According to him, Glafkos fell the victim of intra-Macedonian political disputes.

Though in his sixties, Vladimir (a pseudonym he used in his underground work) had strong, handsome features carved by sea brine and years of adventure. He kept talking about how they had unjustly "eaten" my compatriot, Thrassakis, and how guilty he felt for having unwittingly played the role of intermediary. But there was no way he could have foreseen the tragic outcome. He had been fond of Thrassakis. He had wanted the best for him. But ten years of life experience with shipping magnates (he had worked on Niarhos's "Creole") had taught him that the big bosses play hardball. If you don't do what they want, you lose your inside spot—and not just as Glafkos had, but in a way that keeps you from doing anything at all after that.

It was true that he and Glafkos had met in prison in Rotterdam. Glafkos was there because his alcohol abuse had reached dangerous levels; Vladimir had been picked up for smuggling. But it wasn't true that Thrassakis had introduced Vladimir to the pastor. The pastor was a member of an organization based in New York that sought to liberate Montenegro of Yugoslavia from Tito's yoke. No, not just a member: an agent. He worked for them.

Marshall Tito, with the longevity of a true dictator (from all those Caudillo sweets, his enemies said), was taking forever to die, a fact which served to heighten his adversaries' exasperation. Periodic assassination attempts and other terrorist acts brought about the opposite of their intended effects. The assassination of the Yugoslavian ambassador to Sweden, for example, alienated those opposed to the union of the Western and Orthodox churches, while terrorist activity within Yugoslavia just gave Tito's forces an excuse to step up their program of "ethnic cleansing." There was a stiffening of the party line, while Tito's much-celebrated "third road" went the way of those national products you find everywhere but the country in which they are produced. That, more or less, was the climate back then. Though there was one very positive factor working in favor of the struggle for an independent Montenegro: years of American economic aid had resulted in the *de facto* reality of extensive American infiltration, which gave members of the organization basic hopes for the eventual success of their struggle.

Vladimir had me read a statement concerning the Milovan Djilas case addressed to a U.S. Congressional sub-committee and later published in book form. The witness, who would later become Thrassakis's literary agent, openly declares, "Since we provided [Yugoslavia] with economic support, why shouldn't we have a say in its internal affairs?"

Djilas was a symbol for the organization, a sort of Trotsky of the Balkans. The sailor was willing to give me all the material to read concerning the Djilas case, so I could see for myself what had really been going on.

So the pastor had been the one who put Glafkos in contact with the organization, through the man who would later become his literary agent. This man, a wealthy tycoon in the States, arranged for one of Thrassakis's books to be translated into English. The agent's chauffeur came from the same village as Vladimir, and from him the sailor learned that the writer and his agent soon became as inseparable as ass and underwear, so to speak. They agreed on everything—even an independent Montenegro.

"I lost track of him after that," the sailor continued, "I have no idea what happened or how. But knowing how the big fish work, I can imagine that while he was living in America, the Boss must have taken him under his complete protection, winding the Organization's tentacles securely around him—and by the time the agent found out that Thrassakis was not, after all, one of them, it was already too late. He knew too much. So they had to find a way to get rid of him."

It was around that time that the Rockefeller son disappeared. Rumor had it that there had been another white man with him, a man of uncertain identity whom the cannibals had also devoured. Why couldn't Thrassakis be that other man? So they had the pastor make his statements to the press, selling them the same fairytale he had sold me. The pastor had been the font of misinformation that flooded the public with lies.

And the sailor fell silent.

It's true that some elements of his testimony seemed convincing, and certain external facts seemed to support it. First of all, the disappearance of Thrassakis's books from the American market had always struck me as odd. I suppose the only reason *Prinos II* ever came out was that the contract had already been signed. Since a significant stretch of time usually separates the signing of a contract from the book's eventual publication, the contract might have been signed during the golden days of friendship between the agent and the unlucky writer, while the publication would have taken place after their falling-out. And if the publisher doesn't promote a book, it's liable to be entirely overlooked. I had often wondered why, after the American edition of *Prinos II*, none of his other books had ever been published in the States. But could I accept the sailor's story in its entirety, without verification? I had to let it stew for a while before I could adopt it as true.

In the meantime, I had begun almost literally to freeze at the thought that my biography (if it can even be called a biography) was seeming more and more like a book by Thrassakis, that "classic murderologist," as Dimaras called him in his *History of Modern Greek Literature*. Because if he really had been done in by "dark powers," then Thrassakis, in a fateful materialization of his own imaginings, had achieved a complete identification of the fictive with the real. But let's get down to the facts.

The Thrassakises' (though chiefly Glafkos's) dealings with the agent are divided, like Picasso's paintings, into periods of different colors. First, the rose period. Love and kisses, flowers and hugs. They are introduced by a mutual friend and discover that they share the common background of the Vardaris river. Fields irrigated by its waters, women swarming over its banks. Their friend, the match-maker, will later play a cunning role in the whole affair: as always in such situations, he will side with the side of power—which is to say, with the agent. But back then, during that first period, it's all milk and honey; the agent's wife likes Thrassakis, Thrassakis's wife likes the agent. Two couples of the *Who's Afraid of Virginia Woolf?* variety—which is to say, perverted. This rose period is marked by the discovery of common likes and dislikes: "I really like anchovy paste on rye bread, too!" They agree on more expensive foods, too. For example, they both prefer red caviar to black, which reminds the agent of Siberia and the Gulag archipelago. From the very beginning, Glafkos suspects that the agent might be anti-Communist—but that's no reason, he thinks, to spoil things before they've really even begun. Glafkos, who just then is experiencing a kind of personal crisis concerning his beliefs and their application to his time, tolerates the enemy presence beside him, not knowing or even being able to imagine just how dangerous that enemy is.

They're both in Cork, at an international film festival. The agent is just passing through for the day to make some contacts. He and Glafkos are introduced on the terrace of the Carlton Hotel. The match-maker, their mutual friend, has no idea what kind of fire he's lit. Glafkos and the agent really hit it off. It's love at first sight. The agent crosses himself with three fingers, which drives Glafkos crazy with joy. Soon they discover that they share other things in common. For instance, both of their fathers were Jehovah's Witnesses. At this time in his life Thrassakis desperately needs a megaphone that can shout out his name, that can sing it out to the ends of the earth. And he couldn't find a better megaphone, a better amplifier for his record, than the agent, who has a pointy diamond on the middle finger of his right hand that's as big as one of Jane Russell's nipples. He says it's plastic; the real one is in his vault at the bank. Everyone at the nearby tables is staring at him. They all know who he is. They all want to be sitting with him. The power this man wields, not only in wealth but in possible connections, is simply astounding. If he decides to take you under his wing, you've got it made. The next morning you wake up famous. Because he buys space in the papers and time on the radio and TV. He becomes, in other words, the time-space of your promotion. But he's a strange guy. He hates brown-nosing. Just the smell of it makes him sick. Luckily, Glafkos has no idea how powerful he is. And, not wanting to make him nervous, the match-maker, the go-between, says nothing. So Glafkos is completely relaxed, and he and the agent discuss the "Yugoslavian question," and at first they find themselves in complete agreement.

(Great indeed is the writer who knows exactly how to describe a first encounter, inserting disquieting foreshadowings of how the plot will develop without ever telling us anything straight out. However, in fulfilling the joyless role of the biographer, having given the facts straight out beforehand, I seek not to create atmosphere, but just to summarize, with the help of Glafkos's own writings and the testimony of third parties, how the bond was formed—how the knot, so to speak, was tied—and how it was later destroyed. Because the agent grew like ivy on a weak tree—Thrassakis, the slanting olive, the stunted mulberry, the troubled pear—and sucked him dry. Whatever is invested in your work will end up eating away at the work itself, like an acid corroding the metal it's supposed to be treating. The advertisement, that is, eats the advertised. The advertised doesn't eat the advertiser. Only the consumer of the advertised good escapes uneaten from this whole process of consumption, which ultimately boils down to a class conflict between worker and boss. Thrassakis, the worker, was crushed beneath the overwhelming weight of the agent's slogans—"Year of Thrassakis," "Read Thrassakis," "Glafkos of Athens," and so on—which, after the disagreement and ultimate break between them, gave way to utter silence. To the execution-style killing in the dark, the sabotage of the wormlike Thrassakis's every attempt to crawl out into the light from under the rock of anonymity. But we're getting ahead of ourselves. . . .)

Joe, the agent, has to catch an evening plane for London. He leaves the festival early, informed by his chauffeur that striking dairy farmers have blocked the roads and might make him miss his flight. Joe leaves excited about Glafkos. Immediately upon his return to New York, he puts his secretaries in touch with Glafkos to arrange all the technical details of their contract. But even at Cork, Joe is already promising him fantastic success. And of course, Joe tells him as he gets up to leave, if he were ever to write anything about the victims of "leprosy". . . . Glafkos gets the drift. Up until now he has written primarily about the victims of "cholera." By "leprosy," the agent must be referring to the other camp, the "Red Junta." With this last admonishing comment during their first meeting on the terrace of the Carlton Hotel in Cork, we are given to understand that Joe was touching on a theme dear to his heart, without yet going into details.

"What an amazing individual," said the go-between as Joe went off, waving from afar through a cloud of admiring diners, while the sun, setting behind the chimney of some factory, winked off his plastic diamond at the crowd of would-be starlets in this international pageant. "He's a giant of the press and of art," continued the good go-between, an exiled Russian prince. "He has only a single weakness, and such a human one: he melts on receiving even the briefest handwritten note filling him in on your news, even the most superficial, day-to-day things. It really moves him. Because this great man with his huge impersonal office believes more than anyone in human emotions and in maintaining personal contact with his jockeys, or his 'horses,' as he calls the artists he represents." Seeing Glafkos's doubtful look, he continued: "Yes, that's how he sees you. Like a horse. He often goes to the racetrack and bets insane amounts of money. He lights a fire under you and you run. And since he has two hundred or so horses in his stable, there's no way he can keep track of what each of them is doing. That's why a little note every now and then never hurts. In fact it does a lot of good. Believe me, you'll remember this conversation!" he concluded, puffing like the Python on his gold-trimmed pipe.

Glafkos got up and excused himself, not to go to the bathroom—there was no need for that, since he hadn't drunk a thing—but to call Glafka in Brussels and tell her how wonderfully the meeting had gone. "But we'll see what comes of it in the end," he added, thus anticipating failure in order to ensure the opposite, lest his hopes be disappointed. Calmed by the phone call and wanting to enjoy his last night in Cork, he offered to take the match-maker out to dinner. The exiled prince gladly accepted the invitation. They went to a Greek place, where Omar Sharif was eating in the half-light of a dim corner, and the owner, a Cypriot, treated them with special care. Glafkos cunningly slipped the Brazilian lady who entertained at the place—and who had only one breast, which somehow made her unbelievably attractive—into the go-between's arms, giving her like a blood transfusion to the exiled prince.

What followed was indescribably gratifying. Not just one but a dozen secretaries from Joe's office wrote to Glafkos almost daily asking for all the particulars of his life, his habits, his preferences, his personal relations. The fact that so many different people were writing to him from the same address made him believe in the infinity of the Office, an impression that a German comrade, passing through Brussels, did nothing to dispel: "You met the agent? How did you manage that?" He couldn't believe that Thrassakis and the agent had drunk Campari together on the terrace of the Carlton. "I was in New York for two months," he continued, "I stood outside of his office, I went to all the pizzerias and Italian restaurants he frequents, hoping to exchange a word or two with him. But it was just impossible." "We're both from the Balkans," Glafkos replied mildly, but his mind was already running to that martyr of a student he had known in his youth, a kid from Ardaia or Arnea, he couldn't remember, who had needed a certain professor to give him a passing grade in his course and had stalked this professor all over the city. This kid didn't have a dime, but he rented a room at the Mediterranean Hotel and ate at the Naousa Olympus, and followed the professor to concerts and theater premieres. Until one day he found to his despair that he had no more olives to sell, no more fields to mortgage—he had reached the "Amen" of the prayer and still couldn't get his diploma, and all because that one professor wouldn't give him a passing grade. With the guillotine of army service hanging over his head, with his sister pregnant and needing to get married before she gave birth (but in order for her to get married he had to get his diploma, so as to borrow the money for her dowry), he reached the final solution of the truly desperate: he pulled a knife on the professor, an Algerian switchblade, and finally managed to get the grade he needed for his infamous diploma. Then, leaving the inquisition with the desired grade, uplifted and jubilant, he was killed in a car crash. Which gave the rebellious students cause to seek another vindication for his death.

These flashbacks and feedback make Glafkos more tolerant of the present. And this present thickens with correspondence, until the next summer, when they arrange to meet in legendary Deauville. But they can't find a room there, and end up in the neighboring Trouville, where Joe and his wife Joy get to know Glafkos and Glafka for the first time face to face. This, I repeat, is the rose period. They go together to the racetrack and walk side by side along stretches of shore deserted by sea, collecting bucketfuls of mussels. Every now and then a telegraph boy on horseback (since horses can run in the mud) gallops out to the edge of the sea where the four of them are bent over, pulling up clams, and hands Joe an urgent telegram from Japan or Brazil. And Joe, straightening up in his plastic boots, there on a stretch of land which the sea will soon have covered once more, writes his reply, an "O.K.," a signature: "Joe."

But no rose period can remain as it is. Rose is a color whose nature it is to change, fading or darkening according to its relation with the light.

Joe doesn't drink. Joe doesn't smoke. Joe doesn't eat. So what is Joe, exactly? Joy tells them straight out: as a child he had suffered a great deal, and now that he's achieved a position of relative fame, he relives his adolescent experiences of poverty and lack, but in combined form, as the lack of poverty. Which is to say, he can eat but he doesn't, in order to remind himself of the time when he wanted to eat but went hungry. Joe is a mixture of the self-made man and the puppet moved by outside forces. Though Glafkos hasn't quite figured this out, Joe takes orders from reactionary forces, while commanding progressive forces that serve him, albeit unwillingly. He is, in other words, the pivot point of a strange balance in which no one ever gets the upper hand—at least not over him. He could even present himself at a public court, if need be, in defense of his own progressiveness.

This, then, is the mighty agent Joe. According to his wife, though, he's a giant with the heart of a bird, easily conquered. All you have to do is step on his ego and he crumples, dissolves—and then his reactions are simply impossible to predict. Joe, like every self-made man, doesn't like to be contradicted. He doesn't demand that others agree with him, he only demands their tolerance. Besides, a disagreement might upset him. And when he gets upset his blood pressure rises. And when his blood pressure rises he has to take pills. And those pills are bad for his asthma, so he'll have to pull out his inhaler. And then he'll get dizzy and collapse. Joe's immune system offers some measure of protection. But this master of mass media hangs from a single thread, and whoever breaks that thread on a personal level could be responsible for a death: Joe's. According to the match-maker's descriptions, and later those of Joe's wife, Glafkos could become a murderer at any moment. But would he want that? So, with their warnings, Joy and the match-maker clip the wings of any objections Glafkos might have raised to whatever Joe says. While he finds many things about Joe and their relationship unacceptable, he says nothing. Joe remains embalmed in his fairy tale, his void, uneating, unharmed.

At the international book fair in Frankfurt, Glafkos, who will later become the big boss's right hand man, accompanies Joe to receptions where for the first time people smile when Glafkos enters a room, since the agent, intent on selling his big guns, shares a bit of the limelight with Thrassakis, whose role is something like that of the decorative stamp on a Krupp machine gun. What customer could possibly object to that little stamp when shelling out for the gun? Joe's presence reigns amidst the chaos of the book fair. And Glafkos is pulled behind in his wake. Joe's passage through the various stands opens a channel of admiration, and Glafkos follows behind, a pearl of the great "famine," a cultivated writer with his dichot bloom. They greet Joe, only to discover our man standing behind him. Glafkos is like an elevator boy riding up with customers who barely even notice his presence. And, as a compliment to Joe's obtuse angle, Glafkos plays his role to a T. He meets them. They meet him. We meet. You meet. A friend of his sees him and whispers in his ear, "Now that you're with him, you've got it made." Another Greek asks Glafkos to introduce him to Joe—the German publisher the man works for depends on an American house under Joe's control, so he himself depends almost directly on Joe. Glafkos smiles and answers, "You should depend on the motherland, my friend, not on the colonies." (Glafkos refers to this episode in his personal correspondence with Thomas.)

Glafka's morning shopping excursions with the agent's wife also belong to this early rose period. Glafka, who in those days wore shoes that pinched, comes back to the hotel exhausted each day and heads straight for the tub to soak her feet. They are staying, of course, in the same hotel as Joe and Joy, in a room with a circular bathtub and a round bed surrounded in silk netting—in short, a Hollywood movie set, like in a Negulesko film. The luxury excites our hero, who confesses that he wakes up each morning under sheets tented by the rubber pole of an erection. The opulence, the round bed, the elevated bathtub in the middle of the room, all paid for by the agent, belong to one of the couple's oldest fantasies. So one day when Glafkos happens to see Joe leaving the NATO secret service building, he can't believe his eyes. He tells himself—and believes it—that it must have been someone else, someone who just looked like Joe. Glafkos is riding in a taxi past the sad gray building that once housed the Gestapo's General Staff and is now the headquarters for the American Powers of NATO's Central European division. The road rises into a kind of bridge, built to keep the incessant comings and goings of NATO's personal cars from blocking traffic. When the taxi stops at a red light, waiting to cross the current coming from the Manheim side, Glafkos is shocked to see Joe taking his leave of some men who are shaking his hand with infinite respect, almost as if he were their boss. Glafkos freezes. He goes pale. Glafkos's German is awful, so he doesn't manage in time to ask the driver to stop and wait for a while at the side of the road. He's on his way to an early cocktail party, which Joe will also be attending. Glafkos gets there first. Joe walks in a half hour later and, apologizing to both Glafkos and the publisher hosting the party, says he has to leave again right away, to get back to the hotel and place an urgent call to the States.

No relationship rots like one based on unequal dependence. Joe means business. Glafkos observes his boss's business acumen. And the intoxicating interest on his capital. From playing Monopoly he knows that the less you have, the more clumsily you invest. But when you're sure of what you own, you become smarter—which is to say, braver. In the capitalist system, genius depends, more or less, on your degree of certainty. The ability to keep your mind focused in tight spots, the transformation of a conquered region into a base for new operations, makes the attack easier, and condemns your opponent to a position of incessant defense. Joe buys. He makes deals. When someone holds out for a long time, trying to buck him, Joe offers his opponent three times as much as he's expecting, overwhelming him. Joe and business go together. But Joe sees KGB agents everywhere. Perhaps because it takes one to know one?

This is the period when Thrassakis's book *Zeus* (or *Eu-Z*) is selling like hotcakes all over the world. *Prinos II* will come next, and there it will stop. The rig, so to speak, will abandon him. Furthermore, in this first, rose period, we should mention the innumerable glasses of champagne Glafkos and Glafka drink, the enormous bills they run up. Following in a rich man's wake drags you into a whirlpool of expenses which, like it or not, exceed your daily earnings. People of modest means who spend too much time with rich people end up poor, not from treating those friends to meals or buying them gifts, but simply from boarding the train of their lifestyle, since the cover charge for that train is often as much as someone else might pay for an entire meal. The climax of this trend comes with Glafka's gift to Joe's wife of a seventeenth-century Byzantine icon with black angels. And the agent's subsequent invitation for Thrassakis to come to the promised land of bloody America.

≈

THE SECOND period—the gray period—is passed in correspondence. *Eu-Z* and *Prinos II* both enjoy relative success, the first because of its epic proportions, the second because its description of harsh village life in Greece before the appearance of the drilling rigs proves particularly appealing to the average American, who sincerely believes that his tax money can civilize the rest of the world. Glafkos seems to have sent a rough English translation of his new novel to Joe so that he could sell the translation rights to publishing houses in various countries. From the storm of correspondence that followed, we deduce that the novel has something to do with a crime planned and committed by NATO and CIA agents in some fictional Central European country. Naturally, Joe panicked. As a second-class citizen, of immigrant parents, he was afraid of being criticized for supporting works that turn against his adopted homeland, the great America. So, apart from requesting a cleaned-up version of the translation, he also insisted, as their letters clearly demonstrate, that the names of the organizations NATO and CIA be altered:

> *Since your work treats the structural relationship between progressive and reactionary forces, what difference would it make if you were to reverse the givens of the problem? The result of the equation would remain the same. Besides, the writer's universality should arise not necessarily from political incorporation but from his ability to work his way into individual and collective substructures, governed by inviolable rules. The law of gravity is at work in socialist as well as in capitalist countries. Or, to put it more simply, bureaucracy is not just a phenomenon of the East.*

Reasoning which Thrassakis, in all innocence, assumed to be correct. And so he accepted the first concession: "NATO" would be replaced with "OTAN" and "CIA" with its reverse, "AIC." What he didn't know then was that the downward spiral of abridgment has no end. Because censorship works like math: it starts with the general and grows increasingly specific. After Joe, in the course of a truly fascinating correspondence, manages to convince Glafkos to change the names of the organizations, the next step is to ask him why the story couldn't be set in the Soviet Union. Wasn't there also the Warsaw Pact and the KGB? Glafkos answers that Joe must surely be joking, that his last letter—the one in which he categorically states, "This is as far as I go"—must surely have gotten lost in the mail. But Joe, having won the first round, toys with his victim, needling him, goading him on.

In the general confusion of post office strikes, airplane hijackings, the cutting-off of telephone lines—incidents which, according to Joe, demonstrate the subversive nature of left-wing trade unions—certain letters are supposedly lost, letters which in my opinion were never written, letters whose supposed failure to arrive is used to cover up a deliberate silence in the face of burning questions. "What do you mean?" Joe asks, "Didn't I already address that concern? Didn't you get my letter of such-and-such a date?" With repeated responses like this, Joe manages never to answer Glafkos's query. And all Glafkos can say is, "No, I never got it." Meanwhile weeks pass and the old query has taken on a ghostly character, like an ancient, mummified doubt. So Joe, who has another secretary send Glafkos a message every now and again, drives him crazy with uncertainty—until, not knowing how else to escape from this dead end, Glafkos hastens his departure for America, where he believes that everything will work itself out between the slicing of a gigantic steak and the icing of an enormous cake. There, however, we enter the third period of Picasso's work: the black.

This shift from period to period is not a mechanistic process in which the colors continually darken, like the setting of the sun. Taken together, they constitute an x-ray of a society in which independent, unrestricted minds have no place. If Glafkos had enjoyed the protection of some political party or organization, he wouldn't have fallen so easily into the lion's mouth. In crossing the Atlantic, he has already made the biggest mistake of his life: he has agreed to fight in his opponent's ring. He mistakenly believes that his personal presence can save his work from ruin. For Joe, however, his work is practically worthless. Joe's agency is an enormous enterprise in which some singer might bring in twenty times as much as a writer like Thrassakis, who is no more than a blowfly, a worthless mosquito—but one that buzzes a lot.

So, in an effort to push him out of the circle for good, Joe gets Glafkos mixed up in the plot for an independent Montenegro, just as the reactionaries had once interpreted Manolis Glezos's trip to the Soviet Union as an attempt to sell Greek Macedonia to the Communists. Glafkos falls for this trick, just as he had once, while still a young boy, fallen into a bucket of whitewash, and thought it was the spring of Siloam.

≈

SO THERE YOU have it. Characters right out of a Thrassakian novel: the homosexual pastor (he always put one of "them" in his novels to do the dirty work); the sailor-pimp (he always admired those types, because they were, he said, children of the people); the dark forces (the leadership of the anti-Tito movement); and the main character, who, in his state of psychological confusion, gets mixed up in the whole affair for reasons of his own (i.e., the hope of increasing the chances of his books being translated and published abroad). There you have it, all the elements of an unadulterated work by the mature Thrassakis. Even the

ending comes straight out of one of his longer works of prose: they "ate" him,
true—but who?

No, I'd much rather never have gotten mixed up in this affair. My daydreams
that I was him started up again, since I was writing a story just like one of his,
though I knew that what I was writing wasn't a product of my imagination—I
was just copying down the facts of his life, which happened to imitate his art.

Then again, I preferred this version a thousand times to the tale of the cannibals—which, racist and anti-dialectical facets aside, made me as viscerally sick
as the news of those people who managed to survive a plane crash in the Andes
by eating their fellow passengers. It made meat repulsive to me. In fact, I
became a vegetarian soon after I first got involved in the Thrassakis case. And I
have to admit, I lost half my bulk. My better self, as old friends like to tease me.

Yes, I'll say it again. Better a bullet and instant annihilation than that other
way. And if this new plot really is true, one day it will surely come to light. It's
all in the books. And one day they are bound to get opened. After all, the truth
is surely to be found in Thrassakis's manuscripts.

Which means, of course, that I won't find out until the year 2003.

With that thought, it occurred to me for the first time that perhaps the university library had been paid to buy his manuscripts because the responsible parties knew what would soon become of their writer, and they wanted to ensure
the complete secrecy of any surprises those papers might contain. I then discovered, not without a twinge of fear, that Joe, his American agent, had been an
alumnus of that very same university.

Yet a plot like this stood in complete contradiction to the reality I had known,
of Nick Polis and his son and the house where Glafkos had once stayed. No one
can convince me that it wasn't old Polis who pressed the university into buying
Glafkos's papers. Unless Polis and the agent, both alumni of the university,
belonged to the same organization pushing for the liberation of Macedonia,
which would become an American state with its own star—the fifty-third?—on
the American flag.

I plunged into investigations regarding this possibility. I asked a friend of mine,
a Greek-American in New York, to photocopy some "Yogurt Incorporated"
newsletters of the time, in which Macedonian-friendly currents are clearly repre-

sented. When the copies arrived I found nothing significant—except, that is, for a passing reference to the name of Glafkos's agent. Bingo.

And the Tigers? I searched, but found no relation between the two. Despite their wild name, the Tigers seemed to be the most human of all in this jungle of competing interests.

Chapter Eight

Zagreb, 21. Sixteen Croatian nationalists, charged with terrorist acts in various cities throughout Croatia and the planting of bombs in Zagreb itself, are being tried in the Dalmatian city of Zadar. Some of the charged are also being tried in relation to the assassination of several prominent Yugoslavian figures.

The indictment alleges that many of those on trial entered Yugoslavia illegally and met with local extremists, with whom they plotted the assassination of several of the country's leading figures as well as the sabotage of several industrial targets.

The death penalty is anticipated if the defendants are found guilty on either of the two charges.

—Reuters

THE READER must be wondering—and rightly so, I might add—exactly who I am and how I got my hands on all these details. So, to prevent any misunderstandings, let me explain: in the framework of a general atmosphere of political atonement the Americans have recently been showing to us Greeks, I was informed that I could, if I liked, visit the university library to which Thrassakis had entrusted his papers and have a look at some of his unpublished texts. The

notification came to me from the American embassy, along with a note requesting that I contact the department of cultural affairs.

In times like ours you've got to have guts to set foot in the American embassy,
which is still soaked in the hatred of the world, just as it was in Thrassakis's day.
Back then the Turks had devoured half of Cyprus and were threatening to gob-
ble up the rest, too. Man of the world that I am, I personally have nothing
against Turks—on the contrary, I am in close contact with several of our
Turkish comrades—but I am unable to overlook the rapacious role played by
American imperialism, which, disguised by the "interests" of Aegean shelf
rights, sat back and let the Turks take over the island. In 1922, just over a century
after Greece gained independence from them, the pashas started up again with
their program to take back the islands one by one. At the beginning of the nine-
teenth century democratic ideals were sweeping through Europe—but now,
with the dawn of the twenty-first century fast approaching, autocratic ideas,
combined with religious fanaticism, are once again on the rise.

In short, lest I carry on too long: I was so terrified of suffering some "dynamite accident" like Feltrinelli's as soon as I set foot in the American embassy that
before I went I met repeatedly with my lawyer and drafted no less than three separate wills.

The cultural attaché who met with me impressed me, I have to say, with his
breadth of knowledge concerning Greek affairs. He had no particular respect, he
told me, for the Greek writers who had thus far visited the States as guests of various foundations, because their complimentary words about his country convinced no one, much less those with no desire whatsoever to be convinced. He
preferred, he continued, texts that criticized the system, no matter how biased
or unjust that criticism might be—it was enough that they exhibited freedom
of thought. The U.S., which received so much criticism from inside, had no
need, he concluded, of external support. And to clarify his position with regard
to his predecessors, who had wanted nothing more than hired pens, he assured
me that the new administration was seeking independent minds.

I must admit that I was growing increasingly uncomfortable with each passing minute. Even though the incident had taken place long ago, Thrassakis's
story about Angeloni, who met her tragic end while placing a time bomb in the
basement of that very embassy, was still as vivid to me as a nightmare.

Lowering his voice, the cultural attaché finally explained to me that, as a member of the Jewish diaspora, he fully understood my position. He was completely open with me; he wanted nothing more than to be of service.

Aware of the problems I was facing, having read my articles in the press and seen the reports on TV, he had taken pains to find out, not least to satisfy his own personal curiosity, why the three sacks of Thrassakis's papers at the American university had to remain closed. After indescribable exertions, he managed to find out a thing or two from the agent's heirs. How? That's exactly what he had invited me to his office to tell me.

At a general assembly of the university's trustees, the majority proved amenable to the idea of the deceased's manuscripts being examined—in fact, one member added, it might actually prove useful for the preservation of the materials themselves, because (and I quote) "What if some kind of little moth or something were hatching inside the sacks and eating up all the papers without us ever knowing?" Everyone agreed that something of that sort wasn't entirely out of the question, since Thrassakis came from an economically underdeveloped country whose children still suffered from "Malta fever"—and so, all things considered, it wasn't impossible that some strange Tunisian microbe might have slipped into those bags. When one of the members asked, "Why Tunisian?" the chairman answered that Tunisia was in Greece. It took a rather extensive debate to clear up the fact that Magna Graecia was not, in fact, the same thing as Magna Syrti (which, by the way, is in Libya, not Tunisia), so that the Syrti Minore of the *syrtaki*, the drawer, the *fermoir* of Glafkos's manuscripts, was not in Tunisia but in Athens. To make a long story short, the cultural attaché concluded, that was why he had invited me to see him. From now on I could consider myself able, if willing, to open and study the contents of one of the three sacks—after all, they weren't top secret documents concerning the Oswald case.

I must admit that the good attaché left me rather bewildered. I didn't know how to take the offer—as a concession on the part of his government, which was how he himself had presented it, or as my own surrender, my own selling out? I was touched, it's true, and replied with the warmest of thanks, if only in order to escape a few minutes sooner from that minefield of an embassy. At home, entirely alone (my wife had gone to Yiannitsa, where our daughter, or rather her new husband, was completing his military service), I mulled it over, and the next day I decided to accept the invitation.

I didn't even have to pay my way to America. A friend of mine, a reporter, had a free ticket for a 21-day stay in the States, and gave it to me. And so I set off once more for the New World.

Photographers, interviewers, radio and TV reporters, were all waiting for me upon my arrival at the airport. There was a new librarian—brand new, almost electronic, I'd say. Moreover, though he himself hadn't come to welcome me, the agent's son weighed down the atmosphere with a sense of mystery: the representative who came in his stead had a pistol strapped under his vest. Why bother pretending? I was terrified.

This man with the gun, looking very Great Gatsby-esque in his suspenders, was also present at the unsealing of the sack. Once again he came as a representative of Joe Junior and the literary agency that had once represented Thrassakis. And there I was, the conscientious biographer, enflamed by the passion of research. They shot off an air gun to break the wax that had sealed the khaki-colored paper, letting a gust of fresh air into the sack once used for Brazilian coffee, which really should have been worm-eaten by now.

Greek sprang from the sack like the entrails of a butchered ox. The whole place was flooded in the alphabet. Joe Junior's emissary, a common gunman, didn't know where to look first—he couldn't read a single word. "I was the perfect registrar for the dead texts of a living sea" (Thrassakis).

I'd hit pay dirt: the later texts, plus his correspondence with Joe and an entire sheaf of their contracts. One small scrap of innards, slashed with scissors, hung from the sack like some sensitive schoolgirl's hair ribbon:

It was a Saturday evening when my mother was finally freed from the pains I had been causing for many weeks. I came out, they say, with a mask on my face. My father still carries this membrane in his wallet. Once he even showed it to me. So for a long time now I have believed that I'm "Saturday-born and lucky."

I found myself before a stack of letters between Joe and Glafkos. The match begins with a few dizzying hits from Joe, who has a different secretary write to Glafkos each time about the matter at hand. A certain Catharine Lu Tsevas asks him for a *curriculum vitae*. An Ethel Blanche sends him a questionnaire from the publisher. A John Foster asks him to meet some photographer from a large firm that specializes in writers' portraits. A Judith Aslanian (Armenian, presumably Orthodox) sends him the cover for inspection. A Yoase Dagyan sends the text from the back cover, as it's been arranged with the publisher. Naturally this long list of names impresses Glafkos, who keeps sending new work to the agent in Greek. And Joe thanks him. In a letter of March 13, 1972, for example, he writes: "Thanks for *Prinos III*. It's really great that your creative juices are in full flow. With best wishes for Glafka and yourself, Joe. P.S. Joy is feeling better. (She had a cold.) All will soon be well."

When *Prinos III* is finally translated, the haggling begins over the cuts that have to be made "at the publisher's insistence." Thus Glafkos finds himself faced with the superpower of the publisher, for whom Joe is no more than a mediator, the medium through which the wishes of the Unknown Master are made known. Glafkos, then, has no other choice than to submit.

Joe comforts him, promising to do the necessary cutting himself so that the final word won't fall to the publisher. Glafkos can trust in their friendship and their common Balkan heritage.

But when Glafkos finally gets to see the cuts (which are sent during a postal strike in Brussels via a special NATO service that makes deliveries to multinational corporations and international banks), the letter that accompanies them is not from Joe but from someone else, some "–ouvrier," apparently not Orthodox at all but of French descent, as Glafkos deduces from the name. This stranger, putting knife to bone, says that the necessary cuts were made in the spirit of increasing the book's saleability in an English-speaking market. Glafkos's reaction is violent. He threatens to break the contract if Joe dares to send this distorted text to the publisher.

Joe replies that the go-ahead isn't given to him, but straight to the publisher. And if Glafkos doesn't send it right away, by telegraph, he is very sorry, truly, sincerely sorry, but he will have to resign from his position as Glafkos's agent.

So their relations have reached a critical point (I hope to be able to explain exactly how later on) when, both sides unyielding, Joe shoots to kill. On March 29, 1974, he writes to Glafkos of his friend Djilas, then endangered by the Titoan "reform" taking place in the Communist League in view of the General's likely succession. Joe writes that he is sending a certain Vladimir there, to provide Djilas with some kind of monetary support, and . . .

Glafkos understands. "I'm ready to help," he answers. His willingness smoothes things over for a while and letters start flooding in again from people Glafkos has never heard of before, about translation rights in foreign countries, Japan, Israel, the Laplands, there's even a letter about the sale of rights for one of his books to be recorded by the Society for the Blind. The interest that rises once more from the ashes truly demonstrates Joe's appreciation of Glafkos's willingness to help. The bombardment continues for fifteen days, until events in Cyprus intercede, and then the disappearance of "cholera" (i.e., the fall of the Junta), and Glafkos's subsequent return to his native land.

For days I sat in the visitor's room of the special collections library, reading, cataloguing, making connections between various bits of information. Whenever I absolutely needed to photocopy something, I went to the machine, filled out a form saying which page I wanted to copy and, in the presence of a staff member, copied only that specific page. I didn't omit. I didn't censor. I didn't prostitute the texts. I didn't put my faith in deceptive lights. I'd like to believe I proved equal to the task of allowing the man to emerge not as his fans would have liked, but as he himself wanted to be. So I worked humbly, unselfishly, eating plain sandwiches for lunch and dinner, a cheeseburger at the most. With my wife in Yiannitsa, my daughter newly-married and perhaps pregnant with her first child, there wasn't much time for fooling around. Faithful to my hero and model, who was faithful to his Glafka, I just sat there in the library, copying down all the supplementary information I was acquiring, belatedly, about his miserable life.

From the letters found in the first sack, we see Thrassakis struggling tooth and nail to save his work from the agent's Supreme Censorship, and with each letter, he loses another inch of ground. It's like the Ali-Foreman match, when two black, Muslim men pounded each other before a black referee somewhere in Africa. Similarly, Joe and Glafkos, both of them Balkan, battle separately over each story. And naturally, Glafkos always leaves each round having lost yet again.

But it never descends into vulgar squabbling. Their correspondence overflows with compliments and pleasantries. Since it's always difficult, Joe says, for short stories to stand on their own in the market, the author must make some concessions. It's only natural. Logical. Entirely different if it were a novel. The public buys novels. These short pieces, on the other hand, have no audience. All the publishers agree on that. The short story ended with Chekhov. Joe, of course, always has a different member of his staff send the bad news to Glafkos—rejections from different publishers, notes regarding the changes he has to make, the elimination of this or that section, which might offend the average American housewife. Glafkos finds desired parts (and how can they be anything other than desired?) missing from the text, such as an entire key chapter concerning the traitorous role played by ITT in Chile. How did that whole section get eaten, so to speak? Telegraphs follow in which he threatens to disallow the circulation of his book if they don't replace that crucial part. And though he actually wins on that particular point, it's only because it isn't in the publisher's interest to withdraw the book from the market at this late stage in the game. But he isn't always that lucky. On the contrary, he's constantly losing. For instance, at one point Joe writes to him about one of the new books that Glafkos sent him in Greek, which Joe gave to some of his Greek reviewers to look over:

I handed over the manuscript to people who admire your work. People who adore you. And not a single one of them believes that this book has any chance of a good reception, at least here in the United States. I read their reports with the growing certainty that if I ever actually managed to find a publisher, I'd be hurting no one but you. What else can I say, Glafie, except that I'm tremendously sorry?

With that kind of tone Joe undermines Glafkos's belief in his own work, making Glafkos his dependent, like a pimp exploiting a girl who loves him. Did Glafkos really love that "sensitive giant"? No. But he needed him. And all his rages, his vengeful thoughts, are as ineffectual as caricatures of the Statue of Liberty, whom nothing can upset, whom no satire can destroy. It is simply there. A statue, forever.

The Big Boss's underlings are sometimes even more diabolical than Joe himself. Once they have decided on the final form of *Zeus II*, one of them writes to Glafkos: "We trust that you will not be unduly upset by the elimination, for practical reasons, of certain of the Twelve Olympian Deities." Naturally Glafkos is "unduly" upset. He had based the work on the principle of the twelve-tone scale and on that year's zodiac symbol (which later will become the emblem of the European Community). How can twelve be collapsed into seven? He has no desire for a seven-month book.

According to the dates of their correspondence, it is only when Glafkos raises unassailable objections that the Big Boss bothers to intervene: "Your book, which is lacking a central emotional core, seems to have been put together hastily." This kind of vague criticism makes Glafkos want to swear, but the agent tries, in the next sentence, to placate him: "I might be completely wrong about this—I hope I'm wrong. But I just don't see any chance of success. I really am sorry I wasn't more lucky for you, Glafie." Joe then suggests that he find a new agent, with the send-off, "I wish you well, as always." But that just makes Glafkos even more dependent on him than ever.

When Joe really wants to be mean, he starts his letters with family stories: how his daughter got married to an upper-class kid, one of Kissinger's nephews from Harvard, and how at the wedding he found himself before a new generation that doubted his views. He felt glad for the liberated youth of the world, who had the courage of their own opinions. And he, the affectionate father, couldn't but . . . . These are all things that Glafkos couldn't care less about—because, in the end, what do they have to do with him?

What concerns him more are some of the postscripts to Joe's letters, in which he writes familiar phrases like, "I'm returning the manuscript to your address in Brussels, so you can look it over more carefully," or "Tell me who you want me to send this to." These notes show how Glafkos has been bound, hand and foot. But in these sadomasochist relations of victim/victimizer, whore/pimp, there is no such thing as a one-sided victory. Glafkos described the situation very well during his rushed trip through Inner Mani:

> *The hawk flies low, holding in its talons a white dove that it surely plans on bringing back to its nest and tearing apart. But the bird's weight pulls the hawk lower and lower, until they reach the height of the flight of the quail, passing low over the bushes, the hawk unable to lift its quarry high, the dove unable to still its predator with its weight.*

As far as Glafkos's relations with the agent are concerned, there is simply no going back. This is the ground zero of writing. Joe's last letter is of the *sihtir* (shit) *pilaf* variety, with sweet-potatoes for garnish. Joe clearly states that your books still haven't covered any of the advances you received from the publishers I found for you, and thus, "It will be difficult to find another publisher willing to take a chance on the book you're working on now. I think some other agent might suit you better. I wash my hands of the whole affair."

Chapter Nine

I HAD MANAGED to complete a modest and proper job at the university, civilized, reliable, absorbed in my research, never becoming a burden to anyone or giving cause for complaint from any quarter. A girl who reminded me of my daughter would come and help me with the photocopy machine. Feeling completely protected by the library authorities and proud to be the first to examine the unpublished works of my hero, I was preparing to finish my work and leave before the expiration of the twenty-one-day stay permitted by my ticket (or rather, the ticket passed on to me by my reporter friend), when I received an unexpected visit from the agent's son. As a second-generation American citizen, he showed no sign of the psychological complexes common among immigrants. He told me that after his father's death the family had divided the agency into divisions, each concerned with a single one of the arts. He worked in publishing, one of his brothers worked in the movies, another brother with the theater, and so on. Since an agent's work is based on individual personality, the Great Father's decisive departure from life put them in danger of losing many of their "horses," so to speak, unless they managed somehow to bind them hand and foot—which they did by not just representing the works for a ten- or twenty-percent commission, but buying up the works themselves. In other words, the agency now bought the rights to a work, as if they themselves were the ones who would publish it. The writer got more or less the same amount as before, but the work now belonged entirely to the agency. And that, the agent's son stressed once more, was designed to reinforce the personal achievements of their dear departed Father. The agency was now a waiting room of sorts, an intermediary

137

point between obscurity and fame, and whoever decided that he no longer had any need of it was free to abandon it entirely.

I hadn't quite figured out why he was telling me all this, when he suddenly broke the news: he wanted to buy the rights to the biography of Thrassakis I was preparing. When I expressed doubts that a book like mine would be of any interest to an American audience, he told me that there had been a move of late, still vague and indeterminate, to reopen the "Thrassakis case," as much because of his mysterious disappearance as out of curiosity concerning his unknown works. The agency would begin by reissuing *Zeus* and *Prinos II*, then put out a selection of his short stories, and the appearance of my biography would be the crowning event of what he called the "Year of Thrassakis." If things went well, they would follow up with his unpublished works, since the first sack had already been opened. They would entrust to me the task of classifying the unpublished material, and would put me on the payroll as an advisor and consultant as to how I myself thought about his presence, chronologically or according to genre, what sort of interest I thought the unknown works of the deceased would have for a contemporary audience, and so on and so forth.

This conversation took place in the same university cafeteria where Glafkos had first come with the librarian all those years ago. The agent's son, relaxed and friendly, dizzied me with his proposals. My first reaction was to decline, to reject all his ideas right off the bat, as soon as he suggested them to me. But that's what makes business lunches so useful. Along with the food you sometimes swallow your anger as well, hiding your discomfort by filling a glass with wine. The second thought that came to replace my first, like an airplane of another model and company taking off on the same runway, was to ask him if he planned on reissuing *Prinos II* based on the full text of the Greek original, or as it had previously appeared in its butchered English translation. He told me (and he seemed sincere) that he hadn't known the translation hadn't included the full text, since it didn't say anywhere on the book that it was abridged. How had I found out? From the correspondence, of course, between Glafkos and his father. Joe Junior was surprised and wanted to know if the sections that were cut were of an "erotic" nature, because Joe Senior had been something of a puritan when it came to things like that. "Not at all," I answered. "The censorship was purely political." Joe Junior seemed doubtful. His father hadn't ever talked politics at home. "They had their differences," I explained, "over Croatia," and I invited him to come that very afternoon to the special collections library where I was working and take a look at his father's letters. They were on a special kind of paper, a cream linen that made a certain kind of crackling noise, so they were easy to find. I just shook the whole sack, and as soon as I heard that noise I stuck in the tongs and pulled out the page I wanted. Joe Junior was moved by the sight of his father's letters being drawn from the sack. By the third letter he had tears in his eyes. "Their friendship was so strong," he said, "I never knew." "Those letters were written during the rose period," I explained. "Their relationship," I added prophetically, "fell into periods, just like the phases of Picasso's work."

As I sat there talking to the son of his tormenter, I felt as if I myself were turning into the son of the childless Thrassakis. Between two offspring there would have been the concord of collusion. But since I wasn't related by blood to the writer, I held a trump in my hand: the lack of passion. Because dispassion puts you in a winning position.

Joe Junior agreed with me that the butchered version of Thrassakis's book should be replaced by a publication of the full text, even if that meant higher costs—but since the protagonists had left the stage, the work of restoration fell to us. When I asked about his father in a rather roundabout way, trying to get some information out of him, he told me that he had "died on the ramparts of battle," without ever clarifying exactly what battle he was referring to, the battle for life or for some greater Idea. (For a Croatia freed, perhaps, from Tito's yoke?) He hastened to add that he himself, born and raised in the U.S., put no stock in his father's nationalistic dreams. I admitted the same to him: I didn't give a hoot about the "Red Apple Tree" of the Greek expansionist dream. So we agreed on that much, at least.

However, I was plagued by the suspicion that, as a loyal son, he might just be continuing his father's work, trying to buy my biography so as to bury it all the deeper, or put it through the shredder. If he managed to destroy the evidence I had amassed, he could close the case forever. Perhaps this man was coming to me dressed in innocence, trying to trick me into trusting him. "How did you know I was here?" I suddenly asked at one point, hoping to catch him off guard. "The university always lets us know about anything happening on campus that's related to the writers we represent," he told me. "Usually it's either a lecture or a semester-long class."

Oh, how the passage of time distances people and things. The money he was offering was a substantial sum. That night I called my wife in Athens to get her opinion. It was the 28th of October—" 'No' Day," on which Metaxas had refused, in 1941, to collaborate with the invading Italian forces—a fact that might explain her negative answer. "No contact with the enemy," she told me, which strengthened my resolve, but also left me hanging. It's easy to say no. The hard thing is to say yes. After all, what good would the absence of my biography do anyone? Whereas if it were to appear, even in censored form. . . .

The old problem of psychological identification, as the clever reader will have guessed, was once again close at hand. After all, Glafkos himself must have had similar thoughts during the period when his publisher was pressuring him to put out a collection of short stories. Should the line I took reflect the legalistic point of view Thrassakis had adopted back then—i.e., better to be in parliament, even if shredded by the electoral laws? Besides, Joe Junior hadn't said anything about cuts. I was the suspicious one. All he wanted was the rights.

I had asked Joe Junior for a night to think over his proposal. After my wife's negative response, I really started to torment myself. Our son-in-law, now completing his military service, kept sending telegraphs from Yiannitsa asking for money. My daughter, that innocent lamb who never loved anyone in her life but me, kept writing to him at his base, "Your bayonet in my loneliness," sketching clusters of spearlike rushes and a bog (her), protected by the sharp, malicious plants. How would we come up with the money to support them? And what if tomorrow our daughter told us she was pregnant again, due to his carelessness, and I ended up a grandfather once more? Wouldn't I have an increased responsibility to the children of my child? What would I ever be able to leave them, apart from the act of leaving?

My little daughter, whom I had nursed through the years and stroked back to health whenever she caught a cold and lay sick in her little bed, was at least a source of difference, warding off those fantasies in which I became Thrassakis. I knew I wasn't living some delusion of "subjective time," because there they were: Yiannitsa, a husband in khaki, and my poor girl, following him like a gypsy from base to base.

I had retreated to my room early on this evening of mental deliberation. Around eleven, nearly bursting with irritation and indecision, I went out to walk alone through the city. Thick leaves carpeted the sidewalks. In the sunlight they would have looked golden or violet, but now, at night, they rustled ominously. Naturally, the only restaurant still open at that hour was the one owned by Nick Polis's son, where Glafkos used to go for fresh oysters. Polis Junior knew me from my previous visit, and recognized me right away. We got to talking, and he expressed deep doubts concerning Thrassakis, who was not, he said, a "national writer."

"Why not?" I asked him.

"Because," he replied, "he doesn't concern himself in the slightest with the question of national identity."

"That's precisely why I'm here," I said. "My job is to keep an eye on his work, like a construction worker keeping watch over a half-finished building: I try to keep the dogs from pissing on everything, or the bums from going in to take shelter there. I protect him."

Once more, in that restaurant, I felt myself becoming Thrassakis, my chest swelling to the thickness I had seen in a few photographs, my face sprouting a fuzzy, post-puberty beard, my figure rounding out in the behind. Polis Junior, unlike Joe Junior, was still tied to idealistic delusions. I talked to him like a father. A Croat in his position, I said, would assimilate better in this country we called America. But he, a Greek, just kept spitting out the same old ancestral slogans.

"But our islands," he argued, "are in danger of being taken over by the Turks."

"Both Turkey and Greece," I replied, "get their guns from the Pentagon. So what's the difference? Calm down. Read economics. Then you can talk."

The next day Joe Junior came, having given me the night to think over his proposal. I described my biography for him, explained that it wasn't anything like André Maurois's *Disraeli*, for example, but a rather fumbling investigation, like a book written in Braille. I was constantly coming across new evidence that overturned previous statements I had made, and I had no intention of organizing it all into some kind of overarching, systematic theory, because that would go against Thrassakis's own basic method. Joe Junior couldn't expect my biography to present the kind of text some American academic might produce, in which a footnote on page 112 might refer to another footnote on page 295.

On the contrary, he should expect a text free of narrative conventions, dynamic and unobscured by artificial flavorings or fattening sauces. The development of the "plot" made use of the technological possibilities of neither zoom lenses nor camera tracks, resting solely on the strength and vividness of the subject matter itself. So it went this way and that, digressing into completely unrelated stories, simply because I was holding carrying the camera on my shoulder instead of using a tripod. I had no desire to become the oracle at Delphi, seated on her perch.

Junior Joe, as I called him, agreed with me completely about all of this. He wasn't trying to question my idiosyncratic stance towards biography. The fact that my text imitated the life of my subject, in all his fragmentariness and self-contradiction, was an added bonus, just one more thing I could be proud of. He accepted my book as it was, without changes or cuts. In that he had outdone his father, who, as an agent, always had to keep his customer (the publisher) in mind—which is why he'd been so harsh with Glafkos. Joe Junior, who had taken on the role of publisher insofar as he himself now bought the manuscripts, wasn't afraid of innovations. On the contrary, he sought them out. So there was no reason we couldn't work things out between us.

He caught me, as I've said, at a moment of Thrassakian decline. Whenever Thrassakis wasn't making money, that fact would make him doubt whether he was somebody, whether he had a purpose in life. Now I found myself faced with Joe Junior, who was promising that *Prinos II* would be republished, complete and unabridged, and that all of Thrassakis's stories would be included in the collection. This post mortem justice for Glafkos seemed like a fitting rehabilitation. So I signed the contract.

But I kept something back: I didn't give him the final chapter of my book, in which Glafkos's murder in West Berlin resembles a playing-out of one of his own stories. That I kept to myself, in a safe deposit box in a European bank. In case the sale of my text actually signified its burial, at least the most important part, the yeast, would be left for posterity. (And since the book has yet to be published in the States, my suspicions seem to be justified.)

≈

SILENCE IS CERTAINLY not golden. Whoever claims the opposite is in danger of falling prey to the magnetic pull of some other clause. The fragmentary and, to be perfectly fair to the text itself, not at all representative publication of certain excerpts from my biography in the periodical *New Stove* elicited a thunderstorm of protests. Fortunately the deceased had no direct descendants, because otherwise I wouldn't have known where to hide. Even his distant relatives had died out in a timely manner, so I didn't have to worry about a lawsuit. Nevertheless, friends and enraged fans literally bombarded me with letters, telegrams, phone calls (sometimes threatening), and documents that turned my interest conclusively toward an investigation into the cause of his death. Going back over notes I kept during the time immediately after the publication of third installment of my biography, I find a few sentences that I had jotted down:

> *Athens, early 1989. The publication of my findings to date on Thrassakis had, as one might imagine, unforeseen consequences. Masses of evidence concerning the deceased's activities and relationships have started arriving from all over the world.*

I began to organize and catalogue the material, but that just threw me back on the thankless path of writing. And I who had once declared, as perhaps the well-meaning reader will recall, "No more texts until 2003" (the year in which, I hoped, the other two sacks of his manuscripts would be opened), am here once more with my fistful of pens, tackling yet again the biographer's arduous task.

Besides, there is—why should I hide it?—a masochistic pleasure in writing about this man who no longer exists. Somewhere in my papers I once jotted down this sentence: "As long as I live, I will always be working on Thrassakis"— a frightening phrase, if you consider the consequences.

Chapter Ten

(WITH BORDER DISPUTES raging between Italy and Yugoslavia, and Marshall Tito expected to die from day to day, and encouraged by the actual death of France's President Pompidou, Croat-friendly elements infiltrated all Italian demonstrations not controlled by the Communists in an attempt to prepare the ground for an open conflict to take place in Trieste as soon as Tito bit the dust. His delay in doing so brought about small complications such as the ones affecting Lazaridis-Thrassakis, who paid the damages incurred by others. Later he was transferred, grafted like a Williams pear to the Swiss-Italian border region, from whence the pastor, through Vladimir (an Ustasi agent), collected him and threw him back into the agent's web. At that time the agent was incognito in Spoleto, from whence he sent the fateful telegraph to Thrassakis.)

The message from the agent telling him to get going must have hit Glafkos like a bullet in the gut—he was like a deer in the forest munching happily on leaves or sunning himself in a clearing, blissfully unaware of the hunter who has long had him in the sights of his rifle. The code "UThant" (which stood for "Ustasi") marked the end of his brief respite in Greece. But, one might ask, couldn't he have avoided it? For those unaware of the inner workings of Thrassakis's difficult and unbalanced life, it will no doubt prove impossible to understand how, at that critical time in his own country's history, he could have set out on a mission of such questionable character. On the other hand, the random relations and spur-of-the-moment agreements formed in the course of a lifetime are sometimes paid for indefinitely—until, that is, the final reckoning. Thrassakis had no choice but to obey the agent's telegraph, which instructed him to leave that Thursday by train on the Belgrade-Zagreb-Lubliana line. If he didn't comply, it wasn't that he'd be "done in," as some second-rate detective novel might have it, but that his book would never circulate in the States, or anywhere else, for that matter. His book, his life's work, was in the hands of the agent—who, after trimming it of its "excess ideological fat" (which is to say, all of Thrassakis's most fervent beliefs in the Leftist struggle), would put it on the market—but only if the author could prove his dedication to the (reactionary) Cause "through his active support of the Struggle."

In response to the agent's last letter ("I wash my hands of the whole affair") Glafkos had answered, "Don't abandon me." Thus he joined the dance, deciding to sacrifice his personal ego for the sake of the anonymous ego of art. And indeed, as soon as he had achieved a state of complete serenity, in his own country again after so many years, that telegraph from the agent hit him like the Devil's dart. He couldn't just pretend he'd never gotten it. It was slipped under his door, planted there like a landmine.

I attack Time with small stratagems and maneuvers, trying to harness it, to bring it down to my speed, the poor pace of narrative. Life overflows like beer foam trying to escape the narrow glass that confines it. It is the fall of 1974, and the dictatorship in Greece, the so-called "cholera," has fallen, and Glafkos and Glafka find themselves back in their homeland. (We will see his reactions to that return in a subsequent chapter of this book.) And there, in the fair autumn warmth of the Attic sun, in the honeyed atmosphere of Indian summer, when the leaves haven't yet turned, in that vague hour of afternoon before the clouds in the west take on their silver sheen (look at me, turning lyrical myself), Thrassakis receives the agent's coded telegraph ordering him to set out. Everything has been arranged, every word of the telegraph (which I luckily have in my files) means something. I have reason to believe that this specific action is undertaken in view of the pan-Communist conference in Warsaw. If Yugoslavia managed to increase its number of seats, it would then attempt to strengthen first Titoism and then Tito himself. Meanwhile, it is a known fact that Tito had already chosen his successor, a man friendly to the Soviets. The Ustasi figured that an uprising within Yugoslavia during the Warsaw conference would weaken the General's position, showing that the "iron will" with which he sought to rule his multiethnic state was in fact riddled with holes. Italy, on the other hand, confined its protests to Trieste, thus bringing together everyone in the area—Slovenians, Montenegrins, and Yugoslavians—while Greece's secession from the NATO alliance strengthened the position of the likewise non-aligned Titoism. For the Ustasi and those hiding behind them, there was no other choice but to organize some action inside the country in the hope of stirring up the stagnant waters.

So Glafkos throws whatever he can find into a suitcase and gives a goodbye kiss to Glafka, who watches mournfully as he leaves—though it bothers her less, she tells him, now that she's in her own land, among "our people," than those times when he left her alone in the cold solitude of exile. He jumps into the first passing taxi and heads north. Later on we will examine his literary reactions to this trip. But at the time, in the heat of action, he becomes what others want him to be: Agent . . . Double-O-Zero (for as we will see, he never accomplishes anything worth mentioning, though not, of course, through any fault of his own). And the scribbler within him withdraws, retreats into inner chambers, into a swampy, problem-ridden inner space, where in the end he will drown.

The plan, however, is simple. He will spend the night in Belgrade. (So as to eliminate the slightest suspicion that I might be falsifying reality, I include a piece of unshakeable evidence: his receipt from the Moscow Hotel in Belgrade, where Thrassakis stayed for at least one night, in accordance with the "UThant Plan.") The next morning he'll take the first train to Lubliana, which continues on to Paris, Calais and London, and in the first-class section of the car reading "Paris-Nord" (one half of the car is second class), he will find his liaison, a young man sitting by the window with a SHARP transistor radio made in Formosa (also home to the headquarters of the "movement for a capitalist Croatia"). He will go in and sit down (or, if there's no empty seat, stand in the aisle) and wait for the snack cart to pass by. The man with the transistor radio will order, in Italian, a coffee with milk and no sugar, a request which the train attendant will not be able to accommodate, since the coffee served on these trains always has sugar already added, so the liaison will ask for a small bottle of Slivovitz instead. As soon as the cart moves on, Glafkos will give the man a blank sheet of paper, receiving a package in return. The liaison speaks a mixture of Italian and English. They will get off together in Lubliana to attend an underground

Ustasi meeting and learn the details of a certain plan for subversive action to be carried out the following evening. The next morning Glafkos will take the first train on the Trieste-Venice-Milan line, getting off at the last stop to take shelter in the house of a friend who collects Byzantine icons.

This seemingly complex but essentially quite simple plan is carried out to the letter. In Lamia, at the People's Square, Glafkos buys *kourabiedes*, thick, roughly-cut *yioufkades*, and *halva* for his friend in Milan. At Platamona he convinces his driver to make a stop, and at a farmstand at the turnoff for the road leading towards the sea, he buys honey and thyme from Olympus, the tea of Zeus and Hera's chamomile. (Tourism taken to extremes.) Then, passing quickly through Thessaloniki—the "great mother to the poor," which stinks of the bricks being baked in her furnaces—and the brightly-lit suburb of Diavata, he reaches the border, where his train hasn't yet arrived. Thinking to get his business with the border control taken care of a bit early, he takes his passport to the checkpoint, where they take it from him without telling him why. A small wind of worry ruffles the leaves of his tree, but doesn't manage to upset the roots, since Glafkos keeps telling himself, "The dictatorship is over, we have democracy now, we'll eat the enemy's eye before he eats ours." Eventually they explain that they're only holding his passport until the train arrives, at which point all the passengers' passports will go together to the duty officer. The train arrives late, of course, and eventually the process of returning the passports to their owners begins. When Thrassakis doesn't receive his, he goes up to the station-master with ten working-class emigrants who are headed for "the mills of Germany and the mines of Belgium" and have to convert the rest of their drachma to marks or Belgian francs. He is there for another reason, of course, so while they exchange their money he finds himself in the company of a pretty, plump woman, whose passport is also being held because she was in prison for eight years for stabbing to death her unfaithful lover. Glafkos, stuck with a former murderer in this sad waiting room at the border of two countries, watching the workers exchanging their drachma for foreign currency, wonders how a life of slavery can ever be changed for freedom.

They call him into the cubby of the duty officer, who apologizes for the delay. He knows that Glafkos came by taxi, so he must have money, and thus doesn't fall into the same category as the working-class emigrants. Nevertheless, his passport is invalid due to a breach of regulations: it doesn't refer anywhere to the completion of his military obligations. When Glafkos protests that he "served our country, Captain," the officer calmly answers, "I believe you, Mr. Lazaridis. But how can I tell from this?" Glafkos is holding a copy of *The Afterimage,* back cover showing, which a friend and colleague had sent to him and which he had just finished reading. Fortunately he remembers that Glafka had insisted on his bringing along his military discharge papers, which manifestly declare that he's been in the clear with Mother Greece for untold years. The captain flips through them distrustfully, studying them closely, reading them upside-down and backwards, and something written by hand arouses his suspicions—but in the end, unable to bear the clean honesty of Glafkos's face, he gives in and stamps his passport: "EXIT."

The train ride through Yugoslavia is dull, slow and monotonous, just as Glafkos remembers it from his student years in Paris, when he often made this trip. Earthquakes are so frequent in Skopje that every so often the train tracks need to have their gravel bed replaced. So the tracks are constantly being worked on, and the train often has to inch along for long stretches with backwards and forwards manoeuvres, growling the same phrase again and again, like the hero from Camus's *The Plague,* who keeps writing the same sentence with new syntax. Is this insistence on grammatical change really just a disguised desire for a change of direction? Thrassakis the underground agent can't forget Thrassakis the scribbler: he keeps giving superficial events deeper layers of meaning. He himself will write, characteristically:

> *In approaching my old life, I proceed carefully, slowly, steadily, just as [and here, the simile] a river trying out new pathways will move slowly forward, lest it upset the outer layers of flesh, the accumulation of fat, the nerves of roots that have passed through the callous rock—lest, in short, they disembody the spiritual and therefore Dionysian achievements.*
>
> *(CDW, Vol. I, 66)*

≈

EVERYTHING WENT WELL up to Belgrade: the train arrived with its usual delay; it was raining outside, as always; and Glafkos took a cab to the Moscow Hotel.

He opened a small bottle of whiskey from the mini-bar in his room, then went out to wander around and look at the stores. He ate a cheese-pie at a place on the corner, wondering at the astonishing progress the city had made since his last visit. The Belgrade of '74 was nothing like the Belgrade he knew from '55. It was another city altogether, renewed, fresh, throbbing with the blossom of youth and the prosperity of its bourgeoisie. Meanwhile, the sense of his own inconsistency grew inside of him: how could he of all people be working for agents of the counter-revolution? Was it for the money? Though there was, or at least there should have been, a barrier to block the steep slope down: where did Thrassakis begin? Where did Lazaridis end?

Despite the droves of workers leaving to earn foreign currency abroad, Yugoslavia had attained enviable heights of success. People here weren't suffering from any kind of Balkan oppression. After his long absence during the seven years of fascist rule, Glafkos had returned home to find his own country sunk in the poverty of so-called socialist countries, while Yugoslavia, a neighboring country with thirty years of Communism under its belt, was approaching a level of prosperity (at least in Belgrade) equivalent to that found in so-called capitalist countries. Perhaps, then, the theories had opposite results in practice? These were questions that would have to remain unanswered for Thrassakis, the one-night tourist—but they strongly affected his frame of mind concerning the devilish agent's desired goal.

What was more important, in the end, was not what he was going through, but what was going through him. Like the good conductor of progress he is, like it or not, every writer cannot help seeing what he sees and asking himself: what's my role in all this? Perhaps I'm a kind of pitiful policeman, utterly powerless, transferred to the borders as punishment in some intra-departmental settlement? What am I seeking? And why am I in the hands of the Montenegrin agent, who might have his own reasons, personal or hereditary, for seeking the suspension of progress? Yugoslavia, at that moment, is an emergency exit. A slim ray of hope that the means of mass production won't manage to abolish entirely all forms of personal initiative. As the country in which the first World War began and the third would no doubt end, it had every right, as far as Thrassakis was concerned, to his regard and respect. We can imagine with what heart (what longing and what passion) he must have continued the mistake of his mission the next morning. But when you're dealing with international mobs, you can't change anything on your own. You need the godfather's consent—and that was the conflict that brought about his well-known end.

He still hadn't recovered from the shock of the previous evening when a bell-boy woke him from his siesta at half-past five to catch the night train at half-past seven on the Zagreb-Lubliana-Trieste-Milan-Paris line. (The thoughts described above would most likely have occurred to him in hindsight, after his failure. Remorse, as everyone knows, is constructed in the following manner: if the murderer doesn't succeed, he feels remorse and hopes for forgiveness from his near-victim. If he does succeed, he rightly thinks, "What's the use of regretting now?" After all, the victim is already in the next world.)

So Thrassakis found the car with the sign reading "Paris-Nord," searched through the part of the car marked with a yellow line signifying first class, and spotted the liaison, a hefty man fed on malted milk and other such nourishing capitalistic substances, in a red sweater and blue-gray pants with pegged legs, and shoes like those being advertised in western magazines two decades before, perhaps the time of his last trip "abroad." The train swayed on tracks that were constantly being repaired. Then it took a bend toward the horizon, and the liaison settled horizontally into his seat, stretching his long legs over the discarded sports pages of Slavic newspapers tossed on the seat across from him. Soon the snack cart passed by, and everything proceeded according to plan. Thanks to the sugared coffee and the Slivovitz, Glafkos verified that the man he had picked was indeed the liaison, and approached. Just then they were passing through the only tunnel of the entire journey, and the liaison took advantage of the darkness to rise, kiss Glafkos on either cheek, and thank him in French for his enormous contribution to the difficult Struggle.

The landscape unfolded before him, socialist, homogenized, everywhere the same: ducks and cabbages. Lazarus had never seen so much cabbage growing by so many rivers whose banks were home to so many ducks. Once, passing through East Germany, he had witnessed this same ostentatious absence of ostentation that seemed to mark the socialist landscape—after all, in the absence of competition, who needs a storefront display to showcase the goods? Here, however, the cabbages seemed to have no reason whatsoever to exist. They looked like endless green ellipses on black soil, while the ducks, eternal accents above the eternal vowels of eternal sentences, tried to spoil them by leaving foot-prints in the margins, like corrections on a badly-spelt text.

≈

I AM LIKE a spider spinning its thread in the void. You see a drop hanging from space by its legs, but the thread that keeps it hanging there—the spider's dried-up fluid, angst spun into web—is invisible. This first, insignificant spider, which hasn't yet created its nook, its web, shouldn't feel safe, since it's no more than a mouthful for the first beak that happens by, while the second spider—the spider-dream, the yo-yo spider (game and player in one)—can easily destroy the fly. So, though at first it is unprotected and exposed to the madness of whatever beak might happen by, after it sets up its web in some corner or crossroad, the spider becomes, in the new power scheme, deadly. Such a spider, then, am I, hanging suspended in space, trying to dress myself in words. I'm cold!

(*CDW*, Vol. II, 34)

≈

EN ROUTE TO Lubliana he gazes out of the train window at the autumn landscape. After Zagreb—a pretty city, as he sees it through the pane, old, with smoke-stained walls—the train, in order to make up for the delay, stops for only a short time at each station. Thrassakis, the secret agent, can't help remembering that it was on this same nighttime journey that James Bond fought his toughest battle with the evil blond guy, whom he of course ended up beating hands down. He can't help remembering the scene when the train, entering Zagreb, appears on the screen with the name of the city appearing backwards across it: ꓱꓤꓛAꓜ.The train in the movie had been a badly-made model, not at all realistic, as he now has the opportunity to ascertain. His identification with Sean Connery (James Bond), even if subconscious, shows the extent of his own megalomania, and hints at the agent's cleverness in letting him believe that he too is playing on the big screen, in big scenes, while keeping him from realizing the enemy's true strength. But are the Yugoslavians really Glafkos's enemies? Why? They're not Turks, they're not Muslim. He looks so much like them that in the beginning the stewards and conductors start speaking to him in their own language. It's only when they see his expensive, thick-heeled shoes and some trinkets on his wrist that they fall back into their habitual silence.

Throughout the trip, Glafkos notes people's gestures and the expressions on their faces, trying to guess how unhappy they are, what they think of the system, of their lives in this place—but to no avail. From the train all you can see is a city's back, or an arc of waist. Maybe a glimpse of nipple. But nothing more. As for the people, you end up paying more attention to their luggage. When two trains pass and you gaze through the double panes into the cars going the other way, the people seem almost like Polaroid images flashing by.

After Zagreb, he starts to get nervous. Now there is no other stop until Lubliana, where he is supposed to get off. The liaison is fiddling with his transistor radio, trying to get some station to come in clearly. The landscape outside the window is unbelievably beautiful, rivers and mountains, a dreamy Tempi, but Thrassakis, usually moved by beauty, can't enjoy it as he would like to, with carefree ecstasy. He's on the job—*boulot*, as the French say. So he goes into the other part of the car, on the other side of the divider between the first and second class seats, to take his mind off his worries by talking to some Greeks he first noticed at the border control, on their way to Germany. They're going to change trains in Lubliana, they tell him, because this train is going to Paris, "where people study," while they, they explain, are going for "work"—*arbeit*, in German. Where? In the *papiergesacht*, one man says.

The seats in the second class section of the car are smaller, more cramped, less comfortable. In crossing the divide between the two sections, the thing that suddenly makes you feel like you're in some kind of lower-class neighborhood is, as he puts it succinctly in one of his short stories, the sudden

density of every square meter. The economically underprivileged have at their disposal only the smallest space in which to coexist. Since this fact is not ordained by any street plan, the differentiating element in the passage from one class to another must be sought not so much in the priest's cassock as in the priest himself, whose skinniness, a result of malnutrition, makes that cassock hang on him like the sails of a ship.

(CDW, Vol. II, 315)

People hesitate to accept you as one of them if you don't come from their side of the tracks. They wonder (and rightly so), "What does he want from us? Why is he here?" The Greeks sitting in second class are distrustful of Glafkos's approach. The wealthier man's call to abolish the boundaries blocking communication remains unanswered, because the worker, seeing in the first-class traveller all the characteristics of his own boss, can no longer distinguish between the two. For the worker, economic ease is equated with his boss. Which is something that Thrassakis knows, from having lived it long ago—but, beggar for human communication that he is, he never tires of trying again and again, knowing that if you hit a skull repeatedly against the same spot on the wall, the skull won't break, but the wall will weaken bit by bit until it reaches the breaking point and cracks. So the word *papiergesacht*, pronounced coldly by the emigrant, fails to discourage him or make him uncomfortable—on the contrary, since it's something that concerns him directly, he starts up a conversation, saying how much he himself has been hurt by the paper shortage, the *papierkrisen*, since it has kept his works from being published for so many years.

Because ever since joining forces with the agent, he has become the least published writer of his time. The agent, who holds all his clients' strings, keeps telling Thrassakis that the worldwide paper shortage is forcing publishers to cut back their programs. While there is a grain of truth in this, it is nevertheless intended to conceal the agent's decision to ruin Thrassakis, since he has come to believe that Thrassakis is working as a double agent of Communist infiltration in the anti-Tito organization to which the agent belongs. The agent wants to destroy him first as a writer, and then to follow up with his physical annihilation (the annihilation of Lazaridis, that is—a task far easier than the first). In the last years of his life, Glafkos, through the agent, receives countless rejections, always with mention of the paper shortage—and though he tries to escape from the agent's sorcery, seeking a representative in some other agency, Joe has tentacles everywhere, like a Kafkian father or a hundred-armed Buddha who blocks Glafkos's every move. Whenever Thrassakis sends out SOS signals, his would-be saviors reply, "Why are you coming to us? You have the best agency in the world. Your agency loves you, it has your best interest in mind," thus exposing him to the eyes of the agent himself, who follows his moves with an unquenchable, vampiric thirst for blood. In an attempt to placate the beast, Glafkos accepts minor roles in the agent's political schemes—serving as deputy to the Balkans, for instance—understanding neither the ridiculousness of his position nor the extent of the larger snare into which he has fallen.

So he starts up a conversation with this poor working-class emigrant, who knows all about paper (he makes it, after all), though its crisis in the market is nothing compared to his own: he, like so many of his compatriots, conscripts in the New World Proletariat, is in danger of being fired because of the cyclical cutbacks capitalism requires.

The man's entire extended family fills the car. His mother in her black kerchief is old, but still beautiful, the straight-backed custodian of traditions whose place on this train Glafkos questions. The worker's wife looks more harried than her mother-in-law, young in years but not in spirit, perhaps because she has no tradition to guard and is dressed in European clothes that only serve to reveal the bowling pins of her calves, muscled by years of washing and baking. She too will be working in the mills, then coming straight *heim* in the evenings to take care of not only the children, but her mother-in-law as well.

The worker's wife has managed to transform the train car into her own temporary hangout, opening the curtains for the baby, shelling hardboiled eggs and sprinkling them with salt and pepper; she has piles of cassettes in the white plastic coffins of their cases, ready to indulge her family's longing for the homeland they've just left. The son, about fourteen, perhaps from her husband's first marriage, is studying the train schedule and trying to guess how late they will be arriving at each station. He's an old hand at all this—it isn't the first time he has left his homeland. He tries to comfort his black-kerchiefed grandmother, who asks for no comforting from him. He watches the man from first class (Glafkos) talking with his father, and answers question about when they'll be arriving where, figuring out the delays according to the geometric progression of their slow progress. Glafkos doesn't smoke, but accepts a cigarette for fear of being misunderstood. He doesn't light it, but keeps it tucked like a greengrocer's pencil behind his ear.

And thus the family passed their time on the train. The divider between the first and second class sections slid open every now and then. Glafkos need only have taken a step or two to be back in first class, where he belonged. And then . . .

. . . the train seemed to stop. He looked outside and saw the same magical landscape unfolding before him like a movie set. Used by now to these periodic stops—sometimes for the rails to be fixed, sometimes to let a cow cross the tracks, sometimes for the engine to be oiled—the passengers showed no curiosity concerning this additional, unannounced stop. There was a station outside, a small, charming building. Only when the train started up again and the baby whimpered and the kerchiefed grandmother crossed herself for some unknown reason, did Glafkos, returning to his own section, find the liaison's seat empty. He must have gotten off during that short stop—in fact, it might have been made specially for that purpose. Glafkos wondered whether to get off at Lubliana or go on to Venice, where he was eventually supposed to meet up with Joe. He looked through his bags. Nothing had been touched. Then he saw the small transistor radio watching him from its corner. He panicked, not knowing what to do. Finally he picked up the radio and stuffed it into his bag. Perhaps that was the message for the agent. . . . In the meantime, the train kept moving. It arrived in Lubliana. And there Thrassakis made the big decision not to get off. He gazed out at the city's white buildings and the sign for the Lev Hotel that stuck up above the surrounding buildings, marking the place where he was to have spent the night, and counted the minutes until the train would pull out of the station. When the engine finally started up again he took a deep breath, stood up and went back to talk to the family in second class. Only then did he see them—how could he have forgotten!—on the train platform, looking for their connecting train, which would take them to their factory, to the *papiergesacht* and the *krisen*.

≈

GLAFKA IS WAITING for him in Venice, having arrived by boat earlier that day. His appointment with the agent was originally scheduled for the 27th. They had decided on that date because Glafkos was supposed to stay a night in Lubliana. It is now the 25th. Late. Almost the 26th. So the couple has an entire day at their disposal.

What happened happened. There's no going back to might-have-beens. All that matters now is how a couple spends their day in Venice. They get up in the morning and go for coffee at an artsy little café by the Fenice Theater, then walk to St. Mark's. The shops are open and people are strolling through the narrow streets of this floating city. The sanitation strike hasn't yet reached the magnitude of a plague, but it limits the tourists' freedom of movement. Groups of tourists with plastic nametags pinned to their chests follow umbrellas raised like swords, readied for the storming of some museum or restaurant or *vaporetto*. The locals, withdrawn into their shells, seem reconciled to the double flood of tourists and lagoon. The absence of tires, exhaust, and carburetors, gives walking a charm that no motorboat or barge can disturb. Everything seems slightly damp—the leather shops, the windows full of umbrellas, the people bumping into one another on bridges or sudden corners unmarked by the fat, round mirrors that let cars see what's coming from the other direction. The city has outlived its myth. The people have outlived their history. Everything is rooted in water and the water is rooted in a reef. It is difficult to imagine contracts being signed here. Here the strong foundation of dry land that elsewhere supports the signing of signatures is missing. Perhaps the only contract you could imagine being signed here would be for the chartering of boats. The boats, indeed, seem perfectly at home: houseboats like apartments, with halls, living rooms, bathrooms. The sea, domesticated—not an anonymous port lined with cranes, but eponymous piers with antique gates, the inheritance of centuries.

The couple takes the *vaporetto* to Murano, cruising around the back part of the "Manhattan" of central Venice. It isn't a particularly inviting neighborhood: a hospital overlooking a floating graveyard. Line 5 is filled with women in black carrying flowers. Murano is a quiet place, all Dutch canals and quaint barges. The two of them stroll around, window shopping, and buy a pair of socks, since Thrassakis forgot his at the Moscow Hotel in Belgrade. They visit the Crystal Museum and the workshops where craftsmen blow out bubbles of glass as big as beach balls. They buy souvenirs. Glafka also buys an expensive little vase, at a reduced price due to a small imperfection that only a specialist could detect, as a present for the agent's wife, who will be arriving with him the following day.

≈

THE TRAIN, arriving late, missed the rain, which left its mark on the wet earth, like a woman who wets kerchiefs with holy water and leaves, holding her solitude together with clothespins.

(*CDW*, Vol. II, 116)

≈

THE NEXT DAY, Glafkos and Glafka set out from their humble pension to find the Big Boss at the luxurious Baeur Grunenwald Hotel. On their way in the door, the porter, ready to stop them, asks who they're looking for. As soon as they say Joe's name, the porter suddenly becomes as sweet as saccharin, like ice melting into water, bending over backwards to usher them in. Thrassakis has repeatedly stated his dislike for hotels as meeting places, since they symbolize the temporariness of relationships he would like to be more permanent (in this case, his relationship with the agent). Nevertheless, he goes in. The green pasta he ate late the night before didn't sit well with him. Even now, in the lobby of the four-star Baeur Hotel, his heartburn is so bad it makes his knees shake. And though Joe is waiting for him in the lobby, he takes refuge in the bathroom, where the toilet is stopped up. "Such an expensive hotel and they haven't even bothered to unclog the shitter," he says out loud in Greek, sure that no one else in there would understand him. But from the next stall a bass voice answers, "Good things come to those who wait."

Joe is moody. The conversation that follows doesn't go well. Glafkos's mission has failed, of course through no fault of his own, but still, Joe is upset. Joy tries, as always, to smooth things over, to balance the imbalance, offering coffee, cigarettes, extensive observations about everyday things, but she can't manage to save any of them from the shipwreck of Joe's displeasure. Everyone knew from the outset of the operation that Thrassakis would be involved. So either he himself is a double agent, or he's being so closely followed that any further use of him could prove fatal to the organization. That, in short, is what Joe tells him in the privacy of the hotel suite to which they have retreated. A supporter of the organization—a ticket collector on the train—informed the liaison that a trap had been set for him in Lubliana. Glafkos struggles to remember the ticket collector's face, but to no avail. At one point during the meeting Joe goes to the window and gazes in the direction of Istria with the nostalgia of Unamuno looking across the French border at his beloved Spain. "It will be ours again, in time," he sighs, returning his gaze to the room and its gold-adorned ceiling. Glafkos notes that his eyes are wet with emotion. At one time, during his years in exile, such a moment would have moved him, because he would have seen himself in the other's eyes. Now, having returned to his country, his nostalgia cured by a hefty dose of the homeland, he sees Joe as something rather anachronistic—which is, perhaps, why he pities him.

≈

BUT HOW DID he spend the rest of that day in Venice? Though Glafkos tells us very little, now that we are familiar with his style of writing, it isn't hard to guess from his silences all the things he doesn't stress. His fear, for instance, that the Big Boss would be so overwhelmed with disappointment that he might bite the dust in a city not known, shall we say, for its vitality. What if he, an Orthodox, wanted to be buried next to Stravinsky in Venice's Orthodox cemetery, looking out from his marble mausoleum at his parents' Montenegro on the opposite bank of the Styx? Just the thought of it scared him—which is why he was careful about what he said to Joe, and how he said it. He agreed with everything Joe's said, joking with Joy until her husband's anger subsided, as well as his own heartburn. Then, on leaving the Baeur Hotel, he saw some dead rats floating in the canal of his beloved Venice. What he didn't realize was that the agent had already dismissed him. And if I pity Glafkos, it's because he didn't have the slightest clue about was really going on. Like a girl who falls for some professional seducer, whose feelings continue to grow even as he is plotting to abandon her. And we feel sadness and pity wash over us for her pretty eyelashes and slim cheekbones or the green irises of her eyes, from which we can already see the path her tears will soon follow.

Chapter Eleven

WITH MY DEADLINE fast approaching, I had to wrap things up. I wouldn't have pushed forward in search of other conclusions if I hadn't been sure of the one I had already reached: Thrassakis had fallen victim to an ill-starred fate. How, where, and why? My general policy is not to give away the next installment too soon. But the continuity implied by the installment plan isn't easy to handle with a work as capricious and erratic as the one I have undertaken.

I was broken with disappointment. I kept thinking of a friend of mine who had spent his whole life writing a book about Heironymous Bosch, and just as he was putting the finishing touches on his manuscript, he saw a review in the *Times Literary Supplement* of a book that had just come out about the very same artist.

Thrassakis's death hit me hard in the chest, like a boomerang on its backswing, dismantling everything I had found or written up to that point. Should I start over? No, I didn't have the strength—not to mention the time or money. My grandson's upbringing had literally absorbed me, to the extent that people had begun to accuse me of being secretly in love with my daughter. But it was the only way I could avoid madness. Because that was the only point on which I trumped Thrassakis, hands down: he didn't have a daughter. Luck had guarded him. And me.

I went back to Copenhagen with an SAS ticket given to me by that same reporter friend. I wanted to speak with the mad Danish woman again, the sole survivor. She invited me to her country house, which had been a communications tower in Kierkegaard's time. She had faded with the passing years, but her eyes still flashed now and then. Before I said a word, before I so much as opened my mouth, she treated me to a Macedonian salad, fruit salad drenched in a syrup made with liquor. So there was no need for me to say much in the way of introduction; I knew right away that she understood the reason for my visit.

"If you hadn't allied yourself so completely with that pansy of a pastor, God forgive him," she said, "perhaps I would've been able to help you sooner. The Thrassakis case is one of those mysteries like the Markovic affair—he was a close friend of Alain Delon as well as of Pompidou's wife—or the Mavrogenis affair, which took place here in Denmark and provided the inspiration for Thrassakis's novella *Murdicide*. He himself had foreseen his own passage through those dark files. Look."

And she gave me to read:

"Poetic treatment of the phenomenon is insufficient. Journalistic treatment almost non-existent. Prose analysis, essays, can surely prove more fruitful. For the time being, everything is suspended, waiting for better ways of renewal to be found."

With that, he made mention of the Montenegro issue yet again, then collected his papers and stepped down from the podium.

"This note was written in Berlin a few days before his tragic end," explained the Lady of the Seven Gothic Parables. "Not in the Grunwald forest, where Mavrogenis had been murdered, but in the Wansee forest, the Kleinen Wansee to be precise, on the banks of the frozen lake."

"So you agree," I asked, "that I should start looking around there somewhere?"

"I've given up," the old lady said with a sigh. "I searched at the time and found nothing but a few scattered writings. He had dedicated some of his best poems to me. For me, that's enough. The rest is for the dogs."

And she handed me a poem that he had dedicated to her:

Day passed full of food.
Night came full of dreams.
If the dreams have something
to do with food,

it is in their resemblance
to excrement.
Yet I believe
it is self-evident:
The slave who works for his master
in wet dreams each night,
will one day break his chains
and kill him.

As soon as I had read it she threw herself at me, exclaiming that I reminded her so much of Glafkos that she wanted . . . she wanted. . . . As for me, it wasn't that I didn't want . . . but the thought that she saw me as another Glafkos drove me crazy. I couldn't bear that kind of erotic identification. And contrary to my intentions, I once again left at a run.

The old butler standing at the door helped me find a taxi. He'd had a soft spot in his heart for Greeks, he told me, ever since, decades ago, in mythic times, their princess Anna Maria had married one of our kings.

PART II

THE FINDINGS OF THE FIRST SACK

"The man writes: that's his business. I don't read him: that's mine. No one forces the man to write. No one forces me to read: I like reading, but I don't like reading what the man writes. To each his own."

(*CDW*, Vol. 1)

The Misunderstanding

THIS IS THE TITLE of one of the first stories I came across on opening the first sack of Thrassakis's papers in the States. The story describes an actual misunderstanding: A man is wrongly arrested, not with the kind of metaphysical injustice that Kafka's Joseph K. experiences, but rather according to the natural development of the events that the story presents. Ideologically speaking, the text should be placed in a period of decline for the "fighter" Thrassakis, since at the time of its composition he was trying to distance himself from whatever was considered, back then, "active resistance" (i.e., armed struggle). But before we get into any of that, let's take a look at the plot.

The hero, a handsome young *maggiore*, justly believes (or, at any rate, believes that he justly believes) that society has treated him unjustly, and that it owes him something in return. At the beginning of the story he appears as an anonymous aesthete gazing with narcissistic absorption at his own image in the Tiber. He becomes Livio when the river's waters recede and he is forced to return to his name. The place is Rome, the year 1973.

Livio, born poor, wants nothing more than to escape his poverty, by whatever means necessary. His first forays into the realm of the Left are soon discouraged by his personal encounters with various leftist elements whom he sees sitting comfortably by the paternal hearth, willing to give it all up (or so they say) when the time is ripe. But while for them "time" means waiting in the lap of luxury, Livio is living in conditions of extreme poverty and need. The Left is promising him a *future* new order—but until it comes, he will have to endure the exploitation of the capitalist system.

167

If Livio had obtained some degree of education, the author suggests, perhaps he might have joined the "rock of waiting." But Livio is eager to escape his "unjust fate." He wants to live. And just as a lame dog will try, despite its infirmity, to follow the path of the hare, Livio chases after the possibility of a release from poverty.

Because of his good looks, it would be hard for him to get caught up in the arteriosclerotic gears of the leftist leagues, to serve the interests of the labor representatives who end up, in the best case scenario, with no more than a hefty pension. So, having realized that in a capitalist country with a strong leftist movement, the most advantageous political position for an individual to take involves the objective criticism of the cream of both political crops—that of the old inheritance (Pope) as well as that of the new (Party)—and having realized early on that just as a woman is "grounded" (as in the "grounding" of an electrical current) only upon the birth of her child, a man can only be sure of his position once he has achieved economic independence—having realized all this, Livio passes with breathtaking speed through all the phases of leftist alienation. Left of the Italian Communist Party, left of the Party's most left-leaning faction, left of the leftist extra-parliamentarians, left of the most left-leaning extremists among them, he finally ends up becoming . . . an interior decorator.

And there Livio really finds himself, really begins to feel at home, as it were. He is twenty-two years old. As an orphan, he is exempt from military service. He flirts with rich women, Catholics and Communists alike, concerned only with his own success, his own attempt to wash himself clean of the mud and mire of poverty.

It doesn't take long for success to knock on his door. As the narrator tells us, "He is young, handsome and strong, and can do what he likes." Livio soon makes his way into the uppermost climbs of high society, where "ideological boundaries are abolished." "Borders," Thrassakis writes, "are formed by rivers, gorges, ravines. At the summit, there is harmony."

Livio sells his ideas at a high price to his rich women friends. He sells perspective, air. But in stealing from the rich, who live by stealing from the poor, he feels almost like an instrument of justice. Secretly, inside, he despises the class he exploits, and sides with the exploited—ideologically, religiously, or physically—all over the world.

But no one is above corruption, and even Livio begins to develop curious tastes. He likes kitsch, he likes antiques. Thrassakis contrasts his fall to the rise of the working-class movement in Italy. While these two trends aren't actually interdependent within the story, Thrassakis presents the alienation of the individual who insists on his individuality as antithetical to the development of mass consciousness that is strengthening the Party's position with each passing election.

Until we reach the fateful night. It is spring, and as always at that time of year, the rivers of milling people have swelled in the streets. On this particular night a demonstration, organized by the trade unions, is being held in the Piazza Del Popolo. The author avoids telling us the specific cause behind the demonstration, but we suspect it has something to do with Vietnam and Cambodia. Two different groups set out from two different points: the unionists from Piazza San Silvestro, working-class people, mature and disciplined, women with babies in their arms; and the extra-parliamentarians from Piazza Di Spania, torches already lit, shouting rhythmic slogans that startle the tourists. The first group will head down Via Del Corso, the second down Via Del Babuino, and they will meet in the Piazza Del Popolo.

Livio, meanwhile, is standing amidst a scattering of workmen's tools in some rich woman's penthouse, telling her how he and his crew will continue their work the next morning on the fireplace-to-be, now littered with lime and sacks of cement. The woman (whose daughter is not, as her mother believes, at the Law School, but marching with the extra-parliamentarians at the demonstration) is wearing extremely high heels that make it almost impossible for her to walk through the site without stumbling. She is telling Livio about her dream of surrounding the fireplace with translucent stones that would reflect the flames in watery shimmerings of light. Piazza Navona, she tells him, is paved with such stones, by the northeast fountain as you come in from the Campo De' Fiori. They are always damp from the fountain, and easily uprooted. But any theft of state property, she says, is punishable with up to five years in prison.

Then, since the dust from the cement powder is making her cough, and coughing stretches the skin on her face, already stretched to its outermost limit by the facial she just had to smooth out her wrinkles, she suggests that they go out onto the terrace.

The night is moonless but mild. The cries from the demonstration drift weakly up to their ears—the speakers are shouting out slogans, fanning the flames of the crowd, and the crowd shouts back, and a pocket of air brings these cries storming up as far as the terrace on which Livio and his client are standing.

Soon the two part ways, each driving off in his or her four-wheeled bug of a car.

In the second part of the story, the demonstration has officially ended, and the organizers are shouting through their megaphones for the crowd to disperse peacefully and avoid any kind of provocation. Thrassakis offers snapshots of the protesters as the crowd slowly disperses: a chance meeting, a father who has brought his daughter to the demonstration, "We haven't seen you in a while," and, "The kid was sick." But though the extra-parliamentarians pretend to go along with the resolution to break up peacefully, they secretly meet up again in the Campo De' Fiori—unassailable property of revolutionary youth—and from there continue their protests more forcefully (read: more actively). This fact does not, however, pass unobserved by the police, who are keeping tabs on the demonstrators' movements through CB radio. (Thrassakis uses actual documents from a mimeographed magazine put out by an extreme leftist group whose own wireless radio picked up these conversations. Street names are given in code, using the names of plants, while the different groups of protestors are identified by colors, such as "the Yellow" and "the Red.") The police circle closes in around the site of this new gathering, the Campo De' Fiori, right next to Piazza Navona, where Livio is eating ice cream with some of his architect friends. By now it is past ten, and he is eating a *spezialità*, tight as a snowball and dark as dried shit. He has one eye constantly trained on the northwest fountain, which, like its counterpart in the northeast corner, is surrounded by translucent stones. (After all, while a bank teller normally has no need to think about work on an evening out with his friends, the "slave sharpshooter," as he calls the "freelance" professional, never has "free time," even on his day off.) As an airplane passes low over the square, struggling to rise into the air, Livio stands up with his bag in hand, letting the others suppose, perhaps, that he has seen the shadow of someone he knows flickering over the square.

He walks up to the fountain and makes a sudden move. The breeze from his body pushes the hanging globe of water, shifting the umbrella of light. Water runs from the mouths and nipples of plump angels. The fish are unmoving, hypnotized in the artificial pond. A dog trots by. A ball bounces on the pavement. In the background, the familiar humming crowd circles the outdoor painters and benches of glow-in-the-dark necklaces and wind-up birds. The time is ripe. He bends. The stone shines, glistening like a row of teeth. He lifts it out with his pocket-knife. The damp earth offers no resistance. From the side, the angular stone, sharp and pointed downward, looks like an agate tooth. The agile Livio quickly wraps it in a towel and stuffs it into his bag. If someone looking out over the square had noticed him, they would have thought he had bent to tie his shoe. He returns to his friends. No one suspects a thing. To show how little time has elapsed since Livio left the table, Thrassakis tells us that his ice cream has just started to melt around the edges.

Then, at that precise moment, the chase begins. Streams of students start first to trickle, then to pour in through all the entrances to the square. They come running in and then, as soon as they're sure they are safe within the embrace of this place, stop and transform themselves into sight-seeing tourists just passing through. The fact that this square was once used for regattas supports the image Thrassakis constructs of the waters now filling it once more as the flood-gates open and the persecuted protestors stream in, stung by tear gas, thinking they are entering some kind of sacred space, like a church. After all, the *cara-binieri* wouldn't dare chase them into this haven of tourism, this fountainhead of foreign exchange.

The ever-present hippies and caricature artists who have set up shop in the square, the hawkers with their wind-up birds, are all worried and upset. They, Thrassakis tells us, are the first to foresee the mayhem to come.

As indeed it does. Through those very same floodgates stream the shielded, helmeted, plastic-encased instruments of the law. The police vans rush in and line up to take in the hostages. All exits have been closed off. Whoever is in the square is no longer free to leave.

"What's going on?" the peaceful café customers ask, first nervous, then terrified. A student posing as a customer calmly describes, as if he were talking about the weather, how the police had attacked the gathering of protestors in the Campo De' Fiori. Fighting broke out, and everyone who had come here had done so in order to escape arrest. Instead, they had been caught like mice. But even he can't explain why the police are pushing the protestors so violently into the vans. The roundup is, of course, carried out on the basis of age. So Livio and his friends are locked up along with the protestors, even though they offer their ice cream as unshakeable evidence of their innocence. How could they have ordered, eaten, and attended a demonstration, all within a quarter of an hour? The less enraged officers assure them that they just want to check their records, and they will soon be free to go.

And indeed they do let most of them go, but they keep Livio, because they find the translucent rock in his bag.

The third and final part of "The Misunderstanding" is, as the reader might guess, also the most dramatic. The officer who interrogates Livio is convinced that the paving stone found in Livio's possession was intended to be used against the aforementioned instruments of the law. There were at least twenty officers wounded that night by similar stones, pulled up by "long-haired hot-heads" in the Campo De' Fiori. Livio tries in vain to defend himself. If he had planned on throwing it at them, he argues, why would it have been wrapped up in a towel in his bag when they arrested him? The fateful stone is resting on the interrogator's desk like a tooth on a dentist's workspace. Covered in roots, dried soil, and marks like bruises, as if blood had collected under the surface of its skin. It is porous, and the interrogation lights irradiate the veins inside. It really would have been magical in the light of the fireplace. But with the threat of five years in prison for the destruction of state property hanging over his head, Livio is unable to explain the real reason he had uprooted it from the square.

Livio's tormentor, staring at the corners of the stone, which might have bashed in the helmet or skull of any one of his comrades, gives Livio a sound beating when he insists on his innocence. Finally the blows come to an end and they send him in, bloodied, to join the other students. But since none of them have ever seen him before, they suspect him of being a spy planted by the police to infiltrate their ranks and nail them from the inside. One first-year student, a Maoist, even puts his finger under Livio's nose to see if the blood is real or just marker. Thus Livio, the victim of one misunderstanding, now suffers a second.

In the morning the chosen victims appear in court, where they are given harsh sentences in an attempt to discourage future anarchist uprisings. So Livio spends a while in jail, until the rich woman comes to get him released. Her skin is stretched so tight that she can neither cough nor laugh. She is the only one who knows the truth.

≈

ONE OF THE ISSUES Thrassakis raises in this story, which I retold rather poorly, is that there can be no "individual" freedom independent of the "church" of the state. History, he means to say, isn't just what we make of it, but what it makes of us. In Ancient Greek, an *idiotis* (the source of the English "idiot") was a man who didn't take part in the affairs of the community. Someone who, during earth-shattering eras, kept on building his fireplace, so to speak. Though he was too young to take part in Greece's civil war, our author was nonetheless a victim of that historic confrontation, since his generation had to pay the damages incurred. Hence his deeply-rooted belief that there is no such thing as an innocent observer. Everyone is a participant of one sort or another. Everyone is responsible, actors and audience alike.

Piazza Navona—an irrefutable witness to the flow of history, used in different ways throughout the centuries, whose historical consciousness remains strongly present in the layerings of its architectural foundations (a fragment of ancient years shows through a hole in the road)—provides a perfect setting, a semi-circular amphitheater in which the drama will play itself out. And the side streets that empty into its basin are secret passageways that bring forth from the unknown the protagonists of History: the demonstrators on one side, tear gas on the other.

Thrassakis's story condemns naïveté. For example, just when one of the architects is cracking some joke about his ice cream being "so hard that if you threw it at the cops, it'd be sure to break a few heads," and the others are laughing at his joke, a "secret hum" is heard coming from the Campo De' Fiori, winding them in its spidery web. Soon it will break all their heads and they won't be joking anymore. Before the police rush in, Livio and his friends resemble those summer tourists near the Spanish border who, seeing refugees from the civil war passing over in endless hunted caravans (as the Jews would shortly after), naïvely asked, "What's going on?"—unwilling (and here's the rub) to worry, to get involved. Advocates through and through of the motto, "Don't trouble trouble till trouble troubles you." (At this point I can't say for sure whether Thrassakis was consciously influenced by John Reed's *Ten Days that Shook the World*, in which people are calmly watching a play in a St. Petersburg theater at the height of the October Revolution.) The story censures the kind of people whom Thrassakis elsewhere calls "spatial grays," who believe in neither black nor white, but in a mixture of the two. In this sense the piece is characteristic of the time at which it was written, since back then the critical question hadn't yet been answered as to whether or not a peaceful passage into Socialism can be achieved by means of protests, strikes, parliaments and elections. Or if the flexibility of a ruling class that allows for dissent from within the system is actually its greatest strength. (It is, after all, the elasticity of a metal that gives a bridge its give.)

So what about Livio? Is he a positive or negative character? In my mind, he's both. Positive in that he is punished. In prison he is isolated from the other prisoners as well as the guards. He lives in a double solitude. Because history always demands decisions—for or against, with one group or the other. Whoever chooses not to choose sides is sitting, so to speak, between two chairs. But Livio is a negative presence in that he simply adds yet another, perhaps redundant example to the infinite spectrum of bourgeois individualists. What exactly is the author trying to say when Livio starts decorating his prison cell, rearranging it and tidying it up, studying its tiles as if they too were paving stones from Piazza Navona? That there is such a thing as personal redemption? That hard work pays off? If I were Thrassakis, I would surely have cut those scenes in which his hero finds redemption through work. Elsewhere he tells us that Livio's passion for antiques is a symptom of decadence, since that kind of refined taste cannot be justified in a society in which so many basic needs remain unfulfilled. But then, at the end of the story, Livio's renewed passion for interior decoration (now in the context of his prison cell) seems to leave a crack open for individual escape. Which is a clearly anti-dialectical solution.

The fact that Livio can't give a convincing explanation for his possession of the stone drives him to a fateful misunderstanding with the police. If he had admitted to having stolen it, perhaps he might have avoided the worst consequences of that action. But given the recent vandalism of Michelangelo's "Pieta" in St. Peter's, perhaps he was afraid of being convicted of "the removal of an essential part of the square." (Here Thrassakis refers to his own situation with regard to Law 509, under which he was convicted of "the removal of an essential part of the state," the amphora from Thassos which others planted in his bag.)

We haven't yet mentioned the narrative technique. It does not, of course, simply present action, but offers a chemical analysis of action. There are certain memorable descriptive passages, such as the stream of associations flowing

from the stone, which reminds him of the cobbled streets of his youth, in neighborhoods built on steep slopes—by the church of Agios Yiannis, of course, in
Kavala. The size of the paving stones told you how steep the road was: the steeper
the slope, the narrower and smaller the stones, to give the cars' tires more notches
to grab onto, like a cogged train climbing up the slopes of some mountain. And
from there his mind runs to pre-war yogurt in the big ceramic pots, and how the
yogurt maker would slice out servings with a spatula and throw them like stones
onto the scale—and then he returns once more to Livio, after his ramble
through the narrow, sunless streets of his youth.

The Cave

HE AND HIS model, made in his image, the ignorant reader might think in reading the opening paragraphs of this story, unable to anticipate the Thrassakian
developments to come. *Narcissus and his reflection,* I remember thinking as I
embarked upon my first reading of the story in the electronically-monitored
room of the special wing of the American university library.

This story is also set in Italy, and more specifically at the titular Cave of
Tiberius, northwest of Rome, between Gaeta and Teracina, outside of a village
bearing the strange name of Sperlonga (not to be confused with our own island
Spinalonga, the leper colony off the coast of Crete). On the contrary, Sperlonga
is identified by the Michelin guide as quite a touristy place—something, let's say,
between an Aigio and a Xylokastro.

The "he" in the story is a professional fashion photographer, the "she" a
model for fashion spreads—a "photo-model," as it were. Between the "photo"
and the "model" (between the sun and its shadow in this Thrassakian dual divin-
ity with which we should by now be quite familiar) Thrassakis pushes the wedge
of the "grapher," the writer, himself.

The model's agency contacted the photographer's firm and their professional
rendezvous was arranged almost without the knowledge of the two principal characters themselves. One evening shortly before the shoot, the two find themselves
in the same *osteria,* she with her flock, all of them models, beautiful girls and
beautiful boys, clean-shaven or with thick well-groomed mustaches, and he with
his co-workers, all staring at the other table, gesturing wildly, like hunters outside
the hunting season watching their protected prey. As soon as the season starts up

again in August. . . . The thing to note, Thrassakis stresses, is that everyone in these two airtight groups is bored to death, since groups of people who all do the same thing often find they have very little to talk about. It's the outsider who opens a conversation with questions. Anyhow, the reason for this "premeditated" meeting is for him to be able to watch her without her knowing it. He steals her movements, her expressions, snapping pictures in the dark hothouse of his skull, pictures he will later try to recreate on location. The photographer's agency has asked him to present a certain designer's line of long summer skirts, called "Isadora Duncan," which give the sea breeze complete control over the otherwise naked body. The agency has asked the photographer to use the Sperlonga Museum as his backdrop. And maybe the cave. The photographer goes there ahead of time to study the space, and has more or less decided on the museum, where he thinks the model's body type will be shown to better advantage. As for her, all she knows is that on Thursday she's going somewhere for a shoot.

So on Thursday morning they set out in the photographer's Alpha Romeo. She has two suitcases of clothes with her, and he a small case of lenses. She is sad, she tells him, because she's had to part for the day from her faithful companion, her ever-present escort: her bicycle, a faithful dog that doesn't know what barking means, which she keeps chained up in the hallway outside her apartment. The photographer understands right away that she isn't talking about the tires or the handlebars, but, of course, the seat. She even describes it for him, as it feels to her: soft, fuzzy, with an almost metaphysical spring that presses it into her most private, most sensitive parts. She always rides her bike to and from work, from shop to shop, from house of fashion to house of fashion, where all the men are neuter and the women so absorbed in their own images that they barely even notice her. So, in the asexual environment of the modeling industry, the bike keeps her company.

On a curve, she pushes her seat backwards and, feigning confusion, he gets the gearshift—soft, fuzzy—tangled up in her legs. A bit later, shifting gears, he leans over and strokes her freshly-shaven legs. It tickles, and she nudges him, and the steering wheel jerks over and they laugh, while another car, passing them, honks several times, thinking the driver is drunk. (That "The drunk man tends towards love and the man in love tends towards drink" is one of Thrassakis's fixed ideas, which he now takes the opportunity to include, as the Alpha Romeo speeds down an ambiguous road, neither *autostrada* nor country lane.)

The museum is a modern structure built on a mountainside that slopes down to the Cave of Tiberius, in which fragmented statues of the cyclops Polyphemus and of Odysseus and his comrades were discovered just a few decades before. At the entrance to the museum there are photographs showing the excavations, half submerged in water, and workers in enormous rubber boots struggling against the waves to pull up the huge pieces of stone.

In the museum's main room, the carvings have been reconstructed in all their hair-raising majesty, based on the few fragments found in the cave. Those fragments are not incorporated in the reproduction but are exhibited separately, on their own pedestals. In the glazed plaster reproduction, the cyclops is massive, gigantic, supernatural, almost four meters high, reclining as Odysseus prepares to sink his hot staff into the single eye resting beneath the gable of the cyclops's forehead. Odysseus, represented at approximately his natural size, seems Lilliputian in comparison to the monstrous cyclops. On the basis of a fragment of thigh found in the cave, the reconstruction depicts one of his comrades assisting in the throwing of the spear. The reclining Polyphemus—whose massive legs narrow down to huge toes covered in remarkably lifelike masses of hair that end just where the nails begin, while his enormous penis rests on his testicles like a stuffed zucchini atop two stuffed peppers, and his arms bulge with four trifling muscles—looks like "Mister America" in the *Body Building* porn magazine.

In other corners, the real finds from the excavations—an arm, a piece of the cyclops's leg, a chunk of the spear, a fragment from Odysseus's chest—shine with the irrefutable charm of true gold beside the dullness of fool's gold. The recreated statues, on the other hand, transmit no vital force, but simply let the air swirl between them as between the columns of a colonial-style house. Thus the model feels no emotion other than awe before these apocalyptic monsters, as before the hull of the boat with its skeletoned sides in the next room.

Through the museum's enormous windows her gaze caresses the olive trees on the slope, heavy with fruit, rich in colors and shades. A breeze rustles their leaves, a breeze she can see but not feel, since there are no cracks or openings in the museum's walls through which that breeze might find its way—and so, inside, looking out, she feels cut off from reality, as if trapped in a glass sphere. The jointed trucks with their cylindrical tanks seem strange to her as they pass over the road that bisects the mountain, since from inside the museum she can hear no noise from their passing. They look like mammoths slipping between the branches of trees, or like in a movie when the sound is broken.

The photographer, bent over his dark case, is searching for the appropriate filters. She walks once around the reconstructed cyclops ("That," she thinks, "is what makes statues different from paintings: with a statue you can see the work from all angles, you can wrap it in your gaze"), then stops in front of the original arm, broken off at the shoulder and exhibited upside-down on a rectangular cement pedestal, a cyclopean arm with marble muscles, like a mountain range that will soon be shrouded with mist. In her mind the broken arm takes on metaphysical proportions, as at the height of fever the objects in a room and the people bending to kiss your forehead seem gigantic to you—and as a young girl with whooping cough, Thrassakis tells us, she'd had that kind of nightmarish experience. This arm resembles a remnant of her fever, trapped, frozen in some corner of her memory, and she begins again to burn all over.

Her life among the watered-down men of her trade, who are cruel and inhuman, all charm and flashy clothes, diets and expensive colognes, forces her to anthropomorphize inanimate objects, like this cyclops's arm. Not the entire cyclops, which frightens her, but only that familiar part of it, exhibited separately from the plaster reconstruction—that single arm over which she runs her fingers lightly, fingers of mist that solidify into frost at the touch of the cold, sleek marble, as the steam from boiling water might be temporarily trapped beneath the glass lid of a pot.

Reaching the very tip of the arm, the "five-fingered star" (and between thumb and pointer finger she finds a small marble stake that joins them, most likely to prevent their breaking, as in fact they have not broken, through all these centuries, in tempests and in caves) with its exquisitely chiseled fingers, each one as thick as her wrist (her bracelet could have been a ring for one), sure that no one, not even a gull, can see her, she opens her legs, which are at the same height as the hand, and sits down on the arm, driven by a strange desire to make love to the marble. At first it is cold inside her, but once she has warmed it with her heat she begins to feel the pointer finger with its wide nail touching her exactly where she wants to be touched.

Thrassakis is describing the scene in elaborate detail, even referring back to the seat of the model's bike, when the girl hears the photographer's footsteps approaching. Seeing her almost at the height of ecstasy, he immediately begins the nervous clicks of his machine, while the girl, reaching orgasm, raises her hand as if riding a dolphin—and then the acrobatic sparklings of her pleasure transform it into a bird riding a magic carpet, and it drops slowly down to her mouth, and she kisses her fingertips like women in the movies at the final finishings of the man who has made them briefly happy in bed. Then she stretches her whole body along the concave arm, whose muscles form stony pillows, and leans her head against the dismembered shoulder, kissing its wound—and her mouth, transformed by the touch of the stone, seems to be biting, or trying in vain to tell us something.

(But what can this signify, this adoration of the silent, the speechless? And to what extent has Thrassakis—who himself would have been too ashamed to masturbate with a cold, inanimate object in front of the young photographer—disguised himself behind the character of his model?)

The photographer—the artist, in this case—looks at the girl only through the lens of his Nikon. His camera is his shield, the filters a succession of protective defenses. Through his camera, he himself determines his distance from things. He becomes the machine. Only later will we see him becoming aroused, in hindsight, as he prints the photographs in his darkroom. During the act, he is a tool, inorganic, emotionless, while later, alone, he will grow drunk on the memory of immortalized pleasure.

The girl changes her skirt and follows his instructions as he places her in different poses beside the statue, the boat, and the other busts in the museum, each time arranging the Venetian blinds in the windows to create the proper shadows. (This bit of the story is reminiscent of the scene in the Hitchcock film where the main characters are being chased around the monolithic statues of the U.S. presidents in South Dakota, in which the people clambering over the carved faces look no bigger than wild doves nesting in the cracks in the rocks.) The model docilely follows the photographer's directions. She doesn't give a hoot about anything anymore. As far as she's concerned, she came and finished, before they had even begun. So she climbs up onto the monster's knees and perches on his thigh, accidentally resting a hand on his enormous penis, which looks like one of those unused missile shells that metal smiths used to pound into flower vases after the war. The results are better, though, when she joins Odysseus in catching hold of the pike he is preparing to plunge into the cyclops' eye: for her the pike has greater force than the marbleized stuffed zucchini resting on its two stuffed peppers.

As the photographs will later reveal, this adventure with the plaster repro-duction of the cyclops leaves the girl entirely indifferent, because the *spirit*, the *soul* is absent. But since the photographer has no way of knowing the results beforehand, he just keeps on laughing and talking, threatening her that "the tourists are coming," circling around her like a bee around a stone flower, search-ing in vain for a fleshy pistil—while the whole time, as she follows his directions mechanically, she is plagued by a single desire: to return to that broken-off arm, real and true, worn down through the centuries, that slippery marble to which the plaster had once, briefly, caught hold. As a girl she would slide across wide marble landings and her skirt would ride up and her mother would scold her. And when she was still young she had fallen in love with an arm, more than the man they said would make her happy, though he had hurt her, scraped her, bloodied her—and thus her frigidity in sex. Now she can displace all her love, all her kisses on that arm, that hand, because she knows it will never hurt her, it won't rip her up inside, it will only caress her, stroke her, fondle her, soothe her, with its wide thumb and its half-mooned nail—and it is hard, stiff, worked and working, moving between the gates of her clitoris, opening them, exploring the valley of her pleasure—and she likes the hand because it has no sperm, it won't drain her of milk, like a tongue of land in deep water, far from any rivers whose flow might blur the clarity of the depths—the fingers don't ejaculate, don't hurt her, and there are not just one but five of them, which is why she feels such an overwhelming passion for that superhuman arm, with the rippling Apennines of its muscles, and wants nothing more than the moment to come when she can return to it—when the photographer, helping her down from the cyclops, sud-denly finds her in his arms, pressing the light meter against his chest, and, unable to support her, perhaps even crushed by her weight, he stumbles, and they end up in a heap on the floor. The museum guard, bringing them a gift of fresh fruit from his wife, stops short with the plate in his hand, unsure as to what he should do, while all she can see is Odysseus' pike plunging down into her, blinding for-ever her one-eyed love. They are discovered in this compromising position by a group of white-haired tourists who pile out of their bus, come streaming in, and stand there ogling, munching them like chips with their soft drinks.

The vertigo of sex, the dizziness of desire. If the girl suffers all this in the first part of the story, it's because the broken-off arm of the cyclops reminds her of her first lover, a famous one-armed basketball player—famous, at any rate, in her hometown of Poulia—who managed to turn his handicap into a strength, learning to shoot baskets that made their mark on the history of the sport, swishing in so cleanly that the rim of the basket seemed to have drawn the ball in like a magnet. She herself had been a basket case all through her first spring season when she opened herself to his shots, hurting horribly, until he dumped her for her best friend, a classmate at the conservatory. She managed, over the years, to forget him—but she never forgot his arm, which had taken on an almost supernatural power, as when any part of the body is lost and nature's wise balance gives the missing limb's strength to its remaining counterpart. Thus his good hand did the work for those five missing fingers. And since then, she never found anything like it, not in Rome, Milan, Naples, Syracuse, Pescara, Ferrara—nowhere.

Unless they were weak and underdeveloped, men's arms all seemed pretty much the same to her. But that one had stuck with her as a synonym for orgasm—that arm to which she had clung, trying to show her love for the missing one. He had been an expert at developing each muscular unit separately as if they were musical chords, and she would run her fingers along the scale of his muscles, starting with the soft flesh where the veins of his wrist netted over his lower arm like guitar strings, teasing them, strumming chords with the agate pen of her painted nail as those veins hardened up the length of his arm, until she reached the point where her lips would freeze, biting, and her spit would run like blood from the nose of a man who's been hit, and his flesh would grow hard as marble—which is why the marble now arouses her as flesh might have done. She unconsciously finds in this disembodied arm her first lover's hand, which had caressed and massaged her. She remembers how she and her classmates at the conservatory had always wondered how the famous one-armed basketball player could ever manage to make love. She'd been the first of them to chase after him and try to find out. When she found his half-mooned thumb between the gates of her pleasure, she gave herself over entirely, then went back to report that making love with a cripple was disgusting, so as to keep the others from wanting to steal him away from her—which is exactly what happened with the only one of her friends to whom she confessed the truth: that it was, in fact, amazing.

But all that had been over a decade ago, and would have remained no more than an era fixed in her memory if the arm in the museum hadn't revived the forgotten mechanism of desire, now in the form of masturbation on top of an arm. Believing in the continuity of history, she thinks that perhaps her lover's missing arm (which had actually been blown off by an unexploded mine set by the Allies in World War II) had somehow turned to stone, like the petrified arms discovered in the cave. Back then she had always thought of him as a cyclops. Or cyclopean, at any rate. Enormous. His presence overwhelmed her. And now she has fallen upon another cyclops.

They are wrong, then, who say that love is blind. Love, for her, is the one-eyed, one-way road to bliss.

And the photographer? He is aroused by her arousal. The more she offers herself up for exploitation, the better for him. A pimp of representation, he feels the longing of the true creator on seeing his product in ecstasy. The passion of the documentarist is nowhere near as great as the passion of the voyeur. In other words, the artist, the creator, kills his heroine at the same time as he immortalizes her. This simultaneous stopping of motion and of life resembles the ultimate pleasure of the wasp that dies in the orgasm of its sting. For in exhausting the poison it holds in its stinger, it, too, ceases to live.

There is an important element in the story that might pass unobserved in an initial, plot-oriented reading: in both cases, for both the model and the photographer, love is equated with the past. The girl relives her adolescence in her hometown of Poulia, while the photographer becomes retrospectively aroused, alone in his darkroom. The present is merely a conductor for the past. This is the mature Thrassakis. It would have been interesting to have followed him into old age, to have seen what subsequent transformations he might have gone through. But unfortunately, life took him from us.

Another interesting element is the choice of setting. The space of the museum is a space of collection and concentration. For Thrassakis, the statues present the demonstration of historical continuity. In comparing the statues with those of his own land, he doesn't neglect to comment that the barbaric Romans always preferred quantity over quality. No Greek sculptor would ever have come up with a

Polyphemus like that. The girl, though, is no floozy. She understands art. And the photographer is no wandering snapshot artist goggling over sunsets. He has his detachable flash with him, and portable screens, and one of those black sleeves that goes over his head like the ones the outdoor photographers used to have by the White Tower in Thessaloniki. In his story, Thrassakis compares that dark channel of fabric to the passageway that connects an airport gate to the plane: i.e., a thing that transports you from the earthly to the heavenly realm.

If I were asked to connect the author with one of the central characters in his text, I would say that Thrassakis is neither the photographer nor the model, but the cyclops Polyphemus—the one-eyed among the blind.

Any analysis that leads somewhere has significance. Analysis for the sake of analysis is a superfluous form. Furthermore, we should never neglect to consider a story's historical co-ordinates. Geographical settings are, ultimately, of less significance. They are like the seasons, which always resemble one another, year after year—one spring resembles the next, one winter the next—though the years themselves differ essentially from one another. That said, we should make mention of the Roman Emperor Tiberius, after whom the cave is named. Tiberius was the emperor who refused to send his political opponents to the island of exile, Yiaros, because, as the historian Polivios tells us, "it was uninhabitable and devoid of the elements necessary for the sustenance of life." At the time when the story was written, the island, which even dictators wouldn't use, was very much in style. Perhaps Thrassakis, inspired by the sad reality of his homeland and its Makronissos, used the cave, the *grotto*, in order to give the monster a specific, or perhaps symbolic, location? The archaeologist-spelunkers, dressed in (fascist) black and enormous rubber boots, standing in the breaking waves of the (popular) human sea, which finally coughs up the monster, Polyphemus, and Odysseus, the people's avenger . . . . Perhaps we should look for other symbols in the text? Perhaps we should read the story according to another key?

Tiberius, then, refrained from sending his political opponents to Yiaros because the island was uninhabitable, buffeted by winds, crawling with snakes and rats. Fleshy plants bit into the northwesterly winds, and the barrenness of the island, combined with the suffering of its prisoners, made it resemble the antechamber of Dante's Inferno. The fact that the excavation of the cave was funded by Mussolini can be read as nothing other than a historical coincidence in which one monstrosity (the dictator) uncovers another (the one-eyed Polyphemus). As for the girl, she is repulsed by the memory of her first lover, who deprived her of her virginity, and seeks a replacement for his hand, something to supplant it in her mind. But the cave that bore the monstrosity, the mother of the cyclops—who, for the girl, is not one-eyed but one-armed—threatens to swallow the girl up if she takes her son from the darkness of her womb. Odysseus, who struggles to blind the monster, is the "avenger," who saves her by freeing her from both her past and her present. And since he claims to be "Nobody," he must be somebody. Who? The photographer, of course. For it is in front of the young photographer that she is able to relive and replace her past. Precisely because he is ignorant of that past, he allows her, too, to forget it.

Let us review, then, the three interpretations of the story we have offered. In the first, we have the photographer and his model, the mirror and the reflection, the Poet and his Muse, whose ambiguous relationship resembles that of Modigliani with his model-wives: did he paint them because he was in love with them, or fall in love with them through painting them? In our second, Freudian interpretation, the girl, in the psychiatrist's office of the museum, relives her deflowering by choosing the hand as a replacement for the pleasure she could no longer experience with the brutish basketball player. In the third version (*sex und politik*), we have the humanitarian dictator Tiberius (the cyclops, the freak of the empire) and Odysseus (Che, Bolivar, Velouhiotis). Leitmotif in all three of the interpretations is, of course, the relationship between the eye and the seen, the chooser and the choice.

When they leave the museum in the second and final part of this long story, or short novella, they go to a fish restaurant on the shore. It is that uncertain hour when the plates from lunch are being washed, before the first evening customers start trickling in to dirty them again. Normally, in the city, the restaurant would have been closed, but out here in the country things are different, with the reed fence and the boats pulled up by the restaurant's door, wide open to the breeze.

The old woman who owns the place lets them in at this in-between time and takes out the leftovers she's just put away in the fridge. The fish is so fresh it still has blood in its gills, but even if it had been old and dry, the breeze from the sea would have brought it to life again. The woman boils water on the brazier—an Italian custom, Thrassakis explains, for freshly-made pasta. The old woman tells them that everything is fresh, since that evening she is expecting a tour group to come through (the same one they saw in the museum). The two of them are exhausted, the girl because of the spiritual cost of "playing" with a statue as her partner, and the photographer with the physical exhaustion of a machine-gunner who has just emptied several rounds at a moving target. "Your work," he seems to be telling her, "just ended. Mine is just beginning." While they are waiting for the pasta to cook, she climbs onto a bike belonging to the old woman's grandson and rides in circles at the edge of the beach, happy, relaxed, a moving silhouette backlit by a setting sun that drags the air with it as it falls.

After their meal they walk back up to the square where the photographer left his Alfa Romeo. They find it grazing under a tree. (Thrassakis, with his demoticist leanings, uses a verb for an ultramodern car that had been used up to then only for sheep.) They get in and he drives off, leaving the highway, taking her into a forest where he begins to caress her, while the sweet, playful, caressing voice of Yves Montand sings "Bicycle" on the radio.

The story ends with her asking him to flex his muscles, so she can see if he's a real man. Though entirely unfit, he acquiesces, and unbeknownst to him, ends up setting a record. At which point she, utterly happy, laughs and gives herself to his embrace, while from the forest they hear a purring—no longer from the Nikon, but from an actual cat.

The Analysis of a Photograph
(A complete text by Thrassakis)

Nikon F
Ektachrome X
Flash électronique en lumière indirecte
Objectif Nikon 85 mm

THE PHOTOGRAPH SHOWS a tangle of three naked bodies, two female and one male, in a pale pink light against a background of dappled black. A few rose petals are fluttering down, landing on the man's back at the exact moment that the camera's flash immortalizes the pose, while a single petal rests on the mark left on one of the women's thighs by the elastic of her underwear, like a tear fallen from her eyes, which are closed with passion.

Like a tear, because the poor woman cannot share in the couple's joy. Only the man's right arm, passed around her, pulls her toward him. But she touches nothing, can enjoy nothing. One of her hands rests lightly against his elbow, while the other—long, sensitive fingers, heavy with enough rings to light up a whole room with their glittering glow—presses lightly against her groin, as she masturbates next to the couple. Excluded from their orgasm, she has her own, parallel orgasm, the orgasm of the solitary woman, the orgasm of the oppressed. Her face shows the suffering and grievance of unshared joy.

The other woman's expression, however, is one of indescribable joy and satisfaction. Though the two are surely friends (perhaps even lovers), she seems entirely indifferent to the suffering woman's pain. Her eyes, too, are closed, and she is grabbing the man by the hair at his nape, as if trying to pull him just a fraction of an inch away (perhaps because he has penetrated her a fraction of an inch deeper than she would like). Her other arm is wrapped around his back, pushing him upwards, while her hand falls, perhaps unconsciously, between him and her masturbating friend.

But his back is too wide for her arm to wrap all the way around. Her legs, open like a frog's (as if he has nailed her that way in the air), sketch the obtuse angle of release. On video they would have been moving, opening and closing, pressing together and coming apart again, biting and releasing the imprisoned penis. Here, though, they have the stillness of the snapshot. One of her legs passes through those of her friend, suggesting, as with the hand described above, an unconscious desire to block all contact between the man on top of her and the woman at her side.

The central feature of the photograph and perhaps the reason it was awarded an honorable mention is the facelessness of the man who, with his back turned to the lens, thus offers a symbol of faceless violence. While we can read the movement of orgasm in the fluttering of the women's hair and in the expressions on their faces (both have their eyes closed and lips half-open—but while one speaks of joy, the other's lips part with injured pride), his broad back turned is like a closed door with no knob.

A few fingers shorter than both the blond and the brunette, he has only to bend his head to kiss the blond at the base of her neck—a kiss she seems to enjoy, given the facile expression of pleasure on her face. He comes to her easily at this height, his strong, naked body narrowing slightly at the waist, with naked thighs that taper into hairy legs. He is made like a well-built animal: all of one piece (his neck is barely distinguishable from the rest of his body)—and his muscular arms allow him to hold the blond he's fucking with one arm while reaching with the other to grab hold of the masturbating brunette.

His is a body that doesn't suffer; he doesn't even seem to be making any particular effort to fit both of these women into his embrace. The blond, for one, is all his, as she pulls him closer to get the very last centimeter into her, until it hurts. But his true mastery seems to lie in the way he makes the brunette feel that he will soon be hers—as soon as the blond has come to orgasm (which seems likely to happen any second now), after which he will come right over *to her, the brunette, leaving the other to re—* [here there is a word that is impossible to decipher in the manuscript, most likely "recover," "relish," or "relax"]. *He is a master seducer, a pro, a beast, for whom a few conquests like this are no more than his daily bread: refined society girls of the kind one might bump into at cocktail parties or art openings.*

(Like a machine that charges itself with a generator, obeying its own needs and desires, so too do the people in the photograph seem to recharge, in a way. The Discus Thrower of Mironas has been gathering force to throw his discus for two thousand years, and we can imagine neither the moment after the discus leaves his hand, nor the moment before he takes his current pose. In the same way, this blond will be caught for an eternity at the height of pleasure, while the brunette will eternally be preparing herself to be pleased. What I mean is, there is something in successful works of art that dilates the time represented. In real life, in the time it takes for someone to read this description, the orgasm would be over, the bodies would have unwound themselves from their deadly tangle. But it is infinitely more possible that the viewer—or, by extension, the reader—will reach orgasm, than these three, trapped for all of eternity at the threshold of pleasure.)

Looking again at the photograph, it seems to me that I fell disgracefully short in my description of the blond woman's face. There isn't a hint of vulgarity in that face. At the height of pleasure, her cunt as moist as her mouth, her face forms an expression of gratitude for the anonymous man who fills her. Her gratitude overflows into tenderness in her embrace. Hers isn't the kind of clawed, impassioned grasp that tears flesh, that scratches and is scratched. Her passion is marked by a civility that bears no relation whatsoever to pure animal pleasure. Perhaps, finding herself under the control of another woman, she is ashamed to show just how barbaric she really is? After all, if she were to wound him with her nails, wouldn't the other soon come to lick those wounds, to soothe him, to mother him? Perhaps that's why the blond is holding herself back?

In real life, the silence the photograph exudes would have been filled with breaths, gasps, and whispers—the brunette, convulsing like a crooked "I" (as if she had thrown herself at him, hard, and been flung back, finding the spot already taken) seems to be pulling her head back so as not to hear the chirps of the mating birds. She is a proud deer, wounded and humbled in a clearing, trying to manage on her own, but prevented by the arm that has caught hold of her, as if she were a bird about to be slaughtered, caught by the weak spot near the base of its wings. For soon—there's no doubt about it, it's enough just to see how her foot, which seems to have a life of its own, has come sneaking up on the intimité of the other legs, as if to steal a bit of their heat—the sadness and nostalgia on her face will give way before his attack. And her head, now turned toward the heavens in masturbatory fever, will soon be bowed, submissive to her fate. And, satisfied, she will be calmed.

But just as you might see an island from far off and say, "How beautiful," and then when the boat draws near you disembark onto rough, jagged slopes, from close up the brunette's face has a tortured look. For no matter what she might do, she is unable to take within her that which the man does not give. And it's torture, this emptiness, and it shows as clear as day, through all the filters and pink trimmings, the rose petals and other romantic touches. So, just like the woman who thinks that the more she moves the better she's being fucked, though even the slightest, wisely planned movements can often give the greatest yield, in her wild torture, this woman now forms her body into a concave gulf, to make room for the air to enter. And she masturbates beside a real copulation. Perhaps her own arc, touching the other in tangent, was once not quite so far from the circle's center. But now it would be easier for her to find a place in the thoughts of two people making love in the Laplands among bear furs and wild fowl, than with these two bodies in the same bed that exclude her entirely from their communion.

The fact that the "continental" parts of the bodies (breasts, bellies, thighs) don't show, just the outermost reaches (fingers, toes, hips, hair, heads), clears the photograph of whatever vulgarity those inner regions usually confer. At the same time, the photograph's sensitivity to the extremes, the mountain ranges and seashores, captures also the flights, the gushing, the furious release of concentrated energy. So, thanks to them, we are better able to gauge the heat of the great passion.

His hairy legs, next to their soft pink ones, his darkness beside their satiny skin, his immobility, the width of his back, all testify to the fact that he could easily satisfy them both. If there were only one woman in the photograph, happy and satisfied, we would still be aroused by the expression on her face, but it wouldn't have the intensity, the augmentation of pleasure provided by the jealousy of her unsatisfied friend, already grasped in the crab's claw, being forcibly pulled towards him. Soon, the one now happy in his embrace will fall to the right with a tender expression of abandonment, as the unhappy one takes her place.

At the height of pleasure, the blond seems entirely lost in her absorption to the point of reduced self-consciousness, while the brunette's judgment is perfectly intact, and she sees clearly the ridiculousness of her situation—though as ridiculous as it might seem to her, she knows she cannot escape. She is in his clutches, and knows full well that she will follow the laws of submission—and, knowing he will be comparing the two, she will naturally try to seem like a better lover than her friend, to outdo her in tenderness and technique (she is dreaming now, eyes still closed), and for the time being she avoids touching him so as not to give him any pleasure which he might then transfer, perhaps unwittingly, to the other woman. She keeps her distance from them, so that the beast will at least understand the difference in body heat when he moves from one embrace to the next.

As for the brunette's attempt to insert her own leg from the right (the man's left), the blond cleverly blocks this move by throwing a calf between them. The unfaithful blond's whole body becomes a means of self-defense. She has trapped the male body, without the cleverness of her move being at all apparent on first glance: While the dividing line she has put between the man and her friend is actually the product of cold calculation, it appears at first as a move driven by instinct. No logic can compare to the logic of biology. One half of her gives itself over to the man, while the other half wastes its energy trying to make him unavailable to the other woman, drooling with anticipation beside him. And so her calf, angular and ugly, discourages any future approaches on the part of the brunette's thigh.

Of course, the real drama in the blond woman's case is that she has no idea the claw of the man's hand is already clutching her rival—but even if she knew, would she be able to get between them and cut off that contact? Try as she might to pull him to her left (our right) and free him from that black mag-

netism, he, like an octopus hungry for cuttlefish, prepares the other woman for his tentacle, while the blond dreams of beds strewn with rose petals where the two (not three) of them could give themselves over to endless orgies.

(What must the people in the darkroom, the guys who developed the film, have thought of this picture? What did they think of this triangle? These days we're flooded with porn. Porn. Pornopolis. Se faire pomper à Pompei. *Such an outpouring of printed matter, because these days the search is conducted by way of the image. In earlier times you were able to fantasize. Now others fantasize for you. Self service, no tips. They ask nothing of you but that you consume. Thus this photograph, too, belongs to a category, a genre, in which pleasure is never expressed through a man, but always through a woman. The woman taking pleasure helps other women take pleasure, while inviting men to put themselves in the place of the one giving pleasure.)*

The masturbating woman has nails, long nails on long fingers. If the size of a man's nose is analogous to the size of his penis and the size of a woman's mouth to the size of her vagina, then fingers are the prison bars, the railings, the fence. Her beautiful fingers cover almost her entire belly, the tips of her nails touching her pubic area . . . . If she could satisfy herself, then her fingers would take on the smell of blackberries.

    The endlessness of the act resembles an intellectual lover's obsessive attempts to prolong the "moment." Like famous paintings that absorb admiration, this photograph absorbs a never-ending act, because it is frozen forever at its "moment" of climax.

    Nothing can ever upset this endless threesome: not the person coughing beside you, nor rain nor sun. You can look and leave and come back later and the three of them won't have changed in the slightest. Because they live off of your investment, though not necessarily your participation. Just like the subjects of millions of other photographs, these people do not exist; they take on flesh and bone only through the other's gaze. An unseen person or plant doesn't cease to exist just because we aren't aware of their existence, but a photograph, if it isn't seen, doesn't exist. Inorganic, it has the blissful apathy of a rock.

We can't say that the three of them ever tire of making love, because they simply don't do anything if we don't see them doing it. Thus it is we who are making love, through them. They are only the pretext, the provocation, while the masturbating girl, who represents distance, is there only to make our own identification easier.

(If you hold the photograph up to the light you can see a satanic jester smiling at you from behind, making fun of the flames of desire it has lit within you. Its gaze penetrates the translucency of the glossy paper, laughing at the indecency of your position, as a fly might land on a movie screen, marking the characters' faces, allowing for the intrusion of ripe reality into the realm of the imagination. With the difference that the mask that rises to the surface behind the 'threesome' is more of an intrusion of the imaginary into the realm of the imagination, a kind of criticism printed on the printed work, unlike the living, verbal dig of some passerby who says, 'Look at that jerk,' which would be the equivalent of the fly we mentioned earlier.

But today the world communicates in images. The original meaning of the word has been lost. The word has been demoted to the level of the caption, the subtitle, like the geological layers that sink lower and lower as the centuries pile up on top of them. So, in translating the action of a photograph into words—though in the last analysis it really has no need of those words, since it gets the job done without any help on my part—I am essentially turning the clock back to the agricultural economy of the past century, even if with an ultra-modern tractor.

Flinging into words the feelings it arouses in me, I turn the ice into water, dilute the concentrated soup, water the ouzo—in other words, I do the work of analysis, while the firing mechanism of the photograph itself contains all the possibilities that dynamite has to offer.

I went out to pay some bills and send a few letters by express mail at the post office—the doorman and I have always been on the best of terms—and now I'm eager to get back to the small rectangle of love and baptize myself anew in its holy water.

Outside, life is so exhausting. How can you isolate moments as the photo-
graph does? You need limitless time and resources. And then there's the issue of
the organism: tired as I am, I prefer the comfort of the ready-made meal.)

Summing up, I see that their relation neither advances nor retreats with time. The
one woman will always be at the height of pleasure. And the other will always be
jealous. They are like heroines in the great novels of the past century, women-sym-
bols, ageless, undaunted by social uprisings, by new buildings going up, by the after-
math of war. A stopped movement, the quintessence of love invested in a photograph.

Utterly complete and happy, accepting neither his bodily pressure nor the
wet poetry of his kisses, the blond is nonetheless stuck to him almost like a mag-
net, and she can only be thinking unspeakable things, like, Here I am, living
it up in the tree of Evil, the tree of Knowledge. ("After all this knowledge, what
forgiveness can there be?" T.S. Eliot.) The graceful movements, the ignorance,
the childishness, are all finished now. Now knowledge goes deep. She has eaten
the forbidden fruit. So how can she return to the world of ectoplasms? This is
the truth, her truth. And while she gives herself to him in rippling tides, the
other pulls away, like waters receding, grows deeper, seeks to fill the void, rub-
bing herself like a massage, trying to ward off the cold.

But the beast, the werewolf, the dirty man, doesn't let her go so easily. He
holds her with one hand, like people afraid of the water testing it with a sin-
gle hand. As for her, is she afraid of him or afraid because she wants him so
badly? Is she, that is, afraid of her own desires? Otherwise she surely would
have found some way of slipping out of his grasp. And yet she gives herself to
him, though pulling away at the same time, the top half touching him, the
bottom half keeping its distance, like a mermaid pleasing herself alone under
the water, while offering the sight of her breasts, bobbing above the waves, to
whatever sailor happens to look her way.

The brunette is without a doubt the more beautiful of the two, and thus
the more wronged. Beauty goes hand in hand with injustice. How many beau-
tiful girls remain unmarried, unmatchable, and thus doubly alone? And how
many monsters, true horrors, are matched, married, happy?

The fact that she is more beautiful than the blond woman shows itself not
only in her physical form—Atalanta who was caught in the trap—but in the

expression of her character. Surely if she was in the blond's place, she would have offered her friend a helping hand. She seems to be one of those people who can view themselves from outside, even in the height of passion, can see, through the living need of pleasure, the ridiculousness of the human condition. While the blond, with a face full of satisfaction, seems to have completely forgotten the friend beside her, suffering from inescapable loneliness. Surely she has confided in her friend countless times, but now, wrapped like tar around the column that has come between them, she has completely forgotten her friend. Perhaps he is whispering something in her ear, who knows—but it is obvious that she will never unglue herself from him; perhaps he has found her most sensitive spot. Perhaps . . . . Her half-open mouth, licentious, stuffed with unsaid things, looks like a boxer's in the ring, protected in the ring by a mouth-piece. And she isn't even one of those who will afterwards bend to drink at his spring, in order to sooth with his sperm a mouth parched with sighs. No, of the sixty-nine kinds of erotic contact she knows only the three legal ones. And so she gives herself to him without fear, unsuspecting of the various trials and tribulations her lover might submit her to.

As for him, he seems so detached from the act it's as if he were a construction worker plastering walls. (And indeed, he has a workman's hands.) He knows that others inhabit these homes, these two women, and that he is there only to put in motion their mechanisms of desire, to offer the setting in which their own passion, foreign to him, will unfold. And so he doesn't look at all towards the blond, a fact which shows what an insignificant role he plays in her own experience. Unmoved, unparticipating, he takes care to take care of business, with the stance of one who knows they are throwing themselves at him, while on the other hand, a clever ape, he has also caught hold of the brunette, since as soon as he has exhausted the blond, pulverized the last vestige of her resistance, he will turn and destroy the other, too, so he can go back to his part of town and boast to his friends about his conquests among the bourgeoisie.

While for the blond, how heavy it is, my God, how Bovary, to get ready to go out that evening with her husband, to some dinner party or the movies, to boil eggs the next morning for breakfast, not too soft . . . .

This description is like an orgy without end. Just like icons of the Virgin Mary in earlier times, the photograph accepts the adoration, the faith of the masses, in raptures of ecstasy. They even say that icons sometimes cry, ejaculate through the eyes. And they call them miraculous, and flocks of believers run to pray to them and carry them in processions, hoping to heal the hopelessly wounded.

Though this situation isn't quite the same. No, it resembles the badly-printed color reproductions of the saints, sold by the thousands along with short sketches of their life stories. No silver offering graces them anymore.

And so, though condemned to a fate that is not the fate of real icons, which grow old and scratched with time and become museum acquisitions, the photograph passes untouched, unrained upon through the years. While I grow old, change coats, skins, pay my rent, vote in the local elections (the others show no sign of ever taking place), the photograph suffers nothing.

So I will take my leave of these bodies that are given over forever to their pleasure, before they get dressed, before they become bourgeois, before they return to their class and their time. And so, naked, newly-made, before the invention of sin, I give them over to the wax museum of the Word.

The Critique of the Drill

IN THIS STORY, we are given all the elements we need to piece together what Thrassakis elsewhere calls his "khaki self." The main character is completing his military service at the Pavlos Melas base in Thessaloniki-after-the-fire. On the outskirts of the city, the new city, Neapoli. The foothills, their small trees, once centers of attraction where he tested his erotic quadrilles with various girls—the teacher with the plump breasts and grimy cheeks, or the girl from the kiosk, like a magnetic sculpture with her sweaty armpits and glistening lower lip—have now become shooting ranges and fields where attacks are staged against invisible enemies of the state coming down from the North. The landscape is suddenly drained of all its previous erotic significance—the signified of sex has become the signifier of armed service, split between defensive iambs (dig trenches, come together) and trochaic attacks (onward, men of Greece).

The cadet loves his commanding officer. He is emotionally bound to him, as a cadre might be to his party leader. In the best case scenario, the cadre acquires something of the air of his political idol. But the only thing the cadet has picked up from his colonel is, perhaps, his "fox walk."

Unlike Thrassakis's other stories, which exhaust themselves in the effort to create atmosphere and contrast, this one reaches its aim relatively quickly. We get down to brass tacks right away—which is to say, to the titular "critique of the drill." The cadet finds himself under fire from infuriated regiment leaders for ordering a withdrawal ("retreat," as is well-known, is a word the military scorns)—and, moreover, at a point when the enemy (two local donkeys and their innocent drivers) had barely even appeared on the slopes of the mountain.

The cadet (the narrator, and thus, by extension, the author) enters straight into his defense, which is at the same time a critique of the critique. "Since the blanks we fired failed to stop the enemy's advance," he says, "what other choice did I have than to give the orders I gave?" The surrounding hills, according to the givens of the drill, had already been captured by enemy troops (other donkeys with red pack-saddles—for the enemy always wears red). "What else could I have done? Given up my men to certain annihilation, in trenches that offered no protection whatsoever?"

The lieutenant-colonel, a yellow-bellied man who hates the cadet for wearing glasses, tells him that this kind of withdrawal (i.e., before the battle has even been fought) is unprecedented in the army annals. It is unworthy of a Greek officer to turn his tail in flight before a more multitudinous enemy. What ever happened to the spirit the Greek men had shown at Ruppel? Or Vangen? Or Tsataltza? Had they all been fools, those brave men who fought to the very utmost of their ability, giving their all, even their lives, for their country and their cause?

At which point the cadet, biting his lip to keep from laughing, replies that in an analogous situation of actual combat, he too would have fought to the very last drop of blood in his body—which, granted, isn't saying much, since he donates regularly to the Red Cross. During the drill, however, he saw no reason to insist on a sacrifice which was in his opinion unjust, when he saw the donkeys continuing their descent down the hillside.

The misunderstanding is quite simple: the cadet is speaking of the reference, the donkey, in and of itself, while the officers are referring to the referent, the actual enemy. The fact that the donkeys, in this particular case, offer only an *analogy* for the actual enemy should by no means prevent the cadet from completing the appropriate actions such as the leadership that the armed forces expects of him. An actor should always give his all, even during a dress rehearsal. Likewise . . . , at which point the cadet, seeing things a bit more clearly, asks himself if this whole fuss is actually over a military theater of operations or, indeed, a theatrical dress rehearsal. Because the cadet, a scriptwriter by profession (and here we have another clever disguise for the writer, Thrassakis), saw the whole exercise as precisely that: a bad performance of a bad play. Which is why he had said, "All right, guys, pack it in, let's get back to the base. It's high time."

At this point, the cadet's captain steps in, for the first time, to support him. (This involves a resurrection of the dead, since another given condition of the drill was that the captain had been killed in battle and the cadet was to take over leadership of the entire company, though he had never before had to think beyond his own platoon. But as the most senior remaining officer, the heavy lot had fallen to him.) The captain is preparing for an exam in English at the army's School of Foreign Languages in the hopes of being able to go to the States for further training, and the cadet has been giving the captain free lessons. So, indebted to the cadet, the captain, a professor of military semiology at the Halkidas School, speaks up in defense of his young platoon leader, and his words win general approval. He says, then, that "the union of the notion of the 'representation of the representation' with the supposedly essential deconstruction of an ideology is yet another example of "connotative arbitrariness' "—a phrase that works like cough syrup on an inflamed throat. Everyone falls silent. And the captain, "young, handsome, and strong," continues: "The axial line of the mule-drivers, though intended to correspond to a real-life situation, essentially disoriented the cadet, who read the exercise developing before his eyes on the level of meaning and not on the level of the reference." Silence reigns among the boorish, ignorant officers, while the captain, one-eyed among the blind, dazzles them with the anti-Euclidian geometry of a non-representational exercise that gave the cadet the opportunity and the right to develop his individual initiative, and so on and so forth.

That same afternoon, after the critique is over, the cadet will return the favor of the captain's support. During firing practice (this time is with loaded guns), a stray bullet from the captain's machine gun wounds one of his conscripts, a shoemaker from Piraeus. At the hospital to which the poor cobbler (whose wound, fortunately, is not serious) is transferred, the platoon leader testifies to the doctor that the patient had in fact "overstepped the boundaries determined for the attack," so the fault lay not with the captain, who had been holding the gun, but with the wounded man himself.

In the evening, after this harrowing day, the officers head back to the city in the truck that had picked them up one by one from their houses that morning. The good colonel, an affectionate father and peaceful citizen, returns to his spouse and her game of rummy; the captain who dreams of escaping to the States goes home to his young wife, who dreams of his becoming an important general; and the intellectual cadet returns to his life of sin. Today in particular he is so disgusted by the concession of Barthes' ground zero of writing to Klausvitch's ground zero of war, so literally sick of signifiers and signifieds, that he goes and finds a friend of his from high school, and together they give themselves over to the orgies of the night. They go to the bordellos in Vardaris and wake up the old whores, and he has sex with a gypsy silversmith. The gypsy, who has never set foot on an army base and never will, takes particular pleasure in degrading the honorable uniform of the Greek officer. He even sticks plastic glow-in-the-dark stars on the cadet's epaulets.

Later on, the cadet picks up his fiancée and takes her to the movies, then to the Seik Sou forest. After jerking off onto her lap—at which she cries, frightened: "They're crawling, Alekos, they're crawling all over my legs" (referring to his sperm, which she imagines as ants swarming up to the nest of her ovaries)—he goes home and, still in uniform, surrenders himself to sleep.

The next morning he arrives at the base in a foul mood. Since he's on duty that night, he has brought his razor, pajamas, books. After the exercises (that day only two people are killed, during the hand grenade drill, because they're scared of throwing their grenades), he retreats to the Company Command, sitting down by the phone used to communicate with the squads on active duty. The guerilla war has been over for years, but there are always groups of fighters appearing on the slopes of the surrounding mountains, like mosquitoes drawn insatiably to the marshes of remorse. So he is idling by the phone when the sergeant major comes in with the warrant officer, both of them coarse, ignorant career soldiers, and informs the cadet that the next morning he must take part in the execution of a Bulgarian traitor at the Genti Koule prison. Both speak with heavy Macedonian accents and, as prospective executioners, have already begun to live in a state of perpetual drunkenness. When the cadet hesitates to acquiesce, the warrant officer tells him straight out that he is obliged to accompany the firing squad, since he is the highest ranking officer in the unit from which the squad has been selected.

That night the cadet can't sleep at all. And when in the wild dawn he hears the army truck stopping outside the guardhouse to pick him up, he thinks for a moment that they're coming for him, that he's the one slated to die. He climbs with heavy boots into the front seat. The truck, with the squad of recruits in back, drives along the length of the Thermaic Gulf, which lies on the horizon like a still-sleeping bride. The warrant officer and the sergeant major are drinking brandy from a flask. The truck passes a few tripe shops that are already open, a street-sweeper cleaning the sidewalk, the neighborhood of Vardaris, the hotel where he had been two days before—it seems like an eternity—and then the Seik Sou forest, where he had taken his fiancée.

At last they arrive. "But the chains are heavy, the prison heavy," he quotes in a whisper as the doors of the Genti Koule prison squeak open. In the diluted dark, the din of the rising sun sounds like yeast swelling in rising dough.

The squad stands at attention. The verdict of guilt is read aloud to the Bulgaro-Macedonian traitor. There is a line of bureaucratic crows standing there, and a priest, the head crow. The "Bulgarian" doesn't accept last rites. He's an atheist, he says. He believes only in Communism. And his last wish, he says, is his first: "Long live Greece." Then he starts to sing: "A fish can't live on dry land . . ."

The cadet is unable to order the recruits to fire. Fire on whom? This man is Greek. More Greek than Greek. A Cretan, no less, or so it seems from his accent. The warrant officer, blind drunk, orders for him. On the "blo" of "blossom" in his song the man falls, riddled with bullets, and the holes in his greatcoat become the stars of the night that is ending.

That evening after taps, wanting to take his mind off the events of the day, the cadet rushes to the home of a friend of his, a painter who is serving in another unit. But his friend isn't home yet. His mother is worried. The cadet waits there until his friend arrives at around ten, completely exhausted. For half an hour he can't even say a word. What's going on? What happened? Once he has finally pulled himself together, with the help of a smoke, he tells the incredible story. He had been at Kaimak Tsalan for three days, involved in purges of the defeated enemy. When everything had been taken care of and they were about to head back, a shepherd on the mountain suddenly started shouting and waving at them. The cadet's friend was with another soldier, from Mytilini. They stopped. They waited. To make a long story short, the shepherd was trying to tell them that the two of them had walked right into a minefield that ended—look, right there, he said, pointing to a fence. They could thank God and their souls if they came out alive. The other soldiers had gathered on the surrounding hillsides and everyone watched with their souls in their teeth as the two men inched forward, step by step, one foot at a time. Each step might have landed on a mine.

Eventually, they both came out alive. But how will he ever get over the experience of that half hour? His mother makes cold compresses for him and finds some cod-liver oil. He has been given a two-week leave.

The story ends with a conversation between the two friends, who agree that even if the "reds" had won, they, the next generation, would have ended up in the exact same position. Only they would have been executing "agents of the imperialists" and walking through Truman's minefields. Their generation is a generation condemned.

Later on, Thrassakis will write:

My generation was not butchered in World War II or the Civil War. It survived. But it paid a high price for that survival. Without heroism or exaltation, without burning fevers or hypothermia, it endured a slight but constant fever that wore it down slowly, bit by bit. The fact that we ended up mildly cynical instead of tragically disillusioned just shows that we never really believed in anything. Though we did believe in some kind of change or progress, which of course never took place. Instead we slipped backwards, sometimes more, sometimes less—these things are always relative—while TV and radio Americanized us more and more. That, in short, is my generation. As I said, we never had to mourn masses of fallen men. We grew up during the Reconstruction, like orphans always seeking to find out who their real parents are. In the end they believe all versions, from the crudest to the most romantic. Their mother, a princess or a whore. Or neither. Or both.

My generation is like the second son in a family in which all the glory, all the adoration and expectation went to the brave young first-born, who fell fighting on the ramparts of the Struggle. And I, like it or not, am made in his image, according to his prototype. I grow up under his photograph, which is constantly being touched up over the years. The past is idealized, prettified, its glory sung, its story made into a lesson, a moral. So, looking at my first-born brother hanging there in his frame, I ask myself, How can it be that I am shrinking while he stays always the same? I grow old, get wrinkles, and die, while he retains the sculpted stillness of the Beautiful, the Fallen, the Hero. *Historically sentenced to a life in his shadow, I am second-born, second-class, second-rate, first and foremost second—which of course makes me, at least, a step up from third.*

Then again, the third is free of the shadow of our first-born, first-dead brother, because he compares himself to me, and has no cause to be jealous of my past. The same goes for the fourth and fifth: as the generations grow further and further away, they grow freer and freer of these inherited anxieties. I, then, am the only immediate victim of oppression. All my older brother's surviving comrades, still sunk in the times they lived through, are always talking about his manly virtues, with the loquaciousness of the one-time warrior. And instead of truthfully describing the difficult and entirely unromantic conditions under which they served, they idealize the past, turning it into legend for me, weighing me down with their useless, superfluous weight. Instead of analyzing their mistakes for me, instead of examining how and why their generation lost the Struggle, they fob off onto me this heroic confrontation with their own ignorance. And so these men who joined the Struggle as materialists end up as second-rate idealists.

But I was speaking of the fifth, the youngest son, who was killed one day at a demonstration—he was found with a gaping wound in his belly and we didn't have the courage to report his death to the authorities. For the first born, of course, we are in public mourning to this day.

So naturally, the death of this last son is, in many ways, much more important. It shows that the enemy has changed tactics, has become invisible, anonymous. The enemy appeared in the dark. Materialized like an image on a negative. My obligation, then, is to regroup, to start fighting that enemy on his own terms, if I ever hope to conquer him. I too, that is, must become anonymous, a creature of the dark, must stop being the faithful proponent of misleading philology about "equality, brotherhood, and justice"—rake, tractor, scythe—and become wary of the photographers of History. That will be my positive contribution.

And if I have returned again to the issue of generations, it doesn't necessarily mean that I accept their existence as objective fact. After all, what can divide two people at a temporal distance of twenty years, when it takes mil-

lions of light years for the beam from some planet to reach our eyes? Meat is easier to chew if it's cut into small pieces. Ground meat signifies no more than the teeth's unwillingness to work. The same goes for decades, too: a passage through the mill.

There is one thing that remains an undeniable fact: I, whose job it is to express my generation, have always remained true to myself. I neither exaggerated the facts nor shrank them. A victim from birth, I spoke of victims. Suspended between a heroic tradition and some other tradition, as of yet undefined, I balanced myself as carefully as a tightrope walker with no safety net below. A light bulb suspended in the void, I lit up the darkness blindingly.

And yet my youngest brother's fatal wound remains, thus far, the only truth. For now the anonymous killer is finally on the same level as his anonymous victim. Up until now we have had anonymous murderers and eponymous dead. But now, for the first time, we have dead people whose names we don't know, because no one dares report their deaths. The people's fear is measured by the extent of their silence. And that's why I say that a new age is beginning, an electronic, devious age, in which the people's silence has become a new battle tactic. The enemy made a mistake—he said that he was no one. That he never killed anyone.

And so, a lost man, I will not be lost, if I can manage in time to prove myself worthy of my time. The anonymous victims demand revenge. And everything happened the day I was born, "on the eighteenth of November, when the lackeys came out in the transport trucks. And the youngsters from the people's army were waiting for them in ambush . . . "

(With this last sentence, he is most likely referring to November 1973 and the victims of the events at the Polytechnic in Athens.)

Re-enlistment

THRASSAKIS'S SECOND prose manuscript, bearing the title "Re-enlistment," concerns a group of reserve soldiers called in one Sunday for training in the use of new weapons. Every so often, Greece, balanced as it is on the lip of an active volcano (the Middle East), calls its enlisted children to be drilled again in the art of war, so they'll be sharp as pencils, ready as whetted knives or greased bayonets to sink into the enemy's flesh. The narration begins as the men, stretched out on the grass of the shooting range, aim their automatic weapons, which didn't exist back when they had done their military service. The pot bellies they've acquired make it hard for them to "fall flat," as the sergeant major orders, and they're all complaining about something—one guy about his back, another about his heart, his ulcer, kidney stones, arteriosclerosis. They are all men of a certain age, perhaps in their forties, who had planned on spending this Sunday with their families, on some outing with the kids or the in-laws, until that damned order came and spoiled their plans. If they all show up, it's only because the penalties are heavy, as bad as for wartime desertion. There is no immediate threat of war on the horizon, but the sky remains overcast—and here I refer to the political climate, not the meteorological one.

Menelaos, the story's main character and narrator, is a butcher. (This is the first time Thrassakis has decided to examine others from behind the distorting lens of a point of view somewhat distant from his own.) Menelaos closed the shop late the night before, a Saturday (back when the story takes place, the continuous working day hadn't yet been instituted, and stores still closed for a siesta in the afternoon and opened back up again at night). He is full of complaints about the state that hassles its citizens needlessly and, he says, "like clockwork." Sometimes about taxes, sometimes about the meat (he had seen black days, we learn, for illegally inflating his prices), and sometimes, as now, about the defense of the country from "external attack."

Though the story starts in an anti-militaristic vein, it soon crystallizes into a clearly Thrassakian absorption with time. In "Re-enlistment," the former conscripts are endlessly amazed by how much the others have aged, how awful they look. "How'd he get so bald?" "He sure worked up a paunch!" The squadron, brought together again, visibly injured by the intervening years, presents an unprecedented contraction of the element of time.

Their young trainer in his olive drab uniform is slim and dynamic, and has made it his goal for that Sunday to teach them how to shoot the new rifles. The retraining is to last four Sundays in all. Next week he plans on teaching them how to use the new submachine guns. The men will return home that evening, after sunset. The story, then, takes place in a single day, on which old friends and comrades who haven't seen each other in years, almost decades, find themselves together again.

The men have all brought food prepared for them by their wives and packed in three-tiered lunch boxes. Nikos pops handfuls of little fried fish—cold, of course—into his open mouth, where they fall like coins down the throat of a pay phone. When Menelaos asks him what his wife looks like, Nikos pulls out a photograph of a pretty, slim, middle-class woman sitting in front of the weeping willow in their yard. Menelaos can't stop wondering how Nikos managed to put on all those pounds. He remembers him as a trim guy, fresh and strong, in the new recruits' training center, hanging his heavy boots by their laces from his erect dick—and when they were given their first Sunday leave and everyone ran straight to the whores, Nikos, who got there first, kept getting back in line over and over again. But what did that young man, with his high forehead and square, determined chin, have to do with this pot-bellied man tossing fried fish into his mouth with perfect aim?

The rekindling of friendship between the former army buddies takes place over lunch, during their break from drills. While the regulations allow for only a half-hour lunch break, they give these old-timers an hour and a half, so they have plenty of time to eat and rest in the shade of the trees before the afternoon session begins. For most of them it's just a waste of time. But for Menelaos, the butcher, it's a chance to study the "meat," as he thinks of the others, since they've all gotten so fat. They've all changed with time. They are wearing colorful, mottled shirts that barely cover their paunches, pants that are too short or sag, lace-up shoes or slip-ons—clothes of a certain style worn only by men of a certain age. And all the snapshots of kids, wives, houses, dogs—"It's a good thing it isn't hunting season, because then I'd have been a deserter," one man jokes—that they pass around during the break. They take bites of one another's lunches, trying to guess what dishes the others' wives make best: "I bet her *dolmades* have you licking your fingers." For Menelaos, the platoon's body is completely and utterly new.

Thrassakis's title, of course, is inaccurate. The story isn't about re-enlistment, it's about retraining. It isn't about the poor soldier who doesn't know how to earn his daily bread after his dismissal and decides to re-enlist, nor about that forgotten recruit at the border whose discharge papers never arrive. The men in the story are ordered to report to a base outside their city for four Sundays in a row in order to learn how to use new weapons. They proceed from the simple to the complex while chafing themselves with memories.

The alienation inherent in consumer society is represented by each man's attempt to sell his wares to the others. Not only does Menelaos invite them all to his butcher shop for the best livers in town, but the insurance salesmen wants to insure them all, and the car salesmen tries to talk them into buying from him. A leftist importer of Hungarian salami and dill pickles from Prague offers them free introductory samples of his goods. The whole time they are being trained, they never cease trying to convert one another to their respective causes.

But what about the poet? Is he absent from this crowd? Not at all. Thrassakis disguises himself badly behind his awkward narrator, since all the thoughts he attributes to Menelaos can only belong to him. We can't help but assume that it is actually Glafkos, disguised as a butcher, who sees his former comrades as meat—as time has made them, himself included, of course.

The theme of food as a substitute for sex—and indeed, the reserves have brought lots of food with them, fruit and tomatoes, salad, fried zucchini, pureed carrots—links "Re-enlistment" with the next story we will examine, "A-X," in which alcohol becomes a stand-in for the forbidden relation between two characters, Fulvio and Renata. Furthermore, as the reserves go on eating, more and more scenes from "Squall," one of his early stories concerning a bourgeois feast out in the country the success of which is threatened by an impending storm, repeat themselves with the astounding exactitude of obsession: Here, too, something is approaching, and soon will break. A dormant crisis reigns. It isn't hard to figure out what they're all thinking about: "Their plans for their lives, which came out all wrong." How differently they had imagined what their lives would be like after being discharged from the army! Their lives had turned out almost diametrically opposed to what they had hoped. The intervening years had cured them of any delusions. As they eat during the break, before grabbing their weapons again for the afternoon drills, they sing together, "Oh, where are you, youth, who promised I would become someone other than I am now."

THIS UNTITLED STORY examines the two different methods by which firing devices can be assembled: the parallel and the crosswise (A-X). There is no other way for explosive substances (of love as of bombs) to come together. He and she pass through the story like two lines that cross at a single point, then continue along their separate ways.

The setting is, once again, Italian. A hotel in Naples. He, middle-aged Fulvio, is traveling with Sandra and another couple, friends of theirs. They check into a hotel where she, Renata, the whore, the deluxe tart, is practically one of the staff, if not part of the hotel decor.

Fulvio and Renata's fateful encounter takes place that evening. Fulvio comes in with his friend's wife to ask the night clerk if there are any available rooms. Renata, wrapped in her thick fur and sunk in an armchair, looks them over coldly, indifferently, professionally. Fulvio notices her right away—after all, she's a striking woman, and sitting in a very provocative position. Since he is accompanied by his friend's wife and not his own, he is able to study her at his ease, literally devouring her with his eyes. (Later that same night, in Sandra's presence, he can only watch her out the corner of his eye.)

At this time of night Naples is full of American sailors headed for the port to motor back out to the ships of the Sixth Fleet. A few drunken sailors stumble into the hotel asking for a room. The night clerk, a veteran of the underworld with a tough, scarred face, answers flatly, "Full," pointing to the "No Vacancy" sign outside. It's as clear as day he doesn't want that kind of customer. But he does accept Fulvio and his friend's wife. So they park the car and come back, all four of them, each couple with a suitcase, give their passports to the clerk, and go up to their respective rooms to drop off their things before heading out again.

Renata follows all these movements closely as she switches chairs and chats up the different customers, trying to figure out, Fulvio supposes, which one she might get the most out of for the night. He frames her in different poses with his mental zoom lens, like a hawk zeroing in on its future prey—though for all he knows, she could be the owner's daughter, or even a transvestite. Fulvio is burning with curiosity, but not Renata, who sees him and his wife as just another couple. Since all he's doing is looking at her, why should she pay him any attention? A whore doesn't choose, she's chosen. Though she is curious as to which of the women he's sleeping with. As far as she's concerned, all couples are false, fabricated. For her, the only thing that isn't feigned is the selling of sex in the marketplace. How is a hired cab any different from a personal car? They're both cars, they both have four wheels. . . . That's how Renata feels about couples, and when she sees them she shudders, not because she's jealous, exactly, but because they define her own isolation in society—or, better, her necessary position in a society of isolated people. Though she spends her time with taxi drivers, waiters, hotel owners, traveling pimps, and watch-sellers, all she really wants is to go to some relative's home on Sunday afternoon and eat lamb or turkey with thick mashed potatoes, like she did at her grandmother's house when she was little. But given her profession, none of her relatives ever ask her over, lest she sully their homes. Not even her old friends want to have anything to do with her, since her cruel gaze strips off their masks, while her exquisitely painted smile repulses lips that still smack of virginity. "So Renata waited in her armchair for some rich customer, the next buyer—who, in a weekend Naples flooded with sailors, seemed unlikely to appear."

Meanwhile, Fulvio and his friends are wandering through an empty city beneath a blinding moon. They walk through the covered markets, which at this time of night are being hosed down and mopped. Long, high arcades with crossed arches, like abandoned temples. On Rome Street, itinerant hawkers sell flannels and cheap sweaters off the tops of their cars. An old woman selling roasted sunflower seeds protects her legs from the wind with an empty cardboard box.

Though Fulvio tries to participate in the group's nighttime wanderings, he can't forget his real desire: to find a bar somewhere and have a drink, vodka or whiskey, a beer at the very least. But there's nothing open. All the bars close at midnight so the sailors will be forced to head back to their ships. Fulvio gets mad at those underaged sailors, sperm of some puritanical family, half-pint Americans who seem to have absorbed the form and content of whatever show their parents were watching when these kids were conceived in front of the TV. Some look like James Cagney, others like Alan Ladd, with ears sticking out from their heads, others like Mickey Rooney, others like Sammy Davis Junior. What did these poor kids ever do to deserve the job of policing an ancient, historical sea like the Mediterranean, many-faced, with many ports? At the end of their tour of duty they go home, never having understood why they came in the first place. While Renata, in her landlocked fur, waits for an admiral or a captain, chatting up the pimps in the meantime.

Returning empty-handed to their hotel, the two couples see that the Bavarian pub next door, stuck so close it almost looks like an extension of the hotel restaurant, is getting ready to close. The group rushes in. True, Sandra always tries to keep Fulvio from drinking, because he's overweight and has problems with his heart. But her restrictions just force him to drink on the sly—not so much as to make him a confirmed alcoholic, just a drunk man playing the drunk. Now, seeing the beer tap running freely, he gets excited, remembering his student years in Munich, when he couldn't get enough of that abundance of beer that flowed from the barrels like the sperm of an Aryan giant. (Here in the south they serve beer with an eye-dropper, making sure it doesn't overflow the lip of the glass.) The scene that follows is indicative of the way the rest of the story will proceed: the pub closes as soon as Fulvio manages, despite Sandra's complaints, to down a single glass.

The next morning the two couples confer over the phone from their respective rooms, planning a trip to Pompeii. They decide to meet at the little bar in the lobby for a coffee before packing up to leave.

Outside it's raining. After the previous night's full moon, the dawning day brought with it a heavy rain, which clears away the smell of hot tar from the road being paved outside the hotel—but all the same, it's depressing. An almost wintry morning, all sadness and remorse.

Once again Fulvio finds himself alone with his friend's wife (Thrassakis hints that they might be spouse-swappers, though he doesn't insist too strongly on that interpretation). Sandra forgot some kind of cream in the room and has gone back to get it, while his friend is paying the previous night's bill to the morning clerk, not the same scarred man as before. Renata, sitting in her armchair with her fur draped over the seat next to her, seeing him come downstairs with a different woman than the one he had gone up with the night before, is intrigued and looks at him with a wet gaze full of promises, a gaze Fulvio first attributes to some sort of eye-drops, though he soon finds a more poetic explanation: *Her eyes glisten*, he thinks, *like fresh tar in the rain*.

He folds up his newspaper (*Unita*, the newspaper of the Italian left, a clue that Fulvio is politically sensitized), gives it to his friend's wife to read, and gives himself over to Renata's smoldering gaze, which makes him feel like smoking a cigarette—or, since he quit smoking, like having a drink. Around them in the small bar are some German tourists who are already drinking, perhaps out of despair at seeing the rain outside, here in Naples, "the city of sun," as it was advertised by the travel agents who sold them their tickets—and so they sweeten the bitterness of their disappointment by adding alcohol to their morning coffee. But Fulvio doesn't dare follow suit. Sandra will be down at any moment, and if she finds him drinking so early in the morning, there'll be hell to pay.

Renata, in the meantime, has wrapped him in her gaze, piercing him burningly from all sides. Given to vice, she likes men who are like her, as she imagines Fulvio to be, since she sees him playing between these two women. Fulvio, for his part, can't stop thinking about her. Her gaze lights him on fire. He wants to make her his own. His friend's wife is absorbed in the paper, reading an article about the danger of a coup a-la-Greece in Italy.

Just then, Sandra walks in. She found the tube of cream and has come back down. Fulvio's guilt drives him to ask the beautiful stranger (Renata) exceedingly politely if she would mind taking her fur from the chair so Sandra can sit down. Renata does so gladly, pulling at her it as if it were a mute animal, and Sandra, unsuspecting of her husband's connection to the hotel whore, sits down.

So, following their exchange of burning glances, Fulvio's first actual contact with Renata comes with Sandra as an excuse. In asking Renata to pick up her fur

---

so Sandra can sit down, he uses his wife to channel his longing, the way an amplifier channels the sound from a record. He asks her to confine herself spatially, so as to make room for his wife. And so, in response to this attack on her domain, in order to compensate for the ground she has lost, Renata spreads herself over the other woman's husband, doubling the heat and intensity of her gaze as she settles her fur around her "vulnerable shoulders."

From then on things develop rapidly. Sandra is hungry, and says she'd like a sandwich, if there's enough time before they have to get going. Her friend, who is still reading *Unita*, wants one too. Fulvio orders two grilled cheese sandwiches from the barman, an affable young man from Southern Italy. Fulvio, secure between the two women who flank him on the right and left like the balancing fins on a ferry, prepares himself for the big campaign. Renata, in the meantime, has wrapped herself in her fur, transforming herself into a menacing hedge-hog. Since the bar is small and narrow, the four of them are practically sitting in one another's laps. (In fact, this nearness prompts the two women to remark later on that perhaps the whore was a lesbian, because she seemed to be coming on to them. That's how they interpret her smoldering looks—which, if they happened to touch the two women, did so only because Renata was unable to extinguish the fire in her gaze as it passed over them.)

The sandwiches arrive. Sandra starts on hers, but her friend sends hers back because she's a vegetarian and the sandwich came with ham on it. So she buries herself once more in the newspaper. While Sandra calmly eats her sandwich, Renata leans her head back and, protected by her enormous lashes, throws lascivious glances at Fulvio, glances which no one else sees. She is sparking all over. She lights a cigarette and sucks on it deeply, vamp-style, holding the smoke in her lungs for a long time before blowing it out in slow relief. She winks him a signal, then stands.

The rendezvous has been arranged. Stubbing out her cigarette in the ashtray and leaving her fur on the chair, as if promising the other women, "I'll be back soon," she goes to the place she assumes to be the site of all secret meetings—or, at any rate, the place where she's always gone up to now (and where the princess of Uganda was recently caught *inflagrante delecto*): the restroom. Proudly, moving her hips like Silvana Mangano in *Bitter Rice*, she weaves through the Germans, who are drinking their spiked coffee standing up.

Letting a few reasonable seconds pass, Fulvio also stands, muttering an almost inaudible excuse about an umbrella, just a bit of smoke to cover up his departure—after all, he has no one to convince, since no one suspects him of anything. Sandra is finishing her sandwich and her friend is just starting her own, which the waiter brought back without the ham. Fulvio runs into his friend, who has paid the bill and is headed back to join the others, says, "I'll be back in two minutes," and goes not to the bathroom, where Renata is waiting, but to the Bavarian pub next door—which, as a forbidden place, seems to him an entirely logical location for their secret rendezvous. He orders two beers at the bar and is puzzled when Renata doesn't appear.

He doesn't understand his mistake until he gets back to the hotel lobby and sees Renata's chair still empty, her fur lying there like a faithful dog. "Where were you?" his friends ask, "What took you so long?" They head out to the car. They've already put their luggage in the trunk when he sees her returning to her seat. Her gaze is full of a pity, a compassion that undoes him entirely: *Why didn't you come? Why did you trick me like that?*

The narration is concerned with precisely this issue of failure. When he goes to one place and she to another, apart from the individuals themselves, objective circumstances are also to blame. Because whatever it is that forced her to become a prostitute also makes him want to escape the temptation of drink. And if he thinks the site of their illicit meeting is the pub and not the restroom, that stems not from Sandra's prohibition of alcohol, but from his own psychological complex. The two transgressions, of drink and of sex, get confused in his mind—and as a consequence, he gets the place wrong.

The excursion to Pompeii, then, begins under the overcast sky of the failed rendezvous, with which his desires for reality were extinguished. (At the very last moment, Renata threw him an icy, Gillette-super-star glance, which tore him up inside.) For Fulvio, wrapped in the aura of defeat, Pompeii offers a kind of relief. There he sees life stopped in the midst of life, time frozen at the height of spasm. He starts to feel better. *We all live,* he thinks, *at the foot of the volcano. The only unknown is when the lava will set out for any given city, neighborhood, or person.* And like an image trapped and made eternal by a camera's deadly lens, he pictures Renata reclining in her chair, her endless lashes protecting the darts of her eyes, being slowly enveloped by a chocolaty lava that freezes, giving her over to the necropolis of memory.

It's raining, and the ruins are depressing. The beer he drank makes him need to urinate. Breaking away from the others, he goes over to the Lupanari baths where the guards won't see him, and there, against the scraped wall, in the fresh grass of the earth, watches his piss steam like an affirmation of life over stillness and death.

Which of the Two Houses
Should We Get Rid of First, Liuba Dear?

IN THIS STORY, Thrassakis, in the guise of Russian immigrant Raphael Abramov, examines the possibility of return to and resettlement in his longed-for homeland (Odessa, in the story). The story's main character has two small apartments abroad, and is trying to decide which he should get rid of first. Here I will offer a reading of the story that puts Thrassakis back in his proper place, as it were—for if I were to present it with Abramov as the main character, I'm afraid the reader would be hopelessly confused by the double, sometimes even triple masks of reference.

Thrassakis and his wife, then, discuss day and night which of the two apartments (both primarily storage spaces for books and papers, letters and manuscripts) they should get rid of first, the one in Brussels or the one in Rome. The news that the borders have been opened, that the exiles can return, that general amnesty has been granted, even to those prosecuted under Law 509 (and the similarities between Thrassakis's situation back then and my own now makes the whole situation seem like a carbon whose copies are fainter, sicker than the original, but otherwise the same), made the existence of two poles abroad superfluous, since the pivot point of the homeland had been freed. In order for a pendulum to work, it needs two points—otherwise it isn't a pendulum but a stopped watch. Thrassakis's "here today, there tomorrow" attitude, which prevented him from ever really being anywhere, saved him the emotional importunity of having his loved ones nearby. Yet the meaning of "abroad" is, of course, subjective—it depends on your point of view: what is abroad for one person is another person's home. And so the couple discusses and debates which apartment they should keep, the one in Brussels or the one in Rome. The European Council on Refugees and Exiles might let them keep one for a while. But two would be pushing it. New political exiles keep flooding in from other countries—Chile, Argentina, Poland—and they should really hand over the keys as soon as possible.

On first consideration it seems wisest to give up Apartment Number One, in Brussels, since Apartment Number Two, in Rome, is closer to Greece, and is generally more pleasant and more convenient in all respects. But what about the much-discussed possibility of a coup in Leone's Italy? Might all the things of value they've amassed during their time in exile (documents, books, paintings) end up stranded in a country that suddenly finds itself in the same kind of fateful morass as the one from which their own country is just beginning to emerge? And even if the coup doesn't take place, there is the approach of the *Anno Santo* to consider, during which millions of religious pilgrims from all over the world are expected to descend on the Eternal City to visit the Vatican. How can you get around in a city that has literally been occupied by tour groups and busses? It has been estimated that nine million religious pilgrims, above and beyond the normal numbers of tourists, will be visiting throughout the year, with peak periods at Christmas and Easter. Brussels, on the other hand, with its climate of perpetual rain, is NATO's mecca. "How can we live there, now that Greece has withdrawn?" Glafka wonders, and rightly so, while Glafkos, with his obsessive worries about a possible Italian coup, prefers Brussels to the she-wolf's den.

The couple doesn't seem to have any doubts about the political changeover that has taken place in their own country. That year (1974), starting with the liberation of Angola and Mozambique from Portugal, and culminating in Egypt's recovery of lost ground to the east of the Suez Canal in the aftermath of the Yom Kippur War, the world has taken a turn that promises much for the reinstatement of democracy. Only for Greece, that change came with a cost: while Mozambique and Angola were freed, and Egyptian land regained, a part of Cyprus was lost.

Thrassakis's unpublished story ends in a similar climate of unease, of emotional uncertainty, of waiting for developments, a curious stillness of dark winds. The narrator, a nutshell tossed on the roiling waves of History, tries to guess what will happen next in order to act accordingly. He doesn't try to change the flow of history. He just places his bets. He definitely wants to hold on to one of the two apartments abroad. And if Brussels finally wins in the end, it's at the agent's emphatic insistence. Though Glafkos doesn't yet know it, Joe is right at home there, on his own turf—while in Rome, with the geometrical growth of the Italian Communist Party (one and a half million card-holding members, an unprecedented event in the history of the Socialist movement), Joe, with the naïveté of inbred anti-Communism, also fears a coup—not from the Right, but from the Left. (Of course in the story, as explained above, the theme of return is presented in another key: Raphael Abramov returns to Odessa after his dear Liuba assures him that the hunting of Jews has ceased.)

II

UNABLE TO PRESENT my old passport—so full of illegal renewals it was sure to have gotten someone in trouble at the consulate—I presented myself instead, fifteen days after the supposed return of democracy to its ancient birthplace. I reported the loss of my old passport and requested the issue of a new one, with which to return to Greece.

"But where could you have lost it?" asked the terrified bureaucrat, quite at a loss himself, what with all the recent changes.

"Somewhere where I'll never find it," I answered, proud that this was the first time in seven and a half years I was setting foot in the embassy of the nation to which I supposedly belong.

He dared, albeit hesitatingly, to give me that old line about needing police certification verifying the loss of my old passport, and thus legalizing the issue of a new one.

"Why don't we drop the formalities, sir," I replied. "Do you think the colonels were worried about the finer legal points of their actions when they took over control of the state?"

"Of course not, Mr. Lazaridis. You're absolutely right," said the good bureaucrat, glancing fearfully around for that old dog, the military attaché, the junta's bad cop who had carried a gun all these years and threatened gods and devils if the civil servants ever dared help a democrat—"I'll tear you to

shreds, you sons of bitches," he would shout, pacing up and down in the sanctuary of the embassy, thirsting for Royalist-Communist blood (for he had identified the king with the Communists, since the king also took an open position against the "revolutionary government" the military attaché served).

"Mr. Consul," I started.

"Vice-consul," he corrected. "Not quite spoiled, but almost," he said, laughing. After all, the man had a sense of humor, he was an educated guy who seemed to be suffering even more than we were, we professional exiles.

"Mr. Vice-consul, then," I said. "As you must know, I haven't set foot in this building for as long as that anomaly—"

"I know, and I respect you for it," he sighed.

"Let me tell you, then, that I did not, in fact, lose the old passport, but I can't show it to you, because that would mean exposing your colleagues, who, in complete secrecy and at their own personal risk, repeatedly renewed it for me. Think how you would feel if you had done that for someone and he, this guy, were to go and expose you to your co-workers. Would you like that?"

"Of course not. Go on."

"I have nothing to add, and I know how to read," I concluded. "I want a new passport. Here are the photographs. Here's the application. Here's the number of the old one."

And indeed, he gave me the new one right away, apologizing profusely for the colonels' emblem, the phoenix, that was stamped on the cover.

Thus it was that I came across his old, useless passport at the university library. And I dove in with pleasure. A pleasure almost unnatural, as unbecoming as it was illicit. I gaze at his long, thin face, to which his glasses seemed to be trying to lend a bit of curve. There is an artificial light shining on his hair, in the very place where his bald spot will later appear; the lens looks at him a bit slantwise, and from below. "Profession: Writer. Place of Birth: Thassos. Date of birth: 18/11/33. Eye Color: Brown. Hair Color: Brown. Identifying Marks: None. Country for Which This Passport is Valid . . . "

On his new passport, New Zealand, Malta and South Africa are added to the list. The "by way of Yugoslavia" present in the old one ('65) is missing from the new ('74), which means that his mission there, arranged by the agent, must have been incognito. Otherwise he would have needed a visa, which would have been stamped somewhere in his passport. The "Allemagne Occidentale" of '65 is replaced, in '74, by "Allemagne Federale," reflecting not a change in West Germany itself, but a change in the mentality in the land of the passport's issue, i.e., post-dictatorship Greece.

As I flipped through his passport in the monitored room of the American university library (and not, I admit, without some emotion), the stamps that ornamented it looked to me like goose tracks frozen in the snow.

Some words are like untorn, unpunched tickets, unused, dumb. Then there are other words of which you keep only part—the other half is held by the usher, the conductor, the ticket collector. Those words, missing their other half, can complete no sentence, can assist no forward march.

(Thrassakis, "Diary of Return")

Diary Of Return

"THEY TOOK AWAY my analogy, my axis of reference. Now, axle-less, 'how can I proceed, to whom should I report, from whom,' as Karamanlis once said, 'should I enlist support?'"

This cry, which appears in the *Diary* immediately following the restoration of freedom to Glafkos's land, refers to a statement made by former prime minister Karamanlis in his Parisian exile, as he waited hour by hour to be called back to Greece, unsure as to which levels of the army he should apply to for support. A national leader's ignorance as to who is on his side reveals the darkness not so much of an entire era, but of that particular leader, who can't be sure what layer of the populace supports him until that layer, or part of it, demonstrates its support by inviting him back to the ballot-box from his place in exile. In a similar situation, Berlinguer, for example, or Ceriglio, or any other general secretary or representative of a mass organization, would never have to ask himself from whom he should seek support—after all, a real leader knows what specific incarnation of oppression he's up against.

I thought this explanation necessary to prevent the reader from being confused by the phrase, "as Karamanlis might say." On the next page, Thrassakis himself enters into a detailed analysis of Karamanlis' name, with reference to the English "manly," an analysis supported by Karamanlis' physical form: he is a handsome man, strong and robust, though aged by his years in exile. "Kara" is Turkish for "black," and before the elections following the junta's fall, Thrassakis wittily predicts that Center Union candidate Mavros (whose name is Greek for "black") will only get half as many votes as Karamanlis, since he can cover only the "kara" half of "Karamanlis."

As for the substance of the passage quoted above, I believe it speaks for itself. With "analogy" and "axis of reference," Thrassakis refers to the ersatz substitution for the real, the Greek "original" he was unable to enjoy during his years abroad. During those years, he would eat Algerian sweets that were only *like* the Greek *saragli*. Fresh fish abroad *resembled* the fish from his island. A pine tree *looked like* the ones on Mt. Lycavettos in Athens. Roman aqueducts *reminded* him of the aqueduct in Kavala, while the mosaics in Ravenna *resembled* the mosaics at the Church of the Twelve Apostles in Thessaloniki's Old City. All these analogies, which sustained him during the years of exile, collapsed onto themselves with the junta's fall.

In a letter to Thomas, Thrassakis writes:

> *One of the torments of exile is when it finally ends—you have to unlearn habits acquired out of necessity and return to your old daily schedule, now weedy and overgrown with disuse. Waiting for the boat home from Venice, I think of how jealous I used to be of that boat: while my mind could travel with it, my body could not. It was a mental pastime, bringing this "strange lover" back to life again through memory, making it more alive than the real. And now that this dreamy habit is meeting its end, I am left stranded for a while in the void, as if my axle has broken and I can't keep my hold on the wheel* [i.e., the axis of reference].

All these preliminaries to return contribute to a kind of waiting-room agony. For Thrassakis, exile and prison are nearly synonymous in that they both cut you off from reality. Thus he compares himself to a political prisoner who is unable to sleep with the light off after his release, since during his years of imprisonment he had gotten used to sleeping in a room where the light was always on. The thought that his love of the simile ("the endless 'as if' of writing"), overdeveloped over the years by the conditions of his exile, might now be abolished throws him into a panic. What will happen when he can no longer say, "Sicilian olives are like Kalamata olives?" How can he just say "Kalamata olives," without the infamous "like"? Thomas comforts him over the phone: "Come on back, we'll figure something out. We'll say, Kalamata olives are like the Sicilian ones."

This, then, is Glafkos's first reaction to the news that the junta has fallen and Greece has been freed after seven and a half years of enslavement. But let's look more closely at the socio-political climate of the time, before throwing our hero into the fray. Indeed, we are unable to understand or explain many of his notes in the *Diary*, unless we keep in mind the shocking events of that summer of 1974.

Dr. Kissinger's arrival in the international arena heralds a new era which we might characterize as a "remission," since no one is quite sure whether the doctor is opposed to the military or represents the golden peak of its rule. During this era of uncertainty, the wronged Arabs pressure the West by raising the price of oil, thus giving those in favor of nuclear power a chance to prevail. Spiro Agnew's conviction offers hope that the Magician/Pacifier, himself a supporter of nuclear power, will manage to check the monopolistic interests of the multinational oil companies. At that time the world doesn't yet know that he, "Dillinger," was behind the underhanded assassination of Allende in Chile. That comes to light only after the crisis in Cyprus—when, overestimating his omniscience, he doesn't hesitate to link his name with the uprooting of a small but proud people who had managed to live in an equilibrium maintained not by fear but by peaceful co-existence. The island's prosperity and success were crushed in a few days by a Turkish invasion which, though it sparked the liberation of Mother Greece from the junta's reign, also brought about the devastating displacement of the Greek inhabitants of northern Cyprus from their homes, their fields, their places of work. Church bells that had rung in harmony now rang in mourning. The wedding turned into a funeral, though the ritual of the procession didn't change in the slightest detail. Only Archbishop Makarios disappeared, since God took mercy on him and sent down an angel/helicopter to lift him to safety. Unlike the exodus of refugees from Asia Minor in 1922, this one was contained to Cyprus itself, and so its anguish and suffering didn't touch the homeland directly, but only through the newspaper reports and the images shown on TV. In the eddying void created by the invasion and the junta's fall, events sucked Karamanlis back from his eleven-year exile in Paris on the instructions of "Dillinger" himself. The night of his return was marked by public celebration (thus confirming the old adage, "Your death is my life"). A heroic general from the previous regime served as the temporary overseer of this change of scene, like a stagehand making sure the old sets have been struck before the new set designers arrive, the playwrights and actors of the new regime. Or like those overlays on maps, where the black of dry land encroaches on the blue of the sea. A small detail, that is, swallowed up by the great celebration of freedom.

But soon the celebrating began to subside, as they dragged up from the depths monsters and signs that had sunk along with the shipwrecked vessel: mutilated bodies, belts, electroshock machines, martyred sailors, the unknown deckhands of Democracy. As for Cyprus, an attack would have been an admission of defeat, though Karamanlis wisely withdrew the army (if not his own political support) from the NATO alliance. The country started down the road to national elections; investigations began into the events at the Polytechnic; and the members of the junta were isolated and exiled, to be put on trial as soon as a new government came into power, authorized by the all-powerful people themselves. Negotiations over Cyprus got underway as the refugees prepared to pass an inhuman winter on an island where just a short while before they had had the upper hand.

Thus Cyprus, that "unsinkable aircraft carrier," sank, while Greece's "cholera," already in retreat, was finished off by antibiotics prepared in the very same laboratories of the Pentagon that had created the epidemic in the first place. In other words, this is the period of the "melting of the ice," before it freezes again in cold storage, taking on Henry Moore-ish shapes, in which the absence of the model allows for the presence of the work the model inspired. The tragedy of Cyprus passed into small print. Global overpopulation, the specter of famine, disarmament through armament—these were Kissinger's chief concerns. All the rest, for him and the imperialist politics he represented, was small change.

II

ON THE DAY when Glafkos went to exchange his lira for drachma in preparation for his return, the bank was full of tourists jostling before the tellers' windows, returning panicked from the Middle East because of the threat of war between Greece and Turkey. All this was creating problems in transit hubs like Brindisi, Bari, and Ancona. From Venice he writes to his friend Thomas:

Poor Greece, *I thought.* When I see you pushing and shoving in front of the windows of foreign banks . . . . *The little man in front of me cried out in his awful Italian, "I've been here for two hours and you haven't waited on me yet." Everyone turned and looked curiously at this half-pint in glasses twitching and trembling with nerves. I knew right away from his accent that he wasn't Spanish or Portuguese or Turkish or Albanian or Yugoslavian but Greek. We Greeks speak foreign languages with a distinct accent, like imported soil, revealing our background in the joints of words. "I'll have you know I'm a headmaster in my country. You cannot make me wait in line like this!" "Who does he think he is?" someone next to me remarked disparagingly, and those nearby— the familiar blend of foreigners: a robust African couple, a man who seemed to be Austrian or Walloon, two Lebanese, and some old American grannies—all laughed. Our guy, the Greek, was so short that his head only came as high as the marble countertop, which remained indiffer- ent to his rage as he yelled at a sweet-faced young clerk who in Greece would no doubt have been one of his former students and would have bent over backwards to help his old teacher. But this young man just said, "Please wait your turn in line, sir." "But I've been waiting my turn for two hours, the boat will sail and—" "The boat won't leave without you," one of the supervisors told him politely. Then, to placate him, the supervisor took the Greek's passport and promised to go in person to look for the telex he was expecting. At that, the man calmed down right away. He was getting reproachful looks from the oth- ers, but he didn't mind one bit—after all, he had managed to cut the line. The supervisor came back, saying that no telex had arrived in his name. "But how can that be?" our man asked, shattered by the unexpected news. "It was sup- posed to get here two days ago." And suddenly the black cloud of life in a for- eign land (and, moreover, an enemy country—he himself had fought these spaghetti-eaters back in '40) breaks over him. "It's not the bank's fault," the supervisor calmly replied, returning the man's passport with the phoenix on its cover. "It is our duty and our pleasure to serve our customers, but I'm afraid nothing has arrived in your name." Poor Greece, harassed in foreign banks, foreign factories, foreign industries, with a word for everything, but never an act or an object to embody those dreams.*

Judging from this narration, it seems rather obvious that Thrassakis was also unable to exchange any money. Thus, upon his return to his country after eight years of exile, the first thing he asked was, "How much is the lira worth?"

III

"THIS," he will write elsewhere, "is what exile does to us. How much is the franc worth, or the mark?" Every conscientious worker is directly concerned with the exchange value of his labor. He asks not about the quality, as in Cavafy's poem, but about the quantity. An everyday, anti-heroic exchange, but human and justified by the Marxist system of thought.

He refers to this first day every so often in his *Diary*. Like every first contact, it makes an impression on him simply by virtue of being a first. It brands him. He grabs hold of it from early morning, almost by the hair of the night—and it's a beautiful day, after the rain, sweet and scented, and the mark it leaves is like the stamp on a Christmas cake, baked with goat's milk and honey from thyme.

Fragment of a Cycladic statuette

Sidari, Corfu. Twelve years have passed. Morning coffee. The first sharing of drinks with strangers. Conversation. "We'll side with someone," one man says, "now that we're out of NATO."

"Better to stay neutral," says the owner. "Either way, the game is split between the big players."

"We'll take sides," the other insists. "I say they should bury the dictator in cement up to here," he continues, putting a hand to his throat, "and set him up in Omonia Square so everyone can walk by and spit in his face."

Late geometric

The Thrassakises' first day is full of surprises. They stayed awake all night on the ferry—and for once there were no tourists gazing out at the distant lightening flashing above Istria, where all the exiles used to gather with souls starved for their homeland—so no sleep has mediated between the *there* and the *here*, and they disembark the next morning as if into a waking dream. Small lakes of rainwater reflect the sky on the clay of the port. The main square, touched by a slanting light, is deserted except for a few dogs sniffing at trees, and the delivery boy from the coffee shop, straight out of something by Tsarouchis or Vasileos, carrying a tray on his way to fill an order somewhere. The first shock that shakes Glafkos awake comes at the kiosk, where he goes to buy a newspaper. Since the Sunday papers haven't arrived, he buys a weekly magazine instead. "Everything is so expensive," he writes. "Prices are almost unrecognizable. I bought a *Postman* for fifteen drachma. If I ever publish anything in it, I wonder who will be rich enough to read what I write." The new coins seem light compared to the Italian ones he's used to. Stamped with the colonels' phoenix, they reflects their creators' lack of weight. "Like whitewashed ash," he writes.

Early geometric

We laugh. We take pictures. "In a way you're both lucky and unlucky," the owner of the coffee shop tells me. "Unlucky because you had to live far from your country for so many years, and lucky because you were spared the torture, the prisons, the daily humiliation. . . . "

Further on, Thrassakis notes, "Hard to get used to it all." Much harder, certainly, with the people than with the landscape, which remained unchanged through the years, a statue of Time carved by Mother Sea, waiting to welcome him back. The stones of ash-gray marble and embraces of clay in Sidari with its fine sand speak to him of a timeless duration. Glafkos finds fragments of himself in these Henry Moore-ish erasures of rock, in the rounded shapes that harbor and nurture fish, in this village where he once got food poisoning from traces of pesticide on a tomato. Now the faces have aged; new floors have been added to buildings. Young Plutarch, the café owner's son who always wanted to become a sailor and take off on one of the ships, "really did get on a ship and leave, six or seven years ago, and had a civil marriage over in America to a girl from the village, while the old sea-dog, his grandfather, is slowly dying of old age in the shack next door." When Glafka wants to relax, she digs with a pocketknife to unearth rare rainbow-colored rocks wedged into the ground like the tusks of primeval monsters, trying to eat the earth that is eating them.

Everything that happened on that first day—for the first is always important—seemed like a kind of repetition. The rising sun brought people out with it, and the double scallop of the shore was soon strewn with umbrellas, motorbikes, bodies, balls. Like Adam and Eve, having eaten the forbidden fruit of memory, Glafkos and Glafka were entitled to flickerings of memory, of prehistoric selves, seemingly lost, or buried in the silt built up by rain and meteors. They had the right to try and figure out who they had once been, in relation to how things were now. But there are no mirrors in nature. On the contrary, nature has one great power: to heals wounds by incorporating them into its geography. The gashed edges of rocks, rounded by time, had become eloquent curves. Thus time, nullified in the eternity of the landscape, could be nothing but the present. So Glafkos and Glafka were shaken from their hypnotized state by the arrival of the first swimmers—who, it being Sunday, came down in droves to the beach. But for our couple it was enough, that first, immaculate hour.

Wine jug and neighboring large vessel

We pass by the prisons, paying tribute to our friends who spent so many years inside. It is one p.m. and the whitewashed prisons are blinding in the light. Like houses on Mykonos. The guards watch our taxi with curiosity as it writes an "s" in the road and disappears down the same street from which it came.

It is hard for him to get used to the fact that everyone around him is speaking Greek. He is bombarded by fragments of phrases. He feels connected to these people. Even their boredom is his. Their words define his silence.

"Do you not need this chair?" asks a woman in a bikini beside him, stressing the "not." She seems to have taken them for foreigners, and so, like anyone trying to explain something to someone who they suspect doesn't understand their language, she resorts to pantomime, stressing the core of the sentence—in this case the negative, "not." They are at a café in Paliokastrista. Beside a crystalline sea. The kids from the next table are running around, the grandmothers looking out at the topless bathers, the men cracking crayfish and lobsters, all in a happy, animated atmosphere. Glafkos and Glafka listen to the waiters thundering out orders, scolding the younger ones. "My hair is easier to comb," Glafka says, "The water is softer here." And a tear of joy rolls down her cheek.

Headless female torso

Only after lunch do they go back to the hotel and, for the first time, put the marker of sleep between exile and return, dividing yesterday from today in the course of a single day. What matters isn't to fall asleep in a place, but to wake up there. And they sink into sleep.

Attic black-figure oil-flask. Burial wreath of golden oak leaves. Gold earrings and glass ring-stone with representation of charging bull from grave in Arta (Amvrakia). . . .

It is a deep sleep, leaden, heavy with wine and with sun, with the sweet-smelling air and the scent of the earth. When he opens his eyes, Glafkos isn't quite sure where he is. He sees the ruined castle across the way, lacy against the bloody background of the sky, and can't decide if it's a postcard or a set for some Shakespearian play. "The old port" he will write. "Ferries waiting with open jaws for cars to embark. And the chairs at the café in the square waiting for customers. Again, fragments of conversations float up through the window." But just then, on first cracking open his eyes, he wonders if he might not be (another analogy) somewhere else (in Teracina or Porto Ercole, towns in Italy that resemble the old port here). Man lives, as we said, with axes of reference. Without these streaks of memory, he is unable to make sense of what is happening to him. Just as there can be no broadcast without listeners or book without readers, the human mind can accept no image unless it bears at least a marginal resemblance to something with which the mind is already familiar.

The couple gets dressed and goes out. Glafkos observes:

I've been noticing the priests here. They're always out in public. They sit, drink, eat, talk with friends. Unlike Catholic priests, who walk practically glued to

*the walls, like St. Francis, with rosaries looped over their belts, our priests are
a natural part of everyday life. In their black cassocks, they mix with the people like raisins in the rice of a stuffed pepper.*

After dinner they have rice pudding for dessert, with a generous dusting of cin-
namon. The narrow streets are literally jammed with people. It is Sunday
evening.

*This place seems to be waking up from a great lethargy, on an entirely visible
level. The way people read the newspapers shows that for a long time they did-
n't read them—and I stress the "didn't" the way the woman in the bikini asked
me if I didn't need the chair. The newspapers are flooded with bloody scenarios, descriptions of torture, secret trials, unmaskings of scandals and sinecures,
the records kept on innocent citizens. Never in my life have I seen such passionate reading.*

Later in the *Diary*, when the couple is sitting and drinking cold orangeade: "The
fall of the dictatorship opened taps that had been stopped up by fear."

The fact that Thrassakis, as a Greek, is now in the ethnic majority, compared
to the sprinkling of tourists, gives him a feeling of security—"We're in the
majority here"—but one which he quickly gets over with a second glance. At
the Averof Taverna, the waiters "sparkle with agility." They bring plenty of
water to the table. Glafkos had suffered the lack of that water for so many years
in the restaurants and cafés of the Common Market that this lack eventually
came to seem normal to him, and now he appreciates anew this offering of the
cold carafe. On the other hand, used to waiting at least fifteen minutes for his
food to be served, the secretions of his gastric juices don't have time to prepare
his body to take in that food, so everything ends up sitting, quite literally, in his
stomach.

"We're taking it easy," he says a bit further on, concerning his readjustment.
"I tell myself that I'm like floating currency, which, through all the ups and
downs of the market, keeps its cool in adjusting to the new fiscal reality." And
he continues:

Bare, jagged mountains. A reality. And on their bareness, fire. They're burning the trees so the earth will sprout grass when it rains, for the sheep to graze. The stress and strain have made us both nervous. The money flies. But I've promised not to keep track, at least for these first few days. The economics of freedom. The moon is waxing. The earth smells sweet after the rain. The cricket chirps, complains, returns. . . .

Glafkos's first contact with his country's new TV takes place under peculiar circumstances. On their way home from the Averof, they stop for a drink at a coffee shop open late, and there they see it, our mistress the television, in the place where icons used to be kept. Before their departure, there had of course been a few experimental stations showing mountains and waves, the human geography of the country, before the utility poles came and tamed even the wildest of mountains and scrub. Thrassakis, a supporter of MacLuhan's theory that "the medium is the message," soon reaches extreme conclusions equating the dictatorship with television, two evils, "cholera" and "leprosy," nursed on the same milk, found on the same axis of reference. TV and the dictatorship had spread themselves simultaneously over the land, one sterilizing the skin where the other would plunge the needle.

Alkis Steas, flashing a final smile at the camera, relinquishes his spot to some atrocious program in English with Greek subtitles. For Thrassakis, thirsting for his own language—the Thrassakis who wrote, "If Levine were to sketch a caricature of me, he would make me an enormous ear, drinking in the intoxicating nectar of words"—the shock of the (American) occupying forces' televised Vietnamization of his land is hard to swallow. But he forces himself to accept it with a steely, thoughtful resignation:

I tell myself that's how it goes. The Greek has to learn a second language if he wants to survive in this place. I can't look at things egoistically, from the writer's point of view. I have to rise (or sink) to the level of circumstances, and learn to talk like an economist. Learn to say, for example, that movies in English offer the people a means of free education in the English language. . . .

Nevertheless, no matter how hard he tries to overcome the trauma, he can't help comparing these programs to the secondhand airplanes the Pentagon sells to its colonies, causing the deaths of so many trained pilots, so many shining young men. What he means is, the quality of the programming is unacceptable.

And while he knows (and we know) that secondhand cars are often perfectly fine, even comfortable, secondhand airplanes mean suicide. And secondhand movies are like spoiled (choleric) mussels: they poison the body. "TV," he will write, "the opiate of the masses."

≈

Misko Macaroni, how tasty!
Top quality. And it makes more.

Akaaaaakie!
Make sure the macaroni is Sisko.

≈

IN HIS "Dialogues of the Dead" (again, from the *Diary*), Thrassakis assigns the following dialogue to two waiters:

Waiter No. 1 (to Waiter No. 2): That guy [nodding at me] *is one of those who spoke the truth, and couldn't come home because of it.*
No. 2 (to No. 1): So he's Greek?
No. 1 (to No. 2): A hundred percent. Though all those years abroad gave him kind of a European air.
No. 2 (to me): I've got a family. If I spoke up and they sent me into exile, who would take care of my children?

The first Japanese tourist appears beneath the window of their hotel room, quietly taking pictures of an olive tree where a goat is tied, scratching itself against the bark. Glafkos says nothing, thinks nothing, except perhaps, "So they've gotten as far as here"—then calmly goes out for his morning coffee on the waterfront.

My second morning on Greek soil. Without my wanting to, I keep on think-
ing of scenes from Mons, from Charleroix, Namour, Liege, and I shudder at
the thought that those cities could have become eternal cities for me. "Paris,"
Glafka always said, "is a city built by the exiles of the world."

Glafkos is polite, charming, and soon has a ready answer for whoever asks: "Yes,
we came to stay"—though part of his joy in returning is the preparation for
departure. As he writes to Thomas, "If you told me that I could never leave, I'd
be the unhappiest man alive. I like my country, but only on the condition that
I'm free to abandon it whenever I want."

Thrassakis wakes up happy in the mornings, thinking he is "in place." The
hazy clouds of a possible coup can no longer darken the wide sky of his joy.
"Even in prison, I'd be with people who speak my language," he thinks, satisfied, since what had scared him most during all those years abroad was the
prospect of finding himself imprisoned with people who didn't speak the
same language as he.

≈

"IOANNINA. Morning, August 23, 1974. The same clouds."
He sits for hours, he tells us, in the Byzantium Coffee Shop, observing the
movements of the crowds. He detoxifies his gaze in these floods of ordinary people. *These people,* he says to himself, *are my people. We belong to the same nation.*
We defend the same land. We will die for the same country. It concerns me directly
that they read my books. So why do I feel so foreign? So out of it? He has come from
the outside, but would rather not feel "out of it." Just as he drags the rain with
him, he thinks he drags a wall, too. "The seven years that passed threw back not
just the nation but its drachma, too." For him the coffee shop is a watch-tower.
The army recruits walking through the city in uniform seem to have taken
on a mercenary boldness and thuggish attitude. The outside pockets below their
knees make their pants look unkempt, giving their whole body a look of impu-
dence, the mean, scruffy look of recruits in the bordellos. It upsets him to watch
them, because they remind him of Thieu's army in South Vietnam. Instead of

the soldiers seeming out of place among the civilians, the civilians seem out of place among the soldiers.

Parliament of Dodoni

"The officers are responsible for everything." Autumn weather. "If some good program starts up, I'll watch it. What else is there to do here in the winter?" And he orders an almond pastry.

Glafkos watches. His gaze is fixed on unhappiness. He spits sparks like an Ioanninan knife. At this coffee shop he understands, for the first time, the likeness between Greece and Rumania. This realization, he tells us, is sparked by the glint of a gold tooth in the mouth of a farmer sitting across from him eating a piece of *bougatsa*. And so, in his mind, he imagines Tito's "third road" as the only solution. He shudders at the very thought of the General, because it brings everything else rushing to mind. The Croats, the agent. And he swore he wouldn't think about any of that for as long as he was in Greece. He left them like unclaimed baggage at customs, to pick up again on his way out. Just the thought of the agent makes him nervous. So he stands up to stretch his legs, and goes out to get some fresh air.

The afternoon papers from Athens have just arrived at the kiosk on the square. People are falling on them like locusts on leaves. The newspapers become enlarged declarations of political convictions. Promenading with a paper tucked under his arm, each individual shows off what he believes, where his political leanings lie. And he is free to do so, and with each passing day people grow a bit braver. "But it's difficult to defrost the people's fear," says one young man, an architecture student Thrassakis first got to know in Milan.

He sits down again at the Byzantium. Why should he leave? Where better could he possibly go? He has friends here. Company. Tonight there's a soccer match, Ioannina against Athens. Knowing nothing about soccer, Glafkos makes one gaffe after another. A young man with a single long nail tells him it's a friendly match, just a scrimmage, really. At the Philadelphia stadium, the stadium of brotherly love. Thrassakis doesn't even know that this is the first year the Ioanninan team has made the nationals.

Songbirds
New Zealand Rabbit
Sacks for Sale
Meat-producing Fowl
Live Animals

He goes back to the hotel. Glafka wants to rest. On top of the journey, the storm and the lightening—which frightens her as it would a little girl—have worn her out. Glafkos stands on the balcony and looks at the lake, the bald mountain. The garden. On the other side of the garden, a half-finished building. The kitchen balcony, facing him, is covered with laundry lines and plastic dustpans, and a girl is sitting there admiring her wavy hair, waiting for her boyfriend to come up. Thrassakis is in a romantic mood, from the postcards he saw of Ali Pasha and Vassiliki. He goes back into the room. It's pouring outside. Turning on the radio, he hears: *CAN YOU EVER GO BACK TO YOUR OLD DETERGENT?* Answer: *NO.* The speaker concludes: *YET ANOTHER HOUSEWIFE WHO SWITCHED OVER TO JACK.* He changes the station. But the next one is no better: some program about sports in ancient times. And in particular, some "gymnastic writer."

Mobile Examination Office

"Listen," a man selling shoes in a corner store in the neighborhood of Tourkomahala says to him. The others who know him smile. Stroking the pompoms of plastic clogs and slippers. "Listen, the colonel claims to be protecting the honor of the homeland while he sinks his hands into millions. What's that all about? What kind of state is this? All we manage to make are traitors and thieves. That's all. I can't figure out why this state hasn't fallen apart by now."

Glafkos encounters this demand for justice with every step. After mobilization and inflation, it's the third big issue on people's minds. Voices everywhere demand the just punishment of the guilty parties: "Let the people deal with the Junta." "I'm impressed," he writes, "by how thirsty people are to talk, to listen. On the verge of a paid leave and admission of defeat without any leave from the Party. . . . "

It's constantly raining at the Monastery of Philanthropy. The church where it held its Secret School during the years of the Turkish occupation is on the island in the middle of the lake. Frescoes of ancient philosophers in the narthex, and of saints and apostles in the main church, where the windows have been opened to let in some air. On the frescoes, the visiting-cards of vandals: "Soula and Nikos, 1970," "Mairoula, 1969." Glafkos is happy in these little churches, which are barely big enough for him alone: "They contain me and I contain them."

Iron

LAZARIDIS

Tires

LAZARUS

≈

THE STORM HAS kicked up again. It's raining. It seems to me that this is how the weather will be here, most of the time. Monastery of the Prodromou. Ali Pasha's house. "It is forbidden to lie on the couch." I pay for my ticket. Behind me, others don't pay. "We're reserves," I hear them saying, called up by the mobilization. They show the identification cards from their units and are let in for free.

"Do not touch objects." "Lunar calendar in membrane." "Turkish table of Kioutaheia porcelain." "Persis Aise: Organizer of harems of Ali Tepeleni." "Self-loading Browning pistol belonging to Hasan Pasha." "TRAI: back-loading pistol."

≈

"THIS FIG tree usually gives fruit twice a year," the woman says. "But this year, nothing. Not the first time, or the second. The figs all turned yellow and fell. It put out so many that in the end none of them survived."
 A hen waddles by, a fat young thing with a generous behind, a remnant of the age before chickens, too, were industrialized.

"She's young," the woman says. "Just yesterday she hatched her first two eggs."
The woman retreats into her little hut. She is sewing. Her son is sleeping
in one of the rooms, which is why she has been speaking so softly. He just got
back from a 48-hour stint at the border. He was drafted and had to leave
everything hanging, work, money, everything. The house is about as big as Ali
Pasha's house here—which is to say, tiny. The windows look onto the lake with
its thickets of reeds. Lit up by a weak light, the woman looks like something
out of a painting by Nikiforos Litras, influenced by Delacroix.

"There are no more eels in the lake. They drained another lake nearby, and
that seems to have shut the doors of return. Whatever eels there were went
down, deep down, and never came up again."

Portraits of Cabbies

WITH MY OWN title, "Portraits of Cabbies," I have selected from Thrassakis's *Diary* those passages in which he attempts to analyze the Greek mentality by comparing individuals of the same profession (in this case, taxi drivers) from several different regions of the country. This effort reflects his deep desire to cease being merely a Macedonian writer, like so-called Macedonian *halva*, and to become more pan-Hellenic in his approach. "Since all Greeks read my work," he writes in a letter, "I should be writing about all Greeks."

I

THE FIRST in this series of cabbies is a Vlach from Thessaly who married a woman from Corfu and settled down there, since, our writer observes, a wife often comes with a house (from her dowry)—and as everyone knows, everything begins with the acquisition of a permanent place of residence. It's Sunday and the banks are closed, so, after haggling over the price of the ride in Italian lira (in Glafkos's day, western countries, dispensing with the old border disputes, have replaced them with international monetary crises that bring about reciprocal depreciations of currency), Glafkos and Glafka finally get into the taxi to begin their pilgrimage-drive. It is the morning of their return; they've just gotten off the ferry from Brindisi, and the sun hasn't yet risen above the square with its combed trees and freshly-washed stones. Though it is early morning, their driver orders a cognac from the coffee shop on the square, which startles and worries the couple, since he'll be driving in

243

the mountains on curves where the trees have rooted in the asphalt. But they say nothing. For them the moment has a special charm: everyone is still asleep, the shop is almost empty, just a few old regulars and a waiter watering the potted plants with a hose. Glafkos and Glafka look at one another, unsure whether or not they are still living in a dream. Ordering a coffee, in Greek, Glafkos feels a shudder pass through his lips, as in his school days whenever he got the best grade in his class on a foreign language exam. The driver is drinking his second cognac. In the village where they stop later, he'll drink yet another ouzo, so as not to displease the people who own the shop. But he seems to be a stable driver. Mild honks, gentle curves. Apparently the alcohol doesn't have much of an effect on him. This heavy-headed man, a Thessalian of the plain through and through, is unable to get drunk off the island's beauty. Born in the blind, stupid plain, he has to drink first before heading up into the mountains. In order to come out of his shell, to tolerate himself in his skin, he needs to be pushed from the inside. Thrassakis, on the other hand, is all smell (the earth after yesterday's rain) and sight (the kerchiefed old women, the goats, the sheep, the jagged hills), uplifted by these external stimulations. At some point in the journey the driver starts complaining about the price of gas. "Last year it was seven drachmas a liter," he says, "now it's seventeen. Whatever money I make I throw right back into the taxi, just to keep it running. And the taxi stand closes in the winter," he continues. "Here on the island we take what we get working three months a year, during the summer. But this year, what with the business in Cyprus, and the *other*, there was hardly any traffic at all. Not a soul set foot on Corfu."

This description of the dead summer should be compared to the sixth portrait, in which the cab driver likens the square in Navplio to a graveyard. But the most important element in this narration, as the informed reader will understand, is the reference to the "other," which is how the cabby refers to the "cholera" epidemic, the seven years of shame. It has neither name nor gender— it is entirely neuter. At this mention of the junta, Glafkos and Glafka glance doubtfully at one another. (Later, with the experience he has gained, Glafkos will tell us that he would never have opened up to the cabby. But at that point, not knowing, he took a chance.) "The junta," he says, "is the reason we stayed away for so many years." The cab driver accepts this pronouncement calmly, his face

devoid of expression, lighting a cigarette and offering them the pack. "No
thanks, I don't smoke." Throughout the remainder of the portrait, as the day
proceeds, the cabby's form grows darker. When they stop for lunch he orders
spaghetti and drinks two beers, one after the other. Thrassakis, in his bathing
suit, pushes his chair back to escape the sound of the cabby chewing, and is hit
hard on the back by a young kid carrying a crate of fruit to the kitchen. *The
nudge of the homeland*, he says to himself. *In returning, I take up valuable space.
I block the passage of others.* Then, at the journey's end, he hears the braying of a
donkey, turned toward him, and accepts it as a welcome into the small, bitter
love of his homeland.

2

LEAVING IGOUMENITSA, they chose not the best cab but the youngest driver, a
kid who honked at everyone on the road to Ioannina. Of course there weren't
many cars, but he still seemed like lord of the place and the people. He was a carefree, light-hearted guy, though already washed in the slight melancholy that
belongs not just to Epiros but to all of continental Greece. He had no tapes in his
car, just the radio. They took a girl along with them to Ioannina who looked like
anything but the cousin he said she was; she slept in the front seat, waking on the
wild mountain to say she had been dreaming of lightning. But it wasn't a dream,
it really was lightening—a bolt hit the wires that hung in the air before them,
throwing out sparks like fireworks that never go out. After Zalongo and Laka
Souli they descended, while the storm stayed up on the mountain, like a scarf
around a wild man's throat. They stopped at a spring. "It has the best water in this
region," the cab driver told them. "People come all the way from Igoumenitsa and
carry it back in buckets." There was a café next to the spring. An old woman was
mopping the patio with chlorine. The cabby, always cheerful, always in high spirits, pointed out the camouflaged army tents set up in the surrounding mountains.
He himself had gotten away without being enlisted because the army didn't have
enough uniforms to clothe the new recruits. Glafka bought feta from the old
woman. "It's from the Dodoni factory in Ioannina," the old woman told her.
There were hens in the yard, pecking at innards and corn.

3

THEY GOT TO know the third cabby better, if only because the drive was longer—from Ioannina to Athens. They saw him unloading clothes from a washing machine and chose him because his cab was sparklingly new. He was also their only life-long driver up to now. A veteran truck driver, he had "put a cab on the market," as he put it, at a time when in hindsight it would have been wiser to stick to trucks, since the gas prices skyrocketed immediately afterwards. To Glafka's question as to why all the taxi drivers in the city's main square were over fifty, he answered that none of them were lifers at the job. Most of them had gone as young men to work in Germany, and had come back with a bit of money in their pockets, and instead of opening a store or a café, preferred to sink their capital in a cab. Now the profession was bottle-necked. They were even given specific numbers. (One exasperating thing in the "Portraits" is the customer's right to choose his taxi, as he had once chosen horses at the track. But unemployment, you see. . . . So if the square resembles a graveyard, as the cabby from Navplio says, Thrassakis is a ghost who has returned to a place suffering from apparent death.) But hadn't the junta opened up the profession, to send in its spies? No. At least not out here in the country. Of course you had to grease palms here, too, to get a permit. At first the cabby's political stance is hard to gauge. Neither with one side nor with the other. Sure, for the political exiles to return to their villages from the eastern-block countries, "all it takes is for people to need them in the fields." "But haven't they been forgiven by now, thirty years after the civil war?" "How should I know what's going on? Blood is blood. If I were a little kid when so-and-so killed my father, how would I look at him now if he were to come back to the village?" Glafka is sitting in front, the curves make her dizzy. "And our once-strong warrior?" "If he'd been in the 1969 elections, he would've won by a landslide. But as they say, whoever dips his finger in the honey wants to eat the whole dessert." The tape of Epirot songs keeps playing, again and again. He has other tapes, stored in a case, but his passengers always like this one best. Like the previous cabby, he too honks at the traffic cops he knows on the road. He seems to know everyone in Arta, Amfilohia, and Antirrio. But in the capital, he loses it. The roads, the noise, the bright lights and the honking make his head spin. All he wants is to unload them, quite literally, an hour early so he can head back up to his beautiful city on the lake, with its Ioanninian silver and the legendary Mrs. Frosini.

4

THE CABS in the capital look awful. Thrassakis compares them to the ones the Americans abandoned in Cuba when they were kicked out. The companies that made them have since gone under, so they have no spare parts, and sink with time into the gutters of the roads. Headed for Tripoli, they end up in one such cab. The care and kindness of its driver, a young blond kid from Navpakto, aren't enough to make up for the brakes, which sound like the creaky pedal on some ancient piano. After Argos, in the steep mountains, though the moon's light erases the shadows from their cheeks, the air-brushing of this nighttime snapshot can't erase their fears that the taxi might tumble over a cliff as they veer around some curve. And the driver's enormous hands, his words of comfort—"Don't worry, we'll get where we need to go, the worst is behind us"—seem like a camel driver's consolations in the middle of a desert.

5

ONCE AGAIN, the square in Tripoli with its gray taxis. The better the car, the less attention they pay to its driver. The more the engine and shocks and tires protest, the louder, the more emphatic the conversation grows about how horribly the world is going, while what's really going horribly is that particular taxi. And so the driver from Tripoli to Sparta passes unobserved, like a tiny figure in an enormous fresco, while the Spartan's humanism becomes almost emblematic as he embraces our strangers and takes them wherever they want to go. He too has nice tapes. He's blond, an agreeable guy. In Githeo he turns them over to a man from Mani who will take them the rest of the way. This Maniat seems like the best driver of all, because the road, from Githeo to Gerolimena, is all highway. In his *Diary*, Thrassakis often returns to this trip. It stands out in the "Portraits" for the manner in which the driver himself becomes part of the landscape, as he holds steadily to the wheel, guiding his passengers through legendary Mani.

.

6

THE CABBY from Navplio, whom I've already mentioned twice, is distinguished by the following characteristic: he refuses to drop his fares, though all the empty taxis lined up in the square make his insistence seem unreasonable. Work might be scarce, he says, but he isn't going to drop his fares when the prices of everything around him are going up. To make up for it, he takes a new road that passes behind the ancient site of Epidavros—a road, as Glafka comments, which resembles the dictatorship that built it in the manner in which it avoids real life, bypassing villages, looking only on pine trees and rocks—looking, in short, on an inhuman landscape, whitewashed and idyllic, as the dictators wanted Greece to be, without Greeks, populated only by ancient ruins and ladders of light dancing the *sirtaki* to chords from an electric bouzouki. Yes, something like that. The cab driver, guessing that they belong to the "other side," puts in a tape of Theodorakis. The driver is from Peristeri, outside of Athens, and before heading into the city center, they stop to see his sister and his brother-in-law, who has a truck and carries tomatoes to the farmers' markets from Kopaida. When they pay him in dollars, expecting him to be glad, he pulls a scornful face and says, "What if I can't change them?" (Note: Due to "Dillinger," anti-American sentiment in Greece had reached its peak.)

7

A CRETAN, transplanted into Old Greece, is a lost glory when the north wind is blowing. Such a man is the driver who takes him from Athens to Lamia, after calling to tell his wife not to expect him home that afternoon. "As soon as they heard I was going up to Lamia, my little girls told me, 'Dad, bring us back some *kourabiedes.*'" A family man, there's no need to tell him not to speed. In Bogiati, where he stops to get gas, he points to the army base across the way and said, "This is where all the torment took place." "Torment," he says, not "torture."

Exiting Highway I, passing through the second toll, he drops Glafkos off at People's Square in Lamia, where Glafkos rests in the shade of the ancient plane trees, once again, after so many years.

8

THE LAST CABBY is the one who takes him from Lamia to the border, by way of Katerini. A cheerful guy, down-to-earth, with a heavy accent—in short, an old-time cabby. His father is also a cabby and he himself has been on the job for fifteen years. A cab, he declares as he closes the window between the front and back seats to create atmosphere, needs three things, "Tires, upkeep, and heart." He stresses the last. "Without heart even the best cab won't run." He and his father used to have two cabs. Then they sold one, and now only this one is left. He tells stories about last month's mobilization. They took his cab too, of course. "One of the officers says, 'I'll be driving this.' 'Over my dead body you will,' I tell him. For a pro to drive it, sure. They even pulled down the telephone poles in Thessaly, so airplanes could land in the plain." He breaks into laughter. When the cabby went to report for duty, they found him in no kind of condition. So they gave him a truck to drive, filled to the brim with ammunition. "But the truck'll break down, it can't carry this kind of load." How was he to know—and here he bursts again into laughter—that the boxes were empty. . . .

Glafkos notices fires in the fields. They are preparing the ground for the second planting.

≈

AS A GENERAL observation on the "Physiognomies," we might note that all the cabbies turn up the volume on the radio as soon as the news comes on. The cabbies who work out in the country are in contact with the people, the tractors and horses, while the city cabbies might honk at another cabby or two at the most. And from North to South, West to East, their concerns are the same: the skyrocketing price of gas, and the fear of another mobilization.

Thrassakis's dealings with taxis constitute an important element in his intellectual makeup. He is the kind of intellectual whose contact with the common element comes solely in the form of conversation with whatever cabby might be driving him from his house to some theater or demonstration—where, in his capacity as an intellectual, he will address the masses, finding himself once more behind footlights that distance and isolate him from the people. And, respecting the unwritten obligations of the ride, a cab driver usually feels obliged to answer whatever questions his customer might ask.

Such was the situation upon Glafkos's return to Greece, flushed with the agent's money. He took cabs not only within Athens but between cities, paying the double fare for long distances, which, compared to the single fares he was used to paying abroad, still seemed like next to nothing. In Germany the meter started at two-and-a-half marks, while in Greece it was eight and a half drachmas, a third as much. Besides, unemployment was so bad during the summer of his return that the drivers, most of them family men, dropped their prices for long distances. Would it have been cheaper to rent a car and driver? (Glafkos himself, we should note, either didn't know how to drive or was scared to.) Perhaps. If he preferred the taxi, it was because: 1. He could replace it with another at any point along the way; and 2. A cab driver comes into contact with every level of society, from wage earners on their way to the bouzouki joints to whores, thieves, spies. And since Thrassakis's only contact with the lower class came through his dealings with cabbies, he preferred them over some hired driver whose only customers would be people like Thrassakis himself.

The collecting of life from the back seat of a cab; communication with the driver through a window big enough to frame only his eyes; the paid relationship that furnishes him with information; the fleetingness of contact—all this is completely consistent with what Thrassakis notes in "Lazarus's Return": "My frame of mind is like that of the Italian actor who lends his voice to Marlon Brando's face for the dubbing of American movies into Italian." This confession, though awkwardly phrased, constitutes one of my hero's rare moments of sincerity. Indeed, in every country that dubs foreign films into its own language (and Italy is the country *par excellence* of this practice), an actor is chosen from among tens of potentials, with the help of machines that test for compatibility with the voice being dubbed. How must this man feel, speaking from under the mask of another man's face? For this voice-actor, the alienation inherent to the representational arts must take on dreadful dimensions. And Thrassakis, eavesdropping on life, peeping through the closed windows of the everyday, identifies with this man who lends his voice to another, just as he accepts the voice of a life foreign to him, filtered through the impressions of another, of the man in the driver's seat.

Oh, what weather, what weather!
All rain, all longing.

I'll find a voice with which to shout and speak
of the fading of my bitterness.

As I waited through the years
for the sun to shine,
I never noticed the well
they were digging beside me.
And when I finally yelled, "Dawn,
radiant dawn, end of martyrdom,"
I stepped forward, blind,
and slipped and fell.

Lying here in the suspicious whiteness
of lime,
I now look back and wonder,
How could I not have noticed?
The neighbor's kids are grown,
the neighbor inched
into places that once were mine,
and heartlessly they shut me out.

Oh, what weather, what weather!
All rain, all longing.

Lazarus's Return

THE IMAGE, from the *Diary of Return*, of the eels that dove deep down and never came up again because the lake had dried up, helps our understanding of Thrassakis's unpublished story, "Lazarus's Return." (Note, here, the deceptive nature of the title: Glafkos was his pseudonym, Lazarus his real name. Thus the author tries to trick the reader by introducing a hypothetical third person who is none other than the first person of the author himself.) The story speaks of a writer (Glafkos, that is) who returns to his country after a long absence abroad and becomes a neighborhood baker, feeding the people sentences made of bread. And so, in eating, people read.

I summarized the story quickly and poorly, so as not to do it injustice. (Though how many summaries aren't better than the works themselves, how many synopses aren't preferable to the developed scenarios? I'm bragging a bit, but I need to, for courage. It isn't easy to summarize the "Return," a mouthful of a story which, if the deceased had had the chance to look it over again, might have gained a lot from a few necessary cuts, chiefly at points where he tends to get repetitive.) As I have mentioned, there is no doubt that the Lazarus of the story is Glafkos himself, just as Glafkos is, in reality, Lazarus Lazaridis; in this way, beneath a scant camouflage, he seeks to narrate his own personal experiences concerning his return home after years in exile. Which makes the audacious effort to summarize the story quite a difficult task, since I have to pick out the important things while rejecting the insignificant, knowing how much true worth sometimes hides in precisely those seemingly negligible, everyday details. And Thrassakis—the anti-poet *par excellence* of the everyday (Alipastos), or the poet *par excellence* of the anti-everyday (Dimaras)—captivates the reader with his treatment of detail. In fact, that's why he set out to become a writer in the first place. When he was twelve years old (like Christ in the temple, in keeping with the ever-present complex shared by so many Greek Orthodox intellectuals), his middle-school teacher singled him out because of an essay he had written on the theme "My Neighborhood." Lazos lived on March 25th Street, in Eastern Thessaloniki, by the Allatini factory, now famous for its cookies, across the street from Menelaos the butcher who felt up all the housemaids like beasts for the slaughter—"their clothes on meat hooks"—grabbing hold of a girl's kidney or liver or spleen, or the flower of her purity—"ripe with conflict"—and the whole neighborhood went wild and the barber "burst out of his shop with a razor still in his hand, white with his customer's lather." The teacher noticed the detail of that lather and gave Lazarus the following advice: "You, my child, should never abandon your little garden. One day it will yield fine fruit." As indeed it did. From lather to froth—the only difference is a bit of air.

Lazarus's dilemma (that of the intellectual writer) is simple: while the other arts provide the world, the public, with material pleasure—music with sounds, painting with colors, sculpture with textures, cinema with a combination of the above—his own art, writing, can please no one. It is, as Ezra Pound said, just a "damned busyness of the mind." Which is why he becomes a baker. Each day he shapes whatever he wants to say, whatever message or motto or slogan, in soft hot bread, letters for anyone and everyone to eat. Some buy only their own initials, like monograms on luggage. Others buy entire slogans: "Hammer and sickle, it does all jobs." Other customers, the more avid readers, keep track of the paragraph Lazarus writes during the course of the week, eating a bit of it each day, buying as many of these bready letters as they need to feed their families. Thus Lazarus feels that what he himself needs to say, his reader, the other, the necessary third person, buys—and, in eating, reads—or, in reading, eats. And so, just as the streetcorner *koulouri* vendor is happy to see his zeroes of bread disappearing, Lazarus too is glad to see the alphabet vanishing letter by letter from his bakery shelves.

He opens his shop in Kaisariani, a neighborhood built by refugees from Kaisaria (which is why all the streets had names from the lost homeland, the land of

Ionia—New Ephesus, Chrysostomos of Smyrna, Kioutaheia, and so on), on a narrow street that leads to the shooting range where one May Day during the Occupation, the Nazis executed two hundred Greek citizens. In the bakery he also installs a long, narrow refrigerated case with yogurt, Kourtaki *retsina*, soda water and Schweppes, fresh eggs, and—depending on the season—rice pudding or *moustalevria*. The neighborhood grapevine, which comes in the form of a loose-tongued, unemployed man who spends his days at the coffee shop or selling lighters on the street, describes for us the people's reactions to the arrival of this intellectual, "artsy-fartsy" guy who loves poetry and the theater and cinema. At first they keep their distance. Since his appearance in the neighborhood coincides almost perfectly with the fall of the junta, some people think he's a government plant sent there to spy on the thawing of the ancient ice that once encased their daily lives, as an agronomist might be sent to the top of a melting glacier to observe which courageous saplings push out first from under the crust of melting ice. So at first people boycott his bakery, fearing he might be some kind of class enemy.

And so, in the beginning, Lazarus's business goes badly. On the very first day, for example, he notes down in the earnings/expenditures book:

Almost half of the sentence I wrote in bread—"I clench my fists like a station master standing at attention with a red flag under his arm as the train passes by"—was untouched at the end of the day. The bread went stale. I'd like to frame it and hang it up somewhere. The "fists" and "station master" and "red flag" sold fast, still hot, as soon as they came from the oven. But the rest is of no interest to anyone.

The apartment is close to the bakery. He wakes up at dawn, before his wife, and heads to work. Others mix the dough and bake it, while Lazarus composes the sentences and takes care of any corrections in his "texts." From morning to night he comes and goes between the apartment and the bakery. In the beginning, his wife, whose name in the story is Terpi, helps out in the shop. But as soon as he gets settled she starts work of her own, cutting and sewing for neighborhood girls. Their place has enormous balconies and Terpi doesn't hang curtains in the windows, so as to glut herself on the light she had so sorely missed during all those years in foreign lands. Light from light. Light from Imittos that spills lavishly into the house and keeps them from taking their accustomed afternoon nap. But they prefer to be kept awake by light than put to sleep by darkness. "Good morning, sun," Lazarus jots down in his account book. "If work goes well, I'll write a lot. If not, I'll write no more than a rudimentary diary, until I shut down the wreck" (i.e., his bakery).

Though this idea might seem entirely original, it actually isn't. While abroad, Thrassakis had attended the opening of an art show in which the visitors ate sculptures made of sugar, chocolate, almonds, honey, crackers, and unleavened bread (the materials were chosen according to the subject being represented). Thus these constructions were deconstructed, moving from non-existence to non-existence with only a handful of photographs to remind posterity of the brief funeral supper that had come between. The sculptor-confectioner achieved his goal, while the public saw, ate, and left with bellies full, satisfied that their visual feast had been transformed into real heartburn and stomachaches. Glafkos seems to have liked this ritual, and he Hellenized it in his story, just as his predecessor Kazanztakis had, in more epic proportions, transposed German ethics and customs into Cretan villages in *The Last Temptation of Christ*. (The validity of the Hellenization of foreign elements has never been seriously questioned by any Greek critic. Nor by the customs department, whose officials turn a blind eye in such situations, letting the imported goods pass by untaxed. De-Hellenization ("theft") is punished, but never its opposite: e.g., the incorporation of a Bulgarian song into one of Aeschylus' choruses. And Thrassakis most often succeeds one hundred percent in his appropriation of foreign elements.)

The neighborhood inspires Lazarus. It's a squat neighborhood of single-family homes, two stories high at the most, though he himself lives in a newly-built apartment building, from which he looks down lovingly at the surrounding houses. Each morning trucks pass by laden with wares: vegetables, fruit, fish. "Black whitebait, red mullet, fresh shrimp! We take food stamps!" The coffee shop next to the bakery is always full of regulars, all men. Old men and young men sitting inside and outside of the shop, whose large glass pane lets them see and be seen. Tiny basement woodshops, shoe shops tucked into courtyards, big greengroceries with their colorful produce. There are two kiosks on the street, one run by an old man who is young at heart, the other by a young woman, prematurely aged. As a rule, women are pointedly absent from the public life of the neighbor-hood. He sees them in his bakery, where they come to leave pans too big for their own ovens, pans of beef or pork, chicken with orzo or potatoes, crossing the small firmament of the neighborhood like meteors—or, the prettier ones, like diamonds. *Our land is small*, he thinks, *That's why there's room for everyone.*

Soon, much sooner than he had imagined, the newspapers and TV stations discover the baker/writer, Lazarus, come back from the world beyond. Interviews about the Hades he left for this "happy feast of life," articles and pop-ping flashbulbs make him the temporary hero of the morning talk shows. After his appearance on two of the most popular shows, "Invitation to Dinner" and "Salt and Pepper," people start to recognize him in the streets. Just as there had once been a fad among Athenians to buy from the painter who sold roasted chestnuts from a cart, they now go crazy over the baker/writer. Lazarus signs autographs in the street. He is glad that others recognize him. That they know what he represents. Why he came back. Where he is headed. He finds again his guiding light: others. Moreover, he is fulfilling his old desire to participate in pro-duction: he feeds the hungry with bread. (Not having been crucified at the age of thirty-three, now, at forty, he wants to feed the people as Christ did.) And he works with care. He tries to make quality symbols. One day when a tack falls into the dough, he throws out the whole batch. "Closed for reasons of sub-script," he writes outside his shop.

He soon becomes an epicenter of so-called high society. Philippino house-keepers from Kolonaki come to his shop for bread. In the street outside, throngs of cars that belong to important officials, sinister types. Lazarus, who fears that his clientele might be trying to buy him off, rarely makes an appearance in the shop during business hours. "The letters that sell the best," he notes, "are S[ocialism], A[live], I[ndependence], and D[emocracy]. Hardly anyone asks for J[unta]. P[hoenix] is also on the decline." But of course, that which continues to sell the best, as at every bakery, is the life-preserver of the *koulouri*, the zero of dough.

Lazarus's real concern, though, is his ignorance of what went on here during the years he spent abroad. From the time of his departure, he has fallen straight into the era of his return, with no knowledge of the dark days that came between. It's as if he slept through a long tunnel and woke to find himself on the other side of a mountain, where it's still day, but where the slopes cut the light in an almost unrecognizable way. "What did this place go through during those years when I was away?" Lazarus wonders in his bakery, unable to reconstruct the passage of the beast from the tracks left in the streets, the caterpillar treads of armed tanks.

His friend, "All-is-flux," who always believed in the relativity of absolutes ("Didn't I tell you?" he said afterwards, justified by events, "That too has passed"), hasn't changed a bit (as he would say), except that he is no longer the same in anything. His right eyelid still flutters as it always has, like a butterfly pinned to an eye which, after all these years (can he really have entered his fifties already?), still hasn't given up its devilish spark. Lazarus hasn't changed much, he says, or Terpi. He likes the idea of the bakery, but the doctor has forbidden any movement beyond a certain radius, so he unfortunately won't be able to visit them there. Lazarus promises to knead him a poem of his own choosing and bring it to him one Monday or Wednesday afternoon, when the bakery is closed. "All-is-flux" laughs and smiles his old, infinite, bittersweet smile, moved that Lazarus remembers the ancient details of their friendship.

The scene, as Thrassakis describes it, is a difficult one. The setting is the same as in the old days, an old ouzo shop near Omonia Square that hasn't changed a bit. The waiters are exactly the same—just a few more white hairs and perhaps a deeper loneliness in their eyes—and the customers are the same, all in good health (he knocks wood under the marble tabletop)—and yet nothing is the same. The years have left their mark on the faces, the lips, the hands. Only that eyelid, trembling, holds fast to memory.

Then an acquaintance who had shared the bitter bread of exile with Lazarus in Belgium comes and sits at their table. His intrusion between Lazarus and "All-is-flux" comes like interference from a foreign station into their broadcast, filling with static wires already loaded with signals and waves. He brings with him memories that are foreign to "All-is-flux"—the rain and damp of Ambersia, forty days without light in Nemours, the leaky roof in Mons. And while Lazarus is overcome by emotion at finding his old friend, the ancient olive tree, still living, walled up in cement outside the ouzo shop, the intruder pushes himself between them, drumming on the dome of his belly, telling Lazarus (in a phrase we also find in Thrassakis's *Diary*) that "For three months you'll be under clinical supervision." When he had come back during the height of the "cholera" epidemic, the man says, it took him a long time get used to the fact that each morning when he woke up he wasn't still in Brussels. "My work," Lazarus replies, "flours me with the everyday. The here and now. I don't have anything to get used to."

In the evenings he and Terpi sit at a café in the square under a row of short mulberry trees, sunk so deep in their chairs as to be invisible to their neighbors. Early on the square is full of doctors and orthodontists, and later, with young groups of friends discussing what movie to go see. But around eleven a shudder of loneliness passes through the square—the retirees have all gone home, while the late-nighters haven't yet made their appearance. Then, shortly after twelve, the reporters arrive. What fascinates Lazarus is the fact that they already know what everyone else will learn in just a few hours. They've typeset it all, shaped it into headlines, made it into news, just as he too will soon head off to knead the sentences his customers will eat the next day. The reporters speak loudly, used to having to shout to make themselves heard over the noise of the presses. But since they are discussing news still unknown to everyone else, their comments remain incomprehensible to outsiders.

On one such evening Lazarus has pricked up his ears to listen in on their conversation when an old friend from way back passes by, a friend who spent time in prison before being pardoned. Their embraces and exclamations of joy draw the attention of the others in the square. His friend has mellowed with the years. His mother died, he says, and he and his first wife split up, and he remarried— his life has been, in short, a life, and Lazarus comforts him, saying, "I'll make it into bread for you." His friend is carrying a plastic sack. Tonight he is going to sleep in Hideaway Number 3—"I don't want them catching me in my pajamas again, like they did back then." Lazarus is confused. "I have four little apartments," his friend explains, pulling out a fistful of keys as heavy as the worry beads of a monk on Mount Athos. "I split the costs with a few other comrades. We have a rotating system, like in volleyball." "So there are others like you?" Lazarus asks. "All the guys from my neighborhood who paid for the mistakes of our leadership. We're an entire army—unarmed, of course, but organized." *And me,* Lazarus thinks, *where do I sleep? I live in a registered house, I run a well-known bakery. They can come and get me whenever they want.* Luckily Terpi isn't listening, she's talking with some friends at the next table, and besides his friend is speaking softly. He has it from inside sources that there's going to be another coup. Up to now there have been at least five attempts from extremist elements in the army, and not even the slightest hint of it was written up in the papers. The reporters are at the next table. "They must know," says Lazarus, who is growing more and more upset by his friend's calm voice. His friend has spoken with such conviction, as if everything he's been saying is a given fact, and what he's saying makes Lazarus feel as if the ground were retreating from beneath his chair. "What've you got in there?" he asks his friend to change the subject, pointing to the plastic sack. "Nothing. Pajamas, cologne, a razor, a shirt. Just the essentials." Thrassakis remarks:

> *It is an era in which nothing is certain. Fear is deeply rooted in people's minds. Even the prime minister moves around, sleeping one night at the Grande Bretagne, the next at some friend's place. Bit by bit the first descriptions of torture start to come out, and identifications of the responsible parties, which naturally terrify everyone instead of giving them courage. Only when the guilty are punished will people begin to feel courage again. Until now, people have heard a lot, but seen little.*

"What's wrong?" Terpi asks as soon as his friend has gone off, taking leave of them sweetly and heading with his plastic sack to Hideaway Number 3. Lazarus is pale. When he tells her and the others why, they hasten to reassure him. "That's just how Pavlos is," they say. "Don't get him wrong. It stuck with him from back then. He sees coups and centipedes everywhere." (Lazarus understands the former, but they have to explain the latter: the "centipede" of phlebitis that kept Nixon bed-ridden in the hospital.)

Lazarus understands, but says nothing. Later, he will jot down only this: "Time, abridged. The full, greedy light. Thoughts gather inside the walls, then project themselves outwards." Now, on the advice of the vice-mayor of Kaisariani, he projects his messages in little lights in the shop window before his customers come to buy his bread. GREECE FOR THE GREEKS. NO MORE FOREIGN RULE. BREAD, EDUCATION, LIBERTY. OUT WITH THE KINGS. OUT WITH THE AMERICANS. NATO, CIA, TRAITORS. KISSINGER (SS), MURDERER. "The 'B' and the 'R' are simple but complex shapes," he notes in his bakery diary, "offering the pleasure of the braid. And the 'W,' like Kolokotronian knickers, offers the expanse of the full, the satisfied. All my bread sold like *koulouria*."

≈

IN THEIR FREE time, Lazarus and Terpi take trips together. They try to escape the gristmill of work and see a bit of Greece, the real Greece, which they believe lies beyond the limits of the capital. So on their first free Sunday, they decide to go to the nearby island of Aegina. They go down to Piraeus to catch the ferry. Across from the ships, all ready to depart, is a shop with rows of lambs' heads slowly roasting on electric skewers. They walk over and look at them from close up: impaled through their once-glib snouts, the heads turn and turn through unturned time. (Here Thrassakis refers back to a story he had written while still quite young, "First Date," in which the girl, seeing her date (Thrassakis) eating the eye from the lamb's head he has ordered, stammers some excuse about needing to make a phone call, and runs off in a panic.) Terpi, to prove the writer's belief that together two people can conquer their phobias, agrees to share a lamb's head with Lazarus. (For someone involved in research on Glafkos, it is moving to see the same couples reappear in similar situations, but with a new maturity gained with the passage of time.) The head smells good to them. They still don't know that these heads are shipped frozen from the central market in downtown Athens. They will find out later—but until then they accept these heads as an expression and affirmation of the immediacy of the butcher to the butchered.

In stopping to eat the head, the baker and the seamstress miss their boat and have to wait for the next one, the Orange Sun, which leaves a half-hour later. It's a beautiful, sunny day. One of those Sundays that blazes with blinding light. Lazarus, following the Thrassakian cycle of week/month/day/decade, tries to remember what he did on that day ten years ago, the year before, the month before, last Sunday. He goes no further. He can't. The sea, Terpi observes, seems to have fallen quietly asleep, then had bad dreams and woken up in a daze. "Dead calm," he replies as they climb onto the ferry's deck.

At least from the deck, Piraeus doesn't seem to have changed. The port is still utterly egalitarian: Russian, Cuban, and Japanese ships all jumbled together, clinging to the same quays. There are even Israeli and Egyptian ships moored side by side. Everyone on the Thrassakises' ferry is devouring newspapers and magazines. The same vendor who used to sell soft drinks and Pavlides chocolates has now added lucky lotto numbers to his list of goods.

For the couple, Aegina is another site of suffering. As on Corfu, many of their friends did time here, too, in defense of Democracy. Grilled octopus, pastry shops with marzipan in the windows. People selling pistachios everywhere on the streets. "Grown and processed on the island. Five drachma a bag."

The monastery is fine, the pine that was once hit by lightening, and St. Nektarios, performer of miracles, now at rest in the chapel. Even the sponges came up crossed from the depths of the sea, the hierophant insists. Some women outside the monastery are telling one another about the dreams they've had, the angels that graced their sleep. And inside the church, the rows of small chandeliers form a second, crystalline ceiling. There are heaps of little silver boats among the offerings hung on the icons. Nuns walk around watering the potted plants. In a place that needs doctors, there are saints instead. Instead of medicine, holy water and dirty chalices. As for the proceeds, they are invested in philanthropic works, whose primary goal is to breed people to continue the backwardness of religion. No, he can't bear it. The era, tsarist Russia in the Southern Urals. "Who," Lazarus wonders, "will pull this rotten tooth from the mountain?" Dynamite explodes in the mountain's roots, unleashing enormous rocks.

On leaving this Christian place of worship they also pay their respects at the ancient temple of Afaia. The view from up there is magical, and there are hardly any Japanese tourists. Lingering to watch the sun slip behind the mountain, they miss the last ferry as it peels itself from the wharf and launches into the premature night. Now they will have to stay over on the island and catch the first boat back at six the next morning. They find a room at the Brown Hotel, where the window opens onto the floodlit prison—an almost farcical view, since things could so easily have been the other way around. So sleep that night is scant, and bread almost nonexistent the next morning at the bakery. If prison is a place from which you cannot leave, then isn't an island also a kind of prison, if it has no boat for you, no road out?

Still on the island, he picks up the newspaper and reads about an army recruit forgotten somewhere near the border, and his fear at having been trapped on this island brings to mind other, older fears—that his army discharge papers will never arrive, or that he won't pass all his exams and will be left back forever. A few days later when his former principal, now an old man with a wooden cane, stops by the bakery, Lazarus, a sack of flour resting on his head like the brick of his schoolboy days, is terrified by the fleeting thought that the principal has come to make him take some exam he never managed to pass. But the old teacher, once an avid supporter of the Great Idea, just stopped by, he tells Thrassakis, to congratulate him on his service to letters. He remembers him . . . yes, as a young boy, writing that story, "Ripe with Conflict," with the barber who ran from his shop holding a razor covered in lather. . . . Lazarus kneads a phrase for him out of bread: "Fight the years, the ages, fight . . . " "Not only did what we hoped for not happen," says the retired teacher (who has "rosy cheeks and snow-white hair"), "but we keep on losing what we have."

≈

BUSINESS AT THE bakery in Kaisariani depends entirely on Lazarus's relationship with the leftist masses—which, during that period, have split into two factions. Though they will join later on for the elections, it will be a superficial reunion, and each issue has its own partisan opponents and supporters. Lazarus, who suffered the effects of the schism abroad, tries not to take sides. With matters strained in the vulnerable realm of the Left, with its open political wounds—and to top it all off, the crisis in Cyprus (the summer's end saw two hundred thousand refugees still in need of shelter), and skyrocketing inflation—Lazarus is asked to balance the unbalanced by writing, by speaking out. However, given his profound distrust of the act of writing, he becomes a baker instead. Through the bread he bakes, he takes part in the lives of the neighborhood houses. Children learn to read faster now that they know how sweet the alphabet is when you're hungry. At the local school they ask him to write stories in cookies. But Lazarus isn't in it for the money. He kneads to express himself. One day, for example, he comes across this idiotic line in the newspaper: "The reconstitution of the Italian center-left is a sheer impossibility"—and, seeking to purge himself of the stupidity of this sentence, he turns it into flatbread. Because expression doesn't necessarily imply original creation. It can also mean the purging of unpleasant impressions by writing them down—as people say, "Write it to get it off your chest."

Thrassakis moved through the space of his memory the way people walk in old newsreels—fast, almost at a run, with trams whizzing by like bullets. Just as the imperfection of the machine brought about an abridgement of space, the imperfection of memory now causes an abridgement of time—eliminating the gaps, sticking things together.

$$\approx$$

AS A WHOLE, "Lazarus's Return" is a rather static text. The main character is stirred by no internal flame, except for the scene in which he goes in search of the manuscripts of a friend who died during the dictatorship in circumstances that were a bit strange, to say the least. He had fallen (according to the official version) from the sixth floor and died on impact with the sidewalk. A pack of cigarettes was found beside him, though he never smoked. Lazarus suspects from the very beginning that his death had something to do with the events at the Polytechnic. But his friend was from Lamia, and the few relatives who lived in Athens rejected the possibility of murder. Lately he had been depressed, they said, and had decided to take his own life. As for his manuscripts, they refused to admit he had left anything behind. "But he was always writing," Lazarus insisted. "He must have lots of unpublished things." Eventually he got fed up with the relatives (sometimes your closest kin are the people farthest from you) and went to Lamia to find his friend's parents, only to find that his mother had died and the old man was now both deaf and blind. His friend's brother had been in Canada for years. Lazarus tried to probe deeper. To go all the way to the dragon's den. The day after he went to talk to a "tyrannosaur" from the police, he found the front window of his bakery smashed, and on the floor, an empty pack of cigarettes identical to the one that had been found beside his friend.

As I said above, I related the story badly, because its true worth, if there is any, is in the details. And those I left out. For example, the reappearance of old, forgotten names in regard to the upcoming elections—Aidonas, Zardinidis—returns him to the years of his youth. They are the names written on posters glued to a wall where he had once pinned his girl, who was saying, "Not today, I can't." Or the emotional young woman at the advertising agency, who had suffered from depression for years. On seeing Lazarus (an old *amore*) she dissolves in cataclysmic sobs, right there in front of her co-workers. "What we went through here," she tells him, "is beyond description."

But if the story tends to move slowly, it's because Thrassakis himself moves slowly, like a train over tracks that have been taken apart and reassembled over a fresh layer of gravel. It will take some time for the tracks to settle in, to fix again their hold on the earth.

"The times when desire and desired meet," Thrassakis writes, "are as rare as the times when the planet comes into line with its ghostly shadow." This attempt to bridge the chasm is moving. *LONG LIVE THE ARMY. YES TO DEMOCRACY.* Tour busses on the ferry plastered with photographs of the savior Karamanlis. "I've met you somewhere before," someone says to Lazarus, "Don't you remember me?" And Lazarus answers, "Give me some finger of land to catch hold of, some thyme to remember." The other narrates some specific incident from their past. "Yes, yes," the baker says, "But how you've changed." "You haven't changed a bit," his old friend tells him, weighed down with thousands of memories.

No—if his "Return" ended up becoming bread for him, it's because ever since he had become a nomad, he wanted to be a farmer instead.

Sometimes when he and Glafka knead the dough together, they let the flour dust their prematurely whitened hair, trying to trick the trickster, time.

But now I too am in danger of falling into the same trap as those who identify Thrassakis with his writings. I started out discussing Lazarus, the story's character, and ended up talking about Glafkos, the writer, who is someone else altogether. A story follows its own rules. It obliges you, the reader, to work with the tools it gives you and to refrain from looking for things outside the chalk circle of the story itself. We must recognize, then, that unlike his Biblical namesake, the main character, Lazarus—a name symbolic of the world in its double dimension, the here and the there, life after death and life before death (if it exists)—doesn't leave the world of the dead for the world of the living. On the contrary, upon his return, he sees his land as an enormous graveyard. The neighborhood in which he chooses to live is full of funeral parlors, the cemetery just a short way off among the pines.

Though that isn't, God forbid, the reason he chooses Kaisariani. Nor does Alipastos's comment that Thrassakis tends to appropriate other writers' spaces

(Kaisariani, literally speaking, belongs to Marios Hakkas—who, being dead, is naturally unable to defend his property against attack) hold water. The issue is something else entirely. Lazarus answers the ancient question of what role books play in a world where people go hungry (a question that has been answered in different ways throughout the ages) with action. He searches to find a neighborhood—be it lower, middle, or upper class, full of refugees or even illegal immigrants—in need of a bakery. While the smallest possible distance between two dairy stores is fixed at just two hundred meters, the law specifies that a new bakery can be opened only every two blocks. With the help of his lawyer, he locates a few neighborhoods in Athens, all in lower class areas—Kaisariani, Upper Dafni, Aigaleo—and after visiting them with Terpi, they decide on Kaisariani, not because it's the most "red," and home to the bouzouki joints of Tsitsanis and Bellou, but because the air is dry and healthy and smells sweet when it rains. In those days Despina—the dictator's wife who grew up in Kaisariani and went on to climb the highest rungs of the social ladder—is all the rage. "While I," Lazarus writes, "humbly end up in the place from which Despina set out."

≈

(THE SIGN ON the bakery door, reading "Bread or Cakes—Photographs Prohibited—Unpublished," applies to me as well. After all, I'm not allowed to take photographs of the unpublished works I examine. And I don't want to keep meeting Thrassakis at every turn while describing Lazarus. But Thrassakis and I are like two visitors in a museum who every now and then meet in front of another painting. The binding link in the two visitors' solitary wanderings is no longer the statues and the paintings, but these chance, unwanted meetings. As soon as one thinks he has worked free of the other, he sees this replica of himself again, in a corner, a passageway, in front of some roped-off frame. And the museum becomes a distorting mirror of his own activity. That's how I see my relation with the deceased, now that my daughter is getting ready to divorce her first husband and marry one of Thrassakis's fans, and I will find myself yet again on the edge of a primordial loneliness.)

≈

ONE OF THE MOST moving moments in the story is when Lazarus and Terpi finally go to visit Kaisariani's legendary shooting range. It is afternoon and when they first walk in there isn't a soul in sight. Not even the guard. When he appears, they explain who they are and what they want. Yes, the guard, a genial man whose life's work is to protect the memory of the dead, has heard something about their new store, and apologizes for not buying his bread there. But his house is rather far from the bakery, and besides, when he'd first heard about it, he hadn't really taken to the idea. He'd heard that the baker had written something about someone with a red flag under his arm. But a red flag should always be flying high in the sky, an emblem of freedom for the damned of this world. There at the entrance to the shooting range, Lazarus explains that it wasn't at all like the guard seems to have heard. In the sentence he had kneaded, the stationmaster is standing with clenched fists—"That part I liked," the guard breaks in—and holding the red flag under his arm precisely in order to let the train of progress pass.

After the misunderstanding has been cleared up, this man who has been guarding the range for thirty years takes them to see the monument. It is a simple spot, surrounded by a low wall, with cement bases supporting the dusty machine guns that were once used in the executions. Across from their barrels, fifty, perhaps sixty meters away, groups of cypresses mark the numbers of executed men. Signified (dead men) and signifier (cypresses). Where there are five trees, he explains, they shot them in groups of five. Where there are four, they shot them in fours. Where there are three, in threes. This man, this gardener of memory, who himself designed the monument, wanted to salvage something of the manner in which they had been shot. (Who? Greek citizens. By whom? The Nazis.) Lazarus the baker-reader-of-the-message asks this planter-artist-of-memory: "Are these the real German guns?"

There is no wind, and the cypresses stand motionless in the honeyed dusk. There are shouts from children playing ball. Distant gunshots echo in the empty cartridge-case of the cliff. *It must be nice, Lazarus thinks, to be dead and not know what became of your dreams. Nice to have been executed here, under the small cyclamen, and never have to see the bowling alley that the shooting range has become, spreading itself over your soil. Nice to have entered the roots of a cypress and have your thoughts blossom in its pungent cones.*

≈

BUT I'LL STOP my summary here, lest I ruin the entire story. I hope soon to edit it and incorporate it into Glafkos's *Collected Discovered Works*. If I left out a lot— like the exquisite scene in Chateaubriand, or in Omonia, with the Epirot songs—it is because, as Thrassakis says (*CDW*, Vol. I, 1), "In the work of art we proceed not so much by adding new elements as by removing the superfluous."

Three Unedited Pages from "Lazarus's Return"

I

AND I RETURNED, you might say, like a stranger to a world stranger than I. Everything was inconceivably familiar and yet at the same time inconceivably distant—a hard thing to explain. I'm not talking about the people. I expected to find them changed. But the books? How did even the books manage to change as they had? I picked them up, flipped through them, read here and there the warm dedications of colleagues—to an esteemed colleague and poet, with respect, with admiration—but they were no longer the same books. Mysterious spines, with letters I could read, but strange, mystic contents. As in de Chirico's "Mysterious Baths," I found myself surreally silenced before these construction sites of paper. It was, indeed, unimaginably sad. To be no longer able to communicate with them, to have them no longer saying anything to you. Or rather, to have them saying the same things they always had, but to be no longer in a position to understand. My whole library suddenly seemed useless to me. Shelves like an antenna's outstretched arms, here in the room, that catch no message from the outside world. The same thing that happened to me with books I also noticed with respect to certain nooks and corners, which seemed infinitely sad to me, because while they hadn't changed in the slightest detail, they had known eight years that I had not known. Other people used them now. And, ignorant of the prior history of those places, the people also knew nothing of me. But what did I expect? Plaques on the walls? Here lived so-and-so? Such-and-such happened here? No. No, of course not. I wanted nothing to do with that kind of petrified memory, the stone that conceals the worms of damp, ashes of forgetting. I wanted nothing to do with plaques for fallen soldiers. No. For the first time I understood what old age must be like: it's not that you've grown older, but that everything else is suddenly younger. Books, corners, squares of cement, shades of gray beyond change, gray taxis growing older and older without ever following the road to its end, to the wrecking yard, the sheet-metal cemetery. All these things, inorganic but capable of causing pain, testify to the organic nature of the matter, i.e., to the spirit of decay, of corruption, of shock and delusion. Finding myself face to face with my old books, books to which I had once been utterly attached, I have come to realize that I cannot be shot with the patriots who were executed at the shooting range in Kaisariani, because I don't even believe in the executions taking place outside my window, in the shooting range of time, where they seek—oh, yes—the necessary target. They fire, the cracks ring out—but where, at what? The dove is gone, Hakkas is gone. Everything's gone—ha, ha, ha.

2

AND I RETURNED, you might say, to a city that was utterly unrecognizable, because all its familiar details had been erased, just as you might be asked to identify someone killed in a crash and you search in vain for a certain mole under an armpit. You let your gaze rest on this familiar face, transformed by the violent crash. You expected that to be changed, you knew the face would no longer be the same; but that mole, that hidden, secret mole, your mole, the guiding star of your furtive loves—since it's gone, you insist that this might not be the person you knew. And the people around you, and the coroner, all say, "Come on, just sign the form; moles, like all heavenly bodies, just walk off the human form"—but you, idiot of memory, lover of the detail, doggedly deny the words of the coroner, Mr. Kapsaski.

I came back at a time (eight in the evening) when the streets were thick with cars; the central avenues formed long chains of taillights in the night. The riverbanks of sidewalks were packed with people, and I, sailing by on the river's widest part, gazed out at those banks, until I was carried off into the narrow sidestreets. And the mountain's deep-chested sigh at the arrow-shot of the sun.

Later on, from up high, I looked down on the city, which rested like a stone relic in the valley. And I dreamed of a city with heart-shaped manholes and sewer pipes like arteries. I dreamed of little tourist girls carrying enormous packs on their backs, and little dogs, thousands of dogs, sniffing one another, barking.

3

AND I RETURNED, you might say, a man made of dream, to a world that had lived through a nightmare different from mine. The image I had stolen from night didn't suit the exotic illumination of day. The image I had kneaded in the dark didn't suit the bitterer night of a never-ending dawn. She looks at me, eyebrow raised, frozen in time; her innocent hand strokes my own behind the ticket window. Or an agonized voice on the phone—"You're back, you're back!"—and then everything is sunk again in the silent megalopolis. Or our bodies, glued side by side in bed, utterly unable to wipe out seven years of a different life. I understood then that time acts like brakes screeching on asphalt— the violent friction keeps us from being lulled. I realized that the frozen images I had seen on TV would have to dissolve in this new existence, which is the ugliness of life itself. And yet this city rests beautifully at the base of gentle hills topped with a temple, a church and a line of radar towers. It is cradled beautifully in God's outspread clothes, tinted every now and then with a new shade of color. In the mornings, the enormous frame of the sky comes to meet the frame of my window. With no curtain but the day's first cloud, no music but the morning voices of children, with martyrs' clothes for dustcloths and palm fronds from the church for a broom, I set up my house like a shrine. When a storm passes, it always leaves some sad scribblings in the margins. Now it is calm, and the sea still, though a walk by the shore clearly shows that all is not as it seems. And what of it? I am glad to be a mortal once more; I belong to my mortals, and the more irrelevant I am to the new buildings the more these things concern me: the mud, the brick, the sand, the cement—since with those, and only those, are houses built.

≈

GLAFKOS TRIES TO fit as much as he can into his time in Athens. The scattered phrases in his *Diary* don't allow us a full view of the picture. He tries to push the unpushable, to earn the maximum in the minimum amount of time.

And then the telegraph from Joe arrives. Glafka will take the boat to Venice from Piraeus; Glafkos sets out by taxi to catch up with the train at the Yugoslavian border.

That day nature is wearing her autumn best. Burnt Vourla, Lamia, the radar towers of Thermopylae. After Larissa the air changes, weaving that old, familiar lasso around his neck. "*Aman*, save me." Roads he rejects.

The weather is good. Stars in the sky, which is darkening fast. He passes through Katerini, a blossoming city. Wide avenues. Shops. A city he could live in. He feels comfortable there, and not because there are lots of Jehovah's Witnesses living there. He feels comfortable because it's a city he has never seen before.

From there, the road to Thessaloniki has been shortened by sixty kilometers—sixty kilometers fewer of memory. He can't believe his eyes at seeing these Bostonian highways in his land. Unless (he falters at the thought) Tom Papas' Boston were to become his land. No, impossible. And now the lights, white dots on a black background, are filling the rectangular sky, like a crossword puzzle at the bottom of some page. What lines might he write to unite them? And for whom? (The awful stench is from the bricks being fired in Mexican ovens in the earth: *Viva Zapata.*) Then he enters the city. It is a whore whose ass has been laid to waste. In darkened doorways, in the corridors of what is almost an abyss. The driver is completely lost, but Glafkos knows the way. They go to the train station. It has changed. Luckily. The real tragedy would have been if it hadn't. He asks about a place on the sleeping car on the train, which hasn't yet arrived. The sleeping car has been booked for two months. There aren't even any regular seats left. But he's sure to find a seat on the next one, which will be passing through at 2:30 a.m. Glafkos has some time to spare. So he decides to wait until then.

Leaving his bag at the station, he goes into the city. On the waterfront a few boats are floating quietly on a leaden sea. The roads have been widened. It is night now, and from the highest part of the city, looking down, he guesses from the lights where the neighborhood of Papafi must be, and Agia Triada, and Toumba. The stadium is dark. Sikies to the right. Hilia Dendra in the front. The streets—

Kassadrou, Filippou, Apostolou Pavlou—have all been widened. The corners have lost their sharpness, the crossroads lost their snares. Now everything seems to follow a well-regulated street plan. And the increase in population has added new stories to buildings. A forest of antennas above the church of Agios Dimitrios and the Aigli cinema. Tsansali ouzo, and Boutari, and Laios Wine. Metropolitan Iosif Street. *Koulouria* on the streets. Roasted *koumbakes*. Soula Shoes. Mary Lou's. Songbirds. Saki's Sweet Shop. Thrassakis, a tourist in his own town.

Boutiques, lots of boutiques line the central streets. Chic women, dressed to the nines. The Arch of Galerius has sunk. The roads have been widened. The arch's nicest part, the narrow gate, is destroyed, and now there are cars passing through the place where kids used to play on their scooters.

And so, reaching the church of Panagia Xalkaion, close to the old silver shops with their blackened bronze, he happens upon a street, the same street which before the war had been lined with shining bronze. In the depths blossoms a neon sign: "Standard Alibranti." And rubber balloons, just like in 1945. The year when Mr. Prassas told him Ino wouldn't be coming home. Ino and his family lived on the street he is now trying to find, thirty-odd years later, near the church of the Panagia Xalkaion. Ino, the young Jewish kid of Spanish descent who somehow ended up in Thessaloniki, poor, dirt poor. Glafkos remembers. He goes into the courtyard. The dead end is still there. "Romeo, Juliet and the darkness." The darkness remained, surviving both Romeo and Juliet. And what is he looking for now, behind the bright copper, when even memory no longer exists? A wave of depression comes over him. A stony sadness, stone-age, prehistoric. If the balloons hadn't been there to remind him of the old layout, perhaps he could have imagined he was somewhere else entirely. But the sight of that closed inner yard, next to the pewterer, the welder, the polisher—that dark yard whose windows open onto no other light, the yard where he and Ino used to play after school—now hits him hard in the gut. Memory is a gravestone from Auschwitz, Dachau, Bautausen, Belsen. He thinks back to more substantial years, before the grasping Greek vultures illegally auctioned off the appropriated houses of murdered families—the estates of Jews who were killed, because there was no one to inherit, since they too had been killed—and ancestral Jewish memorials, graves, and sanctuaries were sacked, so the good Christians could put up new apartment buildings. Down, he thinks, down with all nations.

A gray-haired shape passes by. He runs but can't catch it. If the banks work well, we'll be able to foresee what convoys will come. That's all that matters. All the rest, all the others . . . .

He makes the train at the station. Old women get on, and old men, poor people with poor memories. He will be detained for a while at the border. He will listen to the last Greek being spoken, something about apples. He will see the sign facing the Yugoslavian side: "Welcome, Greek emigrants." Then he will pass onto foreign land, Yugoslavia, stopping for a night in Belgrade to wait for his connection the following day, in the hopes of fulfilling his mission.

PART III
BERLINER ENSEMBLE

15 Croatian Separatists Sentenced in Yugoslavia

BELGRADE, *17 February (UPI). Today a group of 15 Croatian separatists were assigned prison sentences ranging from 18 months to 13 years for planning terrorist acts aimed at aiding Croatia's secession from the Yugoslavian Confederacy. The court in Zadar, the seaside city where the group had its headquarters, convicted the defendants of having planned robberies, kidnappings, assassinations of Croatian leaders, and bombings of military and political facilities.*

The members of the group are all professors, students, and restaurant owners who resorted to extreme measures in 1971 when President Tito dissolved a movement within Croatia that sought full political self-determination. The Zadar group had close ties to and received monetary support from the Ustasi, the right-wing organization that ruled Croatia as a puppet government of the Nazis during World War II.

The three heaviest sentences were: Josiph Bilousik, student, aged 30, 13 years in jail; Zelimir Mestrovitch, professor, aged 50, 12 years in jail; and Markos Dizdar, student, aged 23, 11 years in jail.

The trial, which lasted three months, was one of a series of recent political trials conducted, according to diplomatic circles, as warnings to separatist movements not to upset the political status quo.

In the past two years, 82-year-old President Tito has been strengthening his central administration, further consolidating the power of the Communist Party. The goal of this effort is to discourage the outbreak, after Tito's death, of the kind of local nationalism that in 1971 rekindled smoldering tensions between Serbs and Croats, Yugoslavia's two largest ethnic populations, bringing the country to the brink of civil war.

Many of the demands put forth by Croatian nation-
alists at that time, such as the representation of Croatia in
the United Nations, were also included in the manifesto
of the Zadar group, whose primary goal was the formation
of an independent Croatia, to include all of Bosnia-
Herzegovina, as well as parts of Serbia and Montenegro.

The Zadar separatists, who call themselves the
"Croatian Revolutionary Army" or the "Group of
Dreams," were presumed to be in close contact with Ustasi
units in Canada, France, and West Germany. The group
received monetary support, weapons and explosives from
supporters both in and outside of Yugoslavia.

Chapter Twelve

IN KEEPING with Thrassakis's zodiac cycle, this twelfth chapter is fated to contain my hero's sad end in Berlin (or West Berlin, which sat there in the middle of East Germany, unabsorbable, like a leech in the flesh of a fat *wurst*), a city I intentionally refrained from mentioning up to now, so as to keep others from catching on and spoiling the research I was still conducting, simultaneous with the writing (or, if you will, the patching-together) of my as-yet unpublished material. I now have good reason to believe that even the opening of the other two sacks will present nothing that might undermine my research. Though there are many ways for a man to live, there is only one way for him to die. And it is that ultimate, certifiable end that I would like now, in brief, to present. (I say "in brief" because if I go into too much detail, there is the fear that someone else might turn what I write into a screenplay, and I'd like to believe that I myself will eventually be the one to make Thrassakis's story into a script, and not some professional who has already gained glory as a screenwriter. So if I don't include *all* the details, it's to keep a card in my hand, since these days, the way our intellectual ethics have ended up, everyone steals from everyone else, the thief from the thief.)

After his departure from Greece and journey by train through Yugoslavia, after the failed rendezvous with the liaison and his meeting with Joe in Venice, a new era starts for Thrassakis. He goes to America, but is unable to relax because there are Croats everywhere. They're almost as bad as the zealous Zionist terrorists. He can't be sure they aren't keeping track of his movements. So while he's in the U.S. he applies for a fellowship to spend a year as a writer-in-residence in what was then West Berlin.

He knows Berlin from way back. It's a city that suits him. There, cut off on all sides, as on an island, he lives with the exile's joy within a second ring of exile (isolated from his comrades in the East). Besides, Thrassakis had been in Berlin during the great youth demonstrations of '68, the mass movements, the violent strikes. Back then the splitting of the city had still seemed viable. When people came to realize that no living organism can be kept alive by injections alone, they started to let things slide, and the city started slowly to die. At the time when Thrassakis (with the agent's help) applied for the fellowship, they were looking for people to give it to. Thrassakis thought that by going to Berlin he could escape the evil demons who were after him. What he didn't know was that Berlin was the largest center in the world for Ustasi training; it was from there that they made their enraged attacks on Sweden. Apart from Arizona, it was the only place in the world where their commandos were being trained right next to the bases of the American forces.

Glafkos is calm. He likes the beginning of winter. The city suits him, it's cut to his measure. It suits his frame of mind. The ruined church, the infiniteness of the streets, the bustle and din of the train station where the foreign workers gather, even the zoo allows him a glimpse of his own reflection. He is a man imprisoned on an island from which he can leave only by plane, or by crossing through the checkpoints of the East. And since he avoids planes at all costs, leaving the city is always a hassle, every time. But isn't that what he wants? To be unable to leave? In the beginning he doesn't write to anyone. He feels safe in his hideout. Having left behind the dark and dismal America, inhabited by every imaginable kind of gangster, he thinks he has found his spiritual balance.

Berlin is a city with two natures, two selves. The day belongs to the old, and the night to the young. Long-haired youngsters pack the *kuchen local*, thick with blossoms of soporific smoke. Glafkos is writing like mad. Since he doesn't understand the language being spoken around him, he is free to think, to let his thoughts wander. Each morning he gets up, takes a hot shower, and fixes his tea, which he drinks with a bit of bread and cheese. His soul opens as he looks out the window at the leafless trees and the leaden sky. Berlin strikes a sensitive chord in him, though even he isn't sure exactly why. He thinks. He finds the city "tomblike." And in this tomb of a town his old dream of being a philosopher comes true.

As soon as his train pulls into the station, his mind and senses come alive. He too, like the city, lives a double life, in a pre-war past and a ravaged present. The doubled time that reigns over the city doubles his life as well. One hour passes like two. Looking, for example, at an old woman's face at the Café Kranzler, he imagines how she might have looked forty years before, sitting at that same café, waiting for her boyfriend. Scenes from *Berlin Alexanderplatz* come often to mind. The fashions of the time, the songs, the trams, all come alive inside him, moving at the speed of old newsreels. And this old woman, as she is now, sitting in a café full of old women like her, lends an incredible richness to the "then" of the past. The "now" doesn't line the "then," like the lining in an overcoat. The "then" lines the "now," exuding that secret odor of old things.

Or in the department store on Kurfuerstendamm where he goes to watch the old women wrapping packages. Each floor has its own counter with five or six of them working all in a row. The product arrives with a duplicate of the bill, which they unpeel, and then cut whatever length of paper the particular item requires. But that isn't the reason why Thrassakis sits in a corner to watch. No, it's the way they tie the ribbon, passing it through the little wooden handle by which the customer will hold the package. The women, most of them sweet old grandmotherly types, once real ladies, now work like the women of Saigon for their American occupiers. Their talent, as far as Glafkos is concerned, lies in their masterly use of the ribbon, which they twist and turn into bows and sturdy knots. He's never seen such nimble fingers, and on such hands, with their bulging veins and unkempt nails—not at all feminine but not really masculine either. He sits and watches them for hours, long enough for his motives to be misunderstood.

So, the city suits him. The cold, the snow, the hot armpits of the U-bahn. The double-decker buses. The aerodynamic taxis. The lake. And across the border, the other country. The Kreutzer with its foreign workers, the Edeka market where he buys frozen trout that smells wonderfully of river as soon as it thaws. Sweden, the great comforting North, just three hours by boat. Whenever he wants to see good theater, he crosses the border between the two worlds and goes to Brecht's Berliner Ensemble. Whenever he runs out of paper he crosses over to buy Socialist notebooks, where his pen glides like a duck in moving water, feet down, neck bent, not even paddling, just following the current. One day on the street he sees an old couple walking slowly but steadily, a large dog tagging despondently after them. They are supporting each other by the shoulders, the man leaning inward and his wife resting on him so they form an upside-down "V," propped on one another and slightly bent, so if one were to swivel a bit the other would fall, and the two of them would topple to the ground in an "X." Both are, or once were, handsome, the woman now very pale, the man with the etchings of death on his face. This sighting provides Thrassakis with the definition of the couple, or of marriage, for which he had been searching for so long: "mutual support in mid-fall." Because only when one really needs the other is there cause for coexistence. Only when one can't manage without the other can there be lifelong copulation. Only when one is unable to walk without the other's support is there real marital communion, and so on and so forth. (As for the despondent dog, it represents the necessary presence of the third party that defines any couple.)

It isn't hard for us to surmise how the Croats came into contact with Thrassakis. Surely the agent would have used the excuse of "What are you working on now?" to keep himself informed of his movements. The fact that Thrassakis chose Berlin as a hideout must have pleased the agent enormously. West Berlin, a center of international intelligence, presented a perfect setting for all kinds of "scientific work." It must have been sometime around Christmas of that year (1977) when the agent came in contact with Glafkos to ask a favor of him.

According to Glafka, the agent's agents were always pestering them for something. Once they asked the couple for a white bean bag chair they had bought in Frankfurt. They hid an escaped prisoner in it, trying to sneak him across the border. When the guard at the border patrol stuck a needle into the cloud-like chair, the Croat didn't let out a peep. But the train was delayed, and a scarlet line appeared on the white vinyl of the chair. The East Germans caught on. And caught the man. And once again Glafkos was blamed for having betrayed the Ustasi.

(But now I'm trespassing again on my wife's terrain—she wanted to use that bit in her own book, and I stole the surprise. However, she has given me permission to include these details, since otherwise my hero's tragic end would be in danger of being left unexplained. I want to make it perfectly clear that Glavka wasn't responsible for his death. He wasn't killed during his attempt to free her from the galleys of East Berlin. His murderers, whose identities we have every reason to suspect, simply took advantage of her absence and his state of distress to deliver their final blow. In short, there had been a leak of information out of Berlin and they suspected Thrassakis of knowing something he shouldn't have. But I have reason to believe he knew nothing at all.)

They had locked Glafka in prison for two days for the illegal possession of undeclared currency: the coin she had won in that year's New Year's pie, which she had kept as a good luck charm in her purse. When they asked her to fill out the declaration form at Checkpoint Charlie stating how much currency she was carrying across, she forgot all about it, and when she was searched (though why they chose to search her that day and not some other woman remains a mystery), the blue eyes of the East German guard who discovered the coin shone with joy. He was blonde, an Aryan type, and Glafka was suspiciously dark, like a Jewish gypsy, so he sent her in to see the duty officer. Glafka, unable to defend herself in his language, explained in English that the coin was anything but smuggled currency, it was just a good luck charm. But the officer didn't believe a word she said.

It happened during those two days when Glafkos was alone. There were no witnesses.

I'm thinking now about those last two days, how he must have run to the East and West Germans alike, trying to explain the Greek custom of hiding a coin in the *vassilopita*, and having them turn a deaf ear to his pleas. How he must have insisted that the coin wasn't smuggled currency, offering as proof a bit of dough still stuck to it from the pie. And the Germans, all *nein* and *nicht.*

His murderers must have approached him the next day to set the trap. Who knows how they managed to lure him to the frozen lake, right next to their base, in order to finish him off once and for all. Free, completely unchecked, who knows what they might have said to him. He must have pleaded with them to leave him alone until his wife was set free (at that point she had already entered her second full day of imprisonment, just a few dozen meters away—from that part of the lake you can even see the top of the building, a miserable Third Reich construction, untouched by the bombings of the war). But no—the agent's agents had decided, it was now or never.

And the next day when the East Germans found the corpse with a note reading, "This is how traitors die," they rushed to set Glafka free, apologizing profusely, hoping they weren't to blame. Another officer appeared, a polite man (unlike the little shit who had searched her), and sent her home with her lucky coin. They wanted to get her off their hands as soon as possible, this woman whom they had held prisoner while her husband was sent to dance his last dance on the frozen lake.

CHAPTER THIRTEEN

AFTER THE SAD events, the Greeks of West Berlin got together and made statements to the press. Thrassakis had celebrated New Year's with them. Most of them were workers in the local mills with irregular jobs and unsettled terms of residence due to the economic crisis of the time, but they didn't hesitate to speak out about the deceased. They said, for example, that on New Year's he had danced the war dance "for a Socialist Greece," fists raised beneath the room's single bare bulb, which they briefly switched off and then on again to light the entrance of the new year. They said he sang Pontic songs. That he drank and his spirits were high. He was expecting good luck in the year to come, since his wife had found the coin in her piece of the pie. He sought a Communist Greece, but one in which the rights of the political minority would be constitutionally upheld. Thus the fact that his body was found between the borders of the two worlds, between the East and the West, symbolically represented the "third road" of multi-party Socialism, or the right to private property in a state-run system.

From the workers' testimonials we glean other useful information concerning his life in Berlin. At six every evening he would climb to the upper floor of the coffee shop to talk politics the way others talk about art. On Saturday nights he would stop by the "Yugoslavian," while during the week he went to Apostolis's taverna, known simply as "the Taverna." (Apostolis was a Greek from Constantinople who had one of the best-known places in Berlin back then. He cooked in the *politiki* style of Constantinople, with sauces he had learned from an uncle from Tatavla, and from his grandmother, a devoted cook.)

I have reproduced the following from *Berliner Ensemble*, the notebook Apostolis kept through the years with almost religious devotion, and willingly handed over to me, when I explained my reason for asking.

I

AND WHILE we were expecting snow, some birds came, as big as gulls and white as snowflakes, and stuck to our panes without melting, without molting their wings. And everything went white as if it really had snowed. On the eight o'clock news they spoke of some inland sea at our northern border that had dried up and the gulls, lost at having lost their homes, flew astray all the way to where we were expecting snow. These were homeless, countryless birds who were given shelter and care by the people here, most of them old men and women who made sure that the birds' old age, too, would be good. For while our lives gave the city a façade of vitality, it still preserved its ruins, like churches where memory could collect in all-night vigils.

Everything in the city worked just fine; the visitor suspected nothing. Only when he came to live did he discover the enormous empty spaces hiding down side-streets and alleyways. The city was vacuum-packed, packed in a vacuum, suffering from apparent death, like those island or mountain villages in Greece that have been bloodlet by emigration. When the shops closed for the weekend they left the lights on in the windows, so the streets would seem less deserted—for at night the city became a field of black clover where the quail of airplanes dipped down to graze. Like all islands, the city was fed from the mainland by convoys of ships and airplanes. Like all islands untouched by tourism, visited only by the boats of a foundering line, the city was slowly withering, just as all the old imperial motherlands are disappearing from the map. For while an empire's old provinces continue to exist after the empire's fall, the mastermind-motherlands are hit hard by worldwide calamities. And so the city was slowly sinking, just like the sea that had once been home to the refugee gulls. And when the day of reckoning arrived and the belltower of the central church rang out to mark the ship's final foundering, all the birds would have flown off, and only the old men and women would sink with their city, and the cripples from the last two wars, the nurses and the physio-

therapists, the policemen and the priests, who had loved this city, their city, so much.

2

THE CITY'S SKY is carved by the passage of planes, which leave tracks like those of a hare. The Ilushin and Boeing jets cut wounds so deep in the blue that no amount of cottony cloud could ever close them again. And the sky doesn't change shirts as the earth does. The sky has no Persephone to bring it spring.

This city has borders, like a country. It is, indeed, an independent state, a state within a state, fed and maintained by air, by planes caught by radar, though not by the enemy's customs officials—like Ke Sahn in times of peace.

"Could you be a bit more clear? What city are you referring to?"

"The one whose walls never forgot."

The houses are scratches on the city's flesh—houses that still, thirty years after the war, continue to look like yesterday's ruins. Bricked-in windows, walls scraped by the nails of cranes, apartments whose windows have been dark for ages, as if blacked out against bombing, and on the walls the indelible marks of the animal that passed, seeking its prey. If you enter the courtyard of some building, you will see on the walls how the battle was fought, step by step— and perhaps you will hear, there in the devout silence of the yard, next to the trash cans, the sound of bursting shells.

These days you sometimes see a band of Hare Krishna in the streets, bald as eggs, decked with the bellpull of a single braid, moving in heat and in cold to the rhythm of some nirvanic dance, handing out pamphlets about the Superlight and collecting fifty-pfennig coins, explaining to anyone willing to listen the new religion of love and non-violence. They are strange birds whom the old women stop to ask what wind brought them here and what wind will carry them off again.

And there are lots of old women in the streets, filling the pre-war cafés, pre-war women, all of a certain type. And their old men: battered cripples with hard, stony faces marked by the injustices that befell them or the injustices they committed.

And the bridges that stretch toward the distant horizon, remnants of Marxism that grow smaller and smaller, linking suburbs once famed for their native workforce but now full of foreign workers. The stagnant waters of canals that once lulled the corpses of Rosa Luxemburg and Carl Liebknecht now reflect the weeping willow's tears.

Sometimes the sky pushes off the grayness—which is no more than a reflection of the city itself—and comes out with a blinding blue, a blue so crisp it hurts your eyes, so resolute in its virginity.

≈

AMONG THE ACCOUNTS from the time immediately following his murder, I found in *Kileler*, the Greek-language newspaper of the diaspora, an investigation into the uncertain causes of his death. I have selected those testimonies that still remain of interest today:

Rug worker A.:

Lazarus was an honest fighter. He never tried to take advantage of circumstances. You could always count on his presence at our demonstrations, our fund raisers, our evenings of dance. Sometimes he even recited poems for us.

Clerk L. from IBM:

His sudden death deprived us of a friend and comrade. He may have been from the upper class, but he had a true understanding of our dilemma. We saw him as an enlightened intellectual who always faced the problems of our class with respect, seeking some kind of solution. A few more Lazaridises in our country and our movement wouldn't hurt us one bit.

Director of Olympic Airways in West Berlin:

I'm surprised that everyone talked to you about Lazaridis and no one said anything about Thrassakis. Thrassakis may not have been very well known by that name, but you can't deny that his books were out there—so either the others want to ignore that, or they're ignoring it because they want to.

The pilot of the helicopter:

I couldn't land on the ice. I wasn't allowed to take that kind of initiative. Because if the ice were to give way, I wouldn't have been able to take off again. How do I know? Because something like that had happened once before, a helicopter had landed on the frozen lake that separates East from West, and the ice gave way, and even though the rotor was going, the helicopter couldn't get free of the ice, it was stuck like a truck in mud, when the wheels spin but the truck doesn't budge. So, in order to avoid that trap, I had to throw down the hook and drag him, like another Hector, as they wrote in Der Tagesspiegel, to the western shore, our side of the lake. For a moment, it's true, there was the danger of a conflict with a patrol helicopter from the East. But the danger subsided as soon as I turned on the radio and said something about suicide . . . .

Glafkos, then, was dragged neither by car nor by ancient horses. And lastly, the medical examiner:

Given the battered condition of the corpse, it is impossible to determine if the split in the individual's cheek was the result of a knife or the wing of a gull trapped in the solid mass of the frozen lake, which might have acted like a knife, splitting the individual's flesh as the helicopter dragged him over the ice.

≈

ACCORDING TO THE evidence I was able to gather, Apostolis's famous taverna was a meeting place for all the third-world immigrants. Thrassakis sometimes worked there as a waiter, just for fun, of course, filling—or, to be precise, overflowing—enormous mugs with foaming beer. Thus he took part in the distribution of revolutionary ideas no longer from the isolated position of the writer, but in the more unassuming capacity of the waiter, a member of the working class. In the heat of conversation, customers would signal to him to bring over another round, and Glafkos would take advantage of this opportunity to listen in on their conversations from close range. Knowing the way he worked, just a few shards from the excavation would have been enough to allow him to piece together the entire amphora, back in the privacy of his workshop.

The smoke-filled taverna had become a target for the police. Aside from the Greeks and Turks, it was a watering-hole for Persians, Iraqis, Syrians, Jews. All of them dark-skinned, curly-haired, and thin, kneaded by the mutual sufferings of their countries. Perhaps that was where the Ustasi elements infiltrated, locating Glafkos and reporting back to the agent, the Grand Inquisitor?

≈

THE EDEKA, which specialized in frozen foods, impressed Glafkos during his first stay in Berlin (in 1971, the stay with which we are chiefly concerned). It was convenient for him to shop there. "Nothing in here smells," Glafkos writes in his notes. The lack of any odor, the absence of any microbe, the waxy freshness of the vegetables, the industrialized offering of fruit in its flawless nets, and, above all, the way in which the machine spat out his change into a tin bowl, offered him a masochistic pleasure in his dark and dismal exile.

On a sheet of paper not included in the *Ensemble*, he writes:

Who inhabits a house before us? And does he leave anything but his marks in the cracks on the walls? Is there such a thing as "caged time"? When a bird flies from its cage, it leaves behind a few feathers to be remembered by. But what does a person leave?

"Berlin, city of absolute love." In Berlin, Glafkos was tied to his Glafka with this kind of absolute bond. Isotopes bound by love. He would take her arm and they would walk together down Kurfuerstendamm, reaching such a point of bodily and spiritual identification that he would imagine, not without a little self-irony, that he was not a two-legged but a four-legged beast of love strolling down the street.

This condition is known among psychiatrists as "the calm before the storm." As for why the storm later broke over the couple, I don't want to go into that now. The thing we should keep in mind is that, in returning to Berlin years later, he sought those memories that were engraved into the beloved walkways of that city. (But I'm already collapsing his two stays into one. Because, I must confess, it gets incredibly tiresome for me to make sure it's always clear to which of the two periods I'm referring. Besides, does it really matter whether it was 1971 or

1977? Time sticks like rubber boots. The attempt to date each event is like the conscientious philologist's need to mark every line with footnotes, while the thirsty reader, the protean lover, wants only the essence, the outline. And I form myself according to my readers' desires.)

≈

THIS CITY IS like a house that has been inherited by two sisters, both old maids, one just as crazy as the other, and instead of dividing it sensibly between them—the top floor is yours, the ground floor and the garden mine—they split it right down the middle and put up a wall between the two halves. And this "wall of shame," as they call it, ensures that the house will never succeed. That's the tragedy of this city—of every city, every person, every snake that is cut in half.

This half-city, then—the one I know, the one in which I live, the one in which they pay me to live (of the other half, I can see only the Marxist ridges of its skyline)—hits you with an awful feeling of entrapment, much as when you find yourself on an island where you know there is no doctor.

An examination of the *Taverna Notebooks*, as I prefer to call the *Berliner Ensemble*, affords an embossed picture of two Berlins, as our poet saw and experienced the city (two, that is, not because of the actual political division, but because of Thrassakis's two separate visits). I know the impatient reader must be wondering what all this has to do with the issue at hand, i.e., the murder of our tragic young hero. But perhaps the relation it bears is simply another way of loving. I have maintained and continue to maintain that Glafkos purposely chose this city as the place in which his life would end. His masochistic desire to end along with the city, his wish for them to breathe their last breath together, made him glad, in 1977, to be living there for a second time—and perhaps, who knows, glad to die unclaimed at the border between two worlds.

"Might a writer's last works," Thrassakis wrote hurriedly by hand, "prophecy his own end?" If *Berliner Ensemble* can answer that question, even indirectly, I believe I will have accomplished my goal.

Chapter Fourteen

IN BERLIN, THRASSAKIS writes character sketches of people he knew in his youth, as he remembers them against the gray background of the void. Could Glafkos have been writing these sketches in preparation for some novel? If so, this is the first time he has done these *croquis*, as painters call them, in preparation for the finished portraits. I can't say for sure. I don't even dare make conjectures.

The years I'm digging through now are the pre-war years. Before the Occupation and our flight into refuge. They are years filled with vague memories—most of them reconstructed from photographs—of big surprise parties. Crowds of people, all of Kavala high society, and the cart driver from Didimoteiho. Back in the days when people still sang "Another jug of red wine" and "Loneliness, you always return . . . "

Until everything changes, on the day when

. . . war broke out. I was on my way home from school with my satchel, it must have been about noon, and I was walking alone up the switchbacks that led to our house. It was a sunny October day and the bells were ringing. As I rounded the last curve in the road, I stopped to catch my breath. Down below was the port, full of big ships and sailboats, and behind the courthouse square, the Ottoman arches with their jackdaws—and I was standing there at the city's peak when Mrs. Patras came rushing down some stairs and told me that war had broken out. It was a strange feeling. I didn't really understand what that word

*meant: "war." And while Mrs. Patras spread the news through the neighbor-
hood—"Look at that path; soon the Bulgarians will be coming down it in
droves"—I looked across at the green mountain where the reservoir shone white
in the sun and wondered what kind of things these Bulgarians might be. Nor did
I know why the word "war" had such a bitter taste. And I wondered, deeply. It
was a wonder I never expressed, like so many others I've held inside since childhood, because it had nothing to do with curiosity. Something was forming inside
of me, the beginning of something I didn't recognize—but knew I would when
it came. By that time I had caught my breath—and, made uneasy but also
pleased by the news, I clutched my satchel tightly and started off again for home.*

A bit further on he will ask himself: "What are the first things that come to my
mind when I remember the Occupation? Cured meat. . . . A room made of qui-
nine and nurses made of aspirin. . . . The feeling that something is ending." And
elsewhere:

*There are lots of things I don't remember, just as there are things happening now,
in the present, that some ancient memory tells me I've lived before. Places I visit
for the first time and it's as if I've been there before in some previous life. Words
that echo in my ears as if I've heard them before. People I meet whom I seem to
recognize from long ago. That kind of thing doesn't happen very often. But when
it does, the feeling is so strong that I really wonder, and stay silent for a long time.*

This confession sends us to a very curious passage found among the papers
of *Berliner Ensemble*, untitled, but typed, with a handwritten note at the top:
"Not to be published, lest I lose my leftist customers." If I'm publishing it today,
it is because the "customers" to whom the deceased refers have themselves now
ceased to exist, the composition of the Left has changed, and such a text no
longer presents any danger to him whatsoever.

*I know I shouldn't have thought what I thought. And I'm willing to make my self-
criticism at the next plenary session. But when you're wrapped in a vacuum—vacuum-packed—you can't always choose what to remember and what to forget.
Besides, all the best intentions proved unequal to the task of preventing a dictatorship.*

So, I was at a demonstration against the dictatorship that is now cele-brating its fourth year [the demonstration to which Thrassakis refers must, then, have taken place during his first stay in Berlin, in 1971], when the sharp, penetrating tone of the voice next to me, shouting slogans like "Out of NATO," "Down with the Americans," "Democracy," and "People's Rule," reminded me of other voices, buried within me for years, yelling, "Out from the mansions!"

The "mansions" to which the slogan referred were, Thrassakis explains, the large apartment buildings on the square by the main post office in downtown Thes-saloniki. There were crowds collecting in the central squares—Plateia Aristotelous, Plateia Eleftherias, Plateia Tahidromiou—shouting with raised fists for the rich to come down from their spacious apartments to make room for the damned of the earth, who slept on park benches at night. And, for the most part, these protestors had a point. But in our narrator's case, as he tells us,

We weren't rich. We were refugees from Eastern Macedonia and Thrace; I have no idea how my father managed to find us that place on the fourth floor, at a time when one-family houses were still the norm, and apartment buildings were few and far between.

One day while he is playing in the churchyard of Agia Thodora, he sees a cart passing by, long, narrow, and covered, "like the ones we used to jump on the backs of for free rides." A man was standing on the cart, pointing to a body lying at his feet that must have been a woman, because her hair was showing from under the white bathrobe that covered her. And the man was shouting, "That's how traitors of the people die!"

In those days young Lazos was used to death, and the cart carrying the woman wouldn't have made any particular impression on him if someone standing next to him hadn't turned to him and hissed, "Run home and see what's happening"—a sentence which, he confesses, made his knees freeze. And, abandoning his friends in the churchyard—Nakis, Boboka, Boubis, and Mihalis (Ino, the little Jewish boy, had been taken away long before)—he ran like a shot towards home.

His building, two stories higher than the half-finished building that the Greek Democratic Left would later rent for its offices, was next to the marketplace, which was across from the churchyard where he had been playing. The front of the building looked over the square in front of the post office, while the back and side looked toward the large, open Plateia Dikastirion and the Fifth Precinct, and the Kapani with its fruit and vegetable stalls, across from the Turkish Baths. The front balcony had a view of the sea, where just a short while before Lazos had seen the old port being blown up by the German forces as they left.

So, turning from Ermou onto Plateia Aristotelous, he was faced with a sight that for a long time afterwards marked him with an otherwise irrational fear of crowds: masses of people, mostly women, were pointing angrily at his balcony and screaming, in voices as shrill as that of the comrade beside him at the anti-junta demonstration in Berlin in 1971, "Let the second fall, too!"

But what second? What first? Who had fallen? Or what? Why was this enraged crowd pointing at his family's balcony? Since his father had been held up in Athens by the December riots, there were just the three women at home: his grandmother, his mother, and a friend whose husband was in the EDES (Greek Democratic National Army) and who was hiding, temporarily, from the guerilla fighters of the Communist-aligned ELAS (Greek People's Army). His suspicion as to what had happened crystallized into certainty within him: one of the two, his mother or her friend, was dead in the cart, the "traitor of the people." And now the crowd wanted the other to fall. Which is why the stranger had hissed at him to run home.

But how could he push through the thick mob of oppressed masses? How would he ever reach the front door of his building? Two columns of guerrilla fighters stretched all the way down Plateia Aristotelous, most of them blond like gods and speaking a strange Balkan tongue, and they helped him push through the crowd. Young Lazos, only as high as their knees, passed from leg to leg until he reached the door of his building. The shouts—"Out from the mansions! Let the second fall, too!"—multiplied within the amplifier of his fear. He asked a thin, weedy woman who the crowd was shouting about, but she didn't know. All she knew is that some woman, a black marketeer, had fallen from that balcony—she pointed to his—and now they were going to throw down another.

The suspicion that the first had been his mother's friend and that the second the crowd was now demanding was his mother herself, had become an unshakeable certainty in his mind. Climbing the stairs, he reached the first landing, which was crammed with armed guerrillas. Grabbing one of the soldier's pistols, the boy made the soldier help him push his way through. As he climbed from floor to floor, the crowd of soldiers grew thinner. At last he knocked on his door, and while he waited for it to be opened, the moment stretched into eons.

But the woman who had fallen was neither his mother nor her friend. The misunderstanding was all too clear. It hadn't been his balcony, but Despina's, which looked north, away from the sea, towards the square, the Fifth Precinct, and the marketplace. It was from that balcony that Despina had fallen, or was thrown, as she threw down some curse at the ELAS troops leaving the city *en masse* on the central avenue of Egnatia, as once the Jews had left. Or perhaps— a more likely account, which Lazarus seems to have supported—on seeing some of the men break off from the phalanx and come running threateningly toward her building, the poor girl had tried to get into some other apartment where she could hide and not be found. In her attempt to get around the divider between her balcony and the next, she had slipped and fallen from the fourth floor, and the soldiers had picked up her dead body, put it in the cart and paraded it around, yelling, "This is how traitors die." The crowd that had gathered in the square, not knowing which balcony the woman had fallen from, but knowing that the higher up someone lived, the richer and more reactionary he was bound to be, started screaming and pointing to young Lazos's balcony on the top floor. Hence the misunderstanding. And the fear that lasted forever.

But who was Despina? The sister of Mr. Klimis, who had a shop with electrical goods in the same building, on the ground floor to the right of the door. She was tall and graceful, with long hair. But why had she decided, on coming out of her bath, to scream what she had screamed? Perhaps, Thrassakis writes, because the ELAS soldiers were after her youngest brother for having cooperated with EDES. The fact that she hadn't been pushed was proven by her slipper, which had fallen onto a second-floor balcony as she tried to get around the divider on the fourth floor. If she had been thrown, the slipper wouldn't have fallen so close to the building. And the bathrobe that had covered her in the cart was her own. She had just come from her bath, her long black hair was still wet. The curse she had thrown from the balcony pulled her down with it like a heavy rock.

Thrassakis concludes:

Now this beautiful comrade and I are holding a banner together—"People's Rule," "Out of NATO"—she on one side, I on the other. We are headed for the Greek Consulate, where we will fight with the German policemen guarding it. I know I shouldn't have remembered that old event. But her voice, the voice of a woman who works in the German factories, seeks a place in the sun. And I'm with her. Besides, I don't think it's anyone's fault for being born bourgeois. What really matters is that he die a proletarian.

≈

AS *BERLINER ENSEMBLE* continues, we learn that most of the people at this anti-junta demonstration were actually Turkish workers. Well, then. The Greeks, scared of getting "nailed," scared that people back in Greece might be punished in their stead, scared that the junta might wreak its revenge on their wives and children—after all, there were lots of photographers at the demonstration, and they weren't all from the Associated Press—relinquished their places to Turkish comrades who resembled them physiognomically, and were thus able to convey the message in lieu of the Greeks. The demonstration was held largely to create an impression, to make the foreigners see that the "Greek question" continued to concern the working class. Four years after its inception, the ordeal of "cholera" still hadn't passed. In the international brotherhood of *gastarbeiter*, substitution was one method of resistance. The Turks who swelled the ranks of the protesters offered a first-class demonstration of solidarity with their Greek comrades, who were in danger of being "nailed" by other Greeks.

Thrassakis can't find words enough to describe the significance of this collaboration. With Apostolis's by-now famous taverna as an epicenter (since Apostolis, from Constantinople, spoke Turkish as well as Greek, his restaurant had become a meeting place for both populations), relations between Turks and Greeks were growing stronger. Glafkos went to a Turkish tailor, who measured him with *sevda*. Glafkos's friendship with this tailor, like Glafka's with her Latvian seamstress, proved that life experience, more powerful than any ideology, can tame even the wildest of pasts. Conversations about the "seat" (in Glafkos's case) or "taking-in" (in Glafka's) can sometimes do more for cooperation between people than any stale proclamation Lenin or Djilas might have to offer.

So, in the Berlin of the early 70s, in the *heim* and the factories, in the hell of the rubber plants where they process rubber the color of hell, the first questions begin to arise, the first doubts concerning accounts written by professional historians, whom someone always pays to write what they write. "What divided us in the past, Turk, Italian, Slav?" "What divided us," the workers will answer with a single voice, "were our masters' interests. But what united us was our common distress." And so, alongside the other international congresses in Berlin in 1970, the First International of Immigrant Workers will be formed by workers from what, back then, are still called "economically underdeveloped" countries. And so, gathering at the invitation of the East on the western side of the wall (the developed negative of the positive), the foreign workers, Turks, Greeks, Slavs, and Italians, will create a solid foundation that no external intervention can undermine. Thrassakis, a witness to this social "becoming," unique in history, will describe it in his *Ensemble*.

In a separate envelope, closed at the top with a clasp, I found a report concerning the execution of certain Turkish fighters by their own junta. The text, a bit awkwardly phrased, must have been translated by his friend the tailor:

May 5, 1971. Yesterday's parliamentary newspaper announced the verdict of guilt and death sentence of three fighters: Deniz Gezmiş, Yusuf Aslan, and Hüseyan Inan.

May 6, 12:40 a.m. All roads leading to the prisons are closed. The prisons are lit by bright floodlights, inside and out. An entire regiment is mobilized in the surrounding area.

The comrades arrive. They are examined thoroughly, down to the socks, shoes, and last undergarments. The public prosecutor informs them out loud that the request for appeal was denied. Then he adds, "All legal processes have been completed." It is one a.m. on May 6, 1971. The lawyers, Ersen Sansal and Müsterin Erdogan, meet first with Deniz, in the chief warden's room. Deniz's head is shaved and his hands and feet are tied. He sits quietly and proudly. He greets them: "We wanted you to be witnesses, so you could tell tomorrow's generations how we went to death, how we greeted it with a smile. Kiss for me all of our boys in prison, one by one. Bury us beside Taylan Olgur."

Then the lawyers meet with Yusuf. He is wearing his ever-present smile. He asks if his father knows about the execution. They tell him he knows. He asks what condition he is in. "He is calm and composed," they say. He asks the counsels to take care of his youngest brother, who is sick because of him. "We believe that the struggle does not end with our death," he tells them. Then he asks to see Deniz and Hüseyan for the last time. The public prosecutor finds this "unnecessary," but the lawyers remind him that "he does not have the right to deny such a reasonable desire of a man who will soon die." The prosecutor gives his permission. First Yusuf sees Deniz, then Hüseyan sees Deniz, then Hüseyan sees Yusuf. They say goodbye.

Hüseyan asks if his father is in Ankara. He wants to know how he is. "He is well and he is proud of you," they say. The prosecutor asks him something and Hüseyan answers: "I will say my last words on the gallows."

In his cell, Deniz dictates his last letter to his father:

Father,

When this letter arrives I will no longer be among you. As much as I might tell you not to be in pain, I know you will suffer. But I want you to face this situation with courage. All people are born, grow up, live and die. What matters is not how long you live, but what you offer during your life. That's why, for me, it is natural that I am leaving life so early. Just like my friends who left before me and didn't hesitate at all before death. Do not doubt me. Your son was not a coward before death. He took this road knowing the consequences. We have different beliefs, but I think you will understand me. I believe that the Turkish and Kurdish people living in Turkey will also understand me. I gave directions to my lawyers about my burial. I will tell the prosecutor. I want to be buried beside my friend Taylan Olgur, who was killed in Ankara in 1969. So please do not try to move my body to Istanbul. The task of comforting my mother falls to you. I leave my books to my younger brother. I particularly would like you to tell him that I want him to become a scientist. Because in working for science you offer something to humanity. At this final moment I want you to know that I do not feel the slightest regret for what I have done. I embrace you with all my revolutionary fervor, you, my mother and my siblings.

Your son,
Deniz Gezmiş

(This letter is typewritten. Deniz dictated it to a prison guard and then signed it.)

For fifteen whole minutes they tried to undo the chains around his feet. Someone from the crowd shouted, "Why bother, put him up in his chains." But the prosecutor intervened, saying, "These kids are all right. Let them take off the chains." They finally took off the chains and dressed him in a white cloak. Deniz said, "When they took us from the army prisons, they didn't even let us tie our shoes. Tie them, so they don't fall off of my feet when you hang me." And they tied them. Then he walked toward the gallows. The tight cloak and his bound hands kept him from climbing onto the high table alone. On the table there was a stool. He got up onto it and tried to put his head through the noose. Then in the silence of night was heard his booming voice: "Long live the independence of the Turkish and Kurdish people. Long live the great ideology of Marxism-Leninism. A curse on imperialism . . . " To keep him from continuing, the responsible parties yelled for the executioner to pull the stool from under him. They didn't let him kick it away himself. Since his feet touched the table, they took that away too. His body swayed in circles and then stopped. It was 1:25 a.m. The warden, the imam and the officers stood at attention. They took him down from the gallows at 2:15 a.m.

≈

THUS FAR WE haven't yet mentioned Mrs. O.'s house, which, in Thrassakis's Berlin, constituted a nucleus and magnetic pole for intellectuals of the East and the West. In this respect it was a unique salon that brought together the cream of the crop from both sides of the Rubicon, so to speak. The Easterners (whose regime trusted them enough not to fear their deciding to stay in the West for good) came on the U-bahn with special twenty-four-hour visas, like students on leave from a nursing school. The test of true Socialism was taking place in their country, and every so often these doctors' aides would venture forth into the world of microbes, so as not to become weakened and sensitized in an atmosphere of sterile gauze and anaesthetics. The fact that the system let them leave, if only for a short time, like good little Marxist cadets, was also a demonstration of power: it knew that none of them would choose to stay in the West, because the true work was taking place in the mind, and the state had managed to change that much, at least: their minds. To Glafkos, these symposia seemed sad, so different and distant were they from the old Berlin, and he always ended up growing melancholy and bored. But he doesn't neglect to observe that Socialism's strength—its ability to let its pigeons fly in the open sky, knowing that when night falls they will return again to the hutch—also marks the system's weakness. Because the "well-rounded individual" is not, cannot be, cannot be allowed to be brain alone, but must have a heart as well. So why does the system distrust the others, the simple, common folk who are not granted those brief exits, as the intellectuals are? (The fact that they had to close the borders because all kinds of agents were slipping through was reasonable and justified, but only up to a point. From that point on, the question of how Socialism could exist in just one country—or, in this case, half a country—remained unanswered.)

Mrs. O. had plenty of stories to tell about her bipolar, bi-natured, bifurcated parties, where the Easterners threw themselves on the whiskey, stunned by Western luxuries they couldn't find in the East, though they tried not to seem deprived, lest they insult their own economy. The Westerners, in turn, drooled at the prospect of an invitation from some East German association of writers or painters, since they knew that for the duration of their stay in the East, everything would be paid for—they would have their own cars and drivers at their disposal, and, generally speaking, would be free of all practical, day-to-day concerns, such as the question of who would be paying the telephone bill. (And in the island of Berlin, a person needed that kind of contact with the outside world.)

Glafkos kept notes on these parties, and based on these notes, reworking certain things and discarding others, I have put together the following.

Mrs. O. had servants from various countries that had fallen victim to capitalism and Communism alike. There was a Vietnamese waiter, all docility and concession, and a butler from Eritrea who took guests' coats at the door. There were others in the kitchen, at the bar, at the telephone: a Czech refugee, a Polish man, a Philippino who mixed the drinks, and a young Cambodian girl who had been tortured by Lon Nol's assholes. According to Glafkos, the staff that served the house ran like clockwork: twenty-four hours a day.

Mrs. O. was a formerly rich, formerly German former leftist who, as a young girl, had attended the salons of "pre-war" Berlin, where, dressed in her schoolgirl frock, she had met almost all the great men of that era whom Glafkos admired: Thomas Mann, Brecht, Erwin Piscator, Kurt Weil—in short, Alfred Döblin's *Berlin Alexanderplatz*. In her heartfelt desire to resurrect this "retro" Berlin, Mrs. O. had the unanimous support of the East Germans, who were indeed, in these matters, maniacs. They would bend over backwards for what had passed and what was yet to come. Only for the present were they less willing to act.

According to Glafkos, Mrs. O.—like the city, like her salon—had two sides: her group self and her individual self. Her group self was the one people saw at her evening get-togethers, where she always made her appearance in a new dress, by the same American designer, rather vulgar, revealing the tropics of her back, the capricorns of her breasts. But her other self, her true self, the Mrs. O. people saw when they came for afternoon coffee or tea, sat hunched over a book on the divan with an unmade face and pulled-back hair, raising her eyes from the page only when her guest walked in. Then she would take off her reading glasses, smile, and, without getting up, stretch out her hand for him to kiss, if he liked. There would be enormous logs burning in the fireplace beside her, and a cat purring happily in its corner. And the same space, the same living room, which seemed cold and impersonal when it was full of guests during her cocktail parties or dinner parties, now, during this *tête-à-tête*, had a homey atmosphere that exuded a certain warmth.

Though she was still the same woman who held those evening parties, the Mrs. O. of the afternoon had a more personal flavor, more down-to-earth, like homemade bread compared to the machine-made loaves you find in the grocery. The indispensable servant in his uniform would appear right away to ask the guest what he would care to drink, and Glafkos, despite the teetotaler spirit of the hour, always asked for champagne with orange juice. Upon which his hostess, to keep him company, would abandon her time-honored tea and have a drink herself, as a special treat.

Her husband, the fourth, who himself had been married twice before (and while Mrs. O, after having loved them, adored them, and made them who they were, had buried all three of her previous husbands without inheriting a cent, since they all had close relatives, her current husband paid alimony to both of his ex-wives—a very complex state of affairs which meant, in short, that they weren't exactly swimming in cash), was always going off on business trips all over the world. He worked in biochemics, an industry in which Berlin, of course, held the scepter. Berlin had more chemical plants per square mile than any other city in the world, except for a certain district in southern Kyoto, Japan. But Mrs. O.'s husband always made sure to be in town when his wife threw one of the parties for which she had become famous in both the West and the East—he liked to see and meet all these people who were drawn in by his wife's magnetic charm.

The conversations at her get-togethers covered a wide range of topics. The Westerners prodded the Easterners with pointed questions about the pressures and persecutions faced in their country by famous writers and intellectuals; the Easterners, most of them seasoned veterans of such interrogations, didn't defend their cops, but diligently explained that the road to Socialism still had lots of obstacles to overcome, and everyone had to pitch in and help clear that road, not by presenting critical portraits "from the outside," but by providing "internal," "constructive" criticism. "Since Communism is such a burning issue for you," they'd say, "why don't you become Communists yourselves and try to apply it more effectively than we have, in your own country?"—a challenge that the unrepentant opponents rejected, saying that there was no way the guinea-pig-intellectuals could ever influence anything the Great Doctor (Ulbrecht, in those days) might do.

So the two sides met at Mrs. O.'s house for conversations and seminars that later developed into congresses. Free of the fear of unassuming informers or underdeveloped agents, there was an ease of dialogue and a freedom of argumentation that was more useful to the secret services than anything else. Because no one doubted that the notorious Mrs. O. was a secret agent. The only question was, for whom.

As hostess, she might not have actually done the cooking herself, but she always peeked into the pots before the dish took its final boil, or opened the oven for a moment to make sure the aluminum foil was covering all corners of the pan. And though she accepted the compliments, she always made sure to pass them on to the chefs in the kitchen. The little flags on the table symbolized not the ethnicity of the guests, but that of the chef who had prepared the day's specialty.

Glafkos often wondered what this woman would be like in bed. And if her current husband, who seemed submissive and almost subservient beside her, might not have some kind of secret charm that kept Mrs. O. fanatically faithful to him. Because Glafkos couldn't discern even the slightest hint that she would ever betray him. Though a European woman might store up lots of erotic adventures while married to just one man, for many American women, the number of men they've slept with is equal to the number of husbands they've had. Mrs. O. wasn't American, but she had lived in the States for several years during her exile from Nazi Germany, and to Glafkos it seemed that the mentality of the women there had rubbed off on her, to some degree.

Mrs. O., always punctual and smartly dressed, with an amazing memory, charming if she liked you, impeccable, her stockings never even a centimeter askew—and you never saw her in the same skirt twice—once "seduced" a Polish man, a regular at her evening affairs, who seems to have made a pass at her during one of her husband's business trips, only to be given the cold shoulder, at first tactfully and then with a bit of heat. This Pole was a veteran of the congresses. For in this, as Thrassakis observes,

> . . . the Easterners who came to Mrs. O.'s house differed from their Western counterparts. They were professionals, state-supported, well taken care of, with no worries about the rent, the electricity bill, their retirement. They were always as sharp as needles at the various congresses and conventions they attended—in fact, they weren't writers so much as professional congress-goers, who had replaced the professional revolutionaries of the previous era. In short,

the kind of men who move from convention to convention, from country to country with badges pinned to their lapels, and since they all see one another so often, they form a sort of family, a family of wandering conventioneers.

The Pole, then, was one of those guys, as women sometimes say about gay men, who are struggling with something on the inside. Only what he was struggling with wasn't sexual desire, but the longing for freedom. To run or not to run, during one of those trips to the West.

As for those who didn't fight it, the state treated them accordingly. "But at Mrs. O.'s," Thrassakis tells us, "there was always a group of people who were ashamed to run off, who said, 'We won't do it because they trust us, they let us leave. Just let them try denying us exit once or twice—then we'll see what happens.'" The guilt, the repression, their Marxist ethics, all urged them to fight the desire to flee, turning them into deeply unhappy people who drank like sponges. The Pole was one of these, and one night when he had drunk too much he made a pass at Mrs. O. in her private room with its double bed, only to be rejected in no uncertain terms. Mrs. O. came bursting out of the room with her lips swollen and her hair a mess, saying, "Your ill-mannered colleague is in there, completely unconscious," though she added slyly that had he been a Chopin, perhaps she would have been able to become another George Sand. . . .

While Glafkos tells us how the others behave, what they say and do, he tells us next to nothing about himself. Fortunately, during that era the *Texas Quarterly* published a column called "Letter from Berlin," of the sort common in literary magazines back then, keeping its readers informed as to the goings-on in the international arena. This column refers explicitly to Mrs. O.'s salon, in which Glafkos seems to have played a leading role. It is obvious (for someone able to read between the lines of the texts by the American columnist—who, like Glafkos, was the recipient of a fellowship) that Mrs. O. displayed a remarkable fondness for Glafkos—until, that is, another companion appeared at his side, an aged but charming Berliner who seems to have caused Mrs. O. to withdraw definitively from Thrassakis, perhaps marking his end. Or rather, the beginning of the end.

Let me offer, here, some quick answers to a few key questions. First of all, why was Mrs. O. jealous of the other Berliner, but not of Glafka? Likely explanation:

since she had met Glafkos and Glafka together, she accepted them from the very beginning as a single being. It was the interloper whom she rejected, the element added after her initial introduction to the Thrassakises. But why would she be jealous, you might ask, of a woman older than she? As I have stressed before, it had nothing to do with age. If Mrs. O. was jealous, it was because the charming Berliner stole her thunder, in a way. After her expatriation, "Charlotte" (as I will call the second woman, whom Glafkos introduced into the salon of the first) only agreed to return to the Berlin of her youth with the proviso that she would be allowed to pass freely from the East into the West. Only when the authorities assured her of this privilege did she return, renting a room in a pension on Kurfuerstendamm that she knew from way back in 1929. It was still owned by the same woman, who was about as old as Charlotte herself, and it doesn't take an architect or a city planner to figure out, just from glancing down Ku-Damm, that the building was one of very few to remain standing after the bombings. Its green dome signaled its pre-war origin. Upon her arrival in Berlin, Charlotte, whom Glafka had become friends with in Montreal, contacted the Thrassakises. For Glafkos, now meeting her for the first time, she represented exactly the period in the city's history that he so adored—Alfred Döblin, Thomas Mann, Kurt Weil, Erwin Piscator. He became quite attached to her, thus living a double life, in his own present and in her past, so rich and up to now so inaccessible. One detail: while Charlotte's pension was in East Berlin, the school she had walked to every day as a girl was now in the West. So, in order to relive a simple walk from her memories, she had to pass through check-points, customs, searches, stamps—thus suffering, masochistically, the end of an era.

"It's all fine and convincing up to here," my daughter (who has been my faithful reader and advisor in this work, since my wife, as I have said, couldn't help me even if she wanted to) broke in, "but there are still two questions left hanging. First of all, why does Glafkos like older women so much? And second, what basis do we have for believing that Mrs. O. was upset by Charlotte's introduction into her salon?"

In regard to the first question, concerning Glafkos's attraction to women older than he, I don't think it requires any particular effort to convince ourselves that he had preferred older women ever since he was young, since they were eas- ier for him to satisfy. In seeking their protection, he knew that even if he didn't succeed in pleasing them, he could always fall back on their motherly support. Preferring not to desire (which would have entailed the kind of active stance he disliked) but to be desired (i.e., the passive acceptance of the other), it was alto- gether logical that he would find in older women the constant understanding that younger women were unable to provide. Perfectly matched in age with his Glafka, he found in women older than she the lost nipple sought by the suck- ling child. And since he preferred for there to be at least a decade of difference in their respective ages, the age of the women he was attracted to shifted with his own passing years. Thus it was perfectly natural for him, at the age of 45, to be attracted to 55-year-old Mrs. O. and even more so to 70-year-old Charlotte.

As for how we know that Mrs. O. was upset by Charlotte's appearance at her salon, certain other texts, which I have decided not to make public for the time being, convince me that while she might have said over the phone, "Of course you can bring Granny along," as soon as she saw her, she started to sweat, unbut- toned the collar of her blouse and wiped her forehead—which, though dabbed with the most expensive perfumes, had gone clammy with jealous perspiration. From that moment on, her relationship with Glafkos deteriorated, and we see the sad repercussions in Glafkos's dealings with his agent.

"That's new, too," my daughter remarked. "It's like solitaire—you never know what the next card will bring."

"The faces on the face cards are given, sweetie," I said, lifting onto my lap the little grandson she had given me, and whom she had given my name. "The fact that they keep showing up every so often shouldn't come as a surprise. The agent and Mrs. O. certainly knew one another. How else would Thrassakis have been introduced to her? The agent must have said, 'As soon as you get to Berlin, your first task is to meet an old friend of mine; she's a wonderful person, and might prove useful to the two of you.' The fact that Mrs. O. was a close friend of the agent is common knowledge, just like the fact that Gertrude Stein and Picasso were friends. Besides, someone must have given him a letter of introduction allowing him into her salon, and I have no idea who else it could have been."

"What about the people who gave him the fellowship? What was Berlin back then, anyhow? Just a handful of people."

"Recent research has shown that Joe and the foundation in Berlin that provided Glafkos's fellowship belonged to the same branch of the secret service. Mrs. O. must have been their local representative."

"But you just said she was an agent, and we didn't know for whom."

"But isn't that the very definition of the double agent? Hating the Easterners for the way they treated Israel and the Jews of their own country, she willingly collaborated with the reactionaries. But hating just as strongly the capitalist exploitation of foreign workers she saw going on in West Berlin, she willingly collaborated with the Easterners in their boycotts of the big multi-national corporations. As with all double agents, each side took what it wanted from Mrs. O., leaving the rest to the other. Glafkos himself draws our attention to the issue of agents and double agents. 'It isn't simple,' he tells us. 'On the contrary, it's quite complex. And we shouldn't try to simplify where there's no room for simplification.' "

"But Dad, what you're saying supports a very simplistic position: Glafkos brought Charlotte to Mrs. O.'s, and Mrs. O. got upset and ordered the agent 'to finish this guy off once and for all.' So when Glafka was arrested by the East Germans, the Ustasi came around and made short work of him."

"That's more or less the plot of a screenplay I'm also planning to write, based on my book. But your version is too schematic; it's missing the element of time. Things ripen slowly. Things never happen according to strictly logical relations of cause and effect. After all, logic—today I woke up with this exact thought in my head—didn't manage to prevent the most illogical of crimes from taking place in our time. Why? Don't we always insist that man is a logical, rational being? Yes. But still, we have to figure in the element of time. Time means the accumulation of a mass of repressed things, hatreds and hostilities that need to take themselves out on something, sometime. That kind of simmering, unconscious hostility is even more dangerous than the conscious ones. And if I'm speaking to you a bit generally, it's because you're still young and don't know how small things, details, can grow with time.

"Glafkos's relationship with Charlotte was clearly romantic. Glafkos, nostalgic for a city now lost, found in the descriptions of this aging German Jew all the fragrance, all the poetry of lost time. Like every artist, he too was searching for a lost Atlantis. With Charlotte as his guide, the past was resurrected, the ruins filled with color, the unknown strands wove themselves into a story.

"Now you'll ask, But wasn't Glafka jealous? Anything but. Charlotte was like a mother to her, and had been so supportive during her difficult time in Montreal that Glafka was pleased to see her husband keeping the old woman company. Mrs. O., on the other hand—a necessary evil for Glafkos in Berlin—didn't think Charlotte worthy of entering her salon, because she wasn't a name, a letterhead. She called Charlotte 'new money' and 'uppity,' though she had a gentleness and a long life experience that was at least a hundred carat. Mrs. O. didn't want nice people in her house as much as she wanted famous names. Or rather, she confused the name with the person. Charlotte, who had held lots of different jobs during her difficult life as a refugee, as she fought to survive without having to depend on a husband, had achieved a fruity essence that had nothing to do with etiquette. Thus Thrassakis's estrangement from Mrs. O. and her salon was either caused by black magic and the evil eye, or had something to do with politics, since he no longer worked for anyone."

≈

THRASSAKIS TELLS us very little about this period in his life. What he does describe in the *Berliner Ensemble* are his dreams. It is a suggestion Charlotte had given him, from her experience when, still quite young, before 1933, she had taken to writing down all the dreams her friends described to her. When she found these descriptions twenty years later in a notebook that had survived the bombings, she was surprised at how accurately people had seen in their sleep all the things that in their waking lives they couldn't even begin to imagine would actually happen: Hitler's rise to power, the war, the concentration camps, the destruction. Glafkos is intrigued by the idea and starts writing down his own dreams, down to the smallest detail.

"If I can manage to get past my dreams," he writes, "I will have become worthy of reality," since he soon reaches the dire conclusion that dreams are unimaginably richer than everyday life. In dreams, past and present, guilt and desire are twined together, while everything seems more self-evident, more well-defined. In his dreams, certain streets return, certain corners, hopes and sufferings, mailmen, mildew, motorcycles, everything, while life is just a poor crop that flourishes only with the magic of memory, the way a stint in the army—wake-up call, mess, drills, mess, drills, mess, taps—is enriched only by nights on watch.

An ordered life is as meaningless as the life of a potato. However, when the potato is mixed with other ingredients, mashed or sautéed or garnished with sunflower seeds or oregano, it becomes something else, is transformed into some-thing more universal, and hence more aberdibama—

(A word which, despite all efforts, I was unable to classify, to fit into some order that might give it meaning. And so I offer it up, like an unclassified rock, to his researchers.)

A dream of air raids. The Soviet planes took care to hit only the strategic targets, keeping the people isolated from the devastation. Glafka and I were at the airport when the attack began. I still don't know why we were at the airport, since we weren't waiting for anyone. Anyhow, knowing nothing, we decided to set out for the city on foot. The land next to the sea was flat and brackish, but with no other defining characteristics. After a while, we crossed a beach reminiscent of Porto Ercole or the southern part of Ostia, with no entrance from the road, just lots of rushes, sand, and seagulls, and eventually we came out onto the highway. We started to walk, still headed towards town, where our hotel must have been, or our house. (From the time when our house became the world and hotels became houses to us, all these things wove themselves together as they do in dreams, forming the real framework in which the painting unfolds, in which art becomes image.)

Then, as we were walking, a bus came by, headed out of the city, back towards the place from which we had set out, and we climbed on.

(Certainly all these movements could be interpreted in light of the couple's lack of a car. Here I remind the reader of Thrassakis's phrase: "Ever since acquiring his own car, he had become sensitized to statistics about car accidents and vic-tims of weekend trips." But things are never as simple as that: in his dreams we often find poetic descriptions of an otherwise repulsive reality, while in waking hours poetry is destroyed by the cheap compromises of the consciousness.)

So the bus took us back to our starting point, where the Russian attack was still going strong. They were hitting their targets with such scrupulous precision that we, three miles away, really had nothing to fear. But then some torn-up bits of cardboard boxes sent flying by the explosions reached all the way to where we were huddled under a bridge, and Glafka got scared and started to panic. And then the refugees began to arrive, confirming our fears that the war would spread throughout the Middle East. After all, why would they bomb a small local airport if they didn't know beforehand that it actually belonged to NATO?

(There follows a detailed diagram, taken from the newspapers, of the most likely locations of the secret bases. This clipping no doubt provided the "kernel" for this dream in which Soviet planes hit their targets without harming a single non-strategic site, while the residents of the Athenian suburbs—Voula, Vouliagmeni, Varkiza, Upper and Lower Glyfada—hasten to distance themselves from the bases. And what frightened the couple wasn't the flight of the eagles overhead, but the womenfolk huddling together under the bridge.)

My mistake, then, was that after I had gone to all the trouble of avoiding the contested region, I took the bus back to my point of departure—a mistake that had its root in reality, since the previous night, caught in a heavy fog, my longing to escape from the ground zero of waiting pushed me onto a bus blazing with lights that was headed in the opposite direction as the bus I was waiting for. So, though I had been headed for the central square, I ended up at the depot, a fact which I explained in the following manner: what I really wanted wasn't to go anywhere in particular, but simply to break free of that thick, Londonish mist. Better the source of danger, a bus station at the very outskirts of the city—like the bombed-out airport at which I found myself once again, in my dream—than the in-between, the middle ground, neither in nor out of danger. In downtown Athens, *I thought*, we wouldn't even have known they were bombing the airport. We would've learned later on, like people listening to the horrors of war over the radio.

"Greece," Glafkos writes a bit further on, "is a land that shrinks you, like grapes into raisins. You get smaller, bitterer, thicker, more substantial—which is why the package is smaller, too. Outside Greece, the extra breathing room allows your lungs to expand."

≈

HE HAD LOTS of dreams during his second self-exile, a surfeit of dreams, dreams that came hard and fast, one after the next, dreams that continued, one from another, dreams so lifelike that they kept him in a state of constant wakefulness in his sleep. With them crowding upon him as they did, or with him crowding them, he would have given anything to free himself from the leeches of his dreams, the Freudian linings of his life, and to find some brief consolation in a deep, dreamless sleep.

The winter days are short. They end fast, before I can wake from the torpor of vision. How fast they descend, the curtains of dusk. And everything has its eye trained on when my eyes will close again. Luckily the lights here never go out. In the cities of the North, where the people live the greater part of the day in night, the electric companies are well equipped to keep up with the demand, so people won't have to live in darkness.

Berlin is my Mount Athos: a city within a city, a state within a state— though here, of course, women are allowed.

During his first stay in his "Mount Athos," he hadn't chosen to lead a monastic life—on the contrary, it had been forced upon him by the ("choleric") conditions of his land. But now he has willingly distanced himself from the worldly affairs of his homeland, and feels guilty over his non-participation, like a disappointed lover who takes refuge in a monastery claiming to have found what his soul had sought, though a thorn in his pillow prevents him from sleeping soundly.

Thrassakis wakes up badly in the mornings. That's all. For no reason. His dreams are folded like onion skins, one within the next. He can find no redemption in this martyrdom, and feels like a rotten lemon hidden at the bottom of a beautiful arrangement made from all the many fruits of the earth—i.e., a deep wound that doesn't show.

In my opinion, this obsession with dreams seems to represent an appeal for annihilation, a preparation for his great communication with the darkness, a tunnel, to use his own beloved image, that he is digging into himself with the diamond drill of sleep, trying to unite it with the passage starting from the other side of the mountain, which in an earlier chapter we called the "there," the "in place."

And so Charlotte's advice that he ease his mind by writing down his dreams undoubtedly offered a kind of relief.

The next dream is another nightmare, related to the one before. I walked in on a party, looking for a newspaper. It was Tuesday and the papers from Greece hadn't yet arrived. The party was in an apartment building that seemed to belong in some poor Parisian suburb—but the strange thing was, it wasn't abroad, it was in Greece. How could that be? All the couples, dancing an anachronistic dance, a Communist dance, were watching me with silent admonition—but what had I done? The host willingly brought me whatever papers he could find, but I already had them all, except for the Sunday edition of Avgi, *which I gladly accepted.*

Some of the guests had just arrived from Greece that very day, and I was hoping they might have brought some of the morning papers with them. But unfortunately, not having the same problems as I, it hadn't occurred to them to do so.

What was really killing me was the look in everyone's eyes—they were glaring at me as if I were some kind of defector. But living here in Berlin, how could I possibly take part in what was going on in my land? Didn't they realize that? Wasn't it enough that I took an interest in reading the papers from home? Or maybe life in print is meaningless, and all that counts is action, participation? In the dream no one spoke. The dancing couples stopped their steps and stood motionless to watch as I came in, asking for newspapers, and the silent, expressionless accusation in their eyes was enough to flood me with guilt, while deep down I wondered how Sunday's Dawn *had ended up here.*

I wasn't quite sure where I was. The building seemed like the Vitri and the city seemed like Berlin, but the party was definitely taking place in Athens. And yet if I was in my own land, why was I so isolated, so alone? Where had I set out from? How had I ended up at that party? I remember that I had gone to find my friend Andreas—in real life he was one of the few comrades I hadn't managed to see while I was in Greece—and in my dream, I was having trouble locating his apartment.

The elevator went too high and I had to walk down half a flight of stairs. I ran into someone in the hall who pointed to Andreas' door, and when it

opened, I found myself face to face with a dance like the one in the movie They
Shoot Horses, Don't They? *where the couples compete to see who can dance
the longest, who can manage to overcome all the adversities and contradictions
of the bitter struggle.* . . . .

≈

THE PLACE WHERE Glafkos lived the last year of his life is of particular importance.
Though ensconced in the neutrality of this city, the writing he did wasn't neutral in
the least. Burning inside, he marked the streets through which he walked like another
Unamuno. Most things I don't know, and they don't interest me. He didn't live this
life because he liked it, but because he couldn't do otherwise.

I find myself unable to speak calmly and composedly about Berlin, since it's
a city about which Glafkos himself was deeply passionate. It changed his way of
life, he said, his entire mode of existence. In Berlin, the syrup, the sweetness of
life, might have been absent. Then again what drew him in was the bareness of
it, the nakedness, the harshness. He felt like a Christmas tree in the middle of
an empty square, weighed down with colored lights and fake snow (his memories, or the false transgressions of the imagination), complete in its isolation. It
was enough for someone else to be paying the electric bill, enough for him not
to take root.

Books paid for with the blood of exile, how can I stand calm and composed
before you, when it was through you that I learned the alphabet, sounding out
the macrocosm through the microcosm of Glafkos himself?

Chapter Fifteen

Amazing recipe for New Year's Pie
(No baking powder. No bacon fat.)

1 cup butter
2 cups sugar
6 eggs
vanilla extract or orange peel
1 package Farina Yiotis flour
1 cup milk
powdered sugar

Blend butter with an electric mixer, gradually adding sugar. Add eggs one at a time, a few drops of vanilla or the orange peel. When mixture is light and fluffy, alternately add flour and milk, mixing constantly. Pour into a No. 30 pan, buttered and lined on bottom with buttered wax paper. Bake at 350° F (177° C) for 50 minutes. When cool, sprinkle with powdered sugar.
—Chryssa Paradeisi

THE PRESENCE HERE of this recipe for *vassilopita* would seem completely inexplicable if it weren't followed by a note that sheds some light on the reason for its inclusion: "The new year is approaching and none of us knows what it will bring. A new year is a new weight." We know Thrassakis didn't look kindly on that year, which was to be his last. And he continues:

Outside the volleys of gunfire continue, firing at the year that is leaving like a deposed tsar, who laughed at our expense, who gave us bitterness and sorrow—while the new year enters like the proletariat whose only power rests in its arms, whose only exclamation points are its upraised fists. . . .

The scene he describes is already familiar to us from the thirteenth chapter of this study: "A group of workers in West Berlin dances beneath a bare bulb with fists raised for a free homeland whose children will not have to live far away in the cold North just so they can earn their daily bread." Then he danced the war dance. And a few days later, probably sometime later that week, while Glafka's coin was still in her purse, the blond barbarian at the East German customs control accused her of smuggling, and . . .

"We did all the usual things," Thrassakis concludes. "We ate lentils so the year would bring wealth, we called people to wish them a happy New Year, we cut the *vassilopita*, and the coin, an old coin from Constantinople belonging to the hostess, fell to Glafka." And who was that hostess, who also gave him her recipe for *vassilopita* as a memento? None other than Doxoula, the worker with the shrill voice who years before at an anti-junta rally had held the other side of a banner that read "Out of NATO" and "Down with the Americans." Anyhow, Thrassakis went to the party, mingled, saw and was seen, listened and talked—but the emigrant workers remained set in their ways, unwilling to budge. In fact they were glad that, given the cyclical crises of capitalism, they hadn't been sent back home.

Conclusion: the political changes, the fall of the junta, the return of the Right, the elections, the reinstatement of democracy, etc., didn't change the fate of these people in the slightest. *Gastarbeiter* they had been, and *gastarbeiter* they remained. Because the changes only affected the superstructure of power, not the substructure, the groundwork of the working class that found itself on the losing end of a relationship of exploitation. Which is why these workers believed that the system needed to be destroyed "from its very foundations," said Knut—who, just as seven years before, had made sure to get hold of some small bottles of *retsina* for the party. So they danced beneath the bulb in hopes of some real change. The giant Ilias who made rugs, *tepiche*, was there, and his young wife, and his kids, whom the junta had kept from leaving the country, and a new baby, to whom Thrassakis must have been referring when he jotted down, "The baby is crying. The bam and boom outside on the street frighten him. He is straddling the threshold of a new year—now they say he is one year old; soon they will call him two." (In the course of my research I tracked down one of Ilias's sons. He's about the same age as my daughter. He works in electronics. Naturally he doesn't remember Thrassakis; he never met him. But he told me his parents often spoke of him.)

Chapter Sixteen

Ich bin ein Berliner.
—J. F. Kennedy

I'd like to ask you
and find out
what longing made you
so down and out.

Have you too loved
and been betrayed?
Come sit with us
and let it fade.

THRASSAKIS USED to listen to Sotiria Bellou's version of this song each night at Apostolis's taverna. It was his favorite song and bridged the transition between two eras: his first stay in Berlin, 1970-71, and his last, 1977-78. Time congealed into a single continuity, which expressed a situation, an experience, not to be found in the words of the song but in the music and the singer's voice, the *signifiant* (signifier) of the listener's emotionally undefined *signifié* (signified). I can't say for sure, but from the information I managed to collect through arduous and dangerous research, I'm guessing that this "experience" had something to do with the use of drugs. During his first stay in Berlin, Thrassakis had quit smoking and the absence of cigarettes from his life made him feel pretty awful for rather a long while. During his second stay, he smoked hashish regularly, before moving on to harder drugs. In the first case, he went to the taverna because he liked the smell of other people's smoke. In the second, he went because (according to Apostolis) it was the only place where he could roll a joint in peace, protected by lookouts who rang a little bell at the door to let customers know whenever trouble was on its way.

Concerning his efforts to quit smoking, we have a description written by Thrassakis himself (*CDW*, Vol. II, 99). Here I will touch on only the basic points. He had been a heavy smoker, two packs a day, and the sudden change was a great one. During the first days he experienced "a diffuse, contagious irritation." Glafka had already quit smoking six months before, and to a certain extent it was her decision that Glafkos quit, too—in a couple, either both partners smoke, or neither. "The nicotine comes out through your fingers," which grow less and less yellow with each passing day. "Then comes an insane desire for a cigarette, which you substitute with food." He gains three kilos. Next comes a period in which he asks others to exhale in his direction—"*Il fume par personnes interposées*," as a Belgian friend put it—and, in general, seeks out places where the air is thick with smoke, of which Berlin has plenty to offer. During this period, characterized by the absence of tobacco, he notices in himself a kind of hypersexuality, as during puberty when his hormones had raged. He punches walls. Or unwinds with masturbatory diversions. But he can't entirely overcome the need for smoke. He buys sticks of Chinese and Indian incense, sets them up like candlesticks under the table by his feet, and breathes in the aromatic smoke. He tries to trick himself with all sorts of ersatz substitutes. And on trains, he always asks for a seat in the smoking section.

As for the role drugs played in his second stay, he himself says nothing. Perhaps he never had the chance? Perhaps his papers were lost? Or have yet to be opened? One thing is certain—it all started in America. Since he believed cigarettes to be more harmful than marijuana itself (one was artificial, made with chemical-soaked paper, the other not), his initiation must have come by way of a cake in which a layer of chocolate gave way to a layer of hashish. He must have eaten it, liked it, loosened up, without having drunk a thing, and thus, given the nervous strain of his everyday existence, found in the drug a much-needed relaxant.

But the downward spiral has no end. And since he couldn't find hard drugs (heroine, cocaine) at Apostolis's taverna, he started hanging out at another place, the so-called "Yugoslavian," on Saturday nights. It was also owned by a Greek, a mysterious character. The police were always arresting him and shutting down his place, and he was always opening it again, even better than before. What kind of a helping hand did he have? Who was protecting him? There were plenty of rumors going around about his dealings with the mafia and all sorts of shady characters. (Might the agent's Croats have numbered among them? It's not out of the question, particularly if we consider that Glafkos's initiation with the doctored cake most likely took place within Joe's crowd.) This Greek was a nice guy, had grown up in Africa, and had an interesting history, and Glafkos might have been studying him in preparation for some book. As a writer, Glafkos was always drawn to the exceptions that prove the rule. Earlier, during his years of political exile, he had never watered his wine, and guys like this Greek had no place among his concerns. But ever since his country had been freed, he had begun to say that he should concern himself not just with political prisoners, but with criminal prisoners as well.

True, the Greek's place (called the "Yugoslavian" primarily to distinguish it from Apostolis's place) reminded him somewhat of the Berlin of Döblin's *Berlin Alexanderplatz*. But still, the underworld of Glafkos's day was nothing like that of the old Berlin. Like everything else, it had gone international. You could find Turkish, Persian, Moroccan, Algerian, Czech, and Polish gangsters, Montenegrins and fanatical Ustasi agents, all of whom had divided the market amongst themselves so as to keep from knifing one another to death. And so, alongside the international proletariat assembly, there was also an international assembly of organized crime.

≈

I HAVE BEFORE me two photographs, one of Glafkos and one of Glafka, standing by the very lake whose frozen waters will soon receive his corpse on a sled. Glafkos is smiling widely, wrapped in a Swedish commando coat of white fur (bought for him by a friend from Oumeo whom he had gone to visit), its wide white collar raised. The collar would be completely indistinguishable from the background of snow if it weren't for a few naked saplings, or oversized shrubs, whose branches, black against the white snow, come between it and the collar. Glafkos is wearing a Russian fur cap (a gift he received in Moscow, he says, before the Party schism) with its two earflaps tied on top (so the cold must not have been unbearable), and though it isn't quite visible, we can deduce from the slant of his shoulders that he must have his hands in his pockets. In the background, the landscape (which still existed back then) seems idyllic. There isn't a single bird on the frozen lake. With a magnifying glass you can make out the East German guardhouse. And behind the trees, the forest where, though Glafkos doesn't know it yet, the Croats have their camps, right next to the American NATO bases. This photograph, taken at the site of the soon-to-be tragedy, is like a man's first introduction to the stage on which his final drama will soon play itself out.

In the other photograph, Glafka also seems happy, a little fur stole around her neck and a Russian cap on her head. Her scarf, caught on the metal fence surrounding the dock, leads your gaze toward the frozen mass that was once a lake. Beneath her cape, closed at the neck, we can see the outline of a Rumanian, or at least Balkan, blouse, perhaps a holiday gift from Joe's wife, Joy. Her gaze, even to me, looking at it today, exudes an immediacy of light—"pollinating the air like pistachio trees," as I once wrote, before I had ever seen this photograph.

≈

"I KNOW THAT MY saying anything against the other Greek's place, where all kinds of strange guys hung out, will just make him think I'm jealous," Apostolis told me. "But I'm sure that's where it all started. This Greek was a handsome guy, and had a thing for nightclubs. He'd opened lots of them, all over Germany. They all looked pretty much the same on the inside: a tiled ceiling made to look like the bottom of the ocean, portholes, fishing nets, ships in bottles, aquariums filled with Japanese fish, a bulwark for a bar, a steering wheel where each spoke was another tap. Really posh places with permits to stay open all night. Our place had to close at two. The police were always after us, as a 'local hotbed of revolutionaries,' they said. As for the other guy's place, when they weren't busy arresting him and shutting it down, he could stay open as late as he liked. Lazarus—because that's what I always called him—used to come to my place to unwind. He went to the other place to work. Sure, he waited tables for me every once in a while. Over there, though, he went by his other name, Glafkos Thrassakis. We all told him to watch out, not because of the other Greek but because of all the gangs that hung out at his place. Lazarus didn't listen. As to what kinds of drugs he was doing, I have no idea.

"If you want to understand, you have to see things the way they were back then. Berlin wasn't going through any earth-shattering upheavals. Just the noise of the airplanes landing and taking off that reigned over the city. And every now and then you might hear some strange explosions, as if the two sides were exchanging fire over the wall. As for the rest . . . .

"For Glafkos, the end of that year promised a better one to come. I had no idea he was mixed up in anything. I saw him, I lived him, on a daily basis. He was a kind man. He seemed younger than he really was, didn't look his age. Probably didn't feel it. 'If a man wants to write,' he used to say, 'he needs a little naïveté.' His plans for the new year, as far as I can remember, all had to do with his work. He had commissions for plays and screenplays and had started some stories he wanted to finish. Thanks to the fellowship, he had temporarily solved his financial problems. It was almost the first time, he told me, that he didn't have to worry about earning his daily bread. His most pressing concern was the need for self-discipline and concentration.

"And how could I forget New Year's? When the new year came, he was still hard at work in a tiny room in the house where the party was being held. Everyone from the old crowd was there. Glafkos, coming in, made an announcement: in the new year that had just begun, after an entire year of political inertia, he was ready, he told us, to dust off his old ideological arsenal.

"Glafkos was really happy when Glafka found the coin in her piece of the New Year's pie. He took me aside and, while we were drinking, described his childhood dreams about the coin in the *vassilopita* they shared each year during the Occupation in his family's apartment building in Thessaloniki. 'Everyone used to gather at the surgeon's place: the merchant, Karpidis; the two old maids from the top floor; a man who used to take me to soccer matches on Sunday afternoons, whose wife was a great businesswoman; Despina, who fell from the balcony; and Mrs. Tesa, who was always pulling me up onto her lap. And each New Year's Eve, for the cutting of the pie, the doctor from the trains would come, and the construction engineer, the hunter with his rifle, a man who was collaborating with the Germans, another black marketeer, the whore, and the dwarf.' Young Lazos would daydream about what he would buy if he found the coin in his piece of the pie— a bicycle or a ball, toys utterly foreign to his world. But each New Year's brought the same disappointment—the coin always ended up in someone else's piece. 'During one German occupation,' he told me, 'I used to dream of a coin. And now, during another, thirty-five years later, the coin fell to my wife.'

"No, during those days before their trip over to the East"—they were going over to buy paper, which Glafkos thought was of better quality in the East— "Glafkos was working calmly. He didn't stop by every day, but we talked on the phone. And when I woke up that Wednesday and saw the picture of him on a sled on the front page of the paper, I was horrified. Yes, his murderers put him on a sled. We Greeks got together, formed a committee, made inquiries, organized ourselves for self-defense, threatened the Greek from the night club to try and make him talk—all to no avail. I have reason to believe that the Greek had nothing to do with it. To be perfectly honest, my first thought was that it must have had something to do with cocaine. But after everything else I found out, it seems to me that things must have been much more complicated than a simple mix-up over drugs.

"Look, here, I want to give you his final manuscripts. I held onto them all these years, waiting for someone like you to come looking for them. His relatives wanted to bury him down in Greece. But Glafka and I insisted on keeping him here. In the end we won—but may you never have such relatives. Take it from me. Though now I suppose you, too, must be thinking about taking his bones back home."

Chapter Seventeen

This notebook is filling up. It's nearing its end, which makes me nervous. While a movie coming to its end makes you glad, a notebook approaching its end upsets you, because there's always a sequel. Once more you will have to shape letters that convey messages. This is why writers who publish infrequently make more money: The rarity of the voice raises the price of that golden silence. Prolific writers, like me, write out of biological insecurity: will I have time?

We're going through a critical period. Don't you all understand? Whoever manages to come out on the other end will be proclaimed a great man. Everyone else will leave behind only the scattered traces of their suffering.

THESE WORDS were, quite literally, Thrassakis's next-to-last.

It isn't hard to understand why I didn't save them for the end. I stated right off the bat that I'm not a fan of "statistical" biographies that start with the person's birth and end with his death. I believe I made my position clear from the very beginning: I would take my material as it came, following whatever path it might lead me down. Thus the reader of my text becomes, in a sense, my ally, my accomplice, as he stumbles into the same pitfalls into which I fall, suffers the same repetitions, and experiences, in general, a "becoming" rather than a life crystallized from the very first sentence—an undertaking which, moreover, would have necessitated extensive preparatory work on the book's structure. I seek neither to criticize nor to defend either of the two methods. I'm only trying to explain how I myself worked. Certainly I could have collected all my material first and then, having completed my research, begun to stitch together the facts. But wouldn't that have been like killing a beautiful butterfly with the stickpin of science? I've always preferred a live butterfly in the collector's net to a "dead soul" pinned to the lepidopterist's table.

Besides, in that case, before writing even a single line, I would have had to wait for the other two sacks in the American university library to be opened. And by then the few eye-witnesses still alive would have disappeared—and who's to say that I myself will be able to hold on until 2003? All theories, like all scientific speculations, are born from the objective conditions of their formation. In this respect I disagree wholeheartedly with Lacan, who claims that objects have lives of their own. No. Objects, like the can of soup to which he refers (I derive the example from Thrassakis's own notes), cannot transmit the stuff of light. Or rather, nothing can be transmitted unless there's an eye to receive it. Thrassakis/Lacan would agree with me on that count: there can be no light without an eye to perceive it. Correct. But, I would add, the eye exists without light—it can see in the dark, too.

≈

SINCE WAKING that morning, he had been thinking about how utterly monotonous his life was. Food, drink, a movie, a walk, a book, perhaps, a bit of work, and the margins of existence were exhausted. Of course every now and then he would watch the sky going bloody with sunset, or the birds mating, pigeons nesting outside his window. He would look at the tongues of butchered animals in the market, or animal heads being eaten at funereal suppers, and wonder how and when his time would finally arrive. . . . This, then, was life? To wake up and work just to go to sleep again because you had worked? How little it all meant, really, defining nothing but the shape of the void. And the newspapers he read made him sick. But when he didn't read them, he thought he was missing out on something he should know. Oh, for the tranquility of the monk on Mt. Athos!

Why do I dislike my face so much? What did it ever do to me? "Nothing," says the mirror. And yet this roundness it's taking on, like a rock losing its corners, can make me nostalgic for hours on end for the jackknives of my old cheekbones and jaw. Longings that once killed have been replaced with doughy yioufkades. The old exploding hand grenades have turned into arti-

chokes. I have no mirrors in the house, so as not to see. Because every time I catch sight of my image in some mirror or glass, I want to flee from that man who's looking at me. I'm like some criminal whose crimes, according to the statute of limitations, can no longer be tried. The criminal can circulate freely, with only himself as an enemy.

No, no, *he said again. Upstairs the dancing continued.* Because I love no one, I hate myself. The absence of love for others is what creates this hate . . .

Since he didn't care for psychoanalysis one bit, he decided to go up, uninvited, to the party being thrown by the girl upstairs. The kids there welcomed him gladly. They treated him to whisky, pastis. He had his eye on a certain black girl. It was the first time he had ever been in the girl's apartment. Her chest was small. She wouldn't have given much milk. The furniture was simple. The Doric bed of love. A shabby room, with rich music. Not much light but lots of youth. He wondered where he had seen that stone vase before. "I don't write for dimes, you know," he said, though no one had asked. "And I can't stand your whining anymore." He left the room. In the street, the clean air brought him around again.

For me, *he thinks,* Berlin was a milestone of a city. Berlin is the center of the world. And if it lives in its prior history, or with it, that doesn't mean the edge is any less sharp in the present. Now a ruined wheel, it still finds itself at the center of a dead diffusion. . .

The narrative, if it can be called a narrative, ends here. The third person singular isn't fooling anyone. Immediately afterwards we find the following cry: "Oh, Germany, Germany. Harsh country, country of calamity. Divided, yet indivisible in your passion for work."

The funny thing is that while Thrassakis seems to pity the immigrants for being forced to work far from their country, the workers themselves, with the looming specter of the recession that has set in, want nothing less than to be sent back home. Setting his sadness as a standard of reality helps neither reality nor his sadness. Apostolis explained to me how the experience with the *Lumpenproletariat* after the *Krach* of 1929 (with Hitler coming to power in 1933) had taught the German citizens this much, at least: by sending away foreign workers, they could protect their own against the blows of the recession. Thus the foreign work force became the scapegoat once again.

Apostolis understood the workers and their problems better than any boss, because he saw them when they came into his taverna to unwind. He spoke to me a great deal about the past. He said that Thrassakis's ties to the workers were political, not actual. In fact, during his second stay in Berlin, he hardly had any contact whatsoever with the working class there. The real change, he said, had to take place within Greece itself, on which the fate of the emigrants depended. And so, with regard to the Greek workers in Berlin, Thrassakis exhibited a desired self-distancing.

≈

I FIND MYSELF in a difficult position. No editor will want my biography before the other two sacks are opened. Which is to say, in fourteen years. Here I am with all these papers and writings, and no idea what to do with them. Joe Junior is the only one who insists that he wants them. But what if he just wants to get his hands on them so as to destroy them? I've reached the end, but still don't know if I'm finished.

≈

THOUGH THE TEMPTATION is great to reopen my research regarding the relations between Glafkos and his agent, I refrain from doing so, lest I bestow too great an importance on a relationship Thrassakis himself might not have considered all that decisive. Yet the new material Apostolis handed over to me (always out of his safety deposit box at the bank) reveals the true extent and heatedness of the conflicts between them. For posterity's sake, I will deposit these letters in the library that is home also to Thrassakis's manuscripts. But I can't resist throwing fleeting glances at the densest period of their correspondence (1971-72) and referring now to just a few highlights from these letters, for the sake of that ideal reader (my daughter) whom I have created in my mind. For example, Joe, in refusing to represent *Prinos II*, writes, "I don't believe that NATO could ever be that clever with its enemies" (i.e., in finishing them off as adroitly as Thrassakis describes in his novel). Another parenthetical phrase refers again to NATO, which "rarely acts only in its own interests." Exactly. Joe hit the nail on the head. Therefore, it must work in the interests of others. But of whom? Why, the multinational corporations, of course. And there we find the agent's fundamental objection to representing *Prinos II*: its brash anti-Americanism. Though Joe, of course, conceals his real reasons for rejecting the book. "I am a dreamer of the American dream," Joe writes, "but I don't reject your anti-Americanism. After all, how could I reject a worldwide phenomenon? Where would we be without it?" So he hits where it hurts. He says that the book is full of political clichés and suffers from a "lack of credibility," and from the inimitable neologism of the "automatic leftism" to which Glafkos is apparently prone. Joe likes Thrassakis's caricatures of idealists and, generally speaking, his ironic attitude toward the progressives. He suggests that Glafkos put the book aside for the time being, and move forward with the next, "which will, I hope, be a novel." And the letter ends with the Sartre-esque curse: "*Eh bien, continuons!*"

I also found a copy of a letter Mrs. O. had written to the agent about how fond she was of Glafkos and how deserving he was of every kind of encouragement. After a talk in her living room during one of those loveless *tête-à-têtes*, moved by the difficulties Glafkos was facing, the generous Mrs. O sat down and dictated a letter to her secretary, and then sent a copy to Glafkos "for your information," which Glafkos kept in his "Joe File."

There is no doubt in my mind, then, that there was contact between Berlin and New York. The instruments of Glafkos's execution must have come from the drug ring. Seeking every now and then to come out of his shell, a shell he couldn't stand, he finally abandoned it altogether to his suppliers in the Berlin underworld.

Immediately after Glafkos's death, the Greek from the nightclub came out and threatened to reveal certain things. They shut down his bar, this time for good. And at least for a while, he went back to work on the ships. He was friends with the sailor Vladimir, Apostolis told me, and through him had met some pastor from Leiden. . . .

Apostolis willingly sat down with me to help identify the names and addresses found jumbled up in Glafkos's papers. As many as he could remember, of course, since a long time had passed. On one page, otherwise blank: "Today I'm trying to quit smoking, for the third time." But the handwriting seems to be Glafka's. On an envelope from the Kaufhaus Des Westens department store, dated December 11, 1971, the name "Lazaridis" is written "Lazarof," though the street name (Eisenzahnstrasse) and number are the same as found elsewhere. "It's a bill for one of those bean-bag chairs, I don't know what they're called in Greek," Apostolis explained. "The kind you sink into when you sit down. We went together, I remember, to pick it out. Glafka liked a cherry red one, Glafkos wanted white. In the end I think they decided on orange. Or was it a more cabbagey color? I don't remember." When I told him the story about the fugitive they had hidden in the chair that was pierced by the East Germans at the border control, Apostolis was stunned. It was the first time he had heard the story. Surely Glafkos had invented the whole thing. He liked for everyday objects to be transformed into elements of suspense. (An acute observation on the part of the taverna owner, who, in the course of his years at the taverna, had learned to read people well.)

Then he broke into a truly torrential description of Glafkos as a Kaufhaus Des Westens enthusiast: "The food was all on the top floor. He could spend hours in there on a Saturday night, when the working class would pour out into the streets and upset the whole universe. Turks, our people, Germans. Anyhow, Glafkos was always trying to apply his principle of milking the system for all it was worth. Every so often they would be advertising something new on the food floor, giving out free samples. Glafkos tried everything, it suited his principle— like at a pay phone where if you figure out the right way to dial, you can make trans-Atlantic calls without paying a cent."

The addresses, names, and scribbled notes changed ink and script, like geological layers that bear witness to the respective eras of their formation. Apostolis was moved to see his old phone numbers among the rest, his home phone and the one at the taverna. "Just think," he sighed, "even I had forgotten them. I can still hear my grandmother's voice as she answers the phone. . . . " Beneath his number there was one belonging to a Kostas, with no last name, just a parenthesis that read "Frankfurt," and the area code for the city. "Kostas, sure, Kostakis," Apostolis said, glad to have remembered him. "He was here in Berlin, too, but then his company—he was an electrician—sent him to work at the airport in Frankfurt on a very delicate job: he wired up those conveyer belts that carry the suitcases to the planes, depending on where the passengers are going. If he made a mistake, a bag destined for Athens, let's say, might end up in Saigon. Kostakis, just think. . . . "

These pages upset him. He didn't want to go on. But for my sake, he mustered his courage. I dressed him in a wetsuit of heartlessness. There were scattered phrases: "The salaries and wages have been fixed," "When will the people be freed," "Very grand, Papandreou's funeral," "The teacher's visiting card," "Ancient Olympia," "The Greek people are like fire—someone needs to light the wick." The phone number for the taxi company, a German name, "Hans," and an address, Langestrasse 78. And then another, "Eleftherios Katsoados, 1 Berlin 36, Wrangel str. 76, *geboren* 4.11.36."

"Oh, sure. Leftherakis, the giant, the one we called 'Whole-hearted.' " Now Apostolis was rushing furiously into the past—and this time I tried to follow him, since Eleftherios was none other than Ilias, the rug worker who used to distribute publications for the resistance and whose kids had been held hostage by the junta. Apostolis explained that Eleftherios must have given Glafkos his date of birth (*geboren*), so Glafkos could use his ins with the "higher-ups" to get him a residence permit for Berlin. The local police were after Leftheris-Ilias-"Whole-Hearted" because they found him too politically "active," and they wanted to get him off their backs in some legal way. Did Glafkos manage to help? Yes, he vaguely remembered that, through Günter Grass, a great anti-fascist and philhellene, right hand man to Willy Brandt, Glafkos had fixed it so that Ilias was able to stay. "Just think," Apostolis sighed, "I never knew we were the same age, me and 'Whole-Hearted'—right down to the same month."

As I turned the yellowed pages, along with these scattered scribblings I was discovering, once again, the futility of my effort to decode a life on the basis of these few remaining crumbs. Elsewhere I found the address of a boutique, and one for Glafka's seamstress Elge. Some more numbers, identified only by first names: Yiorgos, Lela, Alexis, Kostas—"Yeah, the old crowd," Apostolis kept saying, again and again. Somehow I was supposed to create a story out of these, an atmosphere. But how? "I'm ashamed to leave you, but too tired to love you." And above those words, "Athens Grill, Koltbusser Damus 9." "That was the other Greek place," Apostolis told me, "where they made souvlaki in a pita. They did a good business because they were cheap. Of course, the pita wasn't real pita—there are only two companies, back in Greece, that know the real recipe for pita—but for the foreigners, it was what they were used to. Lots of fascists went there, though the owner, Takis, was a good kid, a democrat. No, Glafkos didn't go there too often. But he did like the pizza place that was managed by Greeks. They worked hard, but the Italian who owned it took half their profits. Poor kids. The guy used to have a garage, but he got tired of fixing Greek's cars at half price so he started at the pizza place instead. His wife's cheeks were always red from the ovens. I wonder what ever happened to them." Then I came across these names: Ilioupolis, Euosmo, Kordelio, Harmankii, Dendropotamos, Giftika, Sikies, Neapolis, Polihni, Stavroupolis. Apostolis had only been to Athens, so he didn't recognize them, but I did. They were neighborhoods in Thessaloniki, great mother to the poor.

I had started to get tired, it's true. What was it for, this long, hard journey into a place that would never be able to come alive again? How would my biography be any worse off if these pages weren't included? How would it be any richer if there were as many more like them? I was like a blind man playing an accordion on a streetcorner. I could push it and pull it as much as I liked, but I couldn't see the passersby. Were they mocking me? Did they pity me? The spare change they dropped rang every now and then in my cup, showing me some kind of sympathy. But that was all. And I carried blindly on.

Chapter Eighteen

"I DON'T KNOW whether right is the opposite of wrong," Glafkos writes, "but I am deeply aware of the division between North and South." This was written at the height of the war between the two Vietnams, right next to the dividing line that sliced Korea, too, into North and South.

Seen in this context, this sentence expresses the leading issues of the era in which it was written. "That," he continues, "is why I am unable to understand the distinction between Orient and Occident, East and West." (We see how slowly he develops his theme, how warily he approaches the division of Berlin into East and West.)

"Since the sun's position is static and the earth revolves around it, sometimes the sun seems to be coming up from behind the mountains and other times diving into the clouds." The meaning here is clear: East and West do not exist, in and of themselves. They exist only in relation to the earthly sphere.

West Berlin seems to him like the setting for some play:

> *The set is ready, but the actors are missing. The bus bringing them from the city got a flat tire, and hence this delay. But the borders aren't just any borders. They are the borders of a city that is a state. They searched me at Checkpoint Charlie. They found nothing but a slip of paper with the date, 1933. "That's when I was born," I told them. They didn't believe me. In 1933 they were burning the Reichstag.*

These lines are of interest from several points of view. First of all, the date he refers to is, again, the 33 of Christ at his death, as well as the year of Hitler's ascension to power. Secondly, in this city, where he is destined to leave his bones, they found nothing, he says, but the date of his birth. As if he were preparing his gravestone, leaving the date of death blank.

The battle of Berlin was, as we know, a fierce one. In Glafkos's day, there were still marks of fighting on the walls of the houses. And while the West seems to him like a "pool slowly emptying, uncovering the dregs at the bottom, old fish that never died, scum on the rocks," East Berlin, on the other hand, looks glamorous through his eyes, like a port waiting for its sea, wide avenues waiting to be filled with cars, as soon as the party can throw its resources into their production. (This image is taken from Kostas Kotzias's report on the Siberian port which they built first, and then brought the sea to meet it.) And yet East Berlin is washed with a bitter irony: "Marx Street, Marx Square, Bank of Marx." Marx, a bank? Of course: the Bank of Marxist Faith, the Bank of Asiatic Production, Engels Improvement Works, etc., etc. It's depressing, he seems to be saying, for Brecht to be a museum, Lenin an avenue. And between the two, the wall, "an obstacle to the mind's comprehension of what the retina sees all too clearly." What is it that the retina sees? That one Berlin is slowly dying, while the other hasn't yet begun to live. So leave it free to develop, let nature heal its wounds, "as each spring the trees put out new leaves, conquering the winter anew." Forget all this, he means to say—forget the artificial divisions, the walls of shame, the guard towers with their machine guns that wound the city's body by cutting it in two.

≈

WHY WAS THRASSAKIS, as a poet, so rawly rejected by the Party? What was the mistake that turned him from the bard of the Resistance to a man accused of serving the bourgeoisie?

Of course he was never literally expelled from the Party, because he had never officially joined.

Thrassakis, who answered to the name Thrassos Kastanakis in his underground work (or, in Greek, *paranomia*—"if you leave out the 'm,' " he once noted cleverly, "it becomes 'paranoia' "), didn't cease to exist after his clash with the Party, as did another writer and comrade, ten years older than he, Federico Sanchez, who wrote as Jorge Semprun. Sanchez-Semprun, with whom Glafkos was friendly, once said to him, "If they were to erase you from the city registers, you wouldn't stop existing as a person who eats and sleeps and makes love—who fulfills, in short, all his biological needs. But if they erase you from the Party registers, you suddenly cease to exist, you turn to air, to smoke, you are suddenly a non-being. Friends don't greet you in the street, old comrades turn their backs."

The only intellectuals who become part of the Party machine are the ones who want big funerals. Which is why his own funeral was attended by only a handful of friends.

≈

HERE I WILL STOP my attempts at decoding. The springs have dried up, the crevices are covered with snow. In spring, when the snows melt, perhaps we will speak again. For now, I will let good Apostolis rest from all his efforts to assist me with my work. In the past few days we've been together constantly, running around to see different places, corners, bridges, watchtowers. The Berlin of Glafkos's time is unrecognizable now, but there are still some spots of endless appeal. Some mornings there is a blue so bright it hurts your eyes. And the mist. The snow.

Even his grave was covered in snow, somewhere between the Russian and American cemeteries, in a neutral zone, where they put all the in-betweens—symbolic, perhaps, of my hero's tragic fate. Because despite all his poetic declarations ("may my bones add something to the thistly scent of my homeland"), the fact remains that he left written instructions, found among his papers, that in the case of some accident, he was to be buried at the site of that accident. He loved Berlin. And Berlin won him, in the end, made him its own forever.

I scraped away the hard snow and put down a few flowers, tulips. All the ancient representations of funeral dinners show only tulips, which is why I wanted to adorn his grave with that beautiful flower. The gravestone read, "Lazarus Lazaridis, *geboren* 1933, *kaputt* 1978. Application for residence."

I asked Apostolis to take a picture of me in front of the grave. And then I fainted. They took me to the hospital outside the city, which I left the next day with the idea in my head of removing his bones and his old passport, with which he had left Greece entirely legally before the dictatorship, but with which he would never return.

Here I can't resist the temptation to offer my own interpretation of the events back then, as a kind of last report of my own: the charge concerning the stolen amphora from Thassos, the "essential part of the State," was cooked up by the colonels after his departure, so there would be a reason for his arrest if he were ever to come back. They sought to discourage his return, even when all those in self-imposed exile abroad were told, "Come home, everyone, you're more useful here." Because the judicial decision made in his absence concerning illegal trade in antiquities was not erased by the political changeover. Just as Metaxas's men handed political prisoners over to the German occupiers, the laws back then handed over to the next regime whatever men had been caught by the earlier one. And so, even after "cholera" had passed from his land, the legal obstacle preventing his return continued to exist.

Among the many places he longed for during his youth was, without a doubt, Thassos, the island from which the amphora was supposedly stolen. His grandfather on his mother's side, the one he loved so much, was from Samos. His father was from Thrace. And Lazarus was from Samothrace. As a young man he had written a novel about the return of Wingless Victory to the island of her birth—and now, a mature man, though certainly not old (as he himself said to his contemporaries), he carried with him, in his travels abroad, his own Winged Defeat. . . .

FIRST AFTERWORD
Conversations with Andreas Kalvos

JUST ONE WORD more. As I was tidying up these papers to leave, it occurred to me that I had completely neglected to comment on Thrassakis's seminal text, "Conversations with Andreas Kalvos." Before I begin, I should note that, among other issues Glafkos raises in this text, is the transfer of Kalvos's bones on June 5, 1960 from the cemetery in Kensington where they had lain for ninety-nine years to his "sole, beautiful Zakynthos," on the battleship "Hatzikonstantis." Because this issue might come to concern me as well—in my case, the removal of Thrassakis's bones from the no man's land of the cemetery in which they are currently located, caught between East and West Berlin, to his "sole, beautiful Thassos"—I thought it might be useful to deal more extensively with these "Conversations." Even if it doesn't add anything new to a discussion of his works, it might at least shed some external light on my own internal darkness.

Glafkos himself took an interest (self-prophetic, one might say) in this particular aspect of the life (and death) of the poet of the *Odes*, as if it were something he himself were bound to face later on. Kalvos, as Thrassakis saw him, was no idolater of bones. But though Kalvos took no interest in bones, he nevertheless ended up interesting others in his.

This is not, as we said above, the only issue in Thrassakis's "Conversations." It is, however, the last he examines. And as his own final issue, I am surprised at how I, too, unconsciously managed to avoid mentioning it, thus leaving it to be my own last issue. After all, it will soon become a real concern, what with the approach of the "Year of Thrassakis."

In his admirable introduction to the 1960 edition of Kalvos's *Complete Works*, Spiros Mylonas writes:

> *The life and work of the poet of the* Odes *is surrounded by a great deal of partial and, in many cases, contradictory information. Much of his life is shrouded in darkness. Articles and works of criticism he published on the Ionian islands and abroad do not carry his signature, making a complete assessment of the poet's activity difficult, particularly concerning the period during which he lived on Corfu. Moreover, according to the information we have today, the poet seems rarely to have spoken about himself. He was in his life as he was in his works: difficult to approach. Which is why the task of anyone who undertakes a study of the great hymnest of the Revolution of 1821 is a difficult task indeed. Now, on the occasion of the "Year of Kalvos" and the removal of his bones . . . .*

The limits of this text cannot possibly allow a discussion of all the attempts that were made to locate the poet's grave in the area of Kensington in London. The Cypriot intellectual and Kalvos scholar Antonis Indianos began these investigations on his own initiative in 1924. In 1937, after fifteen solid years of research, he made the following announcement to the Pan-Ionian Assembly: "I finally managed to locate Kalvos's grave. During my visit to Louth I spoke with the oldest inhabitants there, who still remembered the poet, though dimly. They spoke of Doctor Kalvos with great respect." Unfortunately, Mylonas adds (this, as all the rest, is taken from Thrassakis's quotation of the text):

> *. . . despite all the investigations conducted up to now, no portrait of the artist has ever been discovered. From information provided by his biographers we know that he was an intelligent and eccentric man of medium height, with a large head, dark hair, lively eyes, and a heavy step.*

Thrassakis himself writes:

> *Here, lest I overstep the boundaries of this short text, I would just like to mention that the issue of the removal of Kalvos's bones from London to his home-*

*land was raised for the first time in a pamphlet published on Zakynthos in
1881, entitled "Regarding the transfer of the remains of the poet of Zakynthos."*

Mylonas, in his epilogue (subtitled "The Fatherland,") to the *Collected Works*, says:

*The issue was not raised again for many years. But when the First Pan-Ionian
Assembly met in Thiaki in 1938, at the prompting of K. Soldatou, the historian and Kalvos scholar, the issue of the transfer of his bones was raised again,
and a pan-Hellenic committee was formed, to be led by the writer G.
Xenopoulos, now deceased. Unfortunately, however, this noble effort was
frustrated by the advent of war.*

*After the war, in the beginning of 1946, the writer T. Xidis published an
interesting article concerning the transfer of Kalvos's bones in the journal* New
Hearth. *That same year, the Society for Research on the Ionian Islands started
raising money for this cause, though the effort was soon discontinued. . . . In 1952
the issue was raised again by N. Filiotis, the mayor of Zakynthos. . . . In April
of 1957 a rather caustic letter was published in the journal* Epirot Hearth,
*authored by the Levkadian intellectual I. Voukelatos. . . . And in March of 1959,
on the occasion of the ninetieth anniversary of our great Kalvos's death, the
Society for Research on the Ionian Islands once again brought the issue before the
eyes of the Ministry of Education and our nation's cultural community.*

Up to that point, the poet of the *Odes*—who wrote, "May my fate not give
me / a grave in foreign lands; death is sweet / only when you are buried / in your
native land"—had been largely forgotten. No one, neither his island nor the official State nor any of the cultural organizations, took any interest in realizing the
first and last wish of the poet of *Daring and Virtue*.

*The Association of the Museum of Solomos and Other Illustrious Zakythians
initiated a broad consultation of leading social and cultural figures concerning the creation of a committee to organize the celebration of the occasion of
the transfer of Kalvos's bones from London to the land of his birth.*

*After these leading figures examined the general aspects of the issue, it was
decided that a twenty-member committee would be formed, composed of the fol-*

lowing individuals: S. Mitropolitis, honorary president; Marinos Sigouros, president; the senators of Zakynthos; the mayor of Zakynthos, I. Margaris; the abbot of the Agios Dimitrios monastery; the school principal; H. Zois, the president of the tourism committee; L. Karrer; D. Megadoukas; and the editors of the local newspapers. Thirty-five leading cultural and social figures from the island now living in Athens formed the "Zakynthos Committee," while an executive committee, led by G. Kournouto, the head of the Arts and Letters division of the Ministry of Education, undertook to manage the bureaucratic aspects of the transfer.

On March 19, 1960, the poet's bones arrived in Greece, along with those of his wife. Military salutes were given at the airport, and the bones were transferred by a stately procession to the Metropolitan church of Agios Eleftheros. Kalvos's bones were then placed in the chapel of the First Cemetery of Athens, from which they were transferred on the battleship "Hatzikonstantis" on June 5, 1960, to his native island, the sole, beautiful Zakynthos.

At exactly 10 a.m. on that Sunday morning the boat arrived on the calm waters of the Ionian Sea. The bones were accompanied on the Journey from Athens by . . . .

The list of bone-worshippers follows. And Mylonas continues:

A procession was formed in the square by the port, and, to the sounds of the funeral march played by the Philharmonic, it headed for the church of Agios Nikolaos in Mylo. After the memorial service was given by the Honorable Bishop Alexiou, wreaths were placed in the name of the Parliament, the Prefect, the Reserve Officers, the Scouts, the Drivers, the Girls' School, Dr. Stratis Andreadis, General Director of the Commercial Bank, and the city's Pharmaceutical Association.

That afternoon the infinite numbers of invited guests and the local authorities sat down to a banquet given by the local committee and the municipality, in the luxurious dining room of the "Anthi" hotel.

That evening a performance was given with great success at the "Acropol" theater by the students of the Zakynthos grammar school, based on Kalvos's tragedy, Danaids, translated from the Italian by Marieta Yiannopoulou.

And so, Thrassakis concludes, this humble ritual came to an end with the reading of the poet's words in the place of his birth—but, due to a strange coincidence, those words were read only in translation.

And Thrassakis closes his text with two lines of his own: "And when you die they will write you hymns of Easter resurrection. / For now, while you still live, pay your taxes."

I'm not at all certain that Thrassakis, in adding these lines to the end of the "Conversations," wasn't thinking of the conduct of the Zakynthos Municipal Association in 1813, when it refused to give the poet the small economic assistance Hugo Foskolos had requested on his behalf, so that Kalvos might continue his studies abroad. I quote here the relevant part of Foskolos's letter:

> I thought to request from my homeland a yearly fellowship, renewable for five years, to support Kalvos in his efforts to become a learned man so that, upon returning to his island to instruct its youth, his studies would benefit not just himself but his country as well. . . . "

"The Municipality," writes Mylonas, "refused to offer this support."

In Thrassakis's "Conversations," written as an internal monologue but given the form of a dialogue by the "replies" furnished by the poet's texts and various accounts of his life, Thrassakis selects only those events from Kalvos's life that touched him personally. But their greatest similarity is found, in my opinion, in the critic Soldatou's observation, in the 1937 issue of the journal *New State*: "[Kalvos] died in self-exile, forgotten and embittered, and his death passed completely unnoticed in Greece. Not even in the Ionian islands . . . where reports of the struggle were fresh and caught the public interest, was the smallest mention heard." While in his *Early Critical Works* (1888), Kostas Palamas declares: "And how could he not be forgotten, this poor but proud poet who lived and died a premature death far from Greece, as unapproachable in exile as he was in his own lines?" (Thrassakis has underlined the "unapproachable" in this sentence.) "But let us hope, as he hoped," the poet of the *Gypsy* concludes, "that he finds a sweeter life awaiting him in the world to come." "So," Glafkos adds, "when you die they'll write you hymns of Eastern resurrection. / For now, while you still live, pay your taxes."

Kalvos returned to his homeland. But in returning, he suffered a great shock, just as Thrassakis did upon his return to post-changeover Greece. Mylonas writes and Thrassakis underlines:

> *The poet arrived in Navplio in the summer of 1826. But what he found was not at all what he had expected. In Navplio, following the "Mesologghi exodus"* [comparable to the events at the Polytechnic in Thrassakis's day] *the different governing factions were all concerned only with saving their own skins, completing this pilgrimage only to satisfy their own specific interests. . . . The poet, who came to Greece to offer up "one more heart to the Muslim iron," feels a deep disappointment at seeing the most holy goals of the revolution betrayed, seeing the petty transactions taking place and different factions fighting amongst themselves. . . . Earlier, at a distance from the revolution, he had seen things in their ideal form.*
>
> *Thus influenced by the situation he found in Greece, on Corfu he seems to have lost his depths entirely. He fell fighting. As evidence of that we have the fact that the poet's lyre had long fallen silent. He now worked for the good of the "Homeland." He wrote many articles, primarily concerning the reformation of the Constitution in 1847. In doing so, the poet believed he was serving his people. However, he seems to have quickly become disappointed with the reformers, who were working closely with the treacherous English forces of "protection," and in 1852 he left for London. In 1855 he settled in the village of Louth, where he pursued his interest in mathematics and worked on translations from ancient Greek and Italian. He died in November, 1869.*

The similarities between Kalvos's and Thrassakis's respective stories are to be found in even the smallest details. In the "fanatic democrat of Zakynthos, Psimaris, who climbed onto the castle and took down the Venetian flag, symbol of oppression, barbarism and darkness," Glafkos finds the precursor of Manolis Glezos, who along with Santas took down the German swastika from the Acropolis. "The great tables that were laid in all the squares on the islands to celebrate their emancipation from tyranny," and where "all citizens sat on an equal footing"—("burning," Mylonas writes, "the *libro d'oro*, the golden book of the nobility")—remind Thrassakis of the areas emancipated by ELAS where people's courts were established. The Livorno where Kalvos lived from 1801 to 1802 has become a center of the Greek Revolution. "Like my own Angona," Thrassakis observes. The authorities found out that Kalvos had gotten involved with "anarchist elements" in Italy ("the red brigades of my day," Thrassakis comments), and in a letter to Foskolos, Kalvos writes that he is unable to go anywhere because they will not grant him a passport.

Thrassakis feels an even closer connection to Kalvos's travels in Bologna, Milan, and Florence. On June 9, 1816, Kalvos is in Zurich, a city Thrassakis will visit a century and a half later. He then goes to Geneva, where during Kalvos's time various philhellenic societies are being formed. While in Paris (the main center of philhellenism), Kalvos meets a great number of people, reporters and supporters of the movement for national liberation, just as Thrassakis did. There Kalvos publishes his second volume of *Odes*. There Glafkos also published his second volume of poetry, *Laka Souli*.

This, however, is where the likenesses end. For during the time when Kalvos is writing his *Odes*, Greece is under the Turkish yoke. During the time when Glafkos is writing his poems, Greece is under the yoke of other Greeks. And in terms of sentiment, Thrassakis comes closer to Foskolos, who writes to Kalvos: "Why are you speaking and singing again of homeland, of weapons and Greek virtue? Greece, now, is a fleshless corpse."

Then again, Thrassakis is closer to Kalvos in lines like: "The blinder and crueler / the tyranny / the faster the doors of salvation / are opened"—or even, "the cups of injustice run over." And he endorses the Kalvian stanza: "Better, far better / for Greeks to be scattered / to run to all ends of the earth / with hands outstretched / begging for bread/ than to depend on protectors." And he adds the words "of speech" after the first word in Kalvos's "Freedom requires virtue and daring."

I now find myself in a difficult position. Please tell me what I should do. Should I raise the issue of the removal of his bones as soon as 25 years have elapsed after his death? What should I do? Try to put yourself in my shoes. Should I apply to committees for monetary support to help finance the return of Thrassakis's bones, and ask churches to house the return of this "Winged Defeat" to the country of his birth? Apply for financial assistance from the Ministry of Culture? Or from the General Secretariat of Emigrants? Perhaps the Ministry of the New Generation would be more interested? Would Thrassakis himself even want that? Doesn't the basic concept of the international nature of the proletariat rest on the notion of "whatever land and country"? Didn't he himself often say, "The earth is a grave for all men and women alike"? Wouldn't he be bothered by the groups and organizations who would come and present themselves at his funeral? The representatives of local self-rule from his island? As Lazaridis, at least, I believe he would be pleased. "Lazarus, Lazarus," I yell, "come out." And he will come. Not like another Lazarus, just plain old Glafkos, a god of the sea, as he used to be, in ancient times.[*]

---

[*] The god Glafkos, son of the fisherman Polivos from Anthidonas of Boetia, once caught so many fish that when he went to count them, he got tired and left them lying there on the ground. One by one the fish ate the herb that gives eternal life and survived. Glafkos himself also ate from this same herb, and so he became immortal. When he was very old he fell into the sea and there he remained, honored as a god of the sea.

SECOND AFTERWORD

EVER SINCE I lost Thrassakis, I've been at a loss myself. I've lost my crutches, and now all I can do is totter around. I'd gotten used to busying myself with him. Now, the great *now*, looms over me like a void. And I know I've lost my reader's trust: Who knows (the reader must be wondering, and rightfully so) what this biographer will cook up for us next? The film plays in reverse the sequence of a pane of glass being smashed with a rock—the pieces are sucked back into place as if by a magnet, re-forming the original, unbroken pane.

Having identified with him so deeply, isn't it natural that I now feel as if I were hanging, suspended, like a light bulb not quite screwed in all the way? I devote myself to protests and demonstrations, adding my voice to the shouts of the betrayed masses, since my fate is the same as theirs, and not the same as the deceased's. I live in another historical period, and so, though I may be obsessed with him, I am nonetheless formed by other conditions. As Lazarus says in "Lazarus's Return," (written by Glafkos Thrassakis-Lazaridis), a different quality of flour yields a different kind of bread.

The emptiness I now feel, having abandoned my work, is undoubtedly as easily explained as a spasm in the womb of chaos. I ran, I tried, I took action—car races, boat races, chariot races, uphill roads, grassy stadiums, roaring rivers—and look where I ended up: with my car stalled at the edge of a cliff, the two front tires already tasting the taste of nothingness.

Why? Who? Let me explain. I, without Thrassakis, am I without myself. A few drops from his wave fell on me and left indelible marks, burning me like caustic ash. And now, riddled with these holes, I offer myself up like a honeycomb, inviting the bees to fill me with their harvest.

Because in giving myself, I became complete: I was Glafkos, to an extent that he would never have believed, even if given the chance. I find myself stopped, frozen at the point where he gave up the ghost. I try to unstick myself, to disengage, to view myself independently from his model. When he departed, I had barely even started out on this business of life. Isn't it unfair that I should end before I even begin, just because he ended before I really got started? And what about the forty years I lived in peace before I ever knew about him? Happy, healthy years, since I still knew nothing of him. And now, how can I keep going? How?

If I want to keep my hold on life, I have to become a trick, a sham. Until now I was a man with two hearts—mine and Glafkos's. Now that his has stopped beating, I find myself facing the difficulty of landing with just one engine running.

So, sitting in the same chair where I once wrote my descriptions of his stories, but with no more stories left to describe, I'll begin to devour my own flesh, writing, out of necessity, my own stories, as if I were him. I suddenly find myself jealous of my wife, who is still working on Glafka. Every so often I tell her, "You won't understand until you finish. It's an emptiness like no other—you can't even put two and two together to make four, you're lost at the crossroads of five roads, standing at six meters with the barrel of senility pointing your way, and yet seven-lived, like a cat, before the eight-fold paper, celebrating the novena of the ass."

Up until now, I myself remained detached, outside of things. I tried, as much as possible, to keep myself separate from Thrassakis, making rare forays into his territory. Now, able to spread out in my own right, far from the old comparisons between him and me, I'm discovering how little my own self really interests me and how much I seek the "other," as Glafkos would have said, as a means of salvation. So I sit at the same table where I sat back then, gazing out the window at the sun as it plays hide-and-seek with the clouds . . . .

Now, in order to see, I have to wipe the crust of sleep from my eyes. And yet I have loved it well, that crust. Letters are returned to unlucky lovers, but the time spent thinking of the beloved person, waiting, measuring his absence—how can that time be returned?

And since no question is ever posed without regard to some specific circumstance, I ask again: What will my grandson (my daughter's child) say about me tomorrow? Will he say, My grandfather wasn't Thrassakis, but his biographer? Won't he be able to see me independently of him? And if the greatest difference between us thus far has been that I am "living" while Thrassakis is "at rest," what will happen when I too am put to rest? Won't the boundaries between us be even less distinct? Won't people confuse us more easily? And what will my grandson be able to say about a grandfather who wasn't even sure who he was? Thrassakis's grandfather was a living legend in his city, a legend of the hunt and of the mill, a Bulgar-killer and Turk-eater—but what kind of grandfather am I, what embodiment of "grandfather" do I offer my grandson? How can the patricide committed through the adulation of the grandfather—discussed with regard to Lazos and his grandfather in the fourth chapter of my book—happen in my case, since I offer my daughter's son no legend, no fairy tale, no food for his imaginings? Only my scattered existence in print, like the comics I'm always buying for him.

Of course, such comparisons and analogies should be kept in check. The past was one thing, the present is another. With television, with the conquest of the moon and the destruction of wild tribes by the far-reaching octopus of civilization, with the end of colonialism, the easy symbols for "the enemy"—blacks, reds, yellows (always non-white)—have more or less been abolished. No one can really criticize me for not being like Thrassakis's grandfather, who electrified the young Lazos with stories of wild beasts and fires in the Amazon jungles. Yet I can't help from feeling remorse—while I fail to fulfill the responsibilities of the grandfather as I ought, I remain obsessed with the complex of the double.

≈

I AM LIKE THE LAST guest to arrive at a feast where many expensive foods have been devoured—the tongues of birds, suckling pigs, fresh fish, young, incredibly tender lamb—conducting the final inspection of the remains, picking at some bones where a little meat still clings, in a pan half a meter long that's full of inedible bits and pieces: unrecognizable joints, skin, blind heads with the eyes eaten out, necks bent like question marks, which the severe gaze of the all-powerful contemplates from above. Like a churchyard after a weeding. With practiced fingers, I delight in whatever trash escaped the verger's eye.

From "My Childhood Years," for example, I overlooked this:

When I was young, I liked to eat dirt with a spoon, outside the house. Markos [his older brother, Captain Markos of the guerrilla army] *and I would go out to fill up our pails, and out there, even though I knew the dirt was dirty, pissed-on by the greengrocer's donkey, stepped-on by the foot of the priest, I couldn't resist the temptation to take communion from that infernal god, the flesh of mother earth.*

A passage I certainly would have focused on at the beginning of my study, when I still believed that he had been eaten by cannibals, because,

From the most tender age, the children of the first Portuguese colonists to arrive in the Amazon during the 16th century were taught by the natives to eat dirt and lime, one of the most certain methods of committing suicide. They do not consider this earth-eating tendency as a sickness but a vice . . . . (Gilberto Freyre, *Masters and Slaves: the Creation of Brazil*)

What I saw, then, was an atavistic memory, transferred from the wild men to the civilized Glafkos, who naturally didn't eat his kite like the Portuguese children did, but was scared of smiling in front of the nun, because if the nun managed to count all his teeth, he would die. For him to eat soil, or the natives to eat him—for me this expressed the phrase, "Ashes to ashes, dust to dust," perfectly. But I rejected it, just as I rejected the story that Glafkos was eaten at the same time as the Rockefeller son, by cannibals who later became vegetarians.

≈

I'M SLIPPING AGAIN, like a train at a juncture that takes the wrong track because the switchman isn't there. I am ready to re-enter Glafkos's skin. I feel more at home in his hide. Without him, I find myself wrapped in only my own original nakedness, my skin, made sensitive by the introduction of central heating into our society, exposed once more to windswept nature. Light wounds me, and water, air, snow. My protective coat, the "other," is gone. Sitting at the table of the self-punished, I do not exist without him.

Feedback is a method of controlling a system by inserting into it the results of its past performance. Bio-feedback involves reinserting information about the bodily experiences of the subject. Such as. . . .

In a period of self-destruction, the individual, self-punished, finds in the jet of blood that spurts from a desired wound his entire signature, written with the blood of his existence.

Indeed. For me, the three month period during which the dentist was working on my mouth was one of the most fertile of my post-Thrassakian existence. Because the dentist hurt me. I suffered. I became an object in his experienced hands. When I bled, I knew the blood I spat into the basin was mine. I wasn't fooling anyone. Phlegm and blood, and the lie of my life of alienation finally came to an end.

I've always had problems with my teeth. When I was young, my baby teeth were pulled out with pliers. Now it was getting to the point where soon I would hardly even be able to chew. The dentist, a friendly young man from a good family, a Jew with hands of gold, told me, "Teeth grow in opposition to one another. Class struggle, it's all there, upper and lower, one growing into the holes the other leaves"—or, in my case, the cavities of the pulled-out teeth. "A tooth only grows properly if its pair, its opposite, is in its proper place, above or below." (As for who's on the top and who's on bottom, the doctor spoke to me quite openly from the very first moment, as soon as he had finished the general exam. As Heraclitus said, "The road up and the road down are one and the same." Upper and lower, both necessary for the chewing of food. Molars, wisdom-teeth, canines, all words that signified functions, that went beyond the teeth themselves, and aimed instead at the perpetuation of a genre.)

Anyhow, the three months of the metamorphosis of my mouth were, as I said, my happiest. He drilled me, anesthetized me, bridged me, every now and then he would show me my mouth in plaster, and he always explained everything he was going to do before he actually did it—why, for example, he had to support a bridge by drilling a sub-structure into some otherwise healthy tooth, a tooth that was in fact blossoming with shine (Cy . . .), because there was no other place (Cyp . . .) for the bridge (the capitalist air-bridge between Turkey and Israel) to be supported, so he dug out the inside of that tooth (Cypr . . .), sacrificed it, in short. . . . As he explained to me, though we can know everything about a mouthful of teeth, we remain completely ignorant as to how an individual actually chews. So he (my dentist, Kissinger) had to be sure the bridge would hold firm. And so we baptized my sacrificed tooth "Cyprus."

And when at last I acquired my new smile, my new mouth, I finally understood that I had nothing new to say. I was still chewing the same old cud, gathered from earlier grazings. And when I went to admire my new mouth in the mirror, as soon as I opened it to speak I turned into one of those Hollywood beauties about whom we say, "Why did she have to go and talk, and spoil those good looks?" That's how it was with me, too. New teeth to chew the same chow.

THIRD AFTERWORD

UP TO NOW, my most serious critique came from my daughter, who followed the progress of my book though all its incarnations, with all its difficulties and dead ends. She told me in no uncertain terms that if Thrassakis didn't exist, I myself would logically have to be Thrassakis. The contract between reader and writer could be based on one of two assumptions. First, on the assumption that Thrassakis had at one point existed, in which case whatever I wrote would have more or less the sole claim to truth, even if in a fictionalized form—after all, you won't find reference to Thrassakis's name in any literary history, only to Lazaridis Markos, author of *Southern Cross*, etc. (no relation whatsoever to Markos Lazaridis, Glafkos's brother who was killed during the Civil War). Or, second, on the assumption that Thrassakis never existed, that I created him in my image in order to be able to express myself more easily in the guise of the third person. Self-distanced from my own self.

I found you, I found you, said the clever, amorous look in her eyes, just as when she was a little girl and would hide behind the furniture waiting for me to come looking for her.

If that's what she thought, I said, she'd have to take up the issue with her mother, too. After all, how could she have been spending all this time research-ing the wife of a non-existent author? Were both of us just plain crazy? Or was the apple of my eye being poisoned with all these ideas by her new husband, Pierre, who wanted to ruin us in her eyes and take our place in her heart?

"Love is blind," she retorted, like another Sphinx. "Mom pretends to see whatever you want to see. She's blinded by love, and goes along with all your fantasies to make you feel less alone." And with that, she came and sat on my lap. I shuddered at the touch of her firm flesh. When she gave me my second grandson, she lost the virginity of the wild pomegranate tree. But I was still just as drawn to her as before.

Then little Glafkos came in, lurching like a drunk. (As I later discovered, he'd been licking the dregs out of the glasses of whisky left over from a party we had thrown the night before.) My daughter picked him up and pulled him, too, up into the chair, kissing him on the neck.

"Admit it," she insisted as she calmed the spoiled kid on her lap. "One of the narrative styles is yours. Some people use letters, some pretend to have found the manuscript in a bundle somewhere, some write in the third singular, some transplant their characters to some other historical setting. Confessional narrative, dialogue, interior monologue. We learned all that at the Sorbonne."

I was starting to feel dizzy. If Thrassakis was just a figment of my imagination, as my daughter was now boldly suggesting, then who, or what, was I? I knew I couldn't live without him, just as a vain woman can't live without the mirror that confirms her beauty, or her lover's words, even if they're nothing but lies.

Could there be some kind of mother/daughter conspiracy aimed at saving me from myself? Could they, with their womanly intuition, have foreseen that the book was headed for a dead end? Could they have realized that Thrassakis couldn't save me anymore? Were they working together for my own good? I never doubted their love. But one man's good is another man's evil. The tourist's beautiful summer weather is the farmer's drought. The farmer prays for clouds to gather; the tourist blows to scatter them. I'll say it again: I don't know. Because I don't want to know. I want to stay here in this darkness that hatches dreams. In the damp of emotions, where art makes its home.

I soon came to see my daughter's attack not as a criticism of my text but as a confirmation of my victory. Because if she had gone looking in literary histories, if it had even occurred to her to do so, she must have believed in the existence of my hero, the way lots of people think James Bond really exists, forgetting that he's merely the figment of an author's imagination. (My need to compare myself to Ian Fleming indicates just how badly I wanted to impress my audience. I did, however, have one advantage over Fleming: since he was dead, he couldn't continue his hero's life, while I, still living, could use the ectoplasmic tricks of narration to resuscitate mine from the Afterworld, to bring him once more into the present moment.)

There was nothing to do but to continue the deceit. My own unpublished essays and stories sat heavy like spoiled caviar in the belly of my desk. So I decided to publish them as works by Thrassakis. The first volume would be my biography of him, since the new generation clearly prefers non-fiction over fiction. Novels don't interest them, unless they're based on real events. And then, with the snowman of my Thrassakis ready, I would dress him with a cap and pipe.

In the meantime, I was smoking my own pipe like a maniac. When someone comes along and pulls you from your starry world, it can drive you straight to disaster. One night when my astrophysicist friend Nikitas, may he rest in peace, was looking at the stars through his telescope, his wife came into his studio and covered the lens with her palm. "Now you're going to look at me," she declared. And she undressed right there in front of him. For Nikitas, lost in the workings of space, sex was the farthest thing from his mind. His wife grabbed the telescope from him, bent it and started to make love to it. First she mounted it like a broomstick in one of Leonora Fini's *croquis*, then she took it in her mouth, then she lay on her back and spun it before the starry world of her vagina. "Look," she said to him, "milky ways, comets, dippers, whatever you want. Just open the curtains and go wild." It was such a vulgar, torturous, comic scene that it was simply too much for my friend Nikitas to bear. Two days later he jumped off our terrace.

Having been forced to be harsh with me, my daughter, knowing not only what had happened to Nikitas, but how sensitive I was just then, wanted to show me all of her love.

"I had just one problem on my mind," I told her. "How to learn to live without Thrassakis. And you came along and gave me a final push. No, tell me. Is that what they taught you at the Sorbonne? Is that what your enlightened generation is all about? Well, if you did it for the inheritance, I'll tell you right now, I don't have a thing in the world to leave you apart from my work." And I pointed to a stack of papers.

She was smiling as only she knew how to smile, tearing my heart to pieces. That morning I found her so frighteningly attractive that I almost lost control. The room was closing in on me. I had no idea what was happening. And then that sweet satan slipped beside me again, letting my grandson run out onto the very terrace from which Nikitas the astrophysicist had jumped. She took my hand and squeezed it, pressing it against her wedding ring.

"But I went to the States," I insisted. I'm not just imagining it all. I went twice."

"No one's saying you didn't go, Daddy," she whispered, squirming in my lap. (At her touch, that touch, scented with the scent of her body. . . .) "But you did-n't go because of Thrassakis. You went because you had to go. You were invited there, to give lectures."

"And I had a fellowship."

"The fellowship was for you to write, to travel, to see things, you, *you, YOU.*"

Her voice slipped like a hot wind into my ear. The "you" grew, spread out, took control. It gave me a kind of certainty, as if I could punch through walls. "You, you . . . ." Now she was wrapping me in her long, thick hair. Watery shim-merings, lilies, lakes, forget-me-nots.

"And Paris?" I asked in a thin voice.

"You came to see me. That's where you got sick."

"Who got sick?"

"You, *you, YOU.*"

There's no way I could ever find words to describe this sober pleasure. It was like nothing else I've ever felt with a woman. This one here was the flesh of my flesh, my flesh had found hers again, grown up, changed. Her new skin, her new blood, didn't short-circuit my own skin and blood, but on the contrary recharged them. I was father and lover. Everything but husband.

As a companion, husband, father, and lover, Thrassos, despite his obvious eccentricities and authoritarian ideas, his apparent egoism, offers protection. He offers an unassailable fortress that can resist all kinds of attack. Rich in experience, willingness, and genius, a fatherly, loverly guardian, he ensures full obedience and infinite gratitude. (Lili Iakovidi, "Thrassos Kastanakis, the Man," *New Hearth*, Vol. MCVI)

Later, when I tried to free myself of remorse by fobbing everything off on my alter ego, Glafkos, I felt for the first time the impossibility of doing so—after all, my other self, the childless Thrassakis, was free of such incestuous complexes. Indeed, his childlessness was something I stressed throughout my biography. For the first time the guilt was all mine, untransferable, not because I could no longer use Glafkos as an alias, but because I had denied him children—perhaps on purpose, to keep myself from daring to fulfill my own unlawful desires. And so, trying to shake me from my fiction, trying to heal the wounds of my soul, my daughter offered me her body.

That night at dinner her husband seemed to be looking at me with hidden jealousy. I thought my grandson would say something about having seen us on the couch. I thought I heard my wife asking me why I didn't even have the energy to keep my head up and watch TV. I thought my daughter was in love with me.

So, in the state in which I now found myself, unable to refer to some other image, without the lining of that other existence to shield me and soften my contact with the harsh outer fabric, vacuum-packed—"packed in a vacuum," as he might have said—I declared a life strike, something that doesn't fall into any previously existing category of strikes. I eat, so it isn't a hunger strike; I work, so it isn't a sit-in or a walk-out; I sleep, so it isn't a waking strike, either. It's something much deeper. A life strike means that the tape is rolling, but the machine isn't recording. You're in a void; you refuse to accept the deposited coins. The pay phone just spits them out again. It's broken. Out of order. *Guasto. Kaputt. Ne fonctionne pas.* So I found myself at a great advantage: whatever happened to me might have nothing to do with the mythical Thrassakis, but it certainly had nothing whatsoever to do with me, since I was no longer in working order, killing time by studying train schedules.

My daughter's attack had one positive result: The delusion that had been tormenting me for so long, the fantasy that the other was me, passed. I came back to reality. The "you" that her divine spirit had whispered—"you, *you*, YOU"— became my "ego," my irrefutable "me."

Unfortunately, the relief didn't last any longer than a dose of aspirin. Each morning wakes with its demands, it wants you all to itself, it tempts you to devour it. So, once again, I gave myself over to the adulation of my dead hero—though now in a shadowy corner, in secret, where no one was watching. Like a necrophile.

I had imaginary conversations in my head, trying to justify the murder. "Words," I would say, "are created in order to signify things. They are never the things themselves." "Correct," a voice would answer. "Like at the store," I'd continue, "there's a sign saying, 'Canned goods,' or 'Beverages,' but when you go to grab something, you pick up the bottle or the can, not the sign itself." "Correct," the voice answered. "So," I argued, "say another fire comes and destroys the Alexandrian library all over again, and among the few books that survive is my book on Thrassakis. Won't future generations suppose that the *Collected Discovered Works* were lost in the fire, just like all those ancient works we only know about through references to them in other works?" "Correct, but you don't win the present by bluffing with eternity." "I don't want to bluff, I just want to say that with the art of the written word, the extant is as far from the nonexistent as madness is from genius—which is to say, a hair's breadth away." "It's high time they shut you up in a loony bin." "Bite your tongue, jinx. Try to understand that the issue is no longer, 'If it happened, it interests us,' but, 'It interests us because it never happened at all.' There will always be Thrassakises, as long as there are people like me, to bring them back from non-being."

Then, during one of my fits, I started saying that my daughter wasn't really mine; she was an adopted orphan who learned Greek from her father, who had fought in Korea and married a North Korean woman, which is why she had slanted eyes; her parents had been killed in some accident, but she had miraculously survived and was found hanging from a tree, and had somehow ended up in Greece, where I—childless, like Thrassakis, and moved by the reports of her tragedy in the papers—decided to adopt her. It was then that they shut me in a sanitarium for a few weeks, for my own good, until I could pull myself together.